DANCING WITH DESTRUCTION

BAEN BOOKS by JASON CORDOVA

Dancing with Destruction edited by Jason Cordova
Chicks in Tank Tops edited by Jason Cordova
Mountain of Fire
Monster Hunter Memoirs: Fever with Larry Correia

DANCING WITH DESTRUCTION

edited by
Jason Cordova

BAEN

A Baen Books Original

Baen Publishing Enterprises
P.O. Box 1403
Riverdale, NY 10471
www.baen.com

ISBN: 978-1-6680-7275-2

Cover art by Kurt Miller

First printing, July 2025

Distributed by Simon & Schuster
1230 Avenue of the Americas
New York, NY 10020

Library of Congress Cataloging-in-Publication Data

Names: Cordova, Jason, 1978- editor
Title: Dancing with destruction / edited by Jason Cordova.
Description: Riverdale : Baen Publishing Enterprises, 2025.
Identifiers: LCCN 2025007189 (print) | LCCN 2025007190 (ebook) | ISBN
   9781668072752 trade paperback | ISBN 9781964856308 ebook
Subjects: LCSH: Science fiction, American | Imaginary wars and
   battles—Fiction | War stories, American | Space warfare—Fiction |
   LCGFT: Science fiction
Classification: LCC PS648.S3 D33 2025 (print) | LCC PS648.S3 (ebook) |
   DDC 813.0876208—dc23/eng/20250408
LC record available at https://lccn.loc.gov/2025007189
LC ebook record available at https://lccn.loc.gov/2025007190

Printed in the United States of America

10 9 8 7 6 5 4 3 2 1

This is for Jack Clemons.
You were supposed to be in this one.
We miss you, brother. Til Valhalla.

Contents

DANCING WITH DESTRUCTION

Introduction

Shane M. Gries

Since the beginning of recorded history, young people—mostly young men—have volunteered or were conscripted to serve their nations, often finding themselves in mortal danger. All too often they made the ultimate sacrifice, falling to a blade, an arrowhead, a shell fragment, or bullet. Untold numbers of them still lie in unmarked graves, some stacked upon the bones of their comrades, others in situ in collapsed trenches or foxholes, long forgotten. Most of them have one thing in common: they served, fought, and in some cases died, for an elite political and military class that didn't deserve them. This is a trend that transcends the ages and our cultural divides, and just as with King David, Uriah, and Bathsheba, the ruling classes always fall short of those who serve them.

In 2001, a young woman named Leigh Ann Hester enlisted in the Kentucky Army National Guard when she was nineteen years old. Later, on September 11th, before she would even arrive for basic training, the twin towers were destroyed by a gang of bloodthirsty animals who succeeded in murdering 2,977 innocent people. This triggered an outrage that plunged the United States into two decades (and counting) of undeclared war. Young Private Hester, along with millions of others, would ultimately end up on the pointy end of the spear, in a fight against naked aggression and unadulterated evil. They would be sent by a ruling class on both sides of the political spectrum who lacked the moral courage to formally declare a war. A class of people who didn't tell the people to plant victory gardens, but to run up their credit card debt instead.

After completing basic training, Hester was assigned to the 617th Military Police Company, based out of Richmond, Kentucky. Unless deployed, traditional members of the National Guard are part-time soldiers, training one weekend a month and two weeks during the summer. Even though they hadn't received any formal notification, the members of her unit understood it was only a matter of time before they deployed to support the Global War on Terror, so they honed their skills as best they could in anticipation of that. A few years later, Leigh Ann Hester was working full-time as a store manager in Nashville when the mobilization orders came, and she, along with the rest of her unit, deployed to Iraq, right into the thick of things.

The Military Police Corps of the US Army has a couple of core mission-sets; one is law enforcement and the other is area security. On March 20, 2005, Sergeant Hester and the rest of her squad were riding in three Humvees with heavy weapons mounted on top, colloquially known as "gun trucks." They'd been operating in Iraq for months at that point and had seen some serious action. Her company in particular ran into improvised explosive devices two or three times a week and were involved in direct firefights quite regularly. There were so many MPs getting wounded that the battalion commander instituted a policy that after you got your second Purple Heart, you'd get rotated back home to the States. There were several who did just that.

On that particular day, their patrol, designated Stallion 33 and under the leadership of Staff Sergeant Nein, was tasked with route clearance and convoy escort duties. They were to operate along the main road between LSA (Logistics Support Area) Anaconda to CSC (Convoy Support Center) Scania in an area located just outside of Baghdad. They found themselves escorting a convoy of thirty civilian cargo trucks driven by foreign contractors. Along the way, the civilian semi-tractor trailers were ambushed by insurgents who opened fire with machine guns and rocket-propelled grenades. One of the trucks ground to a halt, burning uncontrollably, while drivers from many of the others bailed out of their vehicles, taking cover in the ditches.

In the US Army, the standard practice when caught in a near ambush is not to run, nor is it to go to ground and return fire. When caught in a near ambush, the standard practice is to immediately turn toward the ambushers and attack. Staff Sergeant Nein did not hesitate and ordered the three gun trucks of Stallion 33 to race forward and assault the Iraqi insurgents. All three came barreling up the side of the road, straight into the enemy's kill zone, physically placing themselves between the ambush position and the civilian truck drivers, hammering away with their .50 caliber machine guns.

After quickly taking stock of the situation, Nein ordered them to move out, rounding a corner until they got on the enemy's flank. A rocket-propelled grenade sailed out from a trench, striking the lead gun truck, blowing the gunner off the vehicle, sending him tumbling to the ground. Luckily, he was merely knocked unconscious and would survive the incident.

Realizing they needed all the firepower they could muster, the squad leader ordered them to dismount, leaving the remaining two gunners in place to lay down a base of fire with their crew-served weapons. Once on the ground, Staff Sergeant Nein and Sergeant Hester led a fire team of a half dozen MPs in an assault against nearly fifty insurgents. Hester had an M203 grenade launcher mounted to the handguard of her rifle that she used to good effect, meticulously working their way through the enemy's defensive position, pushing their way forward one meter at a time. Hester would go on to kill three insurgents with her rifle for certain, perhaps taking out even more with the grenade launcher. After an intense forty-five-minute firefight, they would end up killing twenty-seven insurgents and capturing an additional seven, while only suffering three wounded of their own.

For their actions, Staff Sergeant Nein, Sergeant Hester, and one other member of the squad would be given a Silver Star—the third highest award for valor. Nein's award would be later upgraded to the Distinguished Service Cross, and Hester would be recognized for being the first woman since World War II to receive the Silver Star and the first female to get it for participating in direct combat.

Later, Leigh Ann Hester and the rest of her unit returned home and took up the routine of being part-time "weekend warriors" and full-time civilians. They would go about their lives peacefully and quietly, never bragging about what they had done. Their actions in the crucible of war were heroic, though they would never admit it, being the humble professionals they are. She and her battle buddies are true heroes and should never be forgotten.

They are the best of us.

Shane M. Gries
Colonel (Retired)
US Army

Preface

Jason Cordova

Are fates across different universes intertwined with one another? It's a question asked time and time again as we dive deeper into the alternate universe theory, one not so easily answered.

The concept for this anthology was that an omniscient alien species, the Elderwatch, observes humanity across various timelines, watching the parallel universes intertwine at various points of the past, present, and future as an alien invasion begins. Not uncaring, but merely observant, recording everything that they saw, where various nexus points created a singular confluence point.

But the anthology wasn't going to be about the Elderwatch, no. They're nothing more than background players. They're the Multidimensional Editorial Development Team (that's my story and I'm sticking to it).

So the idea became a simple writing exercise: create a series of stories—random, weird stories—based on the anthology's cover art, but have different authors try and tell them. I reached out to some of the best writers I know from both traditional and indie publishing. Rogue CIA agents? Soldiers lost in time who are being hunted? The possibilities, I told them, were limitless. Give me strange, unusual, and make it *hurt*.

And they delivered.

David Weber and Marisa Wolf teamed up to give me a curious case of alien first contact, while Blaine L. Pardoe offered up a twist on the ancient and familiar. We've also got short stories from Joelle Presby, Rick Partlow, and a terrifyingly effective collaborative team-up between Jacob Holo and Edie Skye. Kacey Ezell worked with Melissa

Olthoff and Nick Steverson to deliver a threaded two-part short story, while Jason Anspach and Nick Cole conclude the anthology with an explosive novella set in their WarGate Universe.

Each contribution tells the story of a confluence. How they all end, though, is up to them.

Happy reading!

Jason Cordova

Raleigh, NC

December 2024

All the Little Stars in the Sky

David Weber & Marisa Wolf

Zivhalla had never awakened rested after a long sleep in her travels between planets. Her route to NLX-45 was no exception.

What was an exception, however, was waking to a cacophony of alarms, alerts, and the drone of Bosco. Bosco—her private name for the limited AI that kept the ship functioning while she slept—stuttered, dropped the volume of the blare, then spoke directly into the link embedded in her smallest cranial bone.

"There is a malfunction."

Zivhalla did not curse or shout in response, though a new alert joined the rest as her system spiked at the unhelpful update. "What is it?"

"A malfunction is when—"

"What is the malfunction?" She took a series of deep breaths, an attempt to reacquaint herself with her body, and blinked until her vision began to clear.

"The ship is reporting orbital insertion."

Despite an impressive background in long sleep, during both training and the actual crossing of blank stretches of space that made up the majority of her career, Zivhalla came within a chron of sitting up in astonishment. Which, in her layered biosuit, fastened to the narrow long-sleep tube in some nine hundred places, would have been disastrous. She mentally traced the shape of her body, remembered where each muscle and nerve had set itself, and chose to hold still and keep them uninjured.

"The ship should not attempt orbital insertion without a live pilot." This was exactly the sort of stupid thing one said to Bosco, as Bosco had been built to be excellent with navigational corrections, small repairs, and quality control of the long sleep process, but was absolute excrement at spoken language. Too many decision trees better suited to math, which now and then Zivhalla could appreciate.

At the moment, she'd rather lift the engineers responsible for Bosco by their respective necks, shake them until their bones fell out, and then lock them in a room with their limited conversational model for a millennia. Unfortunately, that was not within her power.

More unfortunately, given her current cramped state, very little *was* in her power.

"The ship did not attempt orbital insertion."

For what felt like an eternity, Zivhalla considered slamming her biosuit-protected head into the top of the tube until it cracked, or she did. She only truly weighed the matter for half a moment, not even long enough for the faint alarms to complete a full cycle of their chorus of concerns, but it was overly tempting all the same.

"But we are in the process of orbital insertion?"

"Correct."

"And you can't reset our navigation?" Very little hope underlined Zivhalla's statement.

"Correct." Bosco's monotone remained as uninflected as ever.

"Is the malfunction in your navigational system?"

"No. I am aware of the proper course and have programmed it several times."

"The malfunction is in the ship's execution of the navigational course?" She stared through the biosuit to the unimpressive stretch of tube above her.

"Correct."

"Finish the cycle so I can get out of the tube and take manual control." If she heard the word "correct" one more time, Zivhalla might be glad to have the ship crash into an unsurveyed planet.

"That is not advised."

Not for the first time, Zivhalla wondered if her interactions with Bosco were recorded, so that its so-brilliant-they-were-indecently-stupid engineers could learn and adapt future models. She rather hoped so, because surely hearing this ever so helpful exchange would cause them to change their programmatic priorities before any other Interstellar Exploratory Corps crew member screamed themselves to death in a tube as they transitioned incorrectly from the haven of space to the greedy claws of planetary gravity.

"It's the only way we're getting out of this without crashing," she said, calm firmly in place. If only by the skin of her suit.

"That is not advised."

"Not crashing is not advised?" Zivhalla squirmed, a hopeless attempt to convince the tubing to disconnect so her encasement would open and she could get out to *do something* besides listen to the alarms and Bosco and be *useless*.

Calm, she reminded herself, and wriggled again.

"Orbital insertion has begun. There is a malfunction. The ship will not deviate from its current course."

"That's why I need manual—"

"The timing is not correct."

Bosco was many things as a conversational partner—frustrating, subpar, mildly ranked above speaking with the food processor—but one thing it did not do was interrupt. That, even more than the subtle increase in alarm volume, stilled Zivhalla in her layers of protective covering.

"We're crashing and there is nothing I can do about it."

"Correct."

"Why did you wake me up?" Frustration kept her from the cliff's edge of introspection—this was not the time to decide if she'd prefer to die unconscious and unknowing, or awake and aware.

"Priority: life of crew. Statistics indicate a higher percentage for survival if crew is alert for non-preferred landing."

"Non... non-preferred landing?" Pressure climbed from somewhere in her midsection toward somewhere near her top, but as she couldn't determine what emotion or state of matter it contained, Zivhalla forced it back down. She hadn't eaten in long sleep, but there were plenty of things circulating through her body that could be expressed. Better not to deal with any of them while layered and strapped as she was.

"Study of living bodies indicates unconsciousness in a rough landing would lead to fewer injuries," she muttered, though she didn't expect an answer. Probably for the better, as unfortunately Bosco was likely correct—after a crash, there wouldn't be time to start the slow process of waking her from long sleep. Nor, depending on how damaged the ship was, would there be a strong likelihood of the system remaining intact enough to wake her.

Bosco did not argue, which left her to lie flat and listen to the ebb and rise of sounds precisely measured to make her leap into action. The long-sleep tube, built to withstand the constant shifts of acceleration and occasional mild collisions, created to keep her functional and safe through near-endless stretches of travel between systems, was an ideal place to shelter through a crash.

If there were such a thing.

Maybe she *would* have time to course correct the ship if she tore everything off the suit, leaving it irreparably damaged but her free, and leapt out, shoved her way into the pilot console, managed to take stock of the situation in a sliver of time, sawed the ship around, and was incredibly, deeply, improbably lucky.

But if she failed at any of that, even by a chron, she'd die, suit or no suit.

Granted, she might very well die anyway, but such was life. Buried in the layers of protection afforded by the tube, she couldn't even perceive the change in speed or direction, so probably she wouldn't know anything until the moment of impact.

"What happened?" While the words put her at risk of further exasperation, her current situation was untenable with only the alarms for distraction.

"The ship is in—"

"What happened to put the ship in orbital insertion?" Zivhalla closed her eyes; they provided no input of interest at the moment.

"A malfunction."

I'm going to pull out your program nodule when we hit the ground and chew it to scrap, were the words she thought quite loudly, but did not communicate audibly to Bosco. After several measured moments in which they did not complete the task of crashing or dying, she formed a more Bosco-appropriate question.

"What was the nature of the malfunction?"

"There were multiple in a small time frame. An unexpected obstacle was detected but did not read on sensors until the ship reached visual range."

The likelihood of such a thing, in all the wide stretches of space, blanked Zivhalla's mind for a brief moment, but Bosco continued, its short phrase module apparently broken.

"The attempt to clear the obstacle was almost immediately followed by an impact, in which key systems were broken."

Obstacle? Impact? Broken? The series of events, recounted in Bosco's unwavering delivery, made strict linguistic sense. The meaning of it did not—each piece held far too much improbability.

But then, Zivhalla operated quite often on astronomical measurements. Why should odds be any different?

By time she processed it, her long-sleep-slowed brain still readjusting, they crashed.

It was awful, and in large part due to the biosuit, she didn't lose consciousness even briefly.

Instead her abused system was forced to attempt to make sense of a barrage of input, all too overlapping to be sensible. Crushing impact, loss of breath. The shriek and tear of metal, stabbing pain in the sides of her head. Colors flashed through tube, biosuit, and her closed eyes, an explosion at such a level those layers made for no barrier at all.

Eventually her midsection heaved, still not under her control but able to cycle the chemicals needed for breath, and a hissing sound pushed through the dull throb left behind her dying ship.

Bosco did not speak, and her dulled thoughts took an unexpected pause to mourn that before the need to continue to survive flooded through her.

Now that she breathed again, each part of her body responded as expected. The biosuit reported only minor faults, and the tube around her remained intact as far as her limited visual field could determine.

"By all the little stars in all the little skies," she murmured. Would she survive crash-landing on a planet she'd seen only in transmitted records, only to die, with inexorable slowness, inside a long-sleep tube she'd seen far too much of?

Bosco, for all its many faults, could run hordes of calculations in a single chron. If it could have timed the tube's release to a precise fraction, enough for her to have the best chance of surviving the landing and still be able to get out before Bosco's program fell to pieces along with the ship . . .

Despite the fact she was most likely in the midst of burning wreckage, she took her time to do the next few things. Careful. Precise.

A flex of her legs, the biosuit moving perfectly with her as it had been designed to do, the hinged joint in the middle of her limbs poised to brush the top of the tube. A stretch of her arms to the side. A breath. Another one, for good measure.

Then she pressed, up and out.

Nothing happened.

She breathed again. The malfunctions hadn't ended her. Nor had the crash. This star-forsaken tube nestled in the midst of what had been a ship somewhere on a planet she'd meant to approach with care and a plan wouldn't—

One more breath. Zivhalla stilled her thoughts, tensed each muscle, mustered every individual firing nerve.

And *pushed*.

The tube unstuck with a dramatic change of pressure, and Zivhalla immediately had several new problems.

The less said of her journey through fiery detritus the better—visibility remained poor even with her biosuit's aid, nothing but her erstwhile tube appeared in useable shape, Bosco did not chirp in her implant, and the path out did not make sense.

Before long she found a gaping hole that made her exit easier and she leapt out, the biosuit flexing around her in case the ground were farther than she'd expected.

She hadn't looked first.

Rookie mistake, and stars be lost in the sky she was too experienced to die because she threw herself out of a crashed, burning ship into a pit of acid or an open volcano.

She told herself this so firmly she locked into place outside what had been her ship, and didn't immediately flee from what could be further impending explosions.

Probably also not her most brilliant experienced-Interstellar-Exploratory-Corps move, but in her defense it hadn't been the most thorough nor ideal wake-up process. Her brain would catch up.

Or maybe it was shock. A slow-moving injury from the crash.

None of that was helpful, and she shoved it all away, then forced herself to take stock.

First, the ship.

She pivoted, paid attention to the flashing alerts of her biosuit, and noted the heat was unsurprisingly high in the area. Burning ship post incorrect re-entry, post incorrect meeting of the planetary surface. It appeared to be in three large pieces, contained in a relatively small area, all of which were on fire. Farther out her display indicated smaller but not insignificant chunks. Also too hot for tactile confirmation.

Second, the area.

A small crater. Probably new, given the shape and how it corresponded to the path of her ship's wreckage. Ground matter solid, colored unexceptionally in her biosuit's current visual spectrum. No evidence of surprise dwellings or life-forms, so probably she hadn't killed anything upon her arrival. That reassured some measure of tension, though the lack of anything identifiable—conveniently whole supply crates, her external equipment, the communication drone meant to make immediate contact with the existing limited AI on the planet from the first wave of non-personnelled exploration...

None of that.

Third...

Her biosuit tightened in a wave over her body, a ripple of motion that didn't cease until she took her first step away from the ship. Even then it only slowed, and she registered the rest of the alerts. Pressure had begun to spike in the area. Nothing around her was stable.

She needed to move.

Once she made the decision, Zivhalla *moved*. The biosuit, predominantly undamaged, would protect her from many things— unexpected atmosphere, small life-forms, most weather. It did all the things the first living member of the Interstellar Exploratory Corps to land on a planet would need—recycled, breathed, adapted, made her stronger, faster, broadened her visual spectrum, ensured she didn't need to eat over-often.

It could not, however, protect her from overwhelming percussive force, and so she *moved*. Out of the crater. Away from what had been her ship, what had been meant to be her base of operations as she conducted a slow and thorough review of the planet.

Instead she would have to fall back to a much-less-desired second location, the beacon where the forerunner limited AI had dug in after completing its initial survey of NLX-45.

She set the biosuit to record as she ran, trusting in her limited cognitive function to keep her momentum forward, if nothing else.

Zivhalla's sense of time stuttered around her, but as she ran through the path her ship had made through the tall plant-adjacent material of the planet, she attempted to remember what native creatures the forerunner AI had noted.

Surely none of them had been so large and mobile as the pack she bowled through some measurement of minutes after she'd left the crater. Her explorer's heart yearned to stop and catalog them, but she was unsure they were far enough from her ship. She roared a warning—wordless, but they were creatures, what would they know anyway—and kept moving. If the stars were kind, she had landed on the correct portion of the planet to make it to the beacon before anything else awful happened.

Simond Graydin had been on worse planets.

Probably.

As the window of their expected communication with *Heracles* opened, closed, and passed wildly behind them, the fact of what planet had been "the worst" blurred.

There'd been Enbidee, where the ground had opened at random intervals and eaten four of his charges before they got reliably airborne. Huson, where the rain cycled from harmless to burning but never stopped. Jeless, more ocean than land and all of it hungry.

He was well-decorated for good reason, but it all meant a hell of a lot of void space for the next idiot planet the genius scientists chose to drop them on. This one, Ceepax, had been perfectly within bounds. At first.

Then Coll Darrey had vanished from camp. Graydin was no slouch—he and his soldiers had been handpicked for exploratory protection duty out of thousands of applicants—but Coll Darrey was the kind of brilliant that didn't leave room for much else.

Like common sense.

Graydin had set up an excellent perimeter. His job was "protect scientists first, contribute to science second" and he was damn near infallible at both. Nothing should have picked off Coll Darrey and gone unremarked. Nor should he have been able to simply wander off, but the fact remained that between one rest stop and the next activity period he'd disappeared.

Then Rober Chysis, while on a trek through the thick almost-forest they'd been surveying for the last near-indeterminable stretch of time. No sound, no struggle, no sign. Gone.

Finally Lani Omerna, which was unfortunate, as she had the sharpest eyes. Scientist first, not a soldier, but very few got into Colonial Service if they couldn't handle themselves in the field. A Coll Darrey, sure, was smart enough he didn't have to be great at keeping himself safe. Brains like Coll's, though, got surrounded by a whole crew that could get him back to the ship in one piece. Not that the captain would be devastated to see him go . . . But Lani, she'd hit ground on nearly as many planets as Graydin, so that one burned.

They all burned, yet the mission continued. Failure might not be avoidable, but it couldn't be consistent. He'd yet to crash an entire mission, and Ceepax wasn't going to be the one that broke his streak.

As the grayed-out dusk that passed for night under the almost-forest's shimmering canopy gathered, Graydin called a halt and his remaining crew of six transitioned into camp setup duties.

They had another three squares to cover in the almost-forest, then they'd backtrack to the plains for another round of calling their late-as-a-deckloader-on-delivery-day ship. Overwatch on *Heracles* had an overlong list of areas for them to survey, so their time wouldn't be wasted, but it would be nice to know their ride was coming, at least.

Graydin could take a delay. He was a damn professional, not a green recruit, he knew timing could be a mess. Especially when the vast quantities of system distance got involved—*Heracles*'s astrographic survey could have been held up by any number of unexpected obstacles, or she could could have tweaked her long orbit and accidentally added five months to her path, or been pulled into a black hole and was currently disintegrating one millennium at a time.

Not the last one. Still, delays were often inevitable. But how hard was it to send a damn wave, beam, message, throw a rock, *something* to let Graydin and his team know what was what?

As he thought it, the light around them changed.

The creeping twilight gray kicked up the luminosity, edging into blue. Instinctively, he craned his head back, peering through the close-linked pseudo branches above them. In a breath's worth of seconds, the sky roared from monochrome to a brilliant blue, and something large passed through the otherwise unmarked atmosphere above them before it all faded back to creeping grays.

Awe. Wonder. Fear. Realization. Each shot through Graydin like a projectile, and he did rough math based on the insertion angle.

"Down!" he shouted, and with admirable, well-trained reactions, everyone dropped.

Whatever was shooting from the outskirts of the planet toward its innards, it probably wouldn't be big enough or close enough to flatten the almost-forest around them.

The shock wave *should* dissipate before it hit them, but "should" and "would" rarely overlapped.

Less than a minute later, whatever it was impacted hard enough for the ground to rumble, the fleshy fronds of the almost-forest to shudder, and his used-to-planetary-nonsense team to blink at each other.

"Meteorite," Ada Casven said, with consideration rather than decisiveness. Too much of a scientist to commit without more information.

"Definitely not a piece of the *Heracles*," Sed Merint muttered, because of course the sour git of regurgitated excrement would.

"Something we should check out, though. Reports didn't indicate Ceepax attracted regular hits, but we should see the aftermath, compare it to topology, see if there are similar artifacts out there." Tom Hetzenberg, good old Hetty, never let Merint's crank linger too long.

"Also Coll Darrey couldn't pass it up," Scom Wodridge offered. Genuine, not being a shit like Sed. No body, no confirmed death, and Wodridge was optimistic enough to lean fully into that theory. "Best bet at finding our wanderers."

"Not wrong." Graydin grunted, cast a sharp look over their barely begun sleep preparations. "Anyone too tired for a march to check out the sky junk?"

No one volunteered to stay behind, and a handful of minutes later, they were on the move.

The almost-forest remained about the same as ever—which was to say, not quite like anything humanity had previously encountered. The scientific side of the expedition had yet to decide if it was technically plant, or animal, or something in between. But Coll *had* theorized that it was mostly one organism, grown all over, which would be a strong explanation for its sameness. Long, curved solid bases, branching about halfway up, coated in pink, brown, green fronds that pulsed at a rhythm they'd yet to assign meaning to. Undisturbed by the humans passing between it, though Graydin ensured no one made prolonged contact after Coll had . . . gone.

So they marched, careful through the almost-forest, touching nothing, complaining not at all, in the direction Ada's handheld sensor narrowed down for the impact. The compact column moved steadily, without further alarms and excursions, and—

It was a good thing Graydin was a damn professional. Because a monster leapt out of the smoke and flames and directly over their head.

Glowing. Long claws. Teeth bigger than his face. Taller than him and Deber Alcoth stacked on top of each other. Burning eyes in front and maybe more of them in spots down its long, tendrilled head.

Monster.

They must have surprised it, because it roared loud enough to ring his ears, then kept running.

Graydin's training locked in—damn professional—and he took all of a fraction of a second to process the evolutionarily unavoidable fear reaction and then shove it in a box.

"Mark it, Hetty," he called, and the people around him snapped to attention. No one shot wildly into the almost-forest. No one ran screaming into the smoke and flame and monster-strewn surroundings.

It was nice, working with damn professionals.

"Drone deployed to mark its path, aye," Hetty replied, his action a fraction of a second ahead of his words.

"It's probably running away from the impact site. Let's see what's what, people. Heads on a swivel in case the fire flushes anything else out."

More monsters. Why not? Ceepax seemed determined to ruin him, but he'd seen worse. Or if he hadn't, he'd survived plenty. This wasn't going to be the thing that punched his ticket.

They crept through the almost-forest, even the three remaining scientists showing their training and holding formation. Weapons were out, but in position to cover the next guy, not accidentally shoot a friendly.

After he'd ascertained that fact, Graydin turned his attention ahead. *Trust the people around you, so you can handle your own shit.* His father hadn't been the only one to say words to that effect, but it was still the old man's voice he had in his head, no matter how many years and parsecs had passed since.

Fifteen minutes of alert march through an almost-forest was enough to blunt the adrenaline, but not instill antsy-ness, which was for the best, because everyone was still on alert when an enormous *BOOM* blasted over them, sending the plantlike forms around them shivering and twitching and his people into wary crouches.

They held position another full minute, each with a quick, silent signal that they were still operational. Nothing else exploded, but that didn't mean it wouldn't.

He gestured for Alcoth and Wodridge to hold in place, then pointed at two of the scientists, Nal Kavers and Ada, to do the same. Hetty and Sed were the fastest, and Graydin himself wasn't staying behind, so in case more things were waiting to go kablooey, it wouldn't take out everyone. That explosion had been *loud*, yes, but hadn't come close to ringing his bell. Likely they could make it to the end of the almost-forest, to the edge of the plains, and get a better eye on what had crashed without getting flattened by its aftereffects.

NLX-45 would be classified as awful. While not one of the Interstellar Exploratory Corps' official designations, "awful" was fitting and perhaps even generous. Zivhalla already had more than enough evidence to make a case that even the most traditional of the Council would accept.

Fact the first: the plant-adjacent matter was oily and shed tiny creatures on a regular basis. This would not be entirely terrible on its own—she'd been the first on TPW-1, and its endless stretches of semi-living pustules—but the tiny creatures *bit*.

Fact the second: there were hordes of tiny biting creatures, and either their strength or the shape of them or the sheer unending *number* of them meant she could feel their bites even through the biosuit.

Fact the third: the biosuit was specifically engineered to keep such things from happening. It should have adapted already, and it hadn't. That might be a result of the recent crash, but more likely was simply due to the overwhelming Awfulness of NLX-45.

Fact the fourth: how under all the stars of all the skies did anything here register her as something *to* bite? It was preposterously unlikely. She should not be food or threat, her alien nature to the planet buying her some grace period. In addition, the biosuit was expressly designed by the best minds at the Corps to render her invisible to the vast majority of small life-forms, based on research from the hundreds of planets in their records. For the few planets with larger, mobile life, which NLX-45 had been expressly noted *not* to have, the biosuit's other adaptations made her less an appealing meal than a fellow predator better avoided.

Fact the fifth: NLX-45 did, in fact, have larger mobile life, and from her playback, they were either wildly malformed, or had evolved enough to attach weapons to their bodies.

Fact the sixth: the bites, even through her biosuit, were beginning to *itch*.

"I shouldn't mark it as awful," Zivhalla muttered, aware absolutely no one and nothing could hear her on this planet. She'd yet to establish a connection to the forerunner AI, Bosco had apparently cracked along with the ship, and the oozy trees did not respond on any wavelength of possible communication attempted by the earlier AI.

"No, I should mark it as 'further investigation required' and maybe even flag it for a supervisor. Let a Council member's favored pet get gnawed on by barely visible pollen-bugs, see how they like it."

She envisioned it with great satisfaction, played out her own surprise, and imagined the many cutting things she could say after the investigation of NLX-45 was over and she was questioned. The biosuit designers and the AI engineers would have no proper comebacks.

Her scenarios threatened to cheer her, despite NLX-45's continued existence, until she checked the time remaining on her chosen course and found it barely diminished.

Fact the seventh: time did not proceed in an orderly manner on this planet.

She struck the last fact from her mental list; it was not true, and would therefore diminish the impact of the others. Her perception of time, however, had gone amok. She should be at the beacon already. Unless her sensors had gone awry, despite the lack of serious errors. Or her computational abilities had broken.

Shock and stress made logical sense, but in the end she was trained for disaster, far better than she was trained for things to go smoothly.

Still, in the privacy of her thoughts, she could blame NLX-45.

At the very least, one thing had gone correctly. Her non-preferred landing had left her on the same hemisphere as the forerunner AI, and it would be only a matter of several local days until she got there. Hopefully she wouldn't even have to sleep, though at some point she should stop and take better stock of the condition of her biosuit.

Her distance-eating strides slowed, and though she would prefer to be fully out of this mass of fleshy organisms and their biting, nasty off-puts, she pulled herself to a halt, surveyed the area through every wavelength the biosuit allowed, and dropped to a squat.

Zivhalla rolled her head back, ensured the recording kept touch on a full range around her, and ran through a systems check of both herself and her biosuit.

It was . . . not within her training, to have waited to do so. Yes, the nonideal cycling out of long sleep followed by a crash perhaps didn't leave her in the best mindset, but all the more reason to rely on her training. How well could she take stock of the planet if she couldn't even take stock of herself?

Shock and stress indeed. As though she hadn't been the sole explorer of dozens of planets, dealing with the unexpected in its infinite combinations.

As if she didn't know better.

The errors were minor. As she acknowledged each—the biosuit's attempt to connect with the various pieces of gear currently some distance behind her in a smoldering crater, a small health alert, an improper disconnect from the long-sleep tube that had left one port open—some measure of tension soothed in the back of her brain.

The biosuit, engineered out of living matter and programmed to adapt to the unexpected, much like Zivhalla herself, would hold them both together for quite some time. She closed her eyes, quieted her senses, and did a more thorough tour of her own body beyond the immediate of limbs and bones.

Nothing screamed an alert. Maybe her consciousness had been shaken over-hard against her oblong skull, but it, too, would heal.

Rattled, but equipped.

Enough, at least. Probably she should go back to the crash site, see if there was anything recoverable once the flames had abated, find and further observe those unexpected fauna.

She stirred, the biosuit's long, probing edges trailing close to the loamy ground, and craned her head back in the direction she'd come.

The indecision was unlike her, and she hated it almost as much as she hated NLX-45.

"Fine."

She straightened, determinedly placed her back to her inauspicious landing site, and planted her feet firmly. She'd go back eventually, but the likelihood that anything of use awaited her remained vanishingly small.

First, the forerunner AI. Her potentially jangled instincts had not been wrong. The beacon would have supplies—in their infinite wisdom and long experience, the Council had long ago instituted emergency backups for their explorers, to better the chances those first living scouts would survive long enough to provide enough information of value to lead to the correct next step for each planet.

Once she replaced her gear, topped off raw matter for her biosuit, and perhaps submitted herself to a full scan, she would return. Properly record both the effects of her arrival, and the life-forms present between her landing site and the forerunner.

Especially these incessant biters.

Another cloud had found her, and she lunged forward, gouging the ground behind her with what might have been a touch more spite than was strictly professional.

Her stride lengthened, her pace increased, and she allowed herself a smidgen of hope. If the stars were kind, the automated data collection would have come up with a feasible work-around to block the plant-adjacent creatures' incursions.

Two things could go right, even on NLX-45.

"Don't need to hypothesize," Hetty said, rocking up on his toes. "That's a ship." He whispered the next, as though he couldn't say what they were all thinking too loudly, "Not like anything we've got."

"Told you it wasn't *Heracles*," Sed grunted, though he kept his attention scanning the area rather than wasting time with further gloating. While he usually found the worst outlook in any scenario, even the crankiest scientist could get distracted by the truly novel.

Graydin might have shushed them, but their voices were an excellent distraction. He scanned their surroundings as well, though nothing but the many-tree moved in the ragged space between the almost-forest and the plains.

Nothing but smoke from a new crater in the plains. An occasional piece of wreckage that rolled off another broken piece of what was unmistakably—never mind science's insistence on conjecture over firm answers—an alien ship.

In pieces. Not likely to snake out an impossibly alien arm and yank them in, or infect them with weird alien viruses, or bristle with a sudden influx of alien soldiers.

But all the same: an alien ship.

Humanity had wandered the stars for centuries, and never found any sign of another spacefaring race. Planet-bound tool using species, yes, although only a handful of them and none far beyond their equivalent of the Stone Age or Bronze Age, but no real evidence of interstellar competitors. The occasional suspiciously repeating signal from a pulsar, perhaps, or a shadow on long-range that might or might not have been a superstructure, a furrow or two on a moon that seemed too regular for standard impacts. But nothing that ever turned out to be demonstrable artifacts of an advanced nonhuman species.

This, though . . . undeniable, clear, irrefutable . . .

Even in pieces, parts still on fire, it was inhuman. Sleek. Rippled and branching and shaped in ways that could be from an unexpected landing but probably . . . maybe . . .

Definitely were not.

Hands like his hadn't made this.

"*In what distant deeps or skies,*" he thought, or said so far under his breath it was about the same thing. With an effort, Graydin locked away the tidal wave of reactions trying to flood through him in favor of the more pressing matter.

"Well, folks, inevitable we'd discover space aliens are real when we're out of touch with the upstairs, innit?" He tilted his head toward the crater. "Say we give it a bit to cool, then get as close as we can, record what we can, and stay alive until *Heracles* limps back for us and we can report all good and proper, yeah." Because *Heracles* was still out there. Hadn't been blown up by aliens, or crashed into this wreck and caused its unplanned landing.

No good thinking about it, nothing they could do. Pressing matter in front of him, not useless wonderings about what was above them.

"Rah, sir," Hetty answered, and Sed set up his equipment to start a record while Graydin kept an alert watch.

The monster that had nearly run them down and yelled a bunch could be native, to be sure.

But Graydin couldn't quite make himself believe it. They hadn't caught a whiff of anything like it, the whole time they'd wandered Ceepax and its nonsense. No. Something had survived that landing. That ship.

And it was out still out there.

Zivhalla stood in the open hatch of the forerunner AI's beacon station and felt the weight of a crashing ship all over again.

The hatch shouldn't have been open.

The storage containers shouldn't have been open. The long-sleep tube shouldn't have been missing.

An awful lot of "shouldn't"—which perhaps she should have predicted for such an awful planet.

"Speaking of shouldn't," she said, once again to no one, "shouldn't be hesitating in the hatch." There were other things to check. The comms pod, additional diagnostic tools, biological mass held in stasis for her biosuit . . .

Another small chunk of time passed before she met her words with the appropriate action, but it didn't matter. Everything she needed was gone.

"Who could have been here to take it?"

"BRRT."

Training and perhaps a low, dull shock kept Zivhalla from whirling on the sudden sound.

"Directive? Forerunner Beacon BZ-O8 ARRRRVERR ZZP DRRR request confirmation."

The forerunner AIs, which she non-affectionately referred to as Bozeo, were not the same model as the ship-Bosco. They had entirely different decision trees for vastly different goals, but in their own way generated a similar frustration as conversational partners. Still, the intermittent loud noises were new.

"Forerunner Beacon, Exploratory Corps Zivhalla." She identified herself with the string of numbers the Council had tagged to her at her commissioning, though her biosuit alone should have registered her with the AI. In fact, it should have connected to the AI long before she reached the hatch, but there she was, should and shouldn't-ing all over the place.

"Zivhalla. Did not BZZPBRP ship." Another string of unintelligible noises followed, and she waited them out with strained patience.

"My ship crashed, Forerunner." *Don't call it Bozeo*, she reminded herself. Some AIs got in a tangle when addressed in terms they didn't expect, and this one seemed already to be in a struggle of some sort.

"Malfunction?"

"There was one, yes. I was in long sleep, and there wasn't time for a full download from the ship AI."

"NLX-45 inhabited." More noises, at a pitch that would have hurt her audial inputs if the biosuit didn't serve as a bit of a buffer.

"Your original report—"

"Original report incomplete." Much like Boscos, Bozeos didn't interrupt. Zivhalla wondered if she still had long-sleep fluid in her system to expel, or if the biosuit had finished processing it. The churning in her middle indicated the former.

"And your current report?" she prompted, when the interruption ended as abruptly as it had begun.

"Native life ZZZIIPSAP BIIING. Incursions."

Though she yanked calm over herself by the tips of her biosuit's reinforced fingers, Zivhalla strongly considered throwing her head back to howl. She also dismissed the following reactions of: scream, claw the walls, smash the Bozeo AI's program house, run at top speed out of the beacon, and set everything on fire.

Training, she reminded herself.

"Incursions of what nature?"

"Native life. Incursions. Standard response deployed."

Standard response? There was none. Either native growth was diagnosed as harmless, and so the forerunner AI signaled the Council for the next round of exploration, or it showed potential for danger, and a different set of next actions were called for.

The latter was not Zivhalla's department. Incursions?

"Detail of standard response?" She didn't have a lot of hope for the results of the question, and therefore was not disappointed when the answer was the longest string yet of oddly pitched nonsense yet.

* * *

They tracked the monster. Whether it was an honest-to-life space alien or some kind of weird pet to an honest-to-life space alien, they could not in good conscience deliver a report that didn't have every possible detail about it.

And if it happened to know anything about *Heracles*'s location, they could not miss the chance to find out.

"It's not hiding its tracks." Wodridge knelt next to the deep furrows they'd found several klicks past their first encounter with the monster. The ground marks were easy to follow—nothing else in the almost-forest had made any markings they'd come across previously—but easier yet was the new bruised color on the edges of the many-tree's tendrils. Graydin hadn't begun to conjecture what had caused it beyond the monster's passage, and none of the scientists had ventured a guess.

"Did you see the size and teeth of it, Wodridge?" Hetty asked, gesturing high above his head. "What's it got to be worried about?"

"Us," Alcoth replied, patting the stock of his weapon with a grin. "C'mon, did you see it run?"

"Yeah." Ada didn't glance back at the rest of them, and frowned at the furrows beside Wodridge instead. "I did. Not sure we'll catch it without the motos, boss," she added, with a tilt of her head in Graydin's direction.

"Motos aren't safe in the almost-forest." Graydin had said it before, as much for his own benefit as the rest. The scientists needed more reminding than the soldiers, to be fair.

They'd left a stash in the plains, and one on the other side of the many-tree, because while overwatch didn't drop a lot of extra manpower, they did understand the need for backup equipment. Over shorter distances, the motos could take three or four people, and the combination of spares and multiple riders meant they could afford to split their supply.

Regardless, it didn't help them in the moment. Neither cache appeared to be on the route the monster had thus far elected to take.

"And we risk losing it if we veer off." Sed noted, back to grumping.

"Is it going to ground?" Nal spoke aloud, but didn't direct his question to anyone in particular. Positing to himself, perhaps. "Finding a burrow somewhere in here?"

"To what end? How would it know about it?" Ada turned on her heel, strode in front of Nal's face to pull his focus back to the group. "Do you think it's been here before? Knows the terrain?"

"Why don't we find it, and then see what we can find out." Sed strode forward and sliced his hand through the air. "After you, Wodridge."

"You heard the man." Graydin pitched his voice to carry, but didn't shout. No need for a pissing match over who was in charge, not when they were all aligned in the next steps.

Besides, with a potential hostile in the area, it was unquestionably him.

The bleeping and blurping worsened, and Zivhalla needed to do *something* with the excess energy coursing between her and the biosuit. She spiraled out from the beacon to search for any of the missing equipment.

As though it would be that easy. As though it had taken itself for a walk. She knew better.

"Incursion" beat around the inside of her brain on a ragged loop, and if she could have dialed her own and her biosuit's senses and sensors any higher, she would have.

As her spiral widened, the windswept ground displayed new tracks. It took half a chron to pull the recording of the mobile fauna she'd passed nearer her crash site, and make a tentative connection between their lower appendages and the marks ahead of her.

The ground closer to the forerunner AI's beacon formed small hills and curving solid edges, populated by small scrubby brush that looked nothing like the oozy trees but dispensed clouds of tiny biting objects all the same.

Truly, NLX-45 would remain forever at the bottom of her list of preferred planets.

To be fair, she didn't need to like a planet to catalogue it appropriately for the Council. And perhaps, at some point in the near future, she would be in a state to attempt to do just that, but that time was not her present.

Her present involved tracking an "incursion" in order to find the materials she needed to either do her job properly, or wrap herself in a tube and wait out the inevitable Council follow-up that would remove her from this morass of biting, sucking, itching, *awful* planetary garbage.

This bias was not her best professional effort, but Zivhalla had been sorely tried, and felt justified to be angry and full of complaint in the privacy of her own head.

Proper job later. Incursion first.

She paused before the crest of each hill, and finally her caution rewarded her. Over the next curve sat three of the fauna she'd encountered earlier. They dug their short, stubby appendages into a pile of equipment recognizably, demonstrably *hers*.

Mobile fauna. Larger than she'd expected to find, but barely half her size, even if she weren't in the biosuit. In theory, her next steps should be straightforward and successful.

Theory, alas, so rarely aligned with reality.

Zivhalla spread her arms and reared to her full height, digging her reinforced feet deep into the ground to propel herself up and over. She yelled at the top of her register, echoing the strangest of noises Bozeo had glitched into, and rampaged toward the trio of native fauna.

But the fauna did not fall back, or split and run, as would have been sensible.

They instead jumped in front of their pile of her equipment, raised their limbs in near unison, and . . .

Fired projectiles at her. They screamed back, the noise far larger than their size would have predicted. Zivhalla recorded the entire encounter for later review, but in the meantime she was, in a word, surprised.

Were they intelligent?

She feinted to one side, and they pivoted together to face her. One made a noise that was so close to understandable she paused, but then additional projectiles impacted the biosuit. A small alert appeared in the corner of her vision and she determined retreat, for the moment, was the best course. It would give her time to consider better next actions.

Incursion indeed.

The tracks grew muddied, messy. Graydin hesitated to put a name to what he thought he saw, and then Hetty did.

"Are those . . . are those *human* prints?"

In a display of unprofessionalism so rare Graydin didn't bother to comment on it, the group crowded close, hovered over the indicated depressions with an overlapping babble of interest.

"Yes," Wodridge said, decisively.

Graydin rubbed the heel of his hand under his helmet and frowned. None of his options were great, but he had to make a call regardless. He was, after all, the one in charge.

"We split. Alcoth, Hetty, take Sed and Nal, and keep on target. Do not engage if you have a choice. Wodridge, Ada, you're with me."

"You think it's Coll, Lani, and Chysis?" Ada asked, then bit her lip. What other humans could there be? Graydin didn't ask the rhetorical question, and couldn't blame Ada for hers. They were dealing with . . . a lot.

"I think it's possible, and you're the one Coll's most likely to listen to if it is. And I'm the one with the most grenades, if it isn't." Graydin made eye contact with each of his people, scientist and soldier both, and each gave a nod in return.

He *wanted* the monster, but he *needed* to know if he'd failed and lost members of his team, or if they'd jeopardized the mission and wandered off on their own. He trusted Hetty and the rest not to feed themselves to giant alien jaws until he had a chance to figure it out and get back to them.

May Ceepax not let him down, this one time.

The team split without fanfare, clicking in over comms periodically to ensure proof of life from both sides.

Not a crackle of connection heralded Coll, Lani, and Chysis when they came into range, but despite all evidence previously gathered, that was who sat around a heat unit, calm as could be. As though they weren't sitting in the open under an alien sky, potentially stalked by an actual monstrous alien, days to weeks after they'd disappeared from camp.

A wild thought, quickly dismissed back into the void from which it had emerged, urged him to shoot them.

He did not, but he had cause to doubt the decision before the debrief finished.

"I had an accident," Coll said, as he scratched the back of his neck and stared somewhere over Graydin's head. "Heard something. Thought it was you all, but it was . . ." His grin did not curve the way it had before, loose on one side and higher on the other. "An alien monument."

"I lost my gear in the almost-forest," Chysis explained, and his fingers tapped an off-rhythm beat against his thighs. "Couldn't find my way back to you. But then I was out on the other side, and I . . . knew I saw Coll."

"I lost track of time." Lani hunched over a large bag Graydin didn't recall from the manifest, and cranked her head so far to the side Graydin's neck ached in sympathy. Or with the beginnings of a dull headache.

"Lost track of time" felt especially egregious. Graydin knew to shipboard standard the number of weeks, days, hours, minutes, seconds they'd been on Ceepax, and so that seemed exceptionally hard to believe. From Lani, the professional that she was, it fell doubly hard.

Between their twitchiness and the odd, discordant noises they made at each other between their explanations, Coll, Chysis, and Lani did not put anyone at their ease. Nor would they let Graydin look inside the bag—"Orders," Coll said with his off-center new smile— and so he signaled the rest of his team that they would stay in place for the night. When the scheduled time came for their debrief, his was clipped and short.

Hetty commed back almost immediately, but clearly he'd listened. *"We have eyes on the monument, boss. We've marked it and will fall back to your position."*

Graydin gazed longingly at his brace of grenades, and agreed that was an excellent plan.

Zivhalla haunted the edges of the strange faunas' camp. Were they nomadic? Had their finding the forerunner AI's beacon been happenstance?

The three she'd failed to scare off clustered around the scavenged gear she needed, and their additional members formed a rough perimeter with them in the middle. The creatures talked amongst themselves, produced gear that was neither hers nor familiar to her, and she was forced to reevaluate her preconceptions.

Intelligent, yes. Fully intelligent, perhaps. Machine-makers. Evolved.

They matched nothing in the forerunner AI's initial report, nor anything she'd encountered in her brief but disastrous time on NLX-45. She had not done her usual thorough duty, given the circumstances, but...

It seemed unlikely they were native to NLX-45, unless other portions of the planet were wildly evolutionarily different from this one and every additional piece the forerunner AI had scanned.

And if they weren't native...

She considered the odd malfunction of her ship. How it had gone so wildly off course, so broken it could not recover before casting her into the orbital grip of NLX-45.

The biosuit tightened around her, and she forced herself back to calm. If the Council had ever encountered evidence of spacefaring aliens, they'd kept it a better secret than history would suggest was possible. Perhaps this was the moment of first contact. And they were unfriendly. She was neither authorized nor trained to—

Her thoughts shattered to a halt, and she froze in her silent prowling around the edges of their camp.

A sound. One of them had made a sound that sounded almost *almost* like language. Like intelligent, intelligible, coherent language.

The same one as before, when there had been only three and they'd shot projectiles at her.

Another one made further noises, louder. They sounded... vaguely like the nonsense the forerunner AI had spouted, in between normal speech.

Zivhalla knew she should stop. Should consider. Should plan.

She was so tired of shoulds.

Instead, she used every advanced speed and strength modification the biosuit provided. She leapt. She grabbed. She leapt again. Her selected fauna yelled, and perhaps a commotion resulted behind her, but she didn't care.

She ran at full speed back to the beacon with her prize.

Graydin had no idea how the excrement-laden monster had taken Coll. How it had vanished as fast as it appeared, blurring until he wasn't sure he'd seen anything at all.

"Sir?"

Not boss, not now. Graydin glared at Lani and Chysis, who gabbled at each other in apparent gibberish, and allowed himself five seconds to process.

Fuck Coll. Fuck this planet.

Apparently they would be left to starve without resources, or perhaps die of old age if the many-tree proved edible. They could wait to see if they were abandoned and doomed, or they could go out guns blazing . . .

What the hell.

"We track the monster. Odds are it took Coll to the monument. We go. We take him back, take *it* out, make our report to *Heracles*." He delivered it calmly, meeting each set of eyes in turn. No sign he knew they were unlikely to survive the attempt.

The monster was huge. And *fast*. It had no right to be either, but facts were facts.

But if he didn't get to strangle Coll himself, he'd be damned if he'd let the monster have the satisfaction of killing the man without a fight.

Chysis and Lani didn't argue, but they were twitchy and half lost to gibberish and Graydin wasn't sure if they truly understood what had or would happen. He tasked Sed to keep watch over them, and the rest of them marched, guns at the ready, back to the location Hetty had marked.

The monument hurt his eyes, as the ship had. It twisted in a way his brain wasn't ready for. Pulsed, even, like it was alive. Like the almost-forest, but worse, because it oozed malevolence. This monument wanted, more than anything, to fuck up Graydin's world.

Maybe he was projecting. Either way, it took a solid reminder to himself that he was a damn professional and couldn't just toss his entire brace of grenades at it.

Might not even help. None of Ada's sensors could determine what it was made of. It didn't even show up right on any of their devices. They only found it because Hetty had put eyes on it, pinned it on the geolocator.

"Vomited excrement on a hot day," he muttered, careful not to put it over comms, but Wodridge snorted behind him. Maybe it was a crazy last stand, but voids take him if he wasn't doing it with the best damn crew he'd ever taken planetside.

"This monument doesn't belong here," Nal said, and it eased something in Graydin, to know they all felt the same way.

Stupid aliens.

Stupid Ceepax.

"Can the drone get eyes on the inside?" It didn't register on sensors, fine, but it *existed*, and damn if they wouldn't do their best not to go in blind.

"On it." Hetty sent three of his smallest drones in, and the fake night held its breath around them.

"Eyes up," he said, and Graydin nodded to Wodridge to take his position so he could move forward and see Hetty's screen.

The monster didn't seem to notice the drones. It loomed over Coll, wild gestures with its claws coming perilously close to the infuriating scientist.

Was it about to sacrifice Coll to the weird looped altar in the corner of the room? Both monster and idiot genius seemed focus on it. Hetty enabled sound and turned the volume up, higher and higher until the noise threatened to impale the center of Graydin's eardrum.

"Is that . . . ?" Hetty trailed off, eyes fixed to his screen even as his shoulders climbed up to his ears.

"Familiar?"

"That's not Coll's voice."

"Who else is talking?"

Ada, who spoke every living human language and a handful of dead ones, made a noise that might have been a laugh. "Something is speaking two languages, on top of each other. And one of them is . . ."

"Ours." Fuck. Fuck fuck fuck fuck. Graydin repeated it half a dozen more times. Aloud. In his head. Didn't matter.

Despite his better judgment, sure he'd end up getting eaten, Graydin signaled his people to hold.

And then he walked into the monster's den, and said the dumbest thing he'd ever produced.

"We're here in peace."

Bozeo had yet to make entire sense, but it made a better effort than Bosco ever had, translating the mouth noises of the weird fauna and speaking Zivhalla's actual words back to it in some sort of shrieking pattern.

"Forerunner AI, do not speak to the creature for a moment. Were they the incursion you indicated?"

"Yes. No."

"Which?"

"Both."

Zivhalla had hated limited AIs before. At the moment, if she could have put her biosuit's extended fingers on even one AI engineer, ripped her limb from limb, and trampled her pieces until they became biomass to feed her biosuit, she would have done it with joy.

As it happened, she could not, so she composed herself, did not squeeze the small creature before her into a pulp, and kept her attention on Bozeo.

"Can you clarify?"

"Local fauna infested the area. Clouded computing. Adaptation required. Created irritant."

That all made sense. The organic matter that composed the AI, and in fact all of Zivhalla's technology, was made to adapt to threats, and turn them away with the least interference possible.

"Was the irritant successful?"

"Irritant sent local fauna away. Larger fauna later returned, with adapted irritant."

That . . . didn't make sense.

"Return to translation. Did you get bitten here?"

The creature gabbled in reply to Bozeo's gibberish. Or alien language.

It made a lot of noise for the answer to be "No," but Zivhalla hadn't waited. She pulled up the readings of the many small bites NLX-45's tiny life had taken from her, and compared that to the awkwardly thin coating of the large mobile fauna.

It wasn't . . . dissimilar.

Zivhalla got about halfway into formulating her next question when another set of gibbered alien language imposed, which Bozeo immediately translated as, "We're here in peace."

She spun around, and long training kept her limbs close so that she didn't accidentally dismember the creature she'd taken. Best to mean one's dismemberments.

"You shot down my ship," she blurted, which was no credit to her training whatsoever, and before she could stop Bozeo, the AI made a string of BLRRT noises and the new intruding creature reared back.

"I did no such thing. We have not had contact with our ship in months, and it is overdue to return. Did you see it?"

"I was in long sleep." Zivhalla cocked her head, but she couldn't tell which noises meant what, so she didn't know how Bozeo conveyed things that might not have a proper translation in creature—alien— whatever speech. Did they use long sleep? How did they travel? Her explorer's heart prompted a hundred immediate questions, but her anger and concern warred above it.

"My people would not have destroyed your ship unprovoked." The alien put its small appendages on the hard shell of its . . . head, probably, and then . . .

Zivhalla reared back this time, a full two steps as it took the top of its head off. What sort of gesture was this? Threat? Display of vulnerability? Would something shoot out of the revealed, softer section?

"We are not here for violence. We are here to learn. Why did you take BLRRT—that one?"

After dialing down every one of her clamoring systems, Zivhalla snapped back to attention. "Bozeo, do not translate. Are you sure that is what it said? They are here to learn?"

"Yes."

"How do you know what they're saying?"

"Translation happened over time. Three of the fauna have embedded adaptable biomass."

It almost began to make sense. The forerunner AI had shooed away local fauna with a small, irritating bioweapon. The local fauna infested the mobile aliens. Mobile aliens returned to the source of the irritating bioweapon for unknown reasons. The infestation allowed the forerunner AI to interface, learn . . . adapt.

And perhaps that series of learnings and adaptations had been why Bozeo hadn't automatically connected to her biosuit upon her abrupt arrival?

"Begin translation again." She would not remove her biosuit the way the new arrival had taken off part of its head, but she shortened her reinforced digits to better match the smaller aliens' appendages. Hopefully the gesture would be taken in the spirit it was intended. "I too am here to learn, not for violence. I took your"—she made her best approximation of the BLRT noise Bozeo had not translated, and gestured at the first alien—"in order to determine what had happened."

"Did you figure it out?"

Was that a joke?

Impossible to tell, in Bozeo's flat lack of inflection. From an alien mouth. But she wanted to believe it might be. That they might come to an understanding, their two spacefaring races. Dangerous, she reminded herself, and held her focus. "I believe I might be . . . close."

Grudgingly, Graydin began to hate Ceepax less. With the efforts of the alien—Zivhalla—Coll, Lani, and Chysis had grown slightly less weird. Still as obnoxious as before, in Coll's case, but far less twitchy.

Through the monument's intelligent system, they found a way to share records, building each other's data store about the planet. His own team's systems had been unable to register the infinitesimally tiny pollen-like creatures of the many-tree, but with Zivhalla's input suddenly several things were made clear.

Ceepax was not a terrific candidate for colonization, despite the suitable atmosphere. The tiny creatures were colonizers of their own, and the human system far too susceptible to them for comfort. After having learned of the infection and the many-mini-tree creatures, Graydin understood Coll and the others hadn't meant to ruin everything and go walkabout. They'd been infected, infested, and driven.

He didn't forgive them, exactly, but he mentally revised his report to be slightly more generous.

Before he could get too carried away at being reasonable, Hetty sprinted out of the shelter they'd built near Zivhalla's tower, waving something wildly over his head.

It spoke to the weirdness of Graydin's recent life that it took him a full breath to figure out what it was: the surface-to-ship comm.

The *Heracles*.

Fucking finally.

The humans were generous, and took their conversation with their ship inside the beacon. Bozeo translated directly to her audial inputs, which allowed her to hide her reactions.

"Apologies for the delay, Ground Team. We were knocked off course

after an encounter. I...am cleared to tell you it was with an alien spacecraft."

Two of the humans—Ada and Chysis—turned sharply toward her, baring their square teeth in their version of a friendly expression. Zivhalla did not share their hopeful sentiment.

Before Graydin could interject, perhaps for the best, the ship human continued speaking.

"It came out of nowhere. About the same time we registered it, it fired on us. We responded with an EMP, in hopes of getting a hold of it."

The humans continued talking, and Coll interjected to ask officious questions but didn't actually reveal Zivhalla's existence yet.

A good thing, because Zivhalla had dealt with Bosco for a very, very, *very* long time and could picture exactly what had happened.

The human ship had not read on any of her ship's sensors until they were nearly on top of it. The "unexpected object" was the human ship. Bosco had attempted to "clear the obstacle" but instead fired on the first other spacefaring race her people had ever encountered.

The AI engineers had never built a decision-tree for potential encounters with other spacefaring races. She couldn't even really blame Bosco. Or the engineers. Not much, anyway.

The human ship's electromagnetic counter had done more damage than the humans could have expected, disrupting the organic links between ship and AI, and navigation had suffered. Operations had suffered.

"It vanished from our sensors almost immediately, though we were sure we made contact... We spent time sweeping the area, and then had to readjust to ensure our message home got out from the best position. Unfortunately, that added more time than we'd expected to our course. We're glad to find you well."

Graydin made the fast scrunch of his facial muscles that indicated he was not impressed, but not angry. Complicated emotions, as befitted a fellow intelligent race. Zivhalla's exploratory heart radiated pride in her success deciphering so much, so soon.

"More important to tell home base we found aliens than ensure ground team was alive. Even with you here," Graydin said, but to Coll, not the comm. Then he gestured to Hetty and spoke to the ship human.

"Happy to tell you we have a lot more information on Ceepax and also aliens than you might have been expecting, *Heracles.*"

"Come again, Ground Leader?"

Sharp, Zivhalla thought. Nervous? Surprised? Bozeo hadn't improved in its ability to inflect, so she had to infer based on the timing of the human words and the AI translation.

"What's your ETA?"

"Repeat, Ground Leader. What's that about aliens?"

"Tell the captain that Coll Darrey's alive. Whole crew, matter of fact. And we got a bonus alien ambassador." Graydin gestured to Hetty again, held his small upper appendage against the side of his mouth and pivoted slightly toward Zivhalla. "Captain hates Coll too. Probably part of why they talked themselves into a delay being fine."

"Graydin, full report, please."

This was a different ship human voice, and from Graydin's snap fully upright, maybe the captain, who was something like a Council member.

Zivhalla listened to the rest passively, recording it for later analysis. Before the humans' *Heracles* arrived, she had her own matters to process.

Such as the fact her people's stupidly smart AIs had twice committed unintentional war crimes on the humans—attacking their ship unprovoked, and then accidentally seeding them with an engineered virus.

If Graydin were successful in soothing his ship people, and they ultimately managed to repair her comms pod...

Where did an ambassador to the first intelligent, spacefaring race they'd ever encountered rank against a Council member?

Maybe she'd have enough power to *finally* fix the fucking AIs.

Old and Broken Gods

Blaine L. Pardoe

Washington, District of Columbia
22 July 1950

The powers that be had relegated David Boyle to the basement of the CIA's offices on E Street. Residents of Washington, DC, did not know what the building housed; to them it was merely another nondescript government office. Aside from a small PROPERTY OF THE US GOVERNMENT sign on the wrought iron fencing surrounding the otherwise boring building, there were only rumors that it was the headquarters of the CIA. David heard rumors of a new headquarters to be built in Virginia, but he liked the old building. *The best place to hide something is often in plain sight.*

David's office in the bowels of the building was intentional. People didn't know what his specialty was, but it seemed to be obscure. Why not shuffle him out of sight? The basement was musty and reminded him more of a dungeon than office space. During the war, he had been with the CIA's precursor, the OSS. Presumably the current director had been told of his unique background and experiences, which was why he hadn't been forced into retirement. Since WWII, his team had been disbanded, leaving only him still working in his specific field of intelligence. While he kept up with his comrades, time separated them. The CIA seemed content to keep David tucked away, out of sight.

His days were spent researching in the musty quiet of his cramped workspace. It wasn't as glamorous as his previous professions, but he enjoyed the work. When his phone rang, he initially assumed it was a mistake. Calls didn't come to him. His supervisor barely spoke to him.

David wasn't sure if it was out of respect or fear, or both. He picked the receiver up slowly, almost cautiously. "Boyle."

"Mr. Boyle, the Director has requested your presence in his office immediately," the woman's curt voice commanded.

His left eyebrow cocked at the news. "Very well. I'm on my way up."

He adjusted his thin black tie on the elevator ride up. He was sure that younger analysts would have been excited to be summoned to meet with the Director. For him, it was an intriguing change of pace. An old ache resurfaced on his upper right abdomen, which he gently caressed. The fact that it gave him any hint of pain was a clue that this was no administrative meeting. *Something is happening... it has to be for them to have called me up here.*

David entered the Director's outer office. His ID was verified by the secretary who ushered him in. As he stepped into the inner sanctum, as some referred to it, he saw General Walter Bedell Smith, who gestured for him to take a seat. It had been years since he had been in the Director's office, prior to Smith's assignment there. He noted the wooden nongovernment-issued desk that Smith used, no doubt an heirloom of some sort. "So, you are the mysterious man living in our basement," the Director said as David sat.

"I suppose that is one way to look at it, sir."

"When I took over for Roscoe, he gave me a rundown on you and the team you led during the war. I have to admit, I was pretty skeptical of what he was telling me. Then he showed me some of the photos and reports. What you did fighting the Germans, well... it is somewhat remarkable."

It was a typical reaction, one he had experienced dozens of times before. "I simply have an area of expertise that is, dare I say, unique."

"Demons and demigods," Smith said. "I never would have thought we'd have an expert in that."

"Threats come in many shapes and forms. Your predecessors felt that having me on staff would be useful should such a threat ever surface." Memories of the last war and his time in the OSS tugged at him.

"Roscoe was a smart man. That's why we're meeting," Smith said, opening a folder with a red stapled TOP SECRET cover page stapled to it. "As you know, the North Koreans have been driving us south. I've had a lot of people chewing my ass, asking how we could have failed to see this coming."

"I can only imagine."

Director Smith cocked his head slightly as he looked at him. "During our redeployment south, one of our people said that the North Koreans had concentrated their forces near Yecheon-gun. We didn't give it much thought, but our recon flights spotted a lot of earth-moving equipment there. Our analysts going over the photos thought it was an archeological dig, which made no damn sense at the time.

"A few days later, we started getting reports of some sort of creature, a monster or some damn thing. It was attacking our infantry."

David leaned in at the word "monster." *The North Koreans were looking for something and found it. Something buried.* Smith slid a photograph in front of him. It was grainy, but he could see three soldiers being attacked by a towering monstrosity. It was reptilian in some respects, with huge claws that looked as if they could crush a human with little effort. Its face was a bony white with rows of sharp teeth and fangs. Bone-like spike projections rose out of the monster's back. The eyes of the creature were pools of obsidian. There were spots that glowed green on its hide. As David pulled the photo closer, he peered into the eye orbs and saw the reflections of fire from all around the troops. There was age there, centuries if not more, mixed with rage.

"What do you make of it?" Smith pressed.

He slowly put the photograph back on the desk. "Are you sure you want to know?"

Smith nodded. "Alright, then. It is a demon, though what kind, I'm not sure." It was odd that it was photographed. *Usually they don't show up on film.*

"A demon."

"Yes."

Smith said nothing for a moment, then nodded. "Assuming you're right, how do we stop it?"

"Not with conventional weapons, that is for sure. My former colleagues and I specialized in terminating or imprisoning demons and devils. This isn't one I'm familiar with, but I know people who are."

"This thing has been hitting us hard. We were lucky that someone from the Signal Corps got a photograph of it before it killed those men. We thought it was a hoax at first. When the word 'monster' came up, one of the older staff members reminded me about you. I always thought this hocus pocus stuff was BS. But this..." He nodded to the photograph.

"An understandable reaction."

"Needless to say, if the press gets ahold of this, it will only make matters worse for us. I can't imagine what we would tell the American people. We need to contain and eliminate this thing."

"I agree. Sir, the best solution is to let me gather my people. We can deal with this. In fact, we may be the best hope you have for dealing with it."

"You're asking a lot. Your team is all over the place, assuming they are still alive. This monster is on some sort of rampage. It is hitting us in key points on the front, as if it knows where to strike us."

It must be being controlled by someone. "Trust me, my people are quite alive," David replied firmly. "We'll need the means to get on the ground in Korea. The rest of what we require we will bring ourselves."

Smith studied his face in silence for long moments. "Is it true, what is in your file about you?"

"I have had this discussion many times in my life. While I don't know the contents of my file, I presume you are referring to my origin. Yes, it is true." Boyle didn't even try and mask the pride he felt.

"I'm having a hard time believing it. I know it's in your official file. It's just ... remarkable."

Boyle extended his right hand, palm up. One moment it was just a hand, the next it held a softball-size orb of fire. The flames were not large, but strangely controlled. Director Smith stared at it, his eyes wide and his mouth slightly agape. He reached out over the desk to the ball of fire, just enough to feel the heat, confirming it wasn't some parlor trick illusion.

David closed his hand and the fire disappeared.

"That's incredible," Smith said.

"It is my gift," Boyle replied with a smile that seemed to melt away his wrinkles. *For all mankind ...*

"I want to send someone to work with you," Smith said.

"That is not necessary."

"No offense, Mr. Boyle, but you are old."

You cannot comprehend how much so. "I know, but my people are more than able to handle themselves."

"That may be the case. The man I have in mind also is fluent in Korean. That might be helpful. I believe that a young, fresh set of eyes and hands may be useful."

David doubted that. Memories of Hank Gordon and Alexi Gruber from September of 1944 came back to him. Before then there was Wally Granite back during the First World War. His death had been heroically tragic, worthy of a poem. Memories of the individual claiming to be Rasputin were hard for him to suppress, but somehow he managed. *Not all people are equipped for the kind of work we do.* Memories of the flames and their screams were things he preferred to not think of.

"What I specialize in is dangerous, in ways that are hard to frame in words. There's no training for what we do."

"Nevertheless, I think it is prudent."

Boyle bowed his head slightly, more out of respect than agreement. "As you wish, sir."

Victor Tanner stepped into his basement office as David finished packing his leather satchel. He was young, in his early thirties, black hair, slicked back. He had a mustache that was pencil thin, almost right out of central casting. "You're Boyle, right?"

"You must be Tanner. The Director sent word you were being assigned to me," he said, extending his hand. Tanner eyed it for a moment, then shook it.

"They told me I am assigned to you. That we're going to Korea."

"That's it?"

He shrugged. "Apparently the rest is on a need to know. So, are you going to tell me?"

Boyle held back a smile. *Where would I begin? Certainly not at the beginning.* "During the Great War, the US encountered some unusual *phenomena.* They were, at the time, not prepared to deal with it. So a unit was formed with individuals who were uniquely equipped to deal with such threats.

"During the next war, Germany and Russia both unleashed more of these threats in an attempt to sway the war effort. I was second-in-command of that unit, under the auspices of the OSS. We went in and did what had to be done. Our efforts were off the books. Great pains were taken to obscure our impact on the war."

"The Russians were our allies."

"So they claimed. We perceived their true intentions long ago."

"Fair enough. What kind of phenomena are we talking about?"

It was a good question. It was proof that he wasn't just writing him off as crazy. "The most appropriate word would be 'supernatural.' Specifically, we helped kill devils and demons, old-world stuff, that the Nazis and Russians decided to awaken."

"You fought demons?" His words dripped with skepticism.

"Yes."

Tanner seemed to be mentally processing the information, almost as if he were cataloging each sentence in his mind. "You do know that sounds insane, don't you?"

"Insanity is a part of the job, at least for those that aren't up to the task."

"How do you do it?"

"It's not something I can describe. Much is dependent on the type of demon summoned. Given the threat in Korea, we are going to have deal with this quickly, before it gains too much power. That means you will have to learn on-the-job."

His young partner nodded. "Alright, fine."

This wasn't the first time he had such a discussion, but it was one of the easier ones, which was puzzling. "If I may, Victor—you seem pretty accepting of this."

Another shrug came with his response. "I've been put on some pretty weird assignments in the last ten years. The way I see it, you are either crazy, which means they put me here to make sure you don't go off the rails; or you are right, in which case, you are going to need all of the help that you can get."

Pragmatic... something that Boyle appreciated. "Very well. We're heading out to Culpeper, Virginia, then up to Brown University in Rhode Island."

"Do you want me to arrange a flight to Japan so we can get to Korea?"

David smiled. "That won't be necessary."

"Then how are we getting to Korea?"

"Trust me."

Culpeper, Virginia

Harry Kyle was using a push mower to cut his grass when David pulled up in front of his house. David got out and saw him and smiled.

Harry's olive-skinned muscles had not lost a bit of tone since the last time they had met. He was sweating, which was something new. *Maybe mortality is finally starting to get a grip on him.* The aroma of freshly cut grass was strangely inviting. *What a strange thing for civilization to adopt, mowing grass for the aesthetics.* Walking up the sidewalk, Victor got out of the car and followed him two paces back. Harry stopped and looked at his old friend.

"This is a surprise," he said with a hint of formality that was always present with Kyle.

"It is good to see you, old friend. Your yard looks good."

"It is grass. This concept of cutting it will never make sense to me, but one must fit in." As a spoke, a falcon flew in and landed on the white rail of his porch.

"I see you still have Isis," Harry said with a nod to the porch.

"It is not a question of me having Isis. It is better to say that Isis still tolerates me. Who is your accomplice?"

"This is Victor Tanner," he replied, gesturing to the agent. Tanner didn't step forward, but dipped his head once in respect.

"It's not like you to bring along luggage, David."

"Even I answer to people."

"That is a choice."

David knew he had to cut to the chase. Harry was not the kind of individual who exuded patience. "A situation has come up; one that I could use your help with." Walking to his friend, he pulled out the photo that Director Smith had given him.

Harry took it and squinted slightly as he looked at it. It was almost as if he were looking through the paper, his gaze was so intense. "Where was this taken?"

"Korea."

"That makes sense," he replied, turning the photo slightly at an angle, as if it offered him a better view. "Strange. Usually they don't show up on film."

"My thoughts as well."

"Someone could be exerting control, which would block its instincts to remain unseen."

"What is this demon? I have never seen one like it."

"It looks to be the natural form of a Dokkaebi."

"I'm not familiar with them."

"As well you shouldn't. They can shape-shift, but this is how they appear naturally. As demons go, they can be quite powerful. Their original naming translates roughly to, 'impossible to kill.' Some like playing the role of tricksters, but some, like this one, are simply vicious killers driven by blood rage. The Buddhists took measures to imprison them a long time ago. Someone must have let this one out."

"The CIA wants it stopped."

"The CIA? How quaint. You may be comfortable with taking orders from mortals, but I do not...not after what we went through in Russian, Holland, and Germany."

"I understand your feelings. I'm not doing this for the US government. This is a demon. Humanity does not have the means to cope with such evil, but we do."

"'We'? I assume you are bringing the others into this?"

"That's the plan."

Harry handed him the photo back. "I won't follow their orders. We are going to need help, someone with the strength. A Dokkaebi will be on par with what we faced with Rasputin."

Memories of the creature in Russia tore at David. *So much blood that night.* "Thank you for reminding me. We will need some strength, brute force. As such, I have some thoughts on that. He's in Valhalla."

"He's always in Valhalla. He won't come."

"I can persuade him."

Harry let loose a thin smile. "Perhaps you can. I will need to do some research. How long until we depart?"

"Two days. I need to persuade Alice to join us."

Harry crossed his massive arms across his chest. "She can be stubborn with everyone other than you. I have tried to visit her twice and been stood up. I trust I can meet with you at Valhalla."

"That was my thinking. And about Alice, she is a force of nature. She will respond well to me, she always has in the past."

"We'll need her. In the meantime, I will do some research on this particular Dokkaebi."

David paused, smiling slightly. "I'm glad you're coming along, Harry."

"Once more unto the breech, old friend."

Brown University
Providence, Rhode Island

David knocked on Dr. Alice Exousía's office door. He had left his new partner behind in DC with a list of gear they might want to bring. The meeting with Alice was something that he wanted to keep private, especially given their past. She could be cordial and venomous at the same time and since he was asking for a favor, he knew privacy would be prudent.

"Enter," came her almost sultry voice. He stepped in and closed the frosted glass door behind him.

She sat behind her desk, framed by a wall of books on shelves. Her black hair had streaks of white in it. Time treated her well. Looking at David, she smiled. "I sensed that you would be coming."

"I thought you might. It is good to see you again."

"I apologize for having to cancel our lunch a few months ago."

"It is understandable, if not disappointing."

She gestured to the chair across from her and David sat down, crossing his legs. "A demon has escaped in Korea. The CIA has ordered me to investigate and resolve the situation. I could really use your help."

"I knew I felt something amiss."

"Harry believes it is a Dokkaebi. It has attacked and killed our troops and is still on the loose."

Alice rested her elbows on the desk, touching her fingertips in the air between the two of them. "Things are not like they were a few years ago. During the last war, we were able to keep much of what we did under wraps. Now that atomic weapons exist, Mars is having far too much fun."

"Mars is a problem for another day. I am more focused on this demon spawn. I know it won't be easy, but I need you there, if you're willing."

There was no hesitation in her response. "Of course. I always found you impossible to refuse."

"I need to go to Valhalla to see if I can get our muscle. Let's meet there at eight PM tomorrow."

"You know he isn't going to want to go. I saw him a while back. He's still brooding about what happened in Holland."

He has every right to still be angry. That's the problem with immortality, you can carry your grudges much longer than mortals. David smiled. "It's not a question of wanting. It's about needing."

"What makes you think I would want to be involved?"

"Come, now. You know what can happen if one of these were to go on a rampage unchecked."

"It isn't my problem, nor is it yours."

"Alice . . ." He struggled using her human name. "Please join us. We need you there."

"We . . . or you?"

He bit his lower lip. "Very well, *I* need you there."

"You are getting soft. If mankind has released this thing, let them cope with it."

"They cannot, and you know it. We are the last bastions of the power needed to bring this thing to bay."

For a few moments, she said nothing, relishing his invitation. "You could have called me," she stated.

"I know. I wasn't sure how you'd react. Also, *I* wanted to see you, regardless of your answer."

"I thank you for that, probably more than you know. The people of today lack much of the formality that we appreciate."

"They do. In the end, I think that lack of civility and respect will be their downfall—but not today. Please come with us. We need your insight and knowledge. None are more equipped."

The older woman sighed. "I agree. But this will be the last time."

"Of course."

"Despite my appearance, time is taking a toll on me. Far too many fights. This time, then no more."

David understood all too well. "I promise. Truth be told, I'm feeling time slowly catching up with me as well. I now have aches . . . something I never expected."

"I suppose I have another good fight in me."

She feels as I do, that Chronos is extracting his toll. "Hopefully this won't be bad."

The nation's capital was dark and wet from an early evening rain that had just ended a few minutes before. The hot pavement made the cooler rain rise as steam, generating a low fog. David and Victor walked down F Street, past the stoic gray government buildings that were dark for the night. Tanner was lugging a heavy green duffel filled with their weapons and gear. David knew they would be of marginal use—with the exception of the grenades—but he hoped it would convince Victor that this was going to be a straight-up fight. He found the alley he was searching for, and turned into it, out of the dim streetlights' beams.

"Where are we going?" Tanner asked, increasing his pace to keep up with him.

"Valhalla," David replied, turning to face a redbrick wall.

"Valhalla? You mean like where the Vikings went when they died?"

"Not exactly," he said slowly, his fingers reaching out and touching the brick. "Myths tend to distort facts over time. There's more than one Valhalla. One is a form of afterlife. This is more like a pub."

"I know of no bar called Valhalla in the District."

He turned to face the younger man. Victor had been patient thus far, a trait that Boyle appreciated. Now he would have to test that bit of his personality even further. "Technically, you're correct. Valhalla exists beyond Earth, in its own space. It intersects the world we live in everywhere. Some of us can open the door to enter it using otherworldly powers."

David waited as Victor stood like a statue. "Like the Buddhist Planes of Consciousness?"

"Close. Think of it as multiple material planes that pass through each other."

"You're telling me there's a bar that exists everywhere . . . some sort of magical pub?"

It was hard to not smile at his summation, since it was technically accurate. "Yes."

Victor nodded his head once. "Okay." *His willingness to accept this does him credit.*

"One more thing. This place was built for the gods. Some are, dare I say, a bit surly about mortals treading in their space. You'll be coming in under my protection. It would be wise to not engage with them if they attempt to taunt you."

"Wait," Victor said, putting his hand on David's shoulder. "Are you telling me that you are some sort of god?"

It was a response that never got old for David. "Yes. So is Dr. Exousía and Harry."

"The CIA employs a god?"

"It's more like former god. It's not like I have worshippers still. It is a long story, one I promise to share when this is done."

A smile rose on Victor's face. "I get it. You older guys like pranking the younger guy. You almost had me going there for a minute. Former god. That's pretty good ... very funny, old-timer."

David matched his grin with his bow. "Hold that thought."

Reaching out with his open palm, he pressed it against the brick wall. A golden light shimmered from his hand, radiating outward to the form of a doorway with an arched top. The brick illuminated by his hand seemed to go dark, then disappeared entirely, opening to a blackness. David stepped through and, as his foot hit the floor, he found himself in the familiar space of Valhalla.

It was a bar, with wooden half walls—built on massive smooth stonework—whose grains seemed etched in time, harkening to ages past. Light came from the lanterns along the walls, eternal heatless flames that flickered and gave life to the space. The bar was long, with bottles both glass and earthenware from many long-forgotten ages. The aroma was familiar to him—heady, tinged with magic and energy. There were a half dozen hand-hewn tables, with only two that had patrons sitting around them. They gave David a gaze of acknowledgment. *I should have come back here long ago. I almost forgot how much I love this place.*

Behind him, Victor stumbled slightly into the room. David moved to help steady him. "The disorientation will fade in a few moments."

"I feel like I'm going to throw up," he said as his face went pale.

"Please don't. Bringing you here is likely going to raise some eyebrows as it is." David left Victor standing alone, fighting his vertigo, and moved to the bar. The archway they had entered through disappeared, replaced by stone and wood as if it had never been there.

"You," the large bartender said. He had a blond beard with streaks of white hair in it, braided at the ends.

David knew him all too well and cracked a smile in response. "Come now, old friend."

"If you are calling me 'friend,' that means you need a favor."

"Can't an old acquaintance come and visit?"

The bartender glanced over David's shoulder to Victor. "Still dragging along your pets, I see."

"This is Victor," David said waving his hand at his partner, who was already getting his color back. Victor moved up next to him at the bar, his eyes clearly trying to absorb everything he saw. "Victor, this is Thor, son of Odin and Jörð, husband of Sif." He stopped there, not wanting to discuss his friend's mistress openly.

Victor stared in awe for a moment, then managed to say, "Nice to meet you."

Thor rolled his eyes quickly, then looked to David. "I still bear scars from our last outing together in Holland."

"As do I."

"You are used to scars. That eagle feasted on your liver for centuries."

"Please, don't remind me. I wouldn't have come, but I need your strength, old friend. Someone has unleashed a terror on mankind that only we are equipped to deal with."

Thor turned to a cask along the wall and opened the spigot, pouring two ceramic mugs, putting one in front of David, and one for Victor. "And why would I care what is happening to mankind? Everyone in this bar has had man turn their backs on them, some more violently than others."

David took the tall mug and sipped the ale, savoring it. Mortal alcohol had little effect on him, but Valhalla had gods' brew. He savored it only for a moment as Victor reached for his mug. David put his hand over the mug and shook his head to warn off his mortal partner.

That made Thor smile, if only slightly. "Come now, he looks to be a sturdy man."

"We both know that what is served here is not for mortals."

"Can't I have a little fun?"

"Yes, you can. Just not tormenting him. Thor, come with us."

"'Us'? Don't tell me you have convinced the others to join you?"

"I did. It didn't even take any effort, really. They will be along shortly."

"Then you don't need me."

David grinned broadly. *He is making me do this dance just to enjoy my effort.* "Come now, we all know that you were a critical member of our team."

"So was Nergal at one time. Holland sealed his fate."

"That was his own doing. This isn't about him, this is about you and what you bring to our little party."

Thor's eyes narrowed slightly, though David could tell that he enjoyed having his ego stroked. He took another long drink of the ale. "I have not tread the Earth since those days."

"And you loved it! Come on, Thor, admit it, you enjoy the sting of battle, the shattering of bones, the thumping of skulls! You always have."

Thor was clearly contemplating the offer, as David knew he would. "What is it we face?"

"A Dokkaebi. A Korean demon, one I assume is particularly nasty."

"Why did they free such an abomination?" The question was a good one that David wanted an answer to as well.

"I do not know. There is a war going on. Perhaps they thought it would aid their cause."

"They are mortal. There's always a war going on."

"True. But this is a demon, Thor! A true test of your might. I'm sure it will present you with challenges in combat. I bet you have not fought a good battle with your life on the line since Holland."

The god of thunder sighed. "Not true! It was not long ago that Erlik came in here with a pet dragon. He refused to leave his pet outside and we fought a glorious struggle to the near death!"

One of the patrons at a nearby table made a *harrumph* sound of derision.

"Erlik?" David said with a sneer. "He only tread on Terra for a few centuries. Hardly a challenge for someone of your stature."

"That dragon was nasty and vicious," Thor countered. "It was a battle worthy of a line in a song, if not two."

"What I am offering you is a real fight. We are talking a demon that has been imprisoned for centuries. Think of it! It will take several gods to capture such a threat. That is something that would surely merit an entire song."

Thor pondered his words, then grinned. "You know me too well. When do we depart?"

"The others are coming shortly. We need to be careful. Demons are infused with the energy of the afterlife. We may need more than brute force to subdue it."

"Excellent!" Thor replied. "I shall go and find a sword worthy of such a battle."

Victor spoke up. "I thought you used a magic hammer?"

Thor shot him an icy glance and walked down to the end of the bar, then through a doorway. David leaned over. "Don't bring that up. His daughter has it. It's a rather sensitive subject."

Victor nodded. "Everyone's words are funny. Their lips don't match what I'm hearing."

"It is the Tongue. We speak a language that is translated in the minds of mortals and others of our kind. It is one of the first powers one obtains as a god rises to power, the ability to spread their message to others. Don't worry, you will get used to it."

"Which god are you?"

David paused for a moment. "Those of us that walk the Earth rarely reference our past lives. It is hard on a god when their worshipers dwindle and when our power fades. We become the things of myth rather than beings that influenced the affairs of mankind. Our long lives mean we must endure being relegated to a status of quasi-mortal. Thor works here, in Valhalla, rather than live among those that no longer recognize or pray to him. Others, like myself, prefer a level of anonymity."

"Can you die?"

"Oh yes. Our powers fade, and eventually our bodies weaken too. Most mortal risks don't worry us, but things of magic from the realms beyond can kill us. Like with this mission: the risks are quite real."

"It must be . . . lonely."

"It can be. Time's tug on us is slower. You see mortal friends age and die, knowing you will continue on. Loves in your life wither away while you adopt a new identity and life." David paused, shaking his head. "You see the wonders of the world, and its most evil creations. I decided to stand against the darkness of my kin, the creatures of the underworld and afterlife. If not people like me, then who?"

Before Victor could ask another question, the doorway arch shimmered and Harry entered. For just a fraction of a second, David saw his friend in his true form, his head transformed to that of a falcon, his skin shimmered of bronze, then he morphed back to his human form. Walking to the bar, he sat down next to David.

Thor returned with a massive broadsword in hand. "Ah, you're on this fool's quest as well?" Thor said as he joined them, setting the sword on the bar top.

"It is good to see you, old friend," Harry said, extending his hand and shaking it with Thor. The doorway shimmered again and Alice stepped through it. Her visage morphed for a moment to that of a much younger woman in a flowing white tunic tied at her shapely waist in a golden belt. He saw the spear she was walking with, but it disappeared as Alice's form returned.

"Thor!" she called out, leaning over the bar for a kiss, which the god of thunder happily gave her.

"It pleases me to see you," Thor said.

"As well it should," she replied with a wink that a far younger girl might cast as a flirt. She turned her gaze to Victor. "A mortal? I would have thought you'd learned your lesson after Holland?"

"Dr. Alice Exousía, this is Victor Tanner of the CIA."

"Charmed," she said, giving Victor a smile. "I used to be in the OSS during the war."

"Really," Victor replied.

"Such times were intriguing. Chasing Nazis gave me a sense of purpose. Of course, killing the occasional devil or recovering dangerous artifacts certainly gave me more spirit than I was accustomed to."

Thor interceded before Victor could probe deeper. "So, what are we facing again?"

"A Dokkaebi," Harry replied. "Nasty little buggers. Asian goblins. Most are pranksters, more annoying than anything else. This one, he's full-blown evil. I checked the Library and found out that the last time he was loose he killed thousands. How they imprisoned it was a marvel of powerful wards and spells."

"Why release it at all?" Alice asked.

"To aid in their war effort. The North Koreans have the UN forces on the run."

"They must have the means to control it," she pressed. "It's a demon . . . they are notorious for turning on those that befriend them."

"I found reference to a set of silver bracers used to, and I quote, 'compel the creature,'" Harry answered. "Whoever is wearing them is calling the shots with this Dokkaebi. They are the demon's leash."

David drank in his friend's words. *So the North Koreans got the bracers, found the demon, and released it . . . does that make sense? It* didn't. The logical part of his mind focused on what they knew and what they didn't. *Few mortals understood the powers arcane. The Dokkaebi in question was a relatively obscure demon. There's more in play than what we know.* Glancing over at Alice, he saw her nod, meaning she was picking up on the same thing he was.

"Since reasoning is out of the question," Thor stated, "I assume we have to rely on brute force." There was a hint in his voice that he was going to be looking forward to that.

"We should attempt to ascertain its purpose," Harry stated.

Alice nodded. "Wanton killing is not the norm for one of these beings. If I recall correctly, Dokkaebi are more into deception and manipulation. From the photo you had, it is clear that this one is being used as a weapon."

"Subduing it for conversation will not be easy," Harry replied.

"You know how demons are once they have had a taste for blood. It will have feasted and its own blood will be boiling as a result," Alice said.

David understood the implications. Once demons had tasted human flesh, they entered a frenzy known as the Boiling. It consumed their thinking and propelled them into more violence, more feeding on mortal prey. *If it becomes too much, they may find that their own control of the creature is impossible.*

"Dokkaebi are crafty beings," Harry said. "It will sense our presence and even if it is in the Boiling, it will suspect a trap."

"We need bait, something that will lure it in. Something that will let the Boiling take over," David said, slowly turning his gaze to Victor.

The usually stone-faced man turned red as all eyes settled on him. "Me? You want to use me as bait?"

"Our blood won't do," Harry replied. "It will want mortal blood."

David saw that the man was overloaded. *A few hours ago he didn't believe that gods walked the Earth. Now he must square off with a demon.* "We will protect you, Victor. We have capabilities that allow us to engage the creature before it can harm you." Despite his assurance, Victor seemed nervous. *It's good that he is fearful. Demons are not easily trifled with.* He turned his attention to Harry. "Can it be drawn in through other means?"

Alice interjected, "I can call to it with blood and power. That will bring it in close. After that, matters will be less certain."

Thor glanced at Victor and saw the trepidation. "Do not fear, little man. I have will be wielding Gram, the blade that slew Fafnir. It is more than enough to pierce the hide of this demon."

David forced a smile to reinforce Victor's fear. "We will be there as well. Have trust and faith."

"How do we get there?" Victor asked, reaching deep in his soul for courage. "I haven't chartered a flight yet and it is an active combat zone. We need to be behind enemy lines. This could take days if not longer to set up. The logistics are a nightmare over there right now, with the Army retreating."

"Valhalla touches Earth everywhere, it is a matter of picking where we exit," Alice told him.

"We should have one more drink before we go," Thor suggested. "We are about to wade into battle. Fighting is always better with the roar of ale in your head."

David gave him a nod of approval. It had been a while since he had squared off against such evil, and he still bore the scars of the last such conflict. "One round, and something a mortal can consume for Victor," he said as Thor wheeled about to find the right libations. *The next few hours are going to be a test of us all.*

Yecheon-gun
Korea

They emerged on an isolated street in the early morning hours. There was a middle-aged man pushing a cart who was only twenty feet away when they stepped out of the wooden wall of the structure that connected to Valhalla. David could feel the humidity in the air and drank in the aroma of rotting garbage from a nearby alley. The man with the cart paused when he saw them, frozen in place for a long four seconds, then turned his head and continued to push on. David wasn't surprised by his reaction, he had seen it hundreds of times in wars spanning the ages. *He's had his country invaded and like so many people, he doesn't want to be involved.*

"We need to get away from the city, head toward the front. That is where our prey will be," Alice said.

"We need to blend in," David pointed out. "Harry, can you take care of Victor?"

"What does that mean?" Victor asked in a whisper.

"We are behind the North Korean lines. White Americans will stand out." As he spoke, David adjusted his own appearance, morphing in a second to appear as Korean, right down to his clothing.

Victor looked worried as Harry waved his hand in front of him. He too took on a new guise, as did Alice and Harry. "So I look like you do now?" Victor asked.

"Some of us," David said, shooting a glance at Harry, "have long hidden our true forms."

They were signs throughout the city of the war: damaged buildings, the presence of garrison troops, an aroma he had not tasted in the back of his mouth since the last conflict. David knew enough to keep his head bowed low and avoided eye contact with the few patrols that cast their gaze in their direction.

They silently made their way out of the town and, once in the countryside, got off the roads and into the forest. This far behind the fighting lines meant that security was thin. Once into the forest he savored the smells of the trees. They marched for miles, heading southeast, toward the war. After hours of silent walking, David raised his arm and the party stopped. While Alice, Thor, and Harry simply stood, Victor dropped the duffel bag of weapons and slumped on a fallen log.

"We need good ground," Alice said, her gaze seeming to penetrate the forest as she slowly turned her head.

"There is a holy spot not far from here," Harry said, his finger stabbing to the south. "A few hours' walk."

"Is it strong enough?" David asked.

Harry nodded. "It is old ground, but with deep roots. It will suffice."

Thor frowned with those words. "You speak as if we are going to return this demon to a prison. I did not come for that. I came for a worthy battle."

"You have not changed," Alice replied.

"Why would I?" Thor's arrogant smile was strangely reassuring.

David interceded. "Holy ground gives us an advantage in the fight. We all know that killing a demon upsets the eternal balance. You will get your fight, old friend, but if it is possible, I'd rather see us imprison the creature rather than merely kill it."

Thor's frown remained. "I was promised battle."

"And you shall have it," David replied.

"What is holy ground? Like a church?" Victor asked.

David turned to his mortal associate. "There are lines of energy that crisscross this universe and this planet. They intersect in many places. These convey strong ethereal energies. In some places multiple lines cross, and in those places mankind often built churches, altars, ritual sites, monasteries...a wide range of places."

"You mean ley lines?"

"Behold," Harry said. "He actually understands."

"Harry, play nice. Victor is a good man," Alice said. "Look at him deeply. He has the blood of Ares in his veins."

Victor looked slightly confused as David jumped back into the conversation. "Pay them no heed, Victor. One of our less desirable traits is our lack of courtesy to mortals."

His partner seemed to understand. "How do you know that there is such a location nearby?" Victor asked of Harry.

"My eyes pierce the forest and through the ages. I can see it."

Victor shook his head. "My father was right," he grumbled. "I shouldn't have pursued this career."

After a few moments of rest, mostly for Victor's sake, they marched on. The forest became hillier, the undergrowth thicker. Thorns tugged at their clothing and flesh as they pressed forward. Thor maintained the lead, occasionally swiping at the vines and brush with his sword. Several hours later, they came to a small clearing that butted up to a large rock formation rising some ten yards in height.

"This is the place," Harry stated, finding a smooth boulder at the edge of the clearing to sit down on.

Victor looked confused, so David moved next to him and started to scrape the soil with his right foot. A few inches down was a stone, carved flat. As he continued more were exposed, revealing that at one time there had been something there. Victor bent down and touched the stones. "Amazing..." he said in a muttered breath.

"That it exists? There are thousands of such places on the Earth. Civilizations may fall, but their places of power don't. Jerusalem, for example, is the nexus for six lines...very powerful ground."

"Not that. I'm amazed that Harry was able to see it."

David nodded. "His sight is great, even better than my own. You see things in the material world. His gaze goes through that and sees far more than even I can comprehend."

Alice used her feet to clear a spot in the center of the clearing. In a matter of minutes she had exposed a circle of stone. As she worked, David addressed the party.

"Once the Dokkaebi senses prey, it will come here. Chances are its handler will come as well. We need to engage the demon. Victor, your role will be to find the one wearing the bracers and kill him. Thor and Harry and I will move in from the perimeter of the ground to keep the beast busy. Hopefully that will give you, Alice, an opportunity to attempt to imprison the creature."

"I can kill the handler far more effectively than this mortal," Thor offered. He glanced at Victor. "No offense."

"None taken," Victor replied.

David forced a fake frown at Thor's words, opting to target his comrade's ego. "A mere mortal? Where is the challenge of that? Besides, we will have our hands full with the demon."

"You take the fun out of this," Thor said. "I can kill both."

"I am sure you can, but I prefer to see you focused." David returned to Victor. "That rock formation at the edge of this ground is the best place for you. If you see anyone, chances are it is the beast's handler. Kill them. After that, remove the bracers from their forearms and get them to one of us, preferably Alice or Harry."

Victor nodded in agreement. "So how am I going to be the bait for this?"

Alice stepped next to him. "Leave that to me."

David looked to the horizon. "It will be dark in a few hours."

"Demons hate the light. Should we wait until morning?" Harry asked.

"It makes sense, but it will take the hellspawn some time to get here," he countered. "Given the distance from where it was last seen, it will arrive here after first light."

"Always the calculator," Thor gibed.

"It has served us well over the ages."

"Not always. Remember Tunguska."

"For the record, that was not a fault of my planning, Thor, and you know it. That was a miscalculation on all of our parts," he said, sweeping his eyes to the other.

Alice nodded; Harry shrugged in response. "Regardless, we should utilize Mr. Tanner here as our bait in a few hours. In the meantime, we can rest, scout the area, and prepare for what is coming." They split up, moving around the forest surrounding the clearing. Victor came back first, pulling an Army bedroll from his knapsack and going to sleep at the base of the large rock formation.

Alice walked over to him, getting close to his face so her voice wouldn't disturb the mortal as he drifted off to sleep. "Your penchant for involving mortals is something I never fully understand."

"The ages of us doing things indiscriminately on our own has long passed," David said. "Mortals need to bear witness to the acts of the gods. It is where great stories and songs are born."

"Are you sure there's not more to it?" she whispered.

"Such as?"

"Perhaps you harbor the thought that surviving mortals might respawn worship in us, restore our powers and our former glory?"

David shook his head. "We cannot go back. We can only long for such things. Having witnesses is only prudent."

"Many do not survive."

"True. But those that do go far in life."

"Always the eternal optimist... the lover of mankind."

David touched a spot on his right torso where the aching of ages still tugged at him. "Someone has to be."

David had walked the terrain surrounding the holy ground, drinking in every detail. He returned and sat down on the grass in the clearing. Sitting felt good. There were centuries at a time that he did not need relaxation, but now, the eternal tug of time seemed to force it upon him. It didn't take much for him to rest, but the mere fact that he needed it spoke volumes. He closed his eyes and let the rest take him.

It was Alice who shattered his rest with a nudge to his shoulder. "It has been a few hours. I think the time has come."

Sunset had started, the beams of light managing to only pierce the foliage in a few areas. Walking to Victor, David reached down and gave him a small shake. He awoke, pistol in hand, ready for a fight. "What... Is something wrong?"

"No, it is time for your role in this affair."

Rolling out of the bedroll, he was drenched with sweat, but seemed to quickly get his orientation back. Victor holstered his weapon and moved to the center of the exposed circle where the rest of the party stood. "What do I need to do?" he asked, cracking his neck.

"I must cut you with the tip of my spear. It will hurt. I will use your blood to entice the demon."

"What spear?"

For a moment the older woman shimmered in a golden light. Gone was her mortal guise. The woman who stood before them wore a short skirt, and a bronze breastplate and helmet. Her knee-length boots were ornately adorned. The gray hairs were replaced by flowing blond. Her face defined beauty. In her hand was a large spear, forged at the heart of the Earth. As David watched her, he thought back to the first time they met, thousands of years earlier.

Victor's jaw hung open in amazement and wonder. "You—you're so... beautiful."

She smiled. "You see me as I truly am."

"Who are you?" Victor struggled to form the words.

"Athena," she replied.

"I—I—I don't know what to say."

"It will pass. You don't need to speak a word. It is rare that mortals have seen me in my true form. Your inability to comment is common. We refer to it as the Awe." She extended the spear between them so that the point was just above his fatigue shirt. "I must cut you for the magic to work. I will be careful, but you should know that this is a weapon of the gods. Even the slightest touch to mortal skin comes with risk."

Victor took a gulp of air and nodded. "After what I've already seen, I think I understand."

Slowly she moved the tip of the spear closer until it touched him. He started to fall, but her cut was lightning fast, across his right breast. Victor wailed in agony and David bent down to help his prone body down.

Blood splattered on the exposed stones of the holy ground. The seams between the rocks shimmered as Athena knelt as well to try and comfort the man as he writhed in agony. The mostly unseen circle of ground throbbed as another drop of blood fell. She muttered a few words, closing her eyes for a moment, evoking the magic of old.

The grass withered brown, then turned to dust as a sudden wind whipped the ground, blowing hard, taking the soil and dead grass away. What remained was a large cobblestoned circle on the ground, now fully exposed. David could feel the power radiating from it as Victor wept. It was like the beating of a bass drum, each pounding pulse spreading out for miles. *It is working . . . the Dokkaebi will not be able to ignore it.*

Athena reached out to where her spear had cut his flesh. Using her index finger, she traced down the cut, the flesh sealing behind it, leaving a perfect pink scar in its wake. When she was done the flow of blood had ceased. Victor was breathing fast, his face was pale, but color was starting to return.

"God, that hurt!" he exclaimed once he managed his breathing.

"My apologies for your pain, but the blood of a mortal was necessary."

David helped Victor to his bed roll. "Rest here. Athena's touch can heal, but there still will be a lingering pain."

"You've done this before, haven't you?"

"It has been many years."

"So this demon will come now?"

"It will sense your blood, amplified by Athena's magic and this site. It will not be able to resist."

Wincing again, Victor locked his eyes on David's. "From what I saw in that photograph, I have to admit, I'm siding with Thor on this. That thing is a monster. Best to kill it."

"There is a balance of good and evil in the universe. If that balance is disturbed, nature moves to correct it. Killing a demon can have unintended consequences."

Victor gave him a single nod. "This is your universe. Until a few days ago, I didn't know that the gods were among us. I'll follow your lead."

"That would be prudent."

"I have seen Athena as she really is. Who are you, really?"

"I am a god that had faith in mankind, and suffered for that vision for ages. I gave humanity a simple gift and was ostracized for it by my peers."

Victor rested, slowly regaining his strength as the rest of the group stood on the now-exposed circle of stone, staring out into the darkness. After the vicious wind that had bared the holy ground, the forest had become still and quiet. There were no animals stirring, no birds, nothing. David understood. *They can sense what is coming.*

The hours passed quickly. The clouds disappeared overhead, allowing the waxing moon to cast a blue illumination on them. David looked into the darkness, his hands hot and sweaty with anticipation. Demons were not mindless creatures; experience had taught him that. They were driven by primal instincts, things they could control, barely. *It's out there and knows where we are, if not more. It will come for blood and death.*

Hours passed, then a cool night breeze blew through woods, a single long gust. He could smell the stench of death on it. "It is close," he said just above a whisper.

"I feel it too," Athena said, holding her spear tightly in both hands.

Thor held out Gram, the massive broadsword he had brought, lowering his stance for battle. "The air reeks of demon."

Harry shifted, keeping his back to the center of the holy ground. "It is coming from the south. It is not alone."

David glanced over to Victor, who rose to his feet. "Get your weapons and seize the high ground of that rock. Hunt its handler and deal with him." The sunrise was just starting, the beams of light casting new shadows on the intended battle site.

In the distance there was the sound of trees creaking, limbs snapping, echoing in the night. *It's closing on us.* Harry's spear would no doubt make an appearance the way that Athena's had. David did not carry one. *I am a weapon.*

There was a pause, another stifling silence dropped on them. No doubt the Dokkaebi could sense them and suspected a trap. Despite that, it would be drawn in. He braced for the fight as his partner climbed to the top of the rock formation along with his duffel bag of destruction.

A snarl reached them, low, guttural, penetrating. "You have made a mistake, luring me here," a voice came. It was a baritone, with a low growl mixed in, like that of a wolf.

It was never wise to engage in dialogue with a demon, but the night was long already and David wanted to see this matter brought to an end. "You're afraid," he said, his voice piercing the darkness. "Run and you might live."

The growl that came back came with what sounded like a chuckle. "I will drink godsblood before this night is through. I will savor your power and make it my own." The words rolled in the air, a taunt meant to infuse fear. *His power is great, but not enough to drive us away in terror.*

"You don't have the courage. Your ilk never does. You slaughter those that cannot defend themselves. We have come to stop you, here and now."

Something sprang from the perimeter of the circle, a blur in the darkness, moving at a speed that obscured its form. It slammed into Thor, knocking him onto the stones, skidding to the edge of the circle. Thor was pissed, David could sense it as the god of thunder sprang back to his feet. A nasty cut on his thigh bled, if only for a few moments.

"He moves to the west," Harry said.

"Come and face us, hellspawn!" Thor demanded.

"You are old and weak, Norssseman," the Dokkaebi replied, hissing as it spoke.

"Test that," Thor respond.

David caught a glimpse of movement from the boulder, barely seeing Victor out of the corner of his eye. His arm arched back and he threw something into the darkness. *No!*

The grenade went off in the night, throwing leaves and twigs into the night. Victor lost his position and fell to the edge of the circle on top of his duffel bag. "Your paltry mortal toys cannot harm me," the demon sneered. "But I can harm you."

The blur charged out of the woods right at Victor. Athena swung her spear in an arc that intersected with the rushing demon, its blade cutting a swath on one of its massive arms. Harry jumped, flying across the large stone dais like a bird of prey, landing between the Dokkaebi and Victor. He spread his arms wide and a bright crimson burst of light formed around him. He transformed to his true form, a falcon head replacing the human one. His body shimmered as if made of golden metal. In his hand was a two-bladed spear: one a straight blade, the other a curved edge. In perfect form, Horus thrust the blade. From his left eye, a burst of bright light, like that of the sun, stabbed in conjunction with the spear, bathing the demon in light.

His spear only caught the shoulder of the monstrosity, but the light made it reel back a few steps.

Thor leaped at it, Gram held in both hands, pointing down. He drove the blade into the demon's left foot, piercing through it and into the stones.

The Dokkaebi swept its ugly clawed hand hard, hitting Thor mid-chest, and throwing his body across and out of the circle. Gram remained stuck upright through its foot, but only for a moment. It pulled it free and threw the blade dozens of yards into the wilderness. Victor scrambled away, moving around the backside of the rock he had been on.

Athena rushed forward, thrusting her spear at him with such speed that David had a hard time seeing her. The demon was just as quick, knocking her thrust aside with one hand as it charged right back at her, its ugly bony maw with glistening white teeth coming at her.

She blocked two biting attempts as Horus thrust into its leg with the curved blade of his spear. Black demon blood hissed and sizzled on the stones. The cracks between them lit up a dully orange.

"Horus, move!" David called.

Athena tried to back up but the demon pounced on her, its teeth biting into her shoulder. She screamed, a sound David had never heard her make. The Dokkaebi thrust a clawed hand on her throat and lifted her up, its claws digging into her flesh.

David was no more. A bright yellow burst of light revealed his true form. Clad in the hide of a dragon's belly, he held his hands in front of him, aiming them as if they were cannons.

Flames burst from his hands—brilliant crimson and orange flames, the fires of Olympus, stabbed out into the creature, roaring as if they were from a blacksmith's forge. The fires hit the demon and it tossed Athena aside, her limp form rolling along the stones that were still illuminated form its blood.

"Prometheusss," the creature hissed, using one arm to block the fire that seared its hide. It was clear that it was going to leap at him as a target.

It sprang at him, right through the fire. Horus was faster. He wheeled in a blur of motion, turning his back to the creature. His skin hardened to that of metal as he transformed. The Dokkaebi hit Horus but did not shake his stance as Prometheus/David stopped his fire blast. It collided with a dull *thunking* sound, bouncing backward.

There was the sound of gunfire, distinct cracking, in the distance.

Prometheus ignored it the moment he heard it. What mattered now was this fight. The demon recoiled and prepared for another pounce as Prometheus moved back from Horus.

The demon once more slammed into Horus, this time knocking him down. Horus skidded on the stone, throwing sparks in the air as he did. The demon's jaw tore into the Egyptian god's head, causing him to wail in agony. The jagged rows of teeth ripped the god's flesh. His metallic hide flickered away to his normal shape, and Prometheus saw his blood squirt from the bite.

Leveling his right hand out, he unleashed another narrow cone of fire right into the white bony skull-like face of the Dokkaebi. He knew the fire had to hurt it, but something else shook it. For a moment, the demon staggered back, holding its claw to its head.

Victor! He must have killed its master! Then, from the edge of the circle came Thor, Gram in his hands. He sprang onto the black-boned back of the creature, grappling with one of the spurs on its armored hide. Thor stabbed the blade deep into it, twisting Gram as it sank into the abomination.

The Dokkaebi whipped about, almost dislodging Thor as Prometheus darted to Athena's dropped spear. The weapon was cold in his hands, but he could feel the power that surged through it. His charge was not as fast as Thor's, but was no doubt much faster than a mortal could move. The point of the spear collided with the demon, knocking it off its feet.

It went to its knees as Horus swept the curved edge of his spear into its neck. More obsidian blood splattered onto the stone and the glowing orange of the gaps of the rocks spiked in their eerie illumination of the night.

The demon roared, so loud that it made his ears ache. It was beyond the noise of an animal, it came from the beyond. Thor pulled out Gram and stabbed down again, this time struggling to penetrate the armored hide for a moment. Thor finally found a weak spot and the blade sunk deep, spraying both the god and his foe with black gore. The unearthly noise of the demon became a gurgle.

The Dokkaebi did another sweep of its arm, a move that caught Prometheus off guard. Its claw tore off his breastplate, shredding the dragon hide as if it were nothing more than silk. Pain tore at him, but agony was an old friend to him. The multitude of scars over his liver, the marks of his punishment, screamed out in agony that Prometheus tried to ignore. He recoiled, suppressing the pains of the past and the new ones he endured.

It was near its end; Prometheus could hear the demon's labored breathing as he moved over it, his hands at the ready. With Athena down, there was no way to imprison it. She alone possessed that magic. *Death . . . that is the only option left to us.* Thor jumped off, sword in hand, and Horus closed the gap as well, swinging his spear around to the straight point, pressing it into the chest of the beast.

"Take my life, upset the scalesss," it hissed.

"We have no choice," Horus said, confirming what Prometheus already knew. *Doing this will be costly, more than we can imagine.*

Thor stepped forward. "We must slay it, before it recovers."

"Know thisss, kill me and you will never know who orchestrated my release. I do not fear the afterlife, it flows through my veins. Send me there, and I will return in another eon. You will never get your answersss."

Before Prometheus could process that information, the creature grabbed Horus's spear, and pulled it into his hide. The body twitched violently for a moment, then collapsed in a heap. It started to smoke, consumed by the fires of Hades or whatever plane of hell it came from. The Dokkaebi crackled like a spring log on the fire and in a matter of moments, it was nothing more than a mound of ash. The wave of heat from the demise of the demon faded fast, returning to the cold morning air of the forest.

He turned to Athena, and as he did, he saw Victor kneeling next to her. "She's hurt bad," he said.

Prometheus leaned over her and saw her once vibrant color draining from her face. Her eyes were only half-opened and when she saw his face, she somehow managed to smile. "It is good to see your true form once more."

"We will go find Asclepius," he said, taking her hand in his.

"I feel the pull of Hades. I will go there. Know this, my friends, I will return."

"Don't say that," Prometheus said, gripping her right hand with both of his. "You will prevail. You always do."

"Not this time, I fear," she said with a gasp.

Before he could respond, her hand went limp in his and her eyes closed. From his knees, he looked skyward at the rising sun and screamed, his voice tearing through the forest. When done, he paused, letting his tears fall onto the dead goddess. *She stood by me when others left my body to be ripped apart daily. She does not deserve to die in this place.* Her death consumed him for long minutes as the survivors left him alone in his grief. Closing his eyes, he muttered a prayer for her. *I will find a way to bring you back from Hades, my love. I swear it.*

Killing the Dokkaebi set this in motion. The scales of good and evil demand balance. Thor put his hand on his shoulder, offering what comfort he could by simply not speaking. Minutes passed as the trio of gods leaned over Athena's form. She started to blur, become incorporeal, then disappeared. All that remained of her was her spear.

"I'm sorry," Victor said. "She was ... magnificent."

"That she was," Prometheus replied, rising to his feet. It tore at him to know she had died. *At least it was for a just cause. No god should perish from something mundane.*

"I killed some Korean officer. He was wearing these." He handed the silver metal bracers to Prometheus.

"You did well," Thor said, "for a mere mortal."

Prometheus held the bracers in deep thought. The Dokkaebi's last words tugged at him. *You will never know who orchestrated my release* ... It wasn't the North Koreans. Someone had used them to release the demon. *There are other forces in play.*

"She will escape your Hades," Horus said. "Many have before her, Prometheus. You will see her again."

"I know. That doesn't make the pain of her passing any easier."

"She would want us to see this through," Horus responded.

"We have," Thor replied. "We killed the demon and its master. She has earned much glory in her passing."

Prometheus shook his head. "Someone led the North Koreans to the demon, told them how to release and control it." He glanced at the bracers in his hand. "Someone manipulated them, fooled them to think that this was a means to an end. There is a greater force playing a game with the humans."

"A trickster," Horus said. "That doesn't narrow the list of gods by much."

"Why would they do this?" Victor asked.

"I don't know, yet," Prometheus replied. "But we owe it to Athena to find out who is behind this and make them pay for what they have done."

"For Athena," Horus replied.

"For Athena," Prometheus responded. As the sun crept into the sky, he realized their mission was just starting and was far more complicated than he could have imagined.

To Win the Final Lizard War

Joelle Presby

"I have to kill Grace and the kids." Jon said that out loud to try to help his own mind grasp the horror of it. "Maybe." He didn't want to. He desperately didn't want to. But he had to. "No. No, I don't. They aren't actually—"

The old-timey chime sounded as the door opened to WeChargeForLess. Jon checked the video cameras for humans, automatically. His cash register rarely had much worth stealing, but anyone on night shift was vulnerable here in this little Northern California town that existed mainly to serve the interstate. And after the latest buyout, corporate had stopped paying for the security company that used to respond to the silent alarm next to the cash register's "open drawer" button.

The four electric vehicle charging stations outside were unoccupied, and the exterior cameras didn't give him a view of the parking spots along the side of his tiny snacks-and-bathrooms building. Neither did the interior cameras' overlapping viewing angles cover the bottom three feet of the front door.

The sudden realization that if he got shot by a dumb kid tonight he wouldn't have to kill his family gave him courage. One local news-level tragedy for him ... And Grace, little Dubya, and baby Liberty could go on living without their bodies becoming national news.

Of course, if they were lizard people for real, it'd be hell for everyone else. They'd grow up and swell larger and join the mass of creatures swallowing whatever goodness was left in the world. But if he died tonight, making that final were-they/weren't-they determination and acting on it would no longer fall on him.

Spurred on by despair, Jon leaned around the endcap filled with potato chips, looking for the dark hole of a gun barrel or the shine of a knife.

He got neither.

And no teenager jumped up from a low crawl position on the floor to attack him with fists either.

A dull gray box-on-wheels bristling with florescent cardboard rolled the rest of the way into WeChargeForLess and let the door close to mute the chime. It was just a stock delivery machine, completely automated. A new pallet of over-the-counter medicines dropped to the floor in the center aisle, blocking customer access to the bathroom. Some new endcap displays filled with snacks clunked down almost in the right place. A pallet of mixed on-sale items landed next to the medicines completing the violation of the fire code. The machine rolled itself right back out again.

Those things used to be remotely operated, and he could exchange a few words of greeting with a fellow working stiff a hundred or two miles away during these mostly empty night shifts. The human-operated machines had, usually, also been driven more wisely. A human knew to go the longer way around the building to where it passed along the glass front closest to his cashier's counter. Enough stocking machine operators had worked nights in little shops too.

They understood that stocking machine wear and tear caused by a startled cashier with a baseball bat could be reduced significantly by not looking like someone low-crawling into the store at two in the morning.

The remote delivery operators weren't all cool, but some of them were pure saints. Hell, one time...

He hadn't known about lizard people then, but he'd been the angriest he'd ever been in his life that evening. Without even talking to him, Grace had quit a waitressing job where they'd let then-infant Dubya play in the back. She'd been making tips so good that he'd only rarely had to work double shifts. The "awesome" job she'd quit for turned out to be a scam, and the restaurant wouldn't take her back. Their rent had been due, so he'd taken every extra shift possible at WeChargeForLess to avoid an eviction. They hadn't realized it yet, but Grace had actually been pregnant with Liberty Ann then.

That night, Jon'd been so sleep deprived on this third shift in a row that he'd been hallucinating. It'd been a Jewish guy from the Bronx running the stocking robot who'd helped Jon give the monitor cameras a glitch. Together they had looped the surveillance feed for ninety minutes. Jon'd gotten a nap right there on the floor of the snack aisle while Levi and the stocker machine refilled the shelves. Levi'd promised to use his bot's horn to wake Jon up if any actual customers arrived. God bless that guy, wherever he was now.

Not that that sort-of-help was possible anymore. A lizard corporate overlord had decided to get new stocking machines that didn't need operators.

Humanity couldn't go on like this. It was bad now, but it was going to get a whole lot worse if people like him didn't act.

But, Grace! She couldn't really be a lizard person, could she?

Hey, at least tonight there weren't fuzzy fronds crawling on the edges of his vision. Before the stocking machine operators had been replaced entirely, one of them had introduced him to the Pugna Lacertilia forums.

Jon logged onto those boards again. These were his friends. They got him. They made him laugh when reality had very little joy in it. And they'd finally opened his eyes to what was really going on: lizard people.

That one crazy guy's profile photo caught Jon's eye. He took a moment to admire it. Clearly painted, it showed two humans running from a fully developed lizard person with one brave human soldier returning fire. Ah, TimeTravelerBilly28. You are absolutely insane, but we love you.

Jon propped his personal comm on a shelf while he transferred the new stuff onto the shelves to replace the expiring unsold merchandise.

Jon scrolled past the usual top posts.

"Pugna Lacertilia is our name. We aren't changing it." Moderator-pinned post. Comments locked.

"*Pugna Lacertilia* DOESN'T really mean Fight the Lizard People!!11!" A thousand-plus new comments there arguing about Latin, mostly written in a style that indicated the posters also didn't understand English. But the spin-off questions about whether the Romans or the Greek were or were not also infested by lizard people, making Latin just as corrupted as English, were interesting.

"WHAT SHOULD WE RENAME THE BOARD???" Also over a thousand new responses.

Jon scrolled on past several posts on the attributes of lizard overlords and a debate on whether it was lizard people or lizard overlords as two distinct groups of nasties, or if they were just alternate names for the same thing. New lists of the attributes of the lizard-DNAed villains and suspected lizard politicians and corporate leaders formed more posts.

He needed a distraction. Or encouragement.

Ah! TimeTravelerBilly28 had a new post up, "my dream of a free world," with a couple dozen responding comments.

Billy often had funny or inspirational things to say.

Jon opened that thread with hope.

Oh, dear. Poor Billy. This wasn't going to be a funny one. It'd be distracting, but Jon wasn't in the mood for watching the active *pugnasts* tear Billy to bits again.

Billy's whole thread had been highjacked by the ones who called themselves "the unbelievers." They didn't disbelieve in lizard people, of course. These were core group *pugnasts*. They did know and firmly believe that the lizard people were the ones ruining society for all the hard-working humans out there. They just didn't believe in TimeTravelerBilly28.

The *pugnasts* of the forum had firm rules for themselves. They didn't see themselves as conspiracy theorists. Jon remembered how when he'd first joined the forums he'd thought they were nuts and had been ready to laugh at everyone. But *pugnasts* didn't buy into things without large amounts of evidence.

Pugnasts didn't believe in a flat Earth. A handful were actually well off enough that they'd gone to Kilimanjaro and used the TCG space elevator where you could see for yourself just how round Earth was.

Area 51 aliens and Bigfoot—okay, well, some *pugnasts* thought those might exist. Jon wasn't sure himself. It was pretty hard to definitely disprove that sort of thing.

But time travel? Jon hoped Billy wasn't about to be banned from Pugna Lacertilia entirely. He was a kind and encouraging sort of guy. And nobody else was as deeply concerned and aware of the dangers posed to humanity by the horrors perpetrated by those with lizard-DNA than TimeTravelerBilly28.

"If you won't believe that I've been to twenty-seven iterations of this world, well, that's on you," Billy wrote.

"So, convince us," Jon (under his forum name of RighteousMan73) typed in.

"Been there. Done that. Got everyone I knew got bitten or eaten by lizard-things," Billy replied.

"What the hell, Billy?" Jon said out loud. Plenty of other *pugnasts* demanded more detailed explanations on the thread.

"I," Billy wrote, "during the first fourteen timeline iterations, convinced everyone of who I was before beginning to build up the rebellion. That takes too long, and the lizards get too powerful before the people can rise up. They swallow us all. During the times after that, I've been trying other combinations. The *lacertilia* infiltrate the other iterations of this forum every time. I've realized that they are searching for me. Being known will lose us the war. I'm trying something new this time."

"What?" Jon didn't have to type that in either.

Billy responded to wave after wave of demands for more detail about his time travel with increasingly cryptic responses about needing to stay undetected. Billy was most likely clinically insane, but he was a nice kind of crazy.

"I'm pretending to be crazy so that they can't use me to track you all down," Billy insisted, "It's too important. I know you don't understand. And I forgive you all. But there are *pugnasts* here who are necessary for humanity to win the lizard wars. For real and final. It all can end right here. But I must stay undetected."

Jon had to laugh at that. Sure why not? But he unhighlighted the star on Billy's post to stop getting notified about it.

Jon didn't think that the lizard wars were actually winnable. Humanity was failing everywhere he looked. But, in a way, Billy was right: if they didn't fight the lizard-DNAed people where they found them, they weren't fighting at all.

But Grace! And little Dubya. Baby Liberty was mostly a ball of screaming infant rage, but she was cute when asleep. She had her mom's nose.

Damn the *lacertilia* for their skinsuits. They were all lizard people. He knew that.

But, what if he were wrong?

And what if he ignored it?

How many more regular human families with little kids would get swallowed up?

Jon decided to write his own forum post. The storefront was still empty and would likely stay that way until after shift change over at 6:00 A.M. Valentina would be here at 5:59 exactly when her grandson dropped her off to take over the register. He wasn't working a triple this time, so Jon could actually go home. Maybe he'd get to sleep a little.

He would take all his concerns and lay them before the *pugnasts* to see what they had to say about it all. Maybe he'd missed something. Tiny bits of hope still glimmered even as he recorded the damning details in his long, long post titled, "Sister's Neighbors: Are they Lizard People or No?"

Yeah, he was anonymizing things for the board. You had to be honest to get honest feedback, but you also had to be cautious, and everyone understood that. After all, the forum had shut down just last month and moved to a new server when some lizard-DNAed infiltrator had filed a report on them. You couldn't be too careful. The lizard people were in power everywhere.

Anonymizing post details had a certain expected format. He didn't make it an "I have a friend who" post. That was too obvious. He invented a sister and said it was her next-door neighbors on the other side of a duplex.

He and Grace and the kids did live in a duplex, and it was a poorly maintained rental with only an automated machine to call for any issues. No local landlord or even a local property manager. Didn't that mean Grace wasn't really a lizard person? He hoped the *pugnasts* would jump on that inconsistency and help him think of some way to get the maybe-human Grace out of the clutches of those overpromising and underdelivering venomous lizard bosses she lived to please.

They needed to get out of the duplex too. The single bathroom smelled like mold all the time. And if Dubya wasn't a lizard baby, that would explain why he got sick more often than a normal child should. They'd likely never be able to afford to buy, even though a lot of the homes in their crumbling town were empty. By the time the prices dropped low enough that he could qualify for a mortgage, the jobs would be completely gone too. Lizard people's boa constrictor economic policies were working as designed. The only way out was to get a remote work job—like Grace's—but with actual income. May all lizard people burn.

Jon returned his mind to the composition of the post. He erased himself and put in a clueless husk of a man. He didn't outright admit the other family members were an adult lizard-DNAed woman-shape and two infected young children. The other details he left completely true.

"Let this be a test," he prayed. If the *pugnasts* on the board said Grace and the kids were human, he'd keep struggling on just as he had been for years. If they said lizard people, well, he already knew what that would mean.

He put in more detail. Grace lived in those body-hugging leggings. He described them. She'd developed a fetish for animal print—including alligator—as if no one could possibly recognize the signs. She put on false smiles and layers upon layers of makeup to sit in front of the screen and attend her work meetings. He'd seen the long eyelashes she glued onto each lid. Her original lashes seemed entirely gone. That could be stress, right? But he knew in his gut that reptiles had no eyelashes. Because it might not be stress of the human sort. Maybe she was letting more of her true lizard-self show through while off-camera.

In their tiny duplex, a trail of discarded clothes accumulated just out of camera view. A stand-in for the comforts of shed lizard-skin while occupying a lair with an uninformed true human? Maybe lizards didn't shed skin? He hoped some *pugnast* would say that.

He included the argument for the company bosses being the real lizard people in case the *pugnasts* would see it that way. Grace's supposed great new job was an unpaid internship with only a potential for glorious salaried pay later. It ate at him every time her work-supplied comm hissed and shook in the middle of their night to get her up to coordinate a business meeting for executives in other time zones. They had to be cold-blooded to think that their new employees should all work for no pay. Standard policy, they'd said, for new hires to do their first three months as interns (unpaid) with an assessment and promotion to full employee status based on job performance at the end of the introductory period. But Grace's internship had been extended and extended again. Fiscal quarter by fiscal quarter. Always with promises that next quarter more of the top performing interns would shift over to "full-time." As if Grace weren't already working close to seventy hours a week for them already! Jon had to step away from his composition and pace the WeChargeForLess store.

The new pallets blocked his way. He shifted the over-the-counter meds to their shelf lines and piled the on-sale mixed closeouts into the appropriate bin next to the door. He never got to pace enough to really calm down.

He straightened the endcap displays, and with a sigh, stacked the two now empty pallets neatly to the side of the front door where he could take them to the side dumpster after clocking out. Stocking product was not in his job description. If Jon got an injury later this month—as had happened to the guy in the job before him when a customer's car hit him while he was troubleshooting an issue with one of the charging stations—corporate would be using the video of this to deny worker's comp based on the evidence that he engaged in unauthorized workplace activity...

Jon knew that Mohammed, who often worked nights when Jon didn't, would be irritated at him for moving the stuff rather than hoping a fire code inspector happened to come in a see it. Mohammed still thought human-operated stocking machines might return. And Mohammed had a bad back from trying to move too many heavy pallets himself. But Jon didn't want to be a lizard leaving messes behind for Valentina to deal with. She would put everything on shelves and walk the empty pallets around back to the dumpster without even checking around the corner first to see if someone was passed on in the little alley between their building and the truck stop.

Jon returned to his cashier's desk and the Pugna Lacertilia post. Where was he again? Oh yeah. The evidence.

Like the programmed-by-lizard-people stocking machine, his children, too, left messes everywhere. Trails of toys or spit-up drool wherever they went. The house had become a reptile den with shed skins and white-crusted proto-venom accumulating everywhere. Animal lizards didn't have venom, but it seemed that lizard people did? Baby Liberty left venom-like milk-spit-up dribbles everywhere. Grace cleaned the messes vigorously, but only in the narrow range of their rental that was viewable by her screen's built-in camera.

Dubya, his beautiful boy little Washington, kept peeing on the floor. Potty training was tough, but this felt personal. Jon put that in the post too. Maybe someone would point out that it was very mammalian and even wolfish to mark your den. Didn't the wild dog breeds near jungles fight iguanas and stuff? Jon scrubbed his face with his hand. He would depend on the *pugnasts* to help him. They would know.

Jon finished the post. He hit SUBMIT with enough force that his comm flipped off the checkout desk and smacked hard on the floor. He checked it for damages. It was fine. Dragon-hide case worked magic, as usual. That small mercy gave him no peace. Jon finished the shift with only a handful of customers coming inside and a growing headache.

He'd always known that life was hard.

It'd been a gradual thing to realize that there might be evil creatures making it hard. That there might really be lizard people, *lacertilia*, monsters in human skin, the lizard-DNAed, the whatevers causing it. Those with real power certainly acted like their veins ran with ice water for how little concern they showed for the people without much power at all.

The concept of lizard-DNA infecting them . . . Well, after enough back-to-back shifts, it just made sense.

If those in power really were a different kind of being, it explained so much. Of course, they didn't care about fellow humans. They weren't human at all.

But as he'd wandered into this understanding during night shifts picked up directly after day shifts, followed by an off-period where he'd again barely slept, only to resume another twenty-four hours of standing at a register, not allowed so much as a stool, and being watched by cameras . . . Even as he'd grown to deeply believe in the many, many lizard people infesting the highest levels of power, he'd never expected to discover he'd married one. He never expected to discover that he'd been used to make two more lizard-DNA babies. He'd certainly never expected to have to kill them.

Jon went home.

Slept only a few broken hours when Grace had a surprise call from one of her matrixed-organization bosses. He'd needed to walk infant Liberty Ann back and forth outside camera pickup range to keep her quiet while Grace smiled so falsely at the people who were on the approvers list for her application to transition from full-time intern to salaried employee. Rage beat in Jon's head against them, and for those stumbling hours he wondered if maybe only those bosses were lizard people and Grace might just be exhausted.

He went to work.

Thank God for the regular humans who'd developed autodrive. He tripped just getting out of their family vehicle. If he'd had to self-drive it, he'd never have arrived safely at work.

Night shift proceeded as usual with almost no customers coming inside for more than a quick in and out to use the bathroom. He sold three overpriced candy bars and a bottle of diet pills to a man in a suit. A tired mom with a crying baby got one package of cheap diapers that WeChargeForLess used as a loss leader to get families shopping there. She put back the package of wipes for sensitive skin and the rash cream when she saw how high her vehicle's charge bill was. Jon got her to take a free hot dog on the claim that he had to throw them out after four hours and they'd been on the warmer for almost that long. Her kid fell asleep on her shoulder and while she lingered over the fixings of nondairy cheese substitute and imitation bacon bits, Jon re-added the wipes, the rash cream, and a better rash cream that had worked on Dubya's butt to her bag.

When he handed her the bag, her eyes widened. She glanced inside it, looked at him, and started to say something.

He nodded at the store cameras and told her, "Have another great day at WeChargeForLess."

She left with a stunned expression on her face like she'd not run into another human in weeks. He had let her believe he'd stolen it from corporate, so she'd take it. He hadn't stolen anything. The cameras had no blind spots at the cashier's table.

He typed in the product codes and charged them against his own account. He and Grace really couldn't afford that, but damn, he couldn't let a baby's rash grow to bleeding blisters.

Then he remembered Grace was probably faking caring about things like that. She was most likely a lizard person. And he was probably going to have to kill her, the kids, and then likely himself. Money wouldn't matter then. *But no,* he told himself, *I'm going to go home and tell her about this, and she's going to scream at me like our first raging fights over money after Dubya was born.* She was a regular human. The *pugnasts* were going to have a good laugh at him and tell him the "neighbors next door" were just people being squeezed by the system, same as everyone.

Grace was going to be so mad. He hoped.

During the next lull in customer activity, Jon logged into Pugna Lacertilia.

The message board flared open. On the Pugna Lacertilia forums, Jon's username of RighteousMan73 had gained a gold ring. It flared and pulsed.

His breath escaped in a hiss of stunned pride at the honor of the gold ring. And his gut clenched at the hundreds and hundreds of replies: "They are lizards. Kill them now."

But hearing the sound—that reptilian noise—come from his own lips, he also bowed his head in shame. He prayed that he hadn't allowed himself to be infected with lizard-DNA too.

The WeChargeForLess station's convenience store was empty, but the cameras were always running. Out of long habit, he kept his comm in the corner and tilted so the lizard people's cameras couldn't read the screen.

Blinking back tears and touching his cheek for the feel of real stubbled skin rather than scales, he brushed away the wetness. Somewhere in his gut, he pushed away the fear that if he went as far as was needed to fight the lizard people, the cold horror of it would seep into his soul and turn him into one of them too. But did reptiles have the ability to form tears?

Jon squeezed his eyes hard and told himself to focus. He didn't have to keep living after this was done. But he couldn't be someone who added more lizard-DNA horrors to this already awful world.

A true warrior shouldn't cry. Not today.

His newly sainted icon had the gold halo that meant someone had donated a full thousand dollars in response to his recent posting. The money went toward site hosting fees and the always complex security programming. The Pugna Lacertilia forums had to balance keeping the online community connected to each other and also keeping them all hidden from the lizard people or *lacertilia* or whatever you wanted to call them.

His pale user-selected image inside that new shining ring was the Statue of Liberty. His wife, Grace, had snapped the photo with her comm during their honeymoon five years ago. They'd made plans to go to Kilimanjaro and take whatever kids they had by then up into space for the first time for their ten-year anniversary. As if they'd ever be able to afford that.

Notifications of replies and emoji responses pinged in with a crackle of fireworks. The *pugnasts* had really taken to his last post.

This one time when he'd been hoping no one would pay much attention to it, and that he could avoid thinking about the rot infecting his life for one more day . . . This, of course, was the day his words bubbled up to the top of the feed to become the Post of the Day.

"Now, now, now!" they all seemed to be howling at him.

His private messages were full of suggestions. Some took into account what he'd need to do in order to hide his tracks. Some wanted photos afterward and talked of a memorial for him as if he'd already been found out and executed by the *lacertilia* in the government. More publicly on the message board itself, they were applauding him for finding the lizards and promising that if they were on the jury, they'd acquit him. Every single one of the *pugnasts* replying assumed that now that he'd found them the only thing he could possibly do was cut them up and burn the bodies.

But.

Grace? His wife! Maybe she'd always been a lizard person but she'd at least pretended to love him. And little Dubya, from before, back when he was tiny and just learning to move, had said "daddy" as his first word. Now he hissed a lot and peed on the floor while refusing to potty-train, but he'd done a great job of passing for human in the beginning. Liberty Ann (middle name after Grace's mother, who'd been dead since before he'd met Grace, and who, now, Jon suspected, might not have existed) mostly slept and burped out spit-up—except for in the middle of his sleep shift when she screeched until he or Grace stumbled out of bed to go walk her back and forth forever in a sleep-deprived haze.

He dithered.

Three days later still at Top Post, Jon's supporters had swelled to over three hundred. They clamored to start a charity fundraiser for him. Ten- and twenty-dollar donations were promised by various *pugnasts*. Others predicted with great confidence that he'd receive over a million dollars once the larger network of patriots heard of his work. Somewhere in the flurry of back-and-forth comments he'd slipped. They all knew it was his wife and kids. But not one of them had blinked at that. They encouraged him all the more.

His gold-halo-giver had been identified: TimeTravelerBilly28.

Billy remained mostly silent with only occasional questions about whether Jon had been able to sleep or if he'd had any breakfast. Jon worked his shift at the charging station's convenience store and sold candy bars he couldn't afford for his own family. Not that lizards would really eat chocolate. Or snakes. Or whatever. He'd never been quite clear on what *lacertilia* looked like in their reptilian form. He'd never seen even little Dubya slip up and let his human skin off while he was home.

Mohammed called in sick and Jon worked a double.

He imagined blowing the overtime payment from this shift (which he'd needed anyway to pay for Grace's non-reimbursed unlimited bandwidth comm connection) on cases of every kind of chocolate. He could feed it to Grace, who used to love chocolate, and to Dubya, who had only had it a handful of times. They'd probably regurgitate the mess into the kitchen sink when he wasn't looking, and he'd have to take apart the disposal again to try to clear it out.

Last quarter, WeChargeForLess Corporate had overbought on some of the pharmaceutical aisle things. A lot of the stuff sold was actually from other stores. So even things with five and ten year use-by periods could arrive on his shelves with just a couple weeks until expiration. They'd run out of Robitussin Silver, Ativan Premium, and all the generics a week early, and the corporate buyer had upped their delivery of everything resulting in a lot of unsold but expiring product. Valentina suggested dropping them in the dumpster. Jon volunteered to take the expired medicines to the distant police department drop-off.

Just because the *lacertilia* serving as county commissioners didn't care about the local water safety didn't mean he would let that stuff go into the regular trash! The dumpster out back only got compacted and stacked at the dump just out of town with no sorting whatsoever. The thoughtlessness of it made him furious. It surprised him not at all that WeChargeForLess corporate didn't care at all about poisoning his little town's water table. Dubya and Liberty Ann needed to still have clean drinking water when they got old enough to have their own kids.

Oh. Wait.

Well, Valentina's grandkids would need that all the same.

The pile of old meds, stripped of shoplifting prevention devices, waited in an anonymous hemp WeChargeForLess tote for Jon to do with them whatever he wanted after shift. He would visit the police station controlled substance drop-off like usual. But, this time, he would also keep back a small pile of the most recently expired sleeping pills.

He used his discount and charged the beater of a vehicle he and Grace shared. All the while, he made guesses about how many sleeping pills it would take to put his *lacertilia* family members into a deep sleep. He had to make sure the dose was high enough for deep sleep for a lizard in an adult woman shape. Lizard-Grace wasn't—despite what appeared to be her best efforts—back to the size she'd been before babies. She could never wake up. The kids could never wake up. Jon didn't think he could follow through if the kids cried at him in human voices instead of hisses.

He'd told Grace he'd gotten a cabin for the long weekend from a friend and they could have a vacation for once without having to pay for it with sleepless day-night-day shifts. Decent vacations or even days off was something they couldn't afford. Not with the bills for Liberty's birth still being drawn out of his paycheck on the bimonthly schedule they'd worked out with the hospital. The internship had promised to provide health care, but they kept telling Grace that the forms hadn't been submitted in time or that they needed another new copy of the bill, notarized (at Jon's cost), or . . .

He put the charging plug back on its hook. Some recent customer had stuck a wad of gum on the underside of the cable rack. Jon peeled it off and dropped it into the trash. He considered just going on without rewashing his hands. But this was to be the last drive he'd ever do with Grace and the kids. He made the trek back in and scrubbed every bit of grime and old-car smell off his hands. Then he got out his comm while still on the borrowed WeChargeForLess connection. He checked Pugna Lacertilia one more time.

TimeTravelerBilly28 had the new Top Post: "What if RighteousMan73 Plays the Long Game?"

There was a halo around Billy too. But Billy always had a halo. He regularly dumped cash into the Pugna Lacertilia forums. This was just the first time he'd paid to Top Post his own original message rather than someone else's. The body of the post was super short too.

"Hey, RighteousMan73, hear me out, please. I've got another idea. Have you ever heard of the Manchurian Candidate?"

Jon replied.

Of course, he had. He'd read the original in school, and enjoyed the *Manchurian Candidate and Zombies* rewrite, the movies, and the many memes on this forum and others claiming various politicians were just that.

Billy suggested Jon single-handedly flip the *lacertilia* script on the entire mass of all lizard/snake/reptilians/cold-blooded-monster-whatevers everywhere.

He suggested a long game. Painted a picture of what it could mean for humanity if some reptile-DNA babies could be raised not as lizards but as dragons: as fierce protectors of humanity.

Jon's profile quote was "Freedom lies in being bold. —Robert Frost." Billy referenced that a lot.

The *pugnasts* were mostly dismissive, but a few who'd been less than enthusiastic about the more gruesome lizard-killing suggestions jumped to support Billy's wild ideas. Most disregarded it and even went so far as to suggest that Billy might be a *lacertilia*.

But the idea latched onto something in Jon's soul and wouldn't let go.

"Fuck, yeah." He replied, "I'd be the fucking Father of the Year. But, I don't see how to actually do it now."

Billy was online and replying immediately.

Others chimed in with a long list of problems, many of which were not real. Jon had not, for instance, already hired a hit man to go after his family.

Did they think he was nuts? Someone like that might accidently kill non-*lacertilia* or hurt decent cops or EMTs responding to a mass shooting. Or what if a bullet went through the wall and hit someone else? There was a duplex on the other side of theirs, after all. Sure it was empty, and that cold unheated space hiked up their heating bill every winter, but the *pugnasts* didn't know that there wasn't some innocent family with kids in it.

Jon explained, "I'd need a real place to take them for the weekend. And, yeah, I'd love to, but how do you actually DO that??!"

Billy's replies hit the board like gasoline on a campfire. Billy posted fifteen different hotels with confirmation codes. Billy explained that his experience in other timelines led him to believe at least one of these locations would be within a five-hour drive of RighteousMan73 and he didn't want RighteousMan73 to reveal where he stayed or supply his address because in some timelines even this message board had *lacertilia* infiltration.

Several *pugnasts* of the unbelievers subgroup spiraled off-topic trying to convince Billy that there were no other alternate timelines, but Billy stood firm.

TimeTravelerBilly28 insisted, as he always had, that Billy's user-icon, that clearly painted image of three human soldiers fighting a horror of an unskinned *lacertilia*, was a photograph of his grandfather's fireteam in the First Lizard War. This time, Billy did not get distracted into the meandering tales of his grandfather's heroism or retellings of how the time machine plans were stolen and stolen back and stolen again.

Billy's time traveler gimmick was silly, but he stuck with it.

Amazingly, though, this time Billy had something new to say. He insisted that only in timelines where RighteousMan73 worked on the inside as father to *lacertilia* babies did humanity prevail in the coming wars. And he had all those hotel check-in codes for Jon to use. Three of the locations were within a day's drive even with frequent stops for diaper changes. They appeared to be valid. Every one of them seemed real and there was a hotel loyalty points account Billy private messaged him that had enough to pay the final amount due for whichever one Jon chose to use. Madman or not, Billy had money. And he was generous to a stranger in need.

Jon used his best encryption and DuckDuckGo-searched the second closest place to get an address and phone number independent of what Billy had posted. He called to confirm. The reservation was real. They didn't have Jon's name or an estimated check-in time, but the full weekend stay deposit hold was already paid.

"No, sir, it is not a scam. Yes, we understand the concern. Yes, those hotel points are valid and would cover the remaining balance in full. Yes, including taxes. Please enjoy your stay."

At TimeTravelerBilly28's urging, the group did create a CashForFriends this time. Billy didn't contribute, claiming direct funds transfer would draw *lacertilia* notice. It didn't reach anywhere near the previous promises for when they'd expected him to kill lizards, but the group did send enough money for a frugal weekend away.

Some *pugnasts* managed to pool charging station reward points so Jon could top-off his vehicle charge along the route without having to choose the second farthest hotel, which had WeChargeForLess stations all the way along the route.

Billy again came through with a complicated fund transfer scheme to allow Jon to get the charging station points as cash on a prepaid debit card. Billy failed to explain why that wasn't a *lacertilia* notice issue. The man was very definitely insane.

A healthy debate on whether or not Billy could really be a time traveler from another timeline briefly overtook Billy's new "Parenting of Dragons" as Top Post. Jon stopped tracking the message board to take his family on vacation.

Little Dubya hissed the whole drive over, but nominally accepted the idea of pretending to be a dragon instead of a lizard. And baby Liberty seemed destined to hiss all her first words too in a desperate effort to be just like big brother. But Grace loved the weekend and seemed almost human by the time they were driving home at the end of it. She smiled for real several times.

She had dimples. How had Jon forgotten she had dimples? Lizards don't have them, they can't. He cried himself to sleep in horror of how close to damnation he'd gone. He came home with new skepticism but also a lot of hope.

Back on Pugna Lacertilia, TimeTravelerBilly28 became a forum moderator. The unbelievers left en masse.

For the rest, it was complicated.

Shame seemed to be an effective motivator. The mods held a purge and rained down twenty-four-hours-blocked-from-posting and seven-day-blocked-from-commenting penalties like candy on *pugnasts* who still wanted to see Jon's family killed. People with blocks in place could still get their words into the forum with cash contributions on the sidebar for gold forum supporters. Forum hosting costs funded at light speed. The moderators managed this sideways way of blockee snark with a ruling that all gold support for the next month would go toward RighteousMan73's new "Teach Them to Be Dragons" fund. Some of the one-dollar gold notes (the minimum) dripped with hostility, even venom, but a surprising number, even from those *pugnasts* currently on the block list, included apologies.

The first *pugnast* support payout was enough to cover one week for Jon with no double shifts.

TimeTravelerBilly28's "Parenting of Dragons" suggestions didn't all work, but he got Jon into several online parenting courses that could be done on his comm during the dead periods of his work shifts. The courses had a ton of useful tips. Nothing directly said "train your kids to overthrow the *lacertilia* overlords" in the course descriptions, but of course they wouldn't. Jon learned things and used them.

Another angry minority left Pugna Lacertilia and set up a new forum, possibly with a better Latin name, but most likely not. The *pugnasts* who remained sent cash when they could. Not a lot but a little bit here and there. Enough that Jon could pay a neighbor to watch the kids three times that summer and take Grace out to watch the minor league baseball team play and eat a few greasy hot dogs. Grace started applying for positions at other companies.

In the fall, donations from the board paid for a family zoo trip. Dubya decided to pretend to be an eagle instead of a lizard, and Liberty's first word, after the hissing, was: "Daddy."

The tone of the boards shifted, and they lost some more regulars. But those who stayed started talking about more real things and ramped up the site security software. They didn't want the *lacertilia* to find out about their efforts to raise freedom-loving kids who also happened to have lizard-DNA. Some got into martial arts. A few tried to get firearms and teach kids competition shooting, but ammo was expensive and the *lacertilia* tracked gun purchases. No one else openly admitted to discovering that their children were lizard-babies, but a lot of them started trading tips on getting kids to sleep through the night. They did a lot of camping.

The old-guard Pugna Lacertilia had a meet-up at a KOA campground five years later. Jon attended without Grace and the kids.

Dubya went by Washington now and had a Boy Scouts event to do. Liberty Ann, now "Ty" to everyone but her daddy, had missed getting a seed spot for the Junior Olympic pentathlon. She was an excellent shot with those laser rifles, but the running killed her scores. Ty was a shark, not an alligator, according to her coaches. She sported red and blue streaks in her blond hair whenever it wasn't bleached out by her constant competitive swim-training sessions, and she was staying home to train.

Oh, and Grace had a new job. A career salaried employee one. She and Jon regularly donated to other *pugnast* families who were going through hard times and needed a bit of help. "Never forget where we came from," as Grace always said.

Grace checked in with Jon by video chat. The new company wanted to promote her again. She wanted to see what he thought of the compensation package and proposed work-hour changes. She updated him on Ty's new personal best swim time and the escapades of their surprise third baby, Billie Hope. She also had some concerns about her sleep-deprived new parent cousin and was trying to remember how they'd gotten through those rough patches themselves. She wished her cousin and her partner could find just one great friend online like Jon's Billy.

Jon choked up, but Grace smiled adoringly at him, told him she loved him, and encouraged him to go have a good time with Billy and the guys.

It was by the grill that night, after Billy and Jon had worked side by side to feed their assorted dozen-plus fellows, that Billy gave Jon a concerned look and dropped the bombshell.

"Uh, Righteous—I mean, Jon, have you ever wondered if maybe this timeline doesn't have *lacertilia* at all?"

"You mean that the ones in charge are just like us?" Jon nodded. He'd seen this one coming. "They don't care who they hurt when they don't have to look us in the eyes as they do it? But they are still human? Could be. Do you think that reality would be a better one?"

"Not about better or worse," Billy said, "just about whether or not it's true. Can't make any good choices if you have bedrock ideas that are all wrong about what reality is."

"You can't?" Jon looked at his best friend in the whole world, who had helped him raise some really amazing children, and who believed himself to be a time traveler because even modern schizophrenia meds can only do so much.

"Nope. Not possible."

"Huh," Jon said, "Wouldn't it be something, though, if you could?"

"Complete nonsense," Billy said. "I haven't been able to figure out if I can go back myself, of course, but that was expected..."

Jon decided to give his friend a lifeline. "Billy, I know you made it up about there having been other timelines where I raised dragons."

"You knew that?" Billy blushed a deep red, visible even with the dimming light from the campfire coals.

"Yeah."

"Well, nothing at all had ever worked in the earlier timelines," Billy mumbled. "I needed something new to try. And Dubya was so much older than he usually was. And still alive. I usually find you after he's, um, you know."

Jon just shook his head. Billy believed what he believed, Jon couldn't change that about him. "Sorry about that, man."

"We always lost before. But now. Winning? Wow. I just don't know what to do. The lizard war is over?"

"Have another beer?" Jon suggested.

"I mean with my life. I didn't realize I'd still have one. I thought I'd be gone." Billy stared into the coals. "The price of success, you know. If you can finally save a timeline, the awfulness that made you also no longer exists. So I thought I'd just vanish. But..." He trailed off, turning to stare in a rather fixed way at the distant glow of the closest city.

"How were you thinking it should work?" Jon asked, tying to keep as much judgment out of his voice as he could.

"I knew it'd be one-way when I was sent," Billy said. "It was the only way to get to all the prospective timelines at once, and we had no way of pinpointing exactly which one of them the *lacertilia* would first learn time travel in—or rather in which other timelines they would also learn it in, after we succeeded in stopping it in the first one."

"Ah," said Jon, "you never did say, who first invented time travel?"

"Oh, that would be Grace Smith. Every single time she goes back and shoots you to save little Washington. But I got to this timeline and Liberty Ann was there too. I'd never arrived late enough that there were two *lacertilia* children involved and the whole family still alive. It made me wonder if this time, we might finally win."

"My wife wanted to kill me and you never said anything?"

He thought he'd known the guy pretty well but at his moment he was strongly considering beating TimeTravelerBilly28 senseless. What a thing to keep from a friend! It took a full second for Jon to remember that time travel wasn't real, so of course Grace had never intended to do anything of the sort. And that in his own way, Billy had always realized that Jon had been the lizard-hearted one who needed to be stopped, not Grace and the kids.

"Well, no," said Billy, who was certainly convinced of the realness of time travel. He blinked at Jon in confusion. "Of course I didn't tell you about Grace Smith at first. She was a *lacertilia* in those timelines. Not like this one here where she's most likely actually human. It all worked out great for everyone. And, I mean, it was actually you who was planning to—"

Jon shut up Billy with a glare.

"Hey, it's war." Billy refused to shut up, but he did pause.

"No one is hurting my wife and kids."

"Hey, man, of course not." Billy glanced over to the campsite where some of the forum members had actually brought family. "And keep it down."

"My voice *is* down." Jon, who had been starting to hiss, checked himself.

"You aren't a *lacertilia*," Billy reassured him.

"Oh, yeah? What about in those timelines where you say I killed my family? Sounds like a lizard-people thing to do, if you ask me."

Billy nodded. "Yeah, maybe you were, in those. That didn't occur to me until much later. If there was a next timeline after this, I thought about contacting Grace instead of you."

"What?" Jon glared at his friend.

"Maybe you were a lizard person," Billy said. "If she wasn't, that is."

"Fuck you."

"But you aren't. And she isn't. So maybe no one is."

"Just shut up."

Billy did. And Jon thought about it all. Nobody in the group ever talked about those before-the-plan posts. The board admins, who were now Billy and Jon, had deleted those old threads and gone back and thoroughly scrubbed all archives and overwritten anything that might have contained duplicates of them. It had been private-messaged about in those darker early years, yeah, but it wasn't going to be something Dubya or Liberty Ann or Billie Hope would ever have splashed across their social media someday after Jon and Grace were long gone and there wasn't even a Billy around to provide context and explain.

Obviously Billy had a recurring schizophrenic delusion about being a time traveler, but he had a good heart. And he did need help from people like Jon to ground him in reality.

"Even if they had lizard-DNA," Jon finally said, "which I'm sure they don't, but if they did, then they are dragons fighting on the side of humanity and I'll challenge anyone who dares to claim different. I raised them right and everyone here has been witness to that."

"Amen," Billy said. But he looked up at the stars and added in a wistful tone, "Still. It'd be nice if I could go back to those earlier timelines and save them too. Or find out how the later timelines with other Billies and Jons did."

"If they saved the kids, they saved the world." Jon shrugged. "If they didn't, they didn't."

"Well, if Grace ever gets a machine working, call me. You've got to stay with the kids. But I could go again. There were twenty-seven Jons who died fighting. Twenty-seven of them."

"Billy, those Jons were *lacertilia*."

"How can you be sure?"

"They killed their kids."

"Oh."

"And that's how we won. You got to me before the infection took me over. Saved me and won the war."

The Joy of the Chase

A Sol Blazers Story

Jacob Holo & Edie Skye

Captain Nathan Kade knew the habitat's one gee could be hard on avions, but he suspected the slump in the man's shoulders had nothing to do with gravity. His wings drooped out the slit-hemmed back of his shirt, white feathers splayed on the floor as if anchored there. Everything else about him was baseline human and dressed in a common, professional style for the Golden Hollow habitat: neat slacks, button-down shirt, and a gaunt, tired face that suggested his superiors sent him for coffee so often he never had a chance to drink any himself.

Nathan didn't hear anyone else beyond the door the man had opened, and within that silence, he saw a new dimness in the man's eyes. His was more than harried fatigue.

"Solomon vaan Tarqeq?" Nathan asked. "Choppa Productions?"

"Yes! Captain Kade! Right?" Solomon clipped each word like he was running out of time.

"You wanted to discuss hiring me and my crew?"

"Yes! Come in."

Solomon dragged his wings out of the doorway and gestured for Nathan to enter.

The building hadn't been what Nathan expected when he'd received a message from the Saturnian movie company, and neither was its inside. Oh, posters of the studio's greatest successes were splayed along the walls behind statuettes of the awards they'd won, but this room wasn't a showoff-ish, sleek lobby. It looked like a converted living room with a circle of well-worn couches surrounding a refreshment-laden table.

Perhaps he shouldn't have been surprised, given what he knew of the studio's history. Aiko Pratti, his second-in-command, had briefed him on Choppa Productions after she relayed Solomon's request to him. The low-budget movie company had been founded as an expensive hobby by a handful of friends, only to rise to sudden prominence when their movies found a cult following, both on Golden Hollow's Saturnian capital and back on the Saturn shell band itself. Their most recent release had turned into a genuine hit, but it seemed the company's physical trappings hadn't quite kept up with its earnings.

It still looked like a hobby company run out of someone's garage.

"Help yourself." Solomon indicated the snacks on the table, and then sat on what Nathan took to be his customary couch cushion, given the two dents in the seat back. The avion fussed with his wings and settled into place. "And thank you."

"I haven't taken the job yet." Nathan sat on the couch across from him and selected a water bottle from the refreshments, if only to be polite.

"I know. But thank you, anyway. For being willing to consider it. And I'm sorry no one else from Choppa Productions could be here."

"Why's that?"

"Because our entire film crew's gone missing."

Nathan paused with the bottle halfway to his mouth.

"Your *entire* crew?"

"For this part of production, at least. All eighteen people."

"Where'd they go missing? And what do you mean 'this part of production'?"

Solomon calmed himself with a deep breath. Or tried to, anyway. His face may have gone slightly placid, but the feathers draping over the couch trembled.

"Let me start from the beginning." He closed his eyes and paused to collect his thoughts. "Are you familiar with our movies?"

"Not really. I'm more into books myself."

Nathan thought it best to leave out that none of his experiences with their movies had been voluntary. They had titles like *Ace Irondark: Going Commando*, *Irondark 2: Terminal Vengeance in the 9th Dimension*, *Irondark 3: The Final Showdown*, and *Irondark 4: The Final Showdown (Again)*, and all the awards they'd earned were either bestowed by very niche fan societies or satirical organizations that "honored" the worst films of the year.

"I was told the last one reached number one on opening weekend. *Irondark 5: Ace of Blades*, was it?"

"That's right. And we're wrapping up principal photography on *Irondark 6: The Darkening*. The plot has the main character—Ace Irondark—and his team of crack Union special forces on a daring rescue mission that takes them to a mysterious jungle habitat. The team then runs into a monster—a spawn of the Devil of Proxima, left over from the Scourging of Heaven."

Nathan nodded, understanding the appeal of such a plot.

The Scourging was the formative event that had led to their current Age of Silence. It was the turning point after which humanity had lost contact with the Pentatheon—the five Guardian Deities who had once granted humanity its every wish. They weren't true supernatural beings so much as unfathomably powerful machine minds, but some still treated them as gods, and anyway, they'd been silenced by *something*. A war with the Devil of Proxima was one of the more popular theories—and thus made the central figure a recurring pop culture bad guy—but really, no one truly knew what had happened all those millennia ago.

The result was what mattered. The Solar System—and humanity itself—had been reshaped according to the wishes granted to those ancient humans. But the Pentatheon—the beings who'd done the reshaping—were either dead or gone or who-knew-what.

"You think the film crew might have run into some trouble?" Nathan asked.

"I don't know. All I *do* know is filming was supposed to wrap two weeks ago, but I've heard nothing from them."

"Where exactly did they go?"

"The Overgrove."

Nathan had never heard of the place—which wasn't surprising, given the hundreds of thousands of habitats within the Habitat Belt alone. He retrieved a vlass tablet from his jacket.

The visual-glass *Solar Almanac* was an essential resource for any self-respecting freelancer. It contained a log of all official habitat surveys, complete with details on their environments, tech levels and baseline deviations for their local populations (when applicable), and overall danger levels.

Nathan skimmed the entry.

The Overgrove was a windowed cylinder with a dense, impenetrable jungle dominating its interior. The survey team had dubbed it the "Overgrove" as a combination of "overgrown" and "grove," which he was certain *someone* had considered witty. The survey had been performed recently—within the past century—but the glaring omission was the survey crew had only studied the interior through the habitat's sun windows.

There hadn't been any boots on the ground.

Nathan looked up at Solomon with hard eyes.

"I *know*," Solomon said. "But the director said he knew a guy who insisted the place was safe. Not even a hint of megafauna. Just really big plants, which sounded perfect for the movie."

"Isn't the company swimming in money? Couldn't you have commissioned your own survey to make sure the interior was safe?"

"Does this look like the kind of studio swimming in money? Yes, *Irondark 5* was a hit, but we spent way more on the marketing than we should have. We only just broke even on it." Solomon pinched the bridge of his nose. "Everything's a mess. But the budget's not my biggest concern."

He produced his own vlass and slid it across the table.

"I want you and the *Neptune Dragon* to go to the Overgrove and bring our film crew back."

Nathan looked over the contract, and his eyebrows rose.

"I'm surprised a company that's barely breaking even could afford us."

"That's a problem for the accountants," Solomon said bitterly. "My friends are out there, and I want to see them back safely. Or to at least know of their fates. But"—Solomon sighed—"if you can't save them all, the execs from our distributor say to prioritize the safety of Orren ven Skoll and Jeremi zuun Tarqeq. The director and the star actor."

"The moneymakers."

"Yes." Solomon bit the word as if he wanted to bite the people who'd made him say it.

Nathan tapped the contract vlass as he thought. He hadn't expected a job offer of this scale to drop into his lap out in the Habitat Belt, and he wasn't operating with a full crew. His engineer and cleric were still off on a local job reactivating one of the habitat's deifactories. It was a low-risk assignment, but it was also a huge time sink. Despite Joshua Cotton's technical skills and Rufus zin Qell's cybernetic sensitivity to the Pentatheon's creations, it'd still be days before they finished. Perhaps even weeks.

That left him, Vessani, and Aiko sitting around, twiddling their thumbs, ready to take on other work. Fortunately, between the former space pirate and the former Jovian commando, they were well-qualified to face whatever dangers Overgrove spat at them.

There was always a chance the job would be simpler than it seemed, that they'd reach Overgrove and find the crew with a malfunctioning ship or downed communications. And even if that wasn't the case, he and his crew had already survived cyborg marauders, Jovian commandos, and a crazed ancient superweapon. A lush, jungle habitat seemed almost timid by comparison.

Nathan set the vlass down and met Solomon's gaze.

"We'll take it."

"*Thank* you," Solomon said, his relief palpable.

"Don't get too excited. We don't know what we'll find."

"Oh, I know," Solomon replied. "It's just . . . you look like the kind of man who's qualified for the job."

Nathan wasn't sure how he felt about those words, coming from a man who worked for a B-grade company that made dumb movies about over-the-top action heroes. Then again, his frame had the kind of muscle that had gotten him through more than a few misadventures. Between that, his rough stubble, the small scars near his right eye, the pistol strapped to his thigh, and the black leather jacket emblazoned with the silhouette of a hawk flying through lightning-streaked storm clouds . . . maybe he did look the part.

The jacket still read *Neptune Belle* beneath its decorative logo, which was inaccurate after the crash that wrecked his old ship and almost killed his entire crew, but he was in no hurry to change it. He liked the sense of nostalgia, and it made him feel like he still carried a piece of his old ship.

He drove back to the New Tarqeq City spaceport and parked the rover in the *Neptune Dragon*'s open cargo hold. *Star Dragon* corvettes were almost unheard-of outside the Jovian Everlife, and it had been quite the battle to get this one declared as legal salvage. But now the sleek, powerful—and well-armed—vessel was his, and he smiled as he took the central freight elevator up to the bridge.

"What's the word, boss?" Aiko asked from the copilot seat.

"*Please* tell me you have work for us!" Vessani griped as she spun around in the pilot's seat.

Both women faced him expectantly, though "woman" was a relative term in one case.

Aiko Pratti had once been organic, but her "meat days" could be considered the Jovian equivalent of adolescence. Unlike her other bodies (which were killing time elsewhere on the ship), this one was geared for combat. And augmented for style. Red armor detailed in gold defined most of her androgynous shape, but she'd accented the triangular head with a vibrant purple. A leather jacket identical to his set off the whole ensemble, still bearing the logo of the defunct *Neptune Belle*.

Meanwhile, the woman in the pilot seat was *definitely* organic, and *definitely* female. Vessani S'Kaari wore a skintight bodysuit open at the chest to emphasize just how blatantly feminine she was. The triangular points of her cat ears poked above her short black hair, and her fluffy tail hung languidly over the armrest. A pair of sharp golden eyes completed her Nekoan divergences from baseline.

Nathan had been initially concerned about how well this unlikely pair would work together, but between their shared love of guns, explosions, and mischief, the ex-space pirate and the ex-commando had become fast friends. Now, they locked their eyes and cameras on him, eager to learn if they'd get to shoot something.

"I do," Nathan said.

"Yay!" Vessani threw up her arms in triumph.

"But it's a rescue mission."

"Boo." Vessani let her arms flop back down.

"The film crew for *Irondark 6* went missing in a habitat called Overgrove. Our job is to find them and pull them out of whatever mess they've landed in."

"Wait a second." Vessani's ears perked up, and her tail flicked. "Did you say *Irondark 6*?"

"I did."

"Yes!" Aiko thumped the air. "Wait, *no*! Wait . . ."

"Why is this complicated?" Nathan asked.

"Because the next Ace Irondark movie is in jeopardy, and I'm having emotions right now!"

"The entire crew?" Vessani added. "Including the star? What kind of situation could stop a beefcake like Jeremi zuun Tarqeq?"

"He's an actor, not a soldier," Nathan said.

"No, he is. Or at the very least was." Vessani sat up, tail wagging. "How do you think he plays Ace Irondark so well?"

"Vess, I've never watched an Irondark movie and thought to myself: 'Wow! This is quality cinema!'"

"That's because you have questionable taste in movies."

"Come on. He's a man who play-fights other men in monster costumes."

Aiko bolted out of her seat so suddenly Nathan flinched.

"Look me straight in the sensors," she began, "and tell me you weren't moved when he chased that dragon toward that exploding volcano dual-wielding two heavy machine guns and said, 'You're in hot water now . . . and I'm the boiling point!'"

"This is not a discussion we're having."

"At *least* admit his catchphrases are fun." Vessani struck a gun-wielding pose and adopted a gruff, gravelly voice, "'You're toast, buttercup.'"

"'Time to split, banana,'" Aiko added.

"'Get ready for the punch-line!'"

"'It's time to be pun-ished!'"

Nathan lowered his head and massaged his temples.

"We cannot allow Ace Irondark to fall," Aiko declared.

"He's an irreplaceable hero of our times!" Vessani added.

"Can you two just get us prepped for launch already?"

Nathan called Joshua and Rufus and informed them of the change of plans. Vessani flew the *Neptune Dragon* above the atmospheric retention walls of Golden Hollow's open ring and then plotted a course through the local habitat cluster. They arrived at Overgrove the next day.

The habitat was a simple affair from the outside—a cylinder spinning in space with three large, rectangular reflectors angling sunlight through three gigantic windows. The interior was filled with green. Lots and lots of green. Over thirty thousand square kilometers of the stuff.

Nathan hailed the film crew from outside, but after several minutes of trying and no responses, Vessani guided the *Neptune Dragon* toward the dock at the far end of Overgrove. The habitat's ancient, automated systems recognized the ship's presence, and the outer door of a massive airlock yawned open.

Vessani brought them to rest next to the only other ship in the dock, and Nathan joined Aiko down in the cargo hold. He donned a hard suit—which served as both environmental protection and body armor—then holstered his wyrmstake heavy pistol to the thigh. Aiko grabbed on her own weapon of choice, a Jovian sinspike assault rifle she'd lovingly maintained since her commando days.

"Let's bring some toys and make some noise!" she declared.

Nathan hadn't paid enough attention to the *Irondark* movies to know if that was a quote, but still glared at her.

"People's lives could be at stake."

"'Then let's find them before they're well-done.'"

The Choppa Productions spaceship was a bulky, practical craft, though Nathan wasn't too sure about the decor. Paintings of winged skulls screamed against a backdrop of explosions, and the name *Skull Exploder* had been emblazoned across each side, "backlit" by huge fireballs.

"Stylish." Aiko nodded approvingly. "Now that's what I'm talking about."

"Can you get us inside?" Nathan tilted his head toward the side hatch.

"Should be able to." Aiko crunched in a small panel beside the hatch. She examined it for several moments before—to Nathan's horror—she ripped the panel off and plunged her arm into the recess. She rooted around in the ship's guts for another minute before the airlock's outer door slid open.

"Was that really necessary?" Nathan asked.

"We can tell them we found it like this."

"*Aiko.*"

"What? You wanted inside, and I opened the way. You really think the crew's going to be picky about how we rescue them?"

"I suppose not," Nathan conceded, then drew his pistol and headed in.

The interior was littered with empty snack wrappers and drink bulbs: the debris of a bunch of guys just having a good time with their surprisingly successful movie business. There were empty spaces in the back where the film equipment might have gone, but no evidence that anything had been taken or wasn't where the crew had left it.

He and Aiko swept through the ship, marching their way to the bridge.

"*Skull Exploder* to *Neptune Dragon*," Aiko said, keying the ship's comms. "*Skull Exploder* to *Neptune Dragon*, do you copy?" Aiko said from the open cockpit.

"They named their ship the *Skull Exploder*?!" Vessani exclaimed. "Hell yeah!"

"Communications still work," Aiko reported, turning to Nathan. "But no one's home to use it."

"Which means they're probably inside the habitat." Nathan sighed. "All right. Let's go try and find them."

Another automated hatch granted the *Neptune Dragon* access to the cylinder's interior, and Vessani guided the ship low over the jungle. The light reflected from Sol cast dramatic rays upon the wild greenery but did little to help with visibility through the thick canopy.

"Where do you want to start?" Vessani asked.

"Hell if I know," Nathan grumbled, then cleared his throat and straightened. "They left the ship in the dock, so I'm hoping they're close by."

"Unless they brought a helicopter with them," Aiko noted. "The *Exploder's* hold was big enough to fit a vehicle or two."

"In which case," Vessani added, ears drooping, "they could be anywhere in this mess."

"Yeah," Nathan breathed more than said.

"What are we looking for again?"

"Something that doesn't belong."

"You mean like that?"

Vessani pointed to a sudden twiddle of red rising above the jungle.

"Yes, indeed." Nathan straightened. "Get us closer."

Vessani banked the *Neptune Dragon* toward it, and as they drew near, the pillar of billowing smoke grew thicker against the canopy's damp greenery.

"No way I can set us down on top of the smoke," Vessani said. "The jungle's too thick for that."

"It's thick everywhere," Nathan looked around. "What about that shoreline? Can you drop us off there?"

"Should be able to manage. Looks like there's enough beachfront property to set the *Dragon* down on. It'll be a bit of a hike for you, though. Call it maybe five or six kilometers."

"We'll manage. Take us down."

Once groundside, Nathan and Aiko took one look at the oppressive jungle and decided to leave the rover behind; they'd move faster on foot. Unfortunately, five kilometers in a spaceship and five kilometers on foot were two different units of measure, especially in a hard suit.

But that wasn't the worst part.

Nathan groaned, not entirely from exertion, as he and Aiko threaded their way between two gnarled trees. Aiko fiddled with her rifle, then turned toward him.

"Please don't," Nathan said without looking.

"'It's gun o'clock...and we're right on time!'"

"Uhh..." He shook his head and trekked on through the jungle.

They marched onward until Nathan pushed a massive branch aside, and it snapped back into Aiko. He glanced back at her, and she once again looked him dead in the eyes.

He waited.

She waited.

The moment he got his hopes up, she said,

"'We should branch out.'"

While Aiko's multiple bodies and electronic consciousness granted her a form of playful immortality, she was acutely aware of the limitations of organic bodies, and that Nathan's mortal meat was a lot more vulnerable than her metal.

She kept her rifle at the ready as they tracked through the jungle, though they didn't bother with silence. Their goal was to reach the source of the smoke—and hopefully, the film crew—as fast as possible, and they trudged as briskly forward as the terrain permitted.

Until...

Nathan stopped.

He looked around, and Aiko searched their surroundings reflexively. The jungle was rife with unusual sights and sounds, but they'd been in far stranger places before.

Why then had he stopped?

Aiko crept close to him. "What is it, boss?"

"Something doesn't feel right."

"Well, yeah. There's eighteen missing people up ahead."

"I mean, right now. It feels like we're being—"

"DON'T MOVE!"

The voice bellowed through the trees in a directionless echo.

Nathan and Aiko snapped their weapons up, back-to-back, covering each other. She didn't see anything unusual, but metal clacked somewhere, perhaps from a weapon being readied. Unusual behavior for a person in need of rescue.

"Care to tell us why we shouldn't?" Nathan shouted back.

"Because this is where the monster hunts." The voice was hard, dry, and deadpan. "I'm coming out, and I'll get you to our camp. Ahead of you."

High ferns rustled, and an unmistakable figure pushed into view, if worse for the wear than he'd ever been. Or, perhaps, more appropriately costumed than he'd ever been.

Jeremi zuun Tarqeq was a baseline human as far as Aiko knew, but his impressive physique would keep him employed as long as cheesy action movies were still selling. His appearance now was much harder than it had ever been on screen with rough tactical clothing torn, muddied, and bloodied. Cuts and scratches marred his exposed biceps and one side of his chiseled face.

Whatever he'd been fighting, he looked the part. His hands clenched his Saturnian rifle like he was ready to fight some more, and the five extra rifles slung across his back ensured he could go the distance.

He jerked his considerable chin toward the red smoke.

"Come with me."

The second man at the signal flare jumped up the moment Jeremi ushered them into a small clearing shadowed by the thick canopy.

"Oh, thank the gods! You found them in time!"

"Time is about the only resource we *do* have," Jeremi replied.

The words weren't harsh, just fatigued, but the other man recoiled from them all the same.

Jeremi turned to face Nathan and Aiko, then placed a hand to his chest.

"Jeremi zuun Tarqeq."

Nathan was about to return the courtesy, but Aiko took the initiative, cocking one hip and propping her rifle on her shoulder like she was the coolest thing ever.

"This is Captain Nathaniel Kade, and I'm Aiko Pratti." She gestured to the other man. "Are you Orren ven Skoll, by any chance?"

"Oh, what a pleasant surprise to be recognized in a place like this!"

Nathan was impressed she'd recognized him at all. He didn't appear on the movie posters, after all, and given the exaggerated character they'd seen of the studio thus far, he'd half expected a man with a surname like "ven Skoll" and a ship like *Skull Exploder* to make ample use of bombastic skull imagery. Instead Orren lurked by the signal flare in dirty slacks, a button-down shirt with its sleeves rolled up, and the kind of hat pretentious art school students wore no matter where in the Solar System they hailed from.

He looked like someone who'd hoped to make his career in art films, only to find that movies he considered beneath him were the ones that kept him fed.

"I'd recognize you anywhere!" Aiko replied. "I've been an Irondark fan since *Going Commando*! That final action sequence with the car chase through the space station was..." She mimed a chef's kiss.

The dark look in Orren's eyes could only be resentment at his unfortunate lot in life.

"Gentlemen," Nathan said, "Solomon vaan Tarqeq sent us to get you out of here. All of you, if possible. First, where's the rest of the film crew?"

"They're gone," Orren said. "And we'll be gone, too, if we don't leave *now*."

"We're not leaving without them," Jeremi grated back.

"Hold up a second," Nathan cut in. "Define 'gone.'"

"It started about two weeks ago." Jeremi stepped in front of Orren before the other man could answer "We'd just finished recording the first major action set piece. Lots of explosions and pyrotechnics. You know the kind. After that scene, the disappearances started." His face grew dark. "I think we may have disturbed something in this habitat. The kind of 'something' best left alone if you hope to reach a ripe old age."

"We were surveying the jungle for our next location when our cameramen went missing," Orren added. "And then one of the stunt doubles followed by the key grip. Naturally, we recognized the severity of the situation, so we sent a team back to the ship. But they never returned! All four of them, gone somewhere between here and the docks! Taken by the jungle! And then more people went missing until our numbers were whittled down to what you see before you. We're the only two left!"

"'Taken by the jungle'?" Nathan echoed.

"We don't know what the creature is," Jeremi said.

Nathan noted how composed the actor sounded compared to Orren. There was a timbre of uncertainty to his voice, but it was much firmer than he'd have expected from a man who made his career *pretending* to be a badass.

"It blends perfectly into the jungle," Jeremi continued. "Silent, invisible. It can sometimes be *minutes* before we realize someone's missing."

"I feel like I've seen this in a movie before," Aiko said.

"Yes!" Orren snapped. "And everyone dies except for the hero! And that's what's going to happen here if we don't leave *now!*"

"Then *you* leave," Jeremi snapped back. "You can fly home and tell the families of our entire crew—our *friends*—that we left them for dead in this gods-forsaken place!"

Orren flinched, but didn't argue back, only broke from Jeremi's gaze, unable to hold it.

"We thought it was safe."

"Tell that to our friends! Look at us! Up to our ears in trouble, and nothing to defend ourselves with but *prop guns!*" Jeremi smashed the gun in his hands to the ground. It clanked against the dirt, heavy but not as heavy as it should have been.

Orren flinched at that sound, again refusing to meet Jeremi's eyes.

"Wait a second," Nathan said. "You came to a barely surveyed habitat and didn't bring any actual guns?"

"Originally, we had two armed guards," Jeremi explained, "just in case we had problems with the local wildlife. But they're gone, along with their weapons."

"If those guns are props, then why carry them at all?"

"Because I can still throw them."

Nathan frowned, unsure if the actor had just told a joke.

"It's better than nothing," Jeremi added, deathly serious.

"I suppose I can't fault you there."

"A few fake guns aren't going to do us any good!" Orren said. "We need to get out of here!"

"I'm not leaving until I find the rest of our crew," Jeremi declared, then looked hard at Orren. "Or their bodies. You do what you want."

"Do you believe they're still alive?" Nathan asked.

"I do," Jeremi replied. "Whatever this creature has done, it hasn't left any blood or corpses. To me, that means there's still a chance."

Nathan met the actor's gaze levelly, saw the sincerity in his eyes, the genuine belief that his friends were still alive. He nodded back.

"All right, then. Let's go find your friends."

"But, the creature—!" Orren began.

"Don't you worry." Aiko hefted her rifle. "Ours aren't props."

"Show us where the last person disappeared," Nathan said. "We'll see what we find and go from there."

"It happened back at our production camp," Jeremi said as he led them deeper into the jungle, prop gun raised, the others clacking on his back.

The camp, when they arrived, was a mess. Tents had collapsed, boxes were turned over, footprints scrambled all over the damp soil. Yet, none of the markings appeared to be the result of direct struggle.

"Where *specifically* did the disappearance occur?" Nathan asked.

Jeremi indicated a tent, still standing and with a fair number of fresh footprints surrounding it. Nathan kept his distance to preserve the tracks as he circled the tent. The prints began at the tent flap and walked around the back, where they stopped, positioned evenly apart as if the man had paused to take a late-night leak and just . . . vanished.

"It's possible he wasn't taken by ground." Nathan looked up. The density of the canopy had as much to do with its webs of tightly interwoven branches as it did the thick foliage, but that network started a good seven meters in the air.

Dropping from that high up, nabbing someone, and fleeing

through the branches—silently and without being seen—was no small task.

"What do you think, Aiko?" Nathan asked, still gazing up into the trees.

"No unusual tracks on the ground. If you're guessing it moves through the trees, then I say you're on to something."

"But how can it do that without being spotted? Or heard?"

"Don't know. But just because I don't have a clue doesn't mean the Pentatheon didn't once design a creature that could do this."

"You think there really is a monster?"

"Maybe. Could be a machine of some kind, following whatever orders the Pentatheon gave it last."

"You see anything through your Jovian optics?"

"Just the big mess that is this jungle. You'll be the first to know if I spot any—"

"Orren?" Jeremi swept his gaze urgently across the camp. "Orren?!"

"Oh, no," Nathan breathed, snapping his pistol up. "Him too?"

"Orren!" Aiko shouted, and her voice echoed through the trees.

No one replied.

"He was right here!" Jeremi exclaimed.

"Where?" Nathan asked. "Show us the exact spot you saw him last."

"Over there!" Jeremi stomped toward the edge of the camp where he'd last seen the man. Nathan and Aiko followed, only to find a similar set of tracks to the one at the tent.

"He was walking this way," Nathan observed, "and then his prints just end."

Nathan crouched beside Orren's last track. It wasn't neatly pressed in; there was upward movement to its planes. Nathan rose, pressed his boot into a fresh patch of mud, then yanked it back up hard, as straight as he could. The contours of the prints looked similar.

He peered up at the canopy.

"I think we found the root of the problem," he murmured.

"Yeah!" Aiko thumped the air. "That's the spirit!"

"What?"

"'The root of the problem'? The . . . you mean you didn't intend that as a cheesy action movie pun?"

"A more appropriate line would be . . ." Jeremi paused in thought, then nodded. "Yes. I'd say this monster has barked up the wrong tree."

Nathan suppressed a groan. *"Really?"*

"I'm a nervous punner, and I'm *very* nervous right now. That's how this whole thing started. I came up with dumb puns to calm myself before my theater elective and then one of my buddies decided to write scripts around them."

"You do all your own stunts *and* your own puns?" Aiko exclaimed. "You're the total package! No wonder you're a star."

"Come on, you two," Nathan grumbled. "Let's see if we can find the trail."

"Jackpot," Aiko muttered once they'd scaled the nearest tree into its web of branches.

Nathan helped Jeremy mount the final branch while Aiko crouched to examine a patch of moss.

The canopy cover hung low above the branch network, but the sunlight was strong enough to pierce through. The rough bark of the branches was covered with slick mosses, lichens, and other fungi, and *something* had left an obvious mess of tracks.

Nathan and Jeremi followed Aiko's gaze downward to find Orren's last footprints directly below.

"There was some kind of device here, too." Aiko knocked on the tree trunk. "The bark's been carved off here and here, like maybe a trap of some sort was anchored to it. Moreover, there's plenty of moss covering the branches, and that means prints. You haven't been able to track this creature because it's been moving *above* you. A lot."

She indicated a set of prints near Nathan, distorted but still fairly clear.

"It's got to be big if it can haul people away like this." He placed his boot in one of the prints for comparison. The print was about five centimeters larger. "And if it's a tool user, then odds are it's humanoid."

"Not necessarily," Aiko replied. "Could be a really weird divergence. Remember the dragon?"

"Aiko, I am *never* forgetting that damn dragon." Nathan glanced around. "At the very least, it's not trying to be stealthy up here, whatever the hell it is." He indicated a trail across the heavy, moss-covered branches. "It should be easy enough to follow."

He eyed the branches ahead, then his gaze turned downward to the drop.

It was a long way down.

Possibly a fatal one. Even if it wasn't, it'd hurt like hell, and he had his hard suit weighing him down.

"Hmm." He grimaced at the precarious path ahead.

"Why don't you two stick to the ground?" Aiko suggested. "I can follow the trail and guide you from up here."

"Sounds like a plan," Nathan replied. "We'll go with that."

Nathan and Jeremi climbed back down the tree, and Aiko guided them forward from the web of branches.

Aiko followed the trail easily enough now that they'd found it, but the jungle's underbrush grew denser as they progressed. The air thickened with humidity and fog, and they pressed on through thickets of cloying branches that left leaves and dirt on their armor. Nathan kept his pistol ready while Jeremi followed, the barrel of his prop gun gripped like the makeshift club it was.

"The question remains," Nathan said quietly as he pushed aside a massive fern, "why pick off a film crew in the middle of nowhere?"

"And where have they been taken?" Jeremy added. "I don't think they're dead. Otherwise, why not just kill on the spot?"

"I'm thinking the same thing," Nathan said. "Surely between seventeen people, you'd have found at least one—wait." He held up a hand, and Jeremi came to a halt behind him.

Aiko caught Nathan's hesitation and paused in the branches above. She readied her rifle and scanned their surroundings.

"What's wrong?" Jeremi whispered.

"Something's different ahead."

An enormous fern blocked Nathan's view, but through it, he saw an unusually strong light for this jungle. Tentatively, he lifted the fern up with one hand and caught sight of a wide-open space, still shaded by the ubiquitous canopy, but not completely.

It was a clearing of sorts, its boundaries composed of knotted vines and collections of dead branches that put Nathan in mind of giant bird nests. Whole walls of them, though mercifully empty. Perhaps for years.

One nest near the bottom drew his attention by being clogged with dead branches.

No, not clogged, but *deliberately covered*. Perhaps to conceal a path to the creature's hidey-hole?

He motioned Aiko to join them, and she dropped down, her commando body absorbing the force of landing with ease.

"Yeah, boss?"

"I think we're getting close." Nathan bobbed his head toward the unusual nest. "Watch my back. I'm going to take a closer look."

"Gotcha covered."

Nathan took one step forward when Jeremi cleared his throat.

"What should I do?"

"You, umm ... you hang back with Aiko. Club anything that gets close."

"You've got it." Jeremi gripped the prop gun tightly, his face cold.

Nathan approached the unusual nest with careful, tentative steps.

If this creature was intelligent—and that certainly seemed to be the case—then the entrance to its lair could very well be trapped. Nathan knew this and his eyes darted across his surroundings, watchful for any detail that might betray some form of danger.

He still missed the trap.

He heard the near-silent click, no louder than a toothpick being snapped—and then a net of vines snapped upward around his body. He hadn't even seen the net.

Something powerful snatched at his net and yanked him bodily into one of the nests, though he saw no hand or other appendage, only felt the jerk.

He came to a rough stop and something sharp pricked against his hard suit, but the deifactured armor stiffened in response, and the attack rebounded off.

He didn't care what it was. He just knew a cold poke inside a hunter's net *wasn't good*, so he wrenched away from the prick and swung his fist. It clanged against a surface as hard as armor and made him glad he'd worn his own.

He couldn't see whatever he'd hit.

What he *did* see was light bending into a vaguely human shape. The shape leaped back, then launched for him.

The creature whomped into him before he could raise his gun, so hard it knocked him backward, swinging in the net. But that put precious space between him and his attacker, gave him the room to raise his pistol.

He snapped off a flurry of six desperate shots. Most blasted branches and vines apart, but two struck his target in radiant flashes of warped light. The shape shifted, giving the vague impression of turning away before fleeing into the jungle.

Aiko and Jeremi both rushed over and scaled the nests to Nathan. Aiko cut him down while Jeremi examined the spot where he'd shot the invisible creature. The actor prodded a conspicuous splotch of blood with his prop gun, then turned to the others.

"If it bleeds, we can kill it, right?"

Aiko pulled Nathan out of the net, and he brushed off his hard suit.

"Sure, we'll go with that," he said.

"Doesn't matter if it bleeds or not." Aiko hefted her rifle. "I can *still* kill it!"

They hustled through the jungle in pursuit of the creature, Jeremi's fake guns clattering against his back, Nathan breathing heavily from the weight of his armor while Aiko ranged ahead of them. They didn't bother with stealth. The monster knew they were coming, and it had two leaking holes to slow it down.

The trail from the creature's retreat led them to a second clearing, and a cave mouth.

Something intangible shifted near the entrance, and both Nathan and Aiko fired.

They didn't hit anything this time, but the commotion had an unexpected effect.

"We're here!" someone shouted, the voice echoing from the cave mouth, followed by a clamor of "Over here! In this cave! Help us!" and similar exclamations.

"Let's go!" Nathan said, and they headed inside.

The hot, verdant light of the jungle abandoned them within the cave, and Nathan switched on his helmet light to supplement the faint glow of bioluminescent lichen. They inched forward, guns ready as they followed the clamoring voices.

"Over here!"

"I see your light! This way!"

"Here! Here!"

"Eyes open," Nathan breathed, pistol up as he motioned for Aiko and Jeremi to follow. "It's in here somewhere."

They eased cautiously around a rocky bend, heads on swivels for anything unusual, and when they turned the corner they found several metal cages, all brimming with scratched and mud-stained young adults who reached through the bars toward their saviors.

Nathan swept his light across the cages, eyes keen for trouble.

But trouble found him first.

A small metal cylinder landed at his feet, and thick smoke blasted out from the device.

"Jeremi, run!" Nathan shouted, unsure what threat the smoke posed. He had his environment suit, and Aiko's synthetic body didn't need air, but the actor had only his skin, his puns, and a collection of fake firearms to defend himself.

But he was already out of time.

A distortion of light plunged from the ceiling, and smoke billowed around the swift shape. Jeremi whirled his gun in a furious circle, and the fake weapon hit with a sonorous clang and *bent*. An invisible blow struck the side of his head, sending a spray of saliva and blood from his jaw, but he gritted his teeth and swung again. His bludgeon cracked against the unseen foe and snapped in half. He snatched another from his back and bashed *that one* into the creature.

Both Nathan and Aiko held their fire, unable to shoot into the light-distorted, smoke-shrouded melee.

The smoke began to dissipate, and Jeremi grappled the beast, one arm flexed around what must have been its neck and the other pinning a distortion that may have been an arm. His muscles rippled even in this low light, tightening against the monster's throat, and in that moment, Nathan was certain he was no longer looking at Jeremi zuun Tarqeq. He was looking at *Ace Irondark*, in the flesh, living up to every stupid story ever told about him.

The monster went limp in the actor's arms.

"I yield!"

"Good, because *I* have the right of way!" Jeremi growled—and then paused. "Hold up. You can talk?"

"Yes, I can talk." The voice was low, husky, and very . . . feminine? "And, again, I yield."

"We thought you were a monster."

"No, I'm not a monster."

"Then what are you? *Who* are you?"

"Permit me to remove my cloak, and I'll show you."

Jeremi glanced to Nathan, who nodded alongside Aiko, guns at the ready.

"All right," the actor snarled. "I'm going to loosen my grip. You make one wrong move, and my friends pump you full of holes. Clear?"

"Very clear."

"Okay, then." Jeremi took a deep breath. "Here goes."

He yanked the captive to her feet and released one of her arms. The shape shifted, reaching for her throat, and a rippling cloak of light dropped to the ground, revealing a woman over a head taller than Jeremi.

Her skin was gray, and there was a lot of it thanks to the bikini top. Flexible plates down one arm formed a legitimate piece of armor, but the rest consisted of hot pants, thigh-high boots, and a lot of fishnet mesh with gear and little bone trophies dangling from it. A helmet obscured her face, styled around the skull of a fearsome fanged creature. Black hair spilled down her back in long dreadlocks.

The gray-skinned woman raised her hands to emphasize her surrender.

Jeremi let go and took a step back while Nathan and Aiko kept her locked in their sights.

"You're, umm..." The actor cleared his throat. "You're not what I was expecting."

"What were you expecting?" the woman asked, sounding sincere.

"Wait," Aiko cut in. "Which version of the series were you lot filming here? Because she looks like someone out of Ace *Irondic*—"

"That series is unlicensed!" Orren's voice snapped from the cages. "We're in the middle of a copyright lawsuit, thank you very much!"

"Aiko?" Nathan said.

"Yeah, boss?"

"That's not really a 'now' problem, if you catch my drift."

"I know. But just *look* at her!"

"It's hard not to," he admitted.

The woman removed her skull helmet, revealing a face as strong and beautiful as the rest of her. Her eyes were a bright, vivid blue.

Jeremi looked up at her with a face full of conflicted emotions, but then coughed and broke eye contact. He didn't have a pun for *this*.

"Now would be a good time for an explanation," Nathan said, keeping his gun trained on the woman while Aiko approached and searched her for weapons. This process didn't take long, given how little clothing there was to search, and Aiko only came away with a pair of drug-coated vibro-knives and a small vlass.

The woman shifted nervously from one foot to the other, eyes flicking to Jeremi more often than anyone else.

"Still waiting for that explanation," Nathan said.

"My name is Rota Perdhet. Of Clan Perdhet."

That meant nothing to Nathan, but the Pentatheon had engineered an enormous variety of divergences into the human race, so a habitat of gray-skinned Amazonian women wasn't out of the question.

"I've been on my coming-of-age safari," Rota continued, "collecting trophies from unexplored habitats."

"You're not from the Overgrove?"

"No, I was born on a habitat on the far side of Sol."

"You're a long way from home, Rota. Why didn't we see your ship in the dock?"

"Because it's not there. I hid it on the habitat's exterior and came in through a different access point."

"Your trophies include other humans?" Aiko asked.

"Not exactly."

"Then what's with the people in cages?"

"That's different." Rota sighed. "I wasn't hunting them—at first. But..."

She glanced at Jeremi, whose expression was both perplexed and perhaps a little entranced by this unusual woman. If the endings of all the Irondark films were any indication, Ace Irondark knew *exactly* what to do with a beautiful woman.

Jeremi, though...

"I came here to hunt this habitat's apex predators, but as you may have noticed, there's not much here in the way of worthy prey. I was about to leave when this crew arrived." She nodded back to the cages. "At first, I didn't understand what they were doing, so I studied them from afar."

"Okay." Nathan nodded. "All that sounds reasonable for, what I presume, is a culture that values killing big game. But where's the kidnapping come in?"

Rota didn't answer as she looked in every direction but Jeremi's.

"Nate, check this out." Aiko handed Rota's vlass to Nathan.

The screen displayed a photo gallery, completely dominated by long-distance pictures of Jeremi, ending with a frantic blur of explosions and gunfight images in which he looked glamorously ripped-up and smudgy for the camera, firing off two rifles at the same time.

Nathan looked up at Rota, whose face darkened in what might have been a blush.

"Don't tell me," he began, "that you took 'Ace Irondark' to be—"

"The alpha of this group," Rota finished, eyes flicking toward the actor. "And an impressive one at that. There were"—her eyes became dreamy—"so many explosions."

"Oh, for Heaven's sake." Nathan lowered his pistol. "You have the hots for him?!"

Rota's cheeks darkened further, and she glanced away.

"So you decided to kidnap his friends?" Aiko asked. "Why not just, I don't know, ask him out?"

"I couldn't possibly do that."

"Oh, yes, you could have!" Nathan said sharply.

"Not without a trophy to impress him with." Rota bit her lower lip, seemingly afraid to meet Jeremi's gaze. "I only just started my safari, and my trophy collection is . . . lacking. I would have tried to hunt something here first, but, again, the local wildlife isn't very ferocious."

"So, what?" Nathan shook his head. "You decided grabbing his friends was the best way to his heart?"

Rota nodded bashfully.

"And how'd *that* work out for you?"

"He didn't seem impressed." Rota sighed, and her shoulders sank. "So, I tried to impress him more." She glanced back at the cages. "Over and over again. But nothing I did seemed to stir him. Clearly, he was even stronger and braver than I'd imagined."

"What?" Nathan blurted. "You thought he was playing hard to get?"

"Wasn't he?" Rota looked over at Jeremi nervously.

"So, let me get this straight." Nathan holstered his pistol. "You kept on kidnapping the film crew in order to impress Jeremi, but he interpreted it the wrong way. Basically, all we have here is one big cultural misunderstanding."

"We have a bit more than that!" Orren snapped.

"Stay out of this, Orren," Nathan snapped back. "You're not helping. You want out of that cage or not?"

"Sorry." The director shrank back. "I'll be quiet."

Rota let out a long, resigned breath as she examined the floor.

"Dating in your culture must be a *pain*," Nathan said.

"I can't argue there," she replied uncomfortably. "And it probably doesn't help that I'm . . . inexperienced with men."

"Didn't you figure out something was off when I shot you?"

"You mean this?"

Rota twisted to reveal the two bullet wounds in her side. Somehow, she'd found time to *staple them shut* before her final stand in the cave.

"They stung a bit."

"A *bit*?"

"I've had worse."

"Are gunfights common courtship rituals where you're from?"

"Depends on how serious the courtship is," she replied matter-of-factly.

"Are you joking?" Nathan asked. "Because I can't tell."

"Why would I joke about something this important?"

She looked over at Jeremi once more, and this time he met her gaze warmly.

"I . . . Listen." He stepped toward her. "I know what you think I am, but that's not me. I'm just an actor."

"You're a professional storyteller, too?" Rota's eyes lit up.

"No, not 'too.' Just a storyteller." Jeremi held up one of his guns. "You see this? It's not even real."

"You've been unarmed this whole time?" Rota placed a hand against her chest, as if she needed to still her fiercely beating heart.

"Look, it's like this . . ."

Jeremi tried his best to explain the situation, but everything he said seemed only to increase Rota's interest in him.

It wasn't that she didn't understand what he was saying. Despite the obvious cultural gap, Jeremi successfully explained what he and the film crew had come to Overgrove to do. But each revelation only served to excite Rota further, and Nathan began to understand why.

Jeremi had been up against a woman who'd trained her whole life to hunt the most fearsome of prey. He'd done so with no weapons or training of his own, and he'd never flinched from his stalwart desire to rescue his friends, even as she picked them off one by one.

He was everything she was looking for in a man.

It took some time, but Jeremi seemed to realize this as well, and the flow of conversation shifted into pleasant—if somewhat awkward—banter.

"Would someone please let us out already?" Orren griped from his cage.

"Sorry!" Rota smiled bashfully at Jeremi. "If you'll excuse me, Ace—I mean Jeremi."

"Of course. Take your time, Rota."

She flashed another smile, then unlocked the cages. The film crew stepped out and gathered around Jeremi. Or rather *behind* him, using the actor as a shield between them and the hunter.

The two resumed their conversation, and neither seemed frustrated by the inevitable misunderstandings. Rota listened with keen interest most of the time, and Jeremi was glad to talk her ears off. The fact that he was speaking to a beautiful warrior woman certainly helped things along, but there was a serious undercurrent to the conversation. As if both were interested in seeing where all this could lead.

"You know," Aiko said quietly, coming alongside Nathan, "*she* might have been flustered this whole time, but *he* hasn't made a single nervous pun."

"You think they'd make a good couple?"

"I've seen worse."

Nathan swept his gaze across the film crew. Most were in rugged outdoor attire or in Union military camouflage, but one was clad in the bulky rubber pieces of the movie's monster costume.

No one knew what the Devil of Proxima looked like, or even if it had existed at all, and that uncertainty was doubled for any of its spawn. Choppa Productions had gone with an unimaginative conglomerate of tentacles, and the actor looked through its open mouth with a face that never wanted to see the inside of a rubber suit again.

Nathan glanced over at Rota, then back to the rubber suit, then to Rota again.

He snapped his fingers, and Aiko tilted her head at him.

"What's up, boss?"

"I've got an idea." He turned to her with a broad grin. "And it might just be crazy enough to work. Oh, Rota! A moment of your time, please?"

＊　＊　＊

Irondark 6: The Darkening watched differently from any Ace Irondark movie Nathan had ever seen.

Oh, Aiko and Vessani still sat beside him, tossing back popcorn (in Vessani's case) and shouting puns with infuriating abandon, but that abandon wasn't quite as unbearable as before. The plush seats of the high-class premiere-night movie theater improved the situation, comfy enough that he could have fallen asleep.

Which was his typical reaction to Irondark films.

But this one held his interest, in no small part thanks to the reshoots.

Rota's culture was too different from Jeremi's for their courtship to proceed at a anything approaching a normal pace...but the combination of her skills and his profession had led Nathan's brain to some interesting conclusions. And *opportunities*.

Fortunately, Choppa Productions' lead writer had been in one of Rota's cages, and it had taken astonishingly few edits to turn their monster movie script into an explosive enemies-to-lovers action romance. Several reshot scenes later, and Choppa Productions had all the material it needed to splice together their revised sixth movie.

"They make a good couple," Nathan declared, propping his feet up.

Jeremi and Rota sat a few rows ahead, holding hands and enjoying the spectacle of their hard work. The chemistry they shared off camera had translated brilliantly to the big screen. Or, at least, brilliantly enough for B-grade schlock like the Irondark series. Rota had a long way to go with the delivery of her lines, but her *screen presence* was undeniably strong.

Besides, most of her time on camera was spent in explosive actions scenes or, later, in more horizontally focused "action" scenes. Her dialogue was a bit of an afterthought by comparison, and she'd nailed all the moaning like a pro.

"It's a unique one," Aiko replied. "I'll give them that."

The movie ended with a bang, and the audience burst into applause as the lights came up. Jeremi and Rota rose from their seats, and the cheering became even more raucous.

"I still can't believe she made you her agent," Aiko said.

"Why wouldn't she?" Nathan leaned back with a smug smile. "She was in unfamiliar territory, and I was a neutral party who could help her navigate it. As for me, I simply saw the opportunity and seized it."

"All out of the goodness of your heart?"

"Well, that and a small percentage of the proceeds from *Irondark 6*. We *are* running a business, after all."

"Of course, of course."

"Besides, I think everyone ended up a winner this time."

"Is that so?" Aiko tilted her head. "You could say we . . . *got lucky.*"

"Or went out with a bang," Vessani chimed suddenly.

"Or came out on top."

"Or nailed it."

The two women faced him expectantly.

Nathan rummaged in his bucket for the last of his popcorn.

"I could say that," he replied at last. "But I won't."

Wilder Kingdom

Rick Partlow

Enforcement Unit Three-Seven became self-aware.

At first there was nothing else to be aware of. He floated in darkness, the biotic fluid in the clone tank warmed to the temperature of his body, so still he might have been in free fall outside the ship. The only connection between him and anything outside the tank was the cable running into the back of his skull, feeding him data.

Feeding him a target. Three-Seven rocked in surprise, feeling the presence of the biotic fluid as it restricted his movements.

Get me out of here, he ordered, the command traveling up against the data stream in the cable. The fluid drained and he sank against the cold metal, suddenly conscious of his own body. He yanked the cable free and waited for the tank to drain, for brand-new lungs to fill with air for the first time in a sensation still intimately familiar.

"How was the Mimic allowed to escape?" he demanded, pushing through the door as it manifested in the side of the tank. The air outside the artificial womb was a bracing chill, sharpening his senses.

"The transport ship was sabotaged by unknown forces," the ship's AI replied, lacking his own sense of outrage. "It has emerged from subspace in a proscribed system and we have lost contact with the crew."

Three-Seven looked down at himself, at the peculiar, bipedal form he'd been given this time.

"A reducing oxygen atmosphere, then." His eyes flickered to the holographic avatar waiting with infinite patience for Three-Seven to adjust to his new self. "Humanoids?"

A nod answered his question, then the AI went on with the brief.

121

"You are aware what will happen if the Mimic is set loose on a proscribed system. Hunting down the fugitive is priority. You've been authorized to eliminate the target."

Three-Seven grunted, flexing his newborn fingers and tightening them into fists.

"It's about time. Get me to the planet."

"We've been talking about primitive man catching animals," Marlin Perkins explained, his gray suit clean and impeccable despite the chimpanzee and peregrine falcon he'd just been handling, "and just taking it for granted that man *always* caught animals. But when did it begin?"

Doug didn't look away from the black-and-white screen even to grab a handful of popcorn from the bowl on the TV tray and barely noticed when a couple pieces tumbled to the carpeting.

"Private Wilson," Sgt. Valentine growled from the ragged couch in the corner of the room, "if I have to tell you one more time to clean up your damn mess, this is the last time we watch *Mutual of Omaha's Wild Kingdom* on the armory TV."

"Yes, Sgt. Val," Doug said automatically, tearing his eyes away from Jim Fowler setting up an antlion trap for Perkins on the screen. "Sorry, Sgt. Val."

He didn't bother taking the kernels to the trash can after he retrieved them, just stuck them in the hip pocket of his olive-drab fatigues.

"I swear to God, Wilson," Val murmured, shaking his head, "if you'd put as much concentration into getting good grades in high school as you do on watching this damned show, maybe you'd be at USC right now studying wildlife and shit." The older man snorted, then wiped at his graying mustache. "Then you'd be *exempt* from the draft and your old man wouldn't have had to finagle you a National Guard slot to keep you out of Vietnam."

Scowling at the NCO, Doug managed to keep his mouth shut this time. He'd let the older man draw him into too many futile arguments since he'd reported to the unit until Corporal Edmunds had taken pity and told him that Val was screwing with him.

"What, Sgt. Val?" he said, the corner of his mouth turning up. "You don't think the storied 184th Infantry Regiment of the

California National Guard is worthy of my service? We kicked ass in W-W-Two!"

When Val burst out laughing, Doug knew he'd scored.

"Oh yeah, right, we're Modesto's finest. That's why we're doing our annual training in the Stanislaus National Forest, to make sure the Viet Cong doesn't invade right through Vietnam and into Yosemite."

"You're just sore that you were too young to fight in the Spanish-American War, Sgt. Val."

Now it was the NCO's turn to scowl. The one sore spot Doug knew he could pick at was Val's age. The man had been a squad leader in the Korean War and *should* have been a hell of a lot higher in rank than a platoon sergeant by now. But this was the Guard.

"Are you watching this shit *again*, Wilson?" Albertson moaned as he stepped through the door into the rec room. "Isn't there *anything* else on?"

"It's just got a few minutes left, Bud," Doug assured him, but the private ignored him and switched the channel.

Robert Conrad punched a cowboy in a bar and the fight was on.

"I said it just had a few minutes left," Doug said, pushing himself up from the folding chair forcefully enough that it almost knocked over the TV table and the bowl of popcorn.

He reached for the dial but Albertson blocked him, shoulders squared up, eyes narrowing. All he needed was a purple, velvet suit and a mean dropkick to be James West. Doug felt more like Ross Martin's Artemus Gordon but he didn't back down.

"That's kid stuff, Wilson," Bud Albertson told him. "Talking about a bunch of stupid animals from Africa. Who cares about that shit? We're grown men!"

"You're a pup, Albertson," Sgt. Valentine corrected him, moving between the two of them and switching the TV off. "Both of you are pups, still wet behind the ears, and I guess I have to play your damn mother and tell you to get your asses to bed. We gotta be up early to load the trucks." He limped out the door, paused halfway through, and pointed back at the two of them. "I hear that TV come back on, I'm gonna beat the shit out of the both of you."

"Nice going, Wilson," Bud growled, shoving Doug back a step. "Now we can't watch any TV the rest of the night. When are you gonna grow up?"

Doug pushed him back, though it didn't have as much effect since Bud outweighed him by a good twenty-five pounds.

"When I get done with junior college," he said, pointing back at the other private as he headed for the door, because retreat seemed a safe bet now that he'd escalated the situation, "I'm gonna go get my degree in zoology and I'll be *in* Africa studying those animals while you're stuck here in Modesto still working on broken-down cars for a living!"

"If you ever *do* get into college, it'll be because your old man has money," Bud sneered. "Not from anything brilliant *you* did. "

"Albertson! Wilson!" Sgt. Valentine's bellow echoed down the hallway. "I said get your asses to your cots! If you're not in your racks with your mouths shut in ten seconds, I'll come down there and make you both wish you'd been sent to the goddamned war!"

Bud mouthed *momma's boy* and Doug responded with a middle finger, but neither said a word on the way to the barracks. Valentine might be pushing forty and had last seen combat fifteen years ago, but Doug had no doubts he could still make good on his threats.

Doug winced, pulling his helmet down lower over his ears as Jacoby Bryant howled the song's chorus again in alto counterpoint to the bass rumble of the deuce-and-a-half's engine. Both of them drowned out the actual music coming from Bryant's transistor radio.

"What?" Bryant asked, frowning at Doug's expression. "Don't you like the Stones, Wilson?"

"No, I love the Stones," Doug told him, yelling to be heard over the ruts in the Forest Service road. "But you're not Mick Jagger, man."

"Don't listen to the nerd," Bud scoffed from just one soldier over on the bench across from them. "He's trying to be like that old stiff on the animal show, the white-haired square who sits in the office and shows videos of shit that other people do."

Doug *should* have kept his mouth shut, but he saw the snickers and sidelong glances from the other young privates. The others didn't care, the older vets who'd taken a reduction in rank to stay in the Guard and stay in California. This was a joke to them, to men like Sgt. Valentine, but the other kids his age—he shouldn't have cared what they thought, but he did. Just like in high school.

"I don't want to be Marlin Perkins," he snapped at Bud. "I want to be like Jim Fowler, the guy who actually goes out and captures the dangerous animals. I don't want to be stuck here doing nothing."

"Ain't there wild animals out here in the Sierras?" Bryant wondered, switching off his radio. "Like mountain lions and bears?"

"Some," Doug sighed. "People have hunted most of them out. Just like everywhere else except Alaska. It's like there's nothing wild left in this country at all."

"You should have volunteered to go to Vietnam, then," Sgt. Valentine suggested, so quietly Doug almost didn't hear him. The older man stared at the canvas on the opposite side of the truck bed, expressionless, knuckles white where he clutched his M1 Garand rifle. It was the same one the older man had used in Korea, not the new M-16s the Army used now. "You know what the definition of adventure is, Wilson?" The corner of his mouth quirked up, though he still didn't look at Doug. "It's somebody else in deep shit far away from home."

Doug said nothing, picked at the wood stock of his own rifle, anachronistic, two generations behind just like everything else the Guard made do with. Twice as useless with the stupid-looking blank adapter screwed to the muzzle. The crimped blank ammo mocked him from the ammo pouches in his belt. He hadn't fired a live round out of the Garand since he'd qualified Expert in Basic Training.

"Don't worry, Wilson," Bud said, as if he'd read Doug's mind. "If we run into any big, bad mountain lions out there, I got ya covered." He slid an en-bloc clip out of his bandolier and Doug's eyes widened at the sight of live ammo before Bud quickly tucked it away.

Not quickly enough.

"Albertson," Sgt. Val sighed, "you are the dumbest son of a bitch I ever had the misfortune to run across. It's bad enough that you brought live ammo on a training exercise, worse that you were stupid enough to flash it right in front of *me*, making me responsible if anything bad happened, but it just takes the cake that you put it right in your damned ammo pouch *right next* to your blank ammo. You really think if you're in the middle of a react-to-ambush drill, you won't screw up and grab the live ammo?"

Bud's mouth worked but nothing came out. He looked as if Sgt. Val had just told him Santa Claus wasn't real. Valentine stuck out his hand, make a "gimme" gesture, and Bud meekly pulled out the clip and passed it across to the NCO. Valentine tucked the live ammo in his fatigue shirt pocket but then put the open hand out again. Bud reddened and produced two more. Valentine looked around at the rest of First Squad.

"Does anyone *else* have any live ammo they want to declare before we get off this damn truck and I have to tell Lt. Pirelli with a straight face that we're good to go for this exercise?"

Before anyone could speak, the trucks' ancient brakes squealed, rusted and overtaxed metal groaning in protest at the sudden stop, echoed by the unenthusiastic sighs from the soldiers inside.

"Everybody out!" Valentine barked, his entire demeanor changing, as if the incident had never happened. "Grab your rucks and get the hell out!"

Away from the shared body heat—and odor—inside the truck, the early morning chill slapped Doug in the face. Dawn glinted above the Sierras and painted the trees gold, so beautiful it almost took his breath away.

"Hey, what's that?" Bryant asked, pointing above the mountains to the northeast.

Doug followed the gesture to a faint red streak trailing down through the thin, wispy clouds, falling to Earth.

"I think it's a meteor," Doug said. "But I've never seen one in the daytime before."

"Wilson! Bryant!" Valentine's ever-present bellow burst the mystery like a soap bubble, dragging them back to reality . . . to the rest of the company tromping out of the other trucks into the muddy, rain-soaked ground and the reality of the next ten days they'd spend living out here with no showers, no indoor toilets, and one hot meal a day if they were lucky. "Get your heads out of the clouds, you knuckleheads! I'm going for the El-Tee's briefing and when I get back, our squad is going on a security patrol, so you better get your bivouacs set up unless you wanna sleep on the damned ground tonight." He turned to the others, holding his Garand over his head like a totem. "Come on, First Squad, get to work!"

"Why do I always gotta be the one on point?" Bud griped, swiping the air in front of him. "I always wind up running through the spiderwebs."

"Yeah, and better you than me, Albertson," Valentine said from just behind Doug. They were in ranger file on the narrow forest trail, the trees shrouding them in shadow, dark enough to conceal the traps arachnids had set for their prey. "Now shut up. If there were enemy around, you'd be advertising our position."

Doug had been asking the same question but with the opposite emphasis, wondering why Bud always got to walk point. As Doug's father liked to say, *If you're not the lead dog, the view never changes.*

Of course, his father said a *lot* of things, most of them having to do with how Doug should go to Cal State where Dad had pull with the board and could get him accepted even with his mediocre high school grades. How Doug should change his major to business or finance and work at his company. He meant well, Doug allowed, but being stuck in an office eight hours a day seemed just as hellish as Bud's prospects for doing the same in a garage.

Ruminating about it wouldn't help, but at least it kept Doug from thinking about how much his feet hurt or how long they'd been walking on this trail. He wasn't good at keeping his pace count even when he was paying attention, but it had to have been at least four miles already, the woods didn't look any less thick than they had for the last half hour and the damned Garand was getting heavy.

"How far does this trail go, Sgt. Val?" he asked, softly less he incur Valentine's wrath.

"All the way to the end," was the predictable response. Valentine checked his watch and sighed. "All right, everyone take a ten-minute break. Drink some water."

Doug shrugged out of his pack and slumped to the ground against a tree, not even caring about the damp grass under his ass. He didn't dare let the Garand fall to the ground, not with Valentine around, but he set it across his lap and closed his eyes. A kick to his boot woke him up.

"I said, drink water," Valentine cautioned, holding up his own canteen in example.

Doug nodded and downed a few gulps from his canteen, which unfortunately revived him before he could enjoy his catnap. Jacoby Bryant pushed off the rock he'd turned into a seat and left his pack behind, slinging his rifle.

"Sgt. Val, I gotta take a dump. I'll be right back."

"You got five minutes, Bryant," Val warned.

Doug tried to shut the exchange out, determined to squeeze in a five-minute catnap. Another kick woke him up. Valentine again and Doug groaned.

"Bryant ain't back," Valentine told him, pointing back the trail in the direction the other soldier had gone. "Go tell that sham artist to pinch it off, wipe it off, and get his nasty ass over here."

Doug responded with a desultory grunt but did it anyway. And took his rifle with him. If he left it behind, Bud would probably hide it in a tree.

"Hey, Bryant!" he yelled once he was out of sight of the platoon, deciding Valentine would prioritize alacrity over stealth. "Come on, man, we gotta go!"

Nothing.

"Come on, Jacoby, I don't wanna have to hunt you down by smell. Let's get going."

How far would Bryant have gone? Doug stood still, held his breath, listening for movement. There was no breeze this morning to rustle the trees, nothing to drown out the rhythmic *tap-tap-tap* coming from somewhere nearby. Into the woods.

"If you're screwing with me, man," he said, hunting for a clear path through, "I'm going to kick your butt."

There. A boot-print heading inward. This *was* the way Bryant had gone. Doug held his M1 in front of him to intercept the dreaded spiderwebs, keeping his eyes on the ground, avoiding tanglefoot vines and roots, until he realized he'd gone twenty yards. He stopped and looked around, saw nothing.

There. That tapping sound, like a faucet left dripping in the middle of the night. Off to the left. Close, somewhere beyond a thick stand of trees. Doug high-stepped around the gnarled roots, wondering why Bryant would go in this deep just to take a dump . . .

Doug froze between steps. The forest floor was splashed in red, a Jackson Pollock painting on nature's canvas. Not completed just yet. Another drip, another *tap*, droplets spattering dead leaves. They came from above. Doug didn't want to follow them to the source, didn't want to know, but his eyes were drawn upward against his will.

What was left of Jacoby Bryant hung by an ankle, tied onto an overhanging branch by the slashed remnants of his fatigue trousers. If Doug didn't scream, it was only because he lacked the breath for it, the air gushing out of him, followed closely by his breakfast. He doubled over and nearly went to his hands and knees but instinctively recoiled from the puddles of blood and stumbled backward instead. His back went against a tree and he *did* scream, spinning around, convinced that whatever had ripped Bryant to pieces was behind him, ready to strike.

The muzzle of his Garand moved up and down with his labored breathing, threatening an unsuspecting oak with its harmless blank adapter.

A hand fell on his shoulder and the only reason he didn't spin around in ludicrous counterpoint was the strength of that grip. It wasn't a monster or a bear or a mountain lion, just a man. Tall, rugged, with the weathered look of someone who spent most of their days outside in the sun and wind, he was dressed in a khaki jacket and matching pants, his brown, leather boots worn and cracked with use. He also wore a large revolver at his hip and Doug yanked out of his grip and swung the useless muzzle of the Garand around to point it at him.

The man's expression didn't change, neither did he react except to tap the badge affixed to his jacket. The ring around the star read UNITED STATES MARSHAL.

"Get that damned thing out of my face," the man growled. "And take me to your leader."

"What the hell do you *mean* he's dead?" Valentine exploded and Doug cringed, seeing the wide eyes staring at the three of them from thirty yards away.

"Get control of yourself, Sergeant," the marshal snapped. His name, or so his ID had said, was James Madison Cooper, though he'd instructed them to call him "Coop." "There's no point panicking your men."

"My *men*?" Valentine shot back, spreading his hands. "What about *me*? These kids are too young to know death is a real thing, but I'm not." He speared Doug with a glare. "You said he was hung up in a fucking tree? We have to get back, tell the captain so he can get the police in here."

"I *am* the police," Coop reminded him. "And you have bigger problems than one dead man. There's a serial killer on the loose.

Escaped during a prison transfer, killed the men guarding him with his bare hands . . . and teeth." The marshal bared his own teeth as if in sympathy. "He stole a truck and killed the owner, but it broke down on a forest service road just a few miles from here."

"Well, ain't that an even better reason to go call the cops?" Valentine demanded.

"The county sheriffs and state police are already combing the area on horseback. I came in on foot because some of the woods I was going through were too rough for a horse. There's no more help to call. They'll be here eventually and nothing I tell them will bring them any faster."

"Okay, okay," Valentine mumbled, rubbing at his temples. "So, we just have to get back to the bivouac area and let the company know what's happening. Yeah, that's it. Gotta get everyone back safe." His eyes snapped up to Doug. "Get everyone gathered together here. I want 'em all where I can see 'em."

Coop sighed before Doug could move to obey.

"Sergeant, you don't understand what we're facing. If you try to make it back, he'll attack again. And now he's armed."

"Bryant only had blanks," Doug blurted. Maybe. The dead man hadn't volunteered any live ammo.

"You all carry bayonets." Coop nodded toward the hilt protruding from the sheath on Doug's belt. "That's all Dracon needs."

"Dracon?" Doug repeated. "What kind of name is that?"

"Hungarian."

Coop's expression didn't change, but Doug couldn't shake the feeling that the man was mocking him.

"Well, what the hell do you suggest, Mr. US Marshal?" Valentine demanded.

"He doesn't know I'm here, with you," Coop said, rubbing his chin thoughtfully. "He hung the body up the way he did to panic you. He thinks you'll take off running. What he'd never expect is for us to hunt him."

"What the hell do you mean *us*?" Valentine yelped. "These kids aren't much better than civilians and all we have is blanks!"

"We got those clips you took from Bud," Doug suggested quietly, not for any great desire to hunt down a psycho killer but more because he'd feel so much better with live ammo.

Valentine glared at him, then began fishing in his shirt pockets. He shoved one of the eight-round clips at Doug, then whistled through his teeth to get the attention of the others.

"Albertson, get over here."

Bud hurried over, not seeming as terrified as the others . . . instead, he was jittery, almost spastic, as if this was exactly what he'd been waiting for.

"Yeah, Sgt. Val?"

Valentine tossed the second clip at Bud, who caught it awkwardly, staring between it and the NCO without comprehension.

"You wanted live ammo just in case. Well, boy, this is just in case." Valentine snorted a humorless laugh. "And don't forget to take off your damn blank adapters."

Leaves and forest detritus crunched under his feet, strangely familiar though his transplanted memories couldn't recall the last time he'd experienced it. This world was like so many other proscribed planets Three-Seven had seen in past lives, primitive and terrible and beautiful.

The sentients here were barely out of the trees. They burned flammables ripped from the ground for heat and power and considered solid-state electronics, nuclear weapons, and chemical rockets the height of sophistication. Given enough time, they'd destroy themselves with their fission bombs, but that was their choice, their destiny and not his concern.

They deserved the chance, but if the Mimic was allowed to roam free, they wouldn't get it. Three-Seven had already seen the carnage the monster had left in its wake, the human butchered like a game animal. According to the file, the creature was usually less elaborate in its kills, more indiscriminate. This one had been planned, designed to send a message.

But is it addressed to me . . . or to the humans?

"Why can't I have some bullets?" Frank Watson whined, checking the bayonet mounted on his Garand for the fifth time in the last ten minutes.

Doug eyed the man sidelong, trying not to move.

"Because you can't split up the cartridges from a Garand clip," he hissed. "Stop talking and stop moving. We're supposed to be setting an ambush." Doug broke his own rules but he couldn't help it—besides, there was nothing in sight. "You're a corporal, dude. You're supposed to be professional."

"If I'm a corporal, why didn't *I* get the live ammo?" Watson muttered, but this time Doug didn't bother shushing him. The two soldiers on either side of Watson said nothing, and Doug wanted to think that it was due to their confidence in him but in reality, they were probably just too damned scared for small talk.

Instead, he settled deeper into the foxhole he'd dug and looked down the barrel of his Garand. In the action of loading the live rounds, it had gone from an anchor dragging him down to a shining sword protecting him from some mythical dragon. It was a comfort, particularly since neither Marshal Cooper nor Sgt. Valentine was with his group. He did have Bud, for all the comfort that was, which gave each team two loaded guns. At least having the only other loaded Garand had kept Bud from whining.

Bud was on one side of their line and he was on the other. The middle three, Watson, Rob Parker, and Chris Hinkley, looked as if they thought they were there to give the psycho killer something to occupy himself until the other two killed him.

Sgt. Val, Cooper, and the other four soldiers were only fifty yards away on the other side of the clearing, tucked into the tree line, the long arm of the L-shaped ambush. How Coop could intuit that this was the path the killer Dracon would take was beyond Doug to figure out, but the man *was* a US marshal. He had to know what he was doing.

"What's this Dracon guy look like, anyway?" Bud asked from the other end of the line, keeping his voice low.

"He'll be the guy covered in blood and carrying Bryant's bayonet," Doug replied tightly.

It was way too bright outside for his tastes. Not that Doug would have felt safer in the dark, but he felt exposed under the late morning sun, the shadow from the trees around them stretching away, as if God were conspiring against them. Still, Valentine and the others were invisible from their position so maybe it wasn't that bad.

Doug yawned. Blinked. There was no way in hell he should have been sleepy, not when they were waiting for a shoot-out with a killer, and yet his head drooped under the weight of the steel helmet and an even greater weight dragged his eyelids downward. If he'd been able to think clearly, he would have shaken himself to awareness, but that point was past and he sagged against the rifle, not quite asleep but definitely not alert.

Time lost all meaning in his half-conscious haze. Minutes might have passed, or hours, before the gunshots snapped Doug alert.

"Where is he?" Bud asked, rising up from his hasty fighting position to try to get a better look into the open field beyond. "What the hell are they shooting at?"

"Stay down!" Doug ordered, though he disobeyed his own directive and rose up to a knee. And saw nothing.

The others were still hidden from view, no muzzle flash accompanying the sharp reports, no movement in the trees.

"We have to go help them!" Bud shouted, jumping up.

"You wanna run right into their fire?" Doug asked, rushing over to grab Bud by the arm before he could move forward. "Sgt. Val told us to stay here no matter what."

Bud grimaced but held back, probably more at the thought of running into a bullet than at fear of disobeying Valentine. Doug brought his rifle to his shoulder, tracking across the field ... and seeing nothing. The gunfire petered out like popcorn in a pan, ending with a last, desultory pop and Doug struggled with indecision. They needed a radio, but the RTO had stayed with the lieutenant and might as well have been on the far side of the moon for all the good he did them.

"Sgt. Val!" he yelled. "Are you guys okay?"

No reply.

Damn.

"Bud, you stay here with the others," he said, the words tumbling out on the heels of the plan. "I'm gonna go see if they got him." Doug spun on Bud Albertson, raising a finger in warning. "*Don't* leave this position until you hear me calling."

"You point that finger at me again, Wilson," Bud warned, his expression sour and defiant, "I'll feed it to you."

Which was as close to an acknowledgment as Doug was going to get, but he looked to Watson and the corporal returned the unspoken question with a nod. He'd try to keep Bud here.

Taking a deep breath and steeling himself with resolve he wasn't certain he possessed, Doug sprinted diagonally across the field. The tall grass whipped at his legs, tickled the backs of his hands where they held the Garand at hip level. No gunfire greeted him, no shouts of recognition, not so much as a sound other than the thud of his boots against the soft ground.

In the few seconds it took him to cross the field, Doug had the thought that Valentine or Cooper had moved the other fire team, had spotted Dracon coming from another direction and chased him down.

He knew that wasn't true when his foot splashed into a crimson puddle. The dark red hit him between the eyes, the color spreading out like Dorothy arriving in Oz. No one was hanging from a tree this time, nor were they skinned like an elk. Doug supposed there hadn't been time for that. Instead, the five soldiers had been ripped to pieces, as if a pack of the mountain lions Bryant had been worried about had leapt upon them and no one even had the chance to scream.

Doug didn't puke this time. Didn't shriek or scream or jump. This wasn't real. None of it. This couldn't be happening. He was still sleeping in the armory, tossing and turning on his cot. That was the only possibility. He'd wake up any second now and this would be a bad dream that he couldn't even remember clearly.

It was a comforting fiction, one Doug could easily have slipped into, the shock warm as a down comforter. Something snapped him back to reality. Maybe the smell. Dreams didn't stink like this, didn't reek of blood and barnyard ordure. They didn't squish under his boots with the sort of thick viscous feel that wasn't water, a feel he'd never experienced before.

He stepped away from the carnage, a few paces back, enough for him to catch his breath without feeling as if he were breathing in the blood. He knew all these men, had known them for months now, but he couldn't tell one body from the other. Except Sgt. Valentine. Everyone else had worn their hair longer than regulation, as if daring the captain to do anything about it, but not Sgt. Val. His was buzzed as if he'd never left Korea. His head was four feet from his body, the Garand still gripped tightly in lifeless fingers, as if it were a crucifix and Valentine a priest giving the last rights. The bolt was locked open, the chamber still smoking. All those live rounds fired but nothing hit. No psycho killer.

But then, no one man could have done this. No man *had*. This was the work of something savage, something inhuman.

"Wilson..."

Doug didn't jump this time. He recognized Coop's voice.

The marshal wasn't dead, at least, but something had torn him up. His right sleeve had been ripped away, bloody gouges on his upper arm and a nascent bruise on his cheek. He didn't look as much the rugged outdoorsman now, more a cornered beast. His revolver was in his hand, a long-barreled .357 Magnum, his fingers clenching and unclenching around the grip.

"Wilson," Cooper said again, shaking his head, his face slack, eyes wide. "It's not human. It's not what they told me..."

"Bud!" Doug yelled, turning back to the other stand of trees. "Bud! Watson! Get everyone over here! Hurry!"

Nothing. No movement. Not even a gust of wind.

"Bud, goddammit, get over here! Corporal Watson?"

Cooper motioned to him with the revolver.

"We should go to them. We have to get out of here, get back to your trucks, get the state police back here... hell, the military, the real military..."

"What is it?" Doug demanded, trying not to let his gaze drift over the bodies. "What the hell did this?"

"A monster," Cooper told him, his voice firming up. He opened the cylinder of the revolver and dumped out a half a dozen brass cases, reloading with a fresh six rounds from a metal speedloader. "It's a monster."

Doug stared at him, wanted to argue, tell him he was crazy, but wanted much more to get back to Bud and the others. There might not be safety in numbers, but stark, gut-level fear loved company just as much as misery did.

He yelled for Bud again, jogging back across the field, then sprinting as he neared the end with the paranoid certainty that staying out in the open would get him killed. He stopped just short of the tree line. Doug's unreasoning fear had been that Bud and the others had run, that Watson hadn't been able to keep them under control. Neither Bud nor Watson had let him down, though.

They were dead. They were all dead. He felt an impulse to check them but didn't bother. If any of the five still had a heartbeat, they wouldn't have it for long. The scene was the same as the other side of the ambush except Bud hadn't even been able to get off a shot.

"Jesus," Doug murmured, crossing himself. "Jesus, oh, Jesus..."

It had started out as a prayer but it wound up a curse. Doug swung his rifle around, searching for the threat, for the killer, whether it was human or not. He expected the threat from the trees. It had to be there. It must have skirted the tree line, flanked Sgt. Val and then followed around behind Bud and the others while Doug had run across the clearing.

There was nothing in the trees except the dead.

"Take me back to your camp," Cooper urged, his handgun held at the ready. "We can't do anything for them. We have to get—"

The creature exploded out of the woods as if it had manifested there, from a spot Doug had scanned seconds ago, crunching deadfall under clawed feet.

Godzilla.

It was the first thought but not an accurate one. The thing was nine feet tall, not ninety stories, and it lacked a tail or those glowing spines on its back, but there was a reptilian nature to the creature, a scaly quality despite its purplish color. And then there were those teeth, jagged and yellow, the eyes amber and slitted. Loping steps brought it five feet closer with each second and Doug knew this was the end, that he'd face the same fate as the others.

Not without shooting back. The butt of his rifle kicked against his shoulder, spiteful and demanding like his high school sweetheart, shocking him with its sudden violence... again, much like his high school sweetheart. He expected the bullets to bounce off, since Valentine's gunfire hadn't done any good, but a surge of hope penetrated his stunned fatalism when the .30-06 rounds punched into the purple, scaly hide. Red flowers blossomed against the violet background on the bulging shoulder and the giant beast staggered backward, roaring its pain.

As if Doug's success had encouraged him, Cooper emptied his Magnum into the monster. Doug hadn't shot many guns besides what the Army had forced on him, but he was pretty sure that even a .357 didn't usually produce a trail of lightning and a static shock strong enough to make the hair on the back of Doug's neck stand on end.

Doug flinched away as if he'd been shot himself, but the effect on the monster was more profound. Charred skin flaked away from its right shoulder and that was enough for the beast. It howled, crashing sideways through the trees, disappearing into the darkness, leaving not a hint it had actually been there other than the ground ripped apart by the claws on its massive feet . . . and the dead men of Doug's squad.

They're all gone. I'm the last one. How the hell am I going to explain this?

"What . . ."

Doug's mouth wouldn't work. His eye twitched and he could barely hold the empty Garand, had to let it drop to the high grass, then followed it down, barely catching himself on hands and knees. Too much. This was too much. Doug's shoulders shook and breath only came in short, sharp gasps, his lungs straining as if he were being suffocated.

"Wilson," Cooper said, kneeling down beside him. He put a hand on Doug's shoulder as if supporting him. "Doug, I haven't been telling you the whole truth."

"No shit." Overwhelmed shock gave way to fury and Doug rounded on Cooper, fists clenching with an uncontrollable urge to punch the marshal in the face. "What the hell is going on?"

"I'm not a US marshal. I do a similar job, but for a . . . higher authority." He pointed upward. Doug squinted at him.

"God?"

"No," Cooper sighed. "I work for a coalition of planets who've banded together to maintain law and order among our members. I came here hunting an escaped murderer."

"You're . . . you're an *alien*?"

Doug wasn't sure why it was such a shock. He'd just watched a nine-foot-tall purple lizard kill his friends, seen it driven away by a *ray gun*. For some reason, he knew he would have disbelieved it less if Cooper had claimed to be an angel fighting demons.

"I'm a Coalition hunter," Cooper confided. "I track down creatures such this one for a living. But this one is different. Most of the ones I hunt down are little more than animals, but this one's smart. Maybe smarter than me." He jerked a thumb behind him. "Look, kid, I know you're hurting and I'm sorry about your friends, but we *have* to get back to your camp. They'll have transportation and they can get me back to my ship. There are weapons there, equipment that can track this thing down and kill it. It's the only hope we have of taking this thing out before it gets loose in one of your population centers and kills *thousands* of people."

Doug watched the man's eyes... *Wait. Is he a man? Whatever.* He tried to judge the truth in them and saw only gray uncertainty.

"Yeah." It felt like someone else was speaking through him, some other Doug Wilson who could still function after seeing nine of his friends die. "Let's go."

Three-Seven had been hurt before, should have been used to the pain, but it felt different in this body. Perhaps he'd chosen poorly. He'd certainly hadn't thought through his dealings with humans well enough. Had they trusted him sooner, had he communicated better the threat, perhaps they would still have been alive.

Now nine of them were dead and the lone survivor was afraid of him.

Perhaps the smart thing to do would be to retreat to the ship, retrieve heavier weapons, and leave the human survivor to his own devices. After all, it wasn't his job to protect any individual human but to guard their isolation as a proscribed system. The regulations were clear. The human had seen too much and protocol was to eliminate him once this was all settled. Three-Seven frowned and winced at the pain of his wounds... as well as the twinge in his conscience.

This was their world. Before he killed the young human, perhaps Three-Seven should give the man a chance to do the right thing.

"How well did you know them?"

Doug didn't answer immediately. He couldn't take his mind off the bloodstains on Bud's Garand. He'd taken it because it held the only live ammo but it also retained the remains of Bud Anderson.

"Not well." It felt like an admission to a priest, with a shadowed, claustrophobic mountain trail as the confessional. "I never hung out with them at all except during drills. I didn't even like most of them, except Sgt. Val. All they did was make fun of me for liking animals and watching *Wild Kingdom*."

The drops of blood on the rifle stock were obscenely warm and the entire weapon seemed to pulse in his hand, objecting to the unkind words spoken about the dead.

"I like animals," Cooper told him. He spoke casually as if this was nothing to him, though Doug noted he constantly scanned their surroundings, his pistol swinging back and forth, following his eyes. "They're more honest than sentient species. They don't betray you. If they're going to kill you, they just kill you."

Doug glanced sidelong at the... *hunter*? Yeah, the hunter. It was a very alien thing to say.

"You work alone?" he asked, just to keep his mind off reality. "Or are there more hunters sitting in your flying saucer, waiting for the call to come riding in like the cavalry?"

"I wish. No, I'm the only one." He offered a smile, forced enough that it made Doug wonder if the expression came naturally to him. "You're doing pretty well with all this. Maybe you should apply for a job."

"I just wanted to be a wildlife biologist." The words might have been plaintive but now they sounded like a lament. *Sgt. Val was right—I should have gone to Vietnam.* "Do you think that... thing will attack us again? What's it called?"

Cooper licked his lips, frowned.

"A Mimic. It's called a Mimic."

"Why?" Doug shook his head. "It didn't look like it was mimicking anything except a *Creature Feature* monster movie."

"I didn't make up the name." Cooper frowned as if the question annoyed him. "I'm given a file and I go apprehend the fugitive. Or kill them. And yeah, if the Mimic recovers from its injuries before we reach your camp, it will definitely attack again. Like I said, it's smart... it knows it has to stop us."

Why was it so dark? It was past noon, it should have been painfully bright. Doug risked a look upward and groaned at the storm clouds rolling in.

"Great, it's gonna rain."

He'd barely gotten the words out before the squall began, great, heavy drops slapping against the leaves overhead a few seconds before the downpour penetrated the tree canopy and drenched them both in seconds. Doug cursed through chattering teeth, the temperature dropping at least ten degrees even before the rain soaked through his fatigues.

"How do you think the rain will affect the Mimic?" he asked, turning to Coop. Then stopped in mid-step.

Where the rain touched the being he called Coop, the edges of his outline shimmered as if it was passing through a mirage. The rugged, Jim Fowler-esque form glitched, fading into static like a TV tuned between stations. Beneath the façade crouched something skinnier, barbed, with skin like an insect's exoskeleton, and the face behind the weathered mask reminded Doug of looking through a microscope at the face of an ant, stretched out into a shape closer to human, with normal, vertical jaws instead of horizontal mandibles. Huge, orange-colored eyes narrowed at him, a gnarled hand going up.

"Doug, wait..."

Doug did not wait. It was too much. The butchered corpses, the giant lizard monster, UFOs and aliens, they'd all built up like downed trees swept by a flood against a bridge. One by one, they'd battered at the abutments of Doug's sanity until there was very little left. The vision of the real face of Coop was the last blow and Doug ran.

Not the way he'd run during the Army PT test, not the way he'd run track in high school. Not even the way he'd run from that bully Ned Frost in middle school when he'd been in fear of getting his ass kicked and his lunch money stolen. Even then, he'd been in control, still rational enough to worry about losing his balance and tumbling head over heels, breaking his fool neck. Not this time. This time, the only limit was how much a human body could move without breaking itself... that and the Garand.

He could have thrown the rifle away, but it was the only power he had left, and he held it out ahead of him like a totem, a crucifix against alien monsters instead of vampires. Green blurred around him, leaves and branches and tall grass filtered through rain and terror, a wall of sameness until a darker blur cut through them, swung straight into him. It hit the Garand, ripping the rifle from his hands and sending Doug flying out of control.

The ground slammed into Doug's shoulder in an explosion of pain, filling his vision with flashes of color, robbing him of breath. Only the raindrops splashing in his face kept Doug conscious and he realized that his helmet was gone, knocked away in the crash. Doug shook water out of his eyes and tried to focus, tried to find his rifle, but all he found was the bug that had been Cooper.

The ray gun was still holstered at its waist but it made no move for the weapon, the talons at the end of its long fingers clicking together in a castanet rhythm like a cicada. All pretense of bonhomie was gone along with the pretense of being human. Except the voice.

"It's a shame," the bug thing said. "You would have been useful to access transportation out of this area. But I suppose I can just *be* you." That mouth stretched into an expression that might have been a smile. "That's why they call me the Mimic, of course..."

Doug felt around at his web gear for his bayonet and the Mimic waited patiently for it, as if the alien thing found his efforts amusing. Anger at the slight firmed Doug's resolve and drove out the lethargy from the pain in his shoulder and back, and he took up a fighting stance just the way Sgt. Val had shown them in training. It was futile, he knew. The big thing had killed nine armed soldiers in seconds, before they could make a sound. But he wasn't going to die flat on his back.

"It's more fun when you primitives try to fight back," the Mimic said, leaning forward like a runner on the blocks.

The alien sprang at him ... then stopped in midair, legs flopping as a massive, scaly, purple hand grabbed the Mimic around the neck. Bug eyes bugged out even wider and the insect-like creature clawed at the gun at its hip, which looked nothing like a .357 Magnum now that the illusion had washed away. The lizard monster shook the Mimic like a hunting dog killing a rabbit and with the same results, the bug's neck snapping with the gut-wrenching sound of a dry twig breaking,

One last, galvanic reflex squeezed a taloned finger on the trigger and the flare of the discharge sent a curtain of steam across the both of them, blocking them from Doug's view for the space of a few seconds. When the clouds settled, squashed flat by the pounding rain, the Mimic lay sprawled out on the muddy trail, its head facing the wrong direction, while the lizard creature still stood like a statue, as if this whole affair had been an elaborate hoax and the dark, scaly monster was nothing but an audio-animatronic from Disneyland.

That illusion was shattered when the giant fell to its knees, the impact a dull thud that reverberated through the ground and up through the soles of Doug's boots. He jumped back at the motion, still holding his bayonet in front of him. The rifle was only twenty feet away and Doug felt an insane urge to run and grab it, but the stock was splintered, the receiver sticking out an angle.

"There is no need to fear me," the purple lizard *spoke*. Its mouth was filled with sharpened fangs and didn't seem constructed to speak any human language, much less English, yet the voice was a steady baritone. "In a few minutes, I won't be a threat to you or anyone else."

The creature had been covering its chest with a massive claw, and when the hand moved, it revealed a charred and smoking hole.

"You..." As surprised as Doug was that the creature was capable of speech, he was almost more shocked that he himself could still manage it. "If that's the Mimic"—he motioned with the blade of the bayonet at the dead bug-thing—"then you must be the Coalition hunter he was talking about."

The point of the bayonet shook in sympathy with his hand and he lowered it, somehow ashamed at the weakness.

"I am." The hunter coughed and blood sprayed from between those sharpened teeth. The alien didn't seem threatening now, despite its fearsome appearance. Doug had seen a picture in his art book of a sculpture called *The Dying Gaul* and if that Gallic warrior had been an alien, the hunter could have posed for the work. "For a few more minutes."

The rain slackened, a last few heavy drops tapping fitfully against the leaves overhead. Just a passing squall.

"What's your name?" Doug asked, though the question was absurd under the circumstances. "I'm Doug," he added in an even more ridiculous counterpoint.

"I'm called Three-Seven." The hunter swayed sideways from its kneeling position, catching itself with a four-fingered hand, fingers the size of a bratwurst squelching in the mud. "I wish I could have reached you sooner. I might have been able to save the others..."

"I'm sorry I shot you," Doug said. "I thought you were a monster."

Eyes as black as a tax collector's soul regarded him with amusement.

"Perhaps I am. If I weren't so badly wounded, I might have been obligated to eliminate you to keep you silent."

"Why didn't you just let the bug kill me, then?" Another dumb question, since it was a chance for the alien to change its mind, but Doug's curiosity wouldn't be restrained.

"Because no one will believe you." The hunter wasn't naked, though Doug had been too frozen in terror when first he'd seen the alien to realize it. It wore a belt around its waist, decorated by what might have been jewelry but Doug sensed were some kind of technology. A finger stained with its own blood touched an amber stone and light glowed behind the faceted control. "There'll be nothing left for them to believe."

Doug swallowed hard, taking an instinctive step back.

"I've set the scalar reactor on my lander to overload," the hunter explained. "You have ten minutes to be a mile away from here." It pointed down the trail in the direction of the camp. "You should go."

"B-but..." Doug stammered, dropping his bayonet and barely noticing when it sank point-first into the mud. "You haven't told me anything! What's out there? What's it like?"

Was it possible for a lizard man to smile? Maybe it was.

"Wild," the hunter replied softly. "Wilder than you can imagine."

The alien gasped out a last breath through scorched lips, then collapsed forward into the mud. Nothing moved except a few last drops of rain.

But the jewels in the belt continued to blink in sequence, reminding Doug the ground was muddy, he sucked at running in boots, and he had about nine minutes to live.

It seemed as if his whole existence had been reduced to flight and despite the pressure of the deadline, he was fresh out of adrenaline, out of breath, his legs as heavy as lead. There were no reserves of energy, nothing to dull the aches in his shoulder, his back, his ribs. He wanted to give up and no sense of duty, no pride in being a soldier, not even the desire to see his family again could make him keep going.

Only one thing did. He was prey, the same sort of desperate prey he'd seen on TV, an antelope being hunted by a leopard, so close he could feel its hot breath on his neck. The prey never gave up, not even when death was certain. Doug turned off these thoughts, turned off his rational mind, and let himself be prey, let one step flow into another, each breath clawing its way into the next.

He'd lost track of time when the world exploded.

Concussion threw him forward, a wave of unbearable heat washing over him, the unmistakable smell of his hair sizzling away not quite overcoming the stench of ozone just before he hit the ground.

Behind him, a ball of white fire climbed into the air, consuming everything, spreading outward in a wall of flame that Doug was sure would swallow him up as well. He tried to think of a prayer but nothing came to mind except the irreverent infantryman's prayer he'd learned in basic training.

For that which we're about to receive, Lord, make us truly thankful...

The white fire faded to yellow, then red, and rather than the raging conflagration Doug expected, the wall of energy simply died away, leaving a line of blackened stumps that had once been trees. Not fire, not any explosion Doug had ever heard of, more like the angel of death descending on Egypt and passing by those who'd painted their doorposts with the blood of the lamb.

Or, in this case, those who could run a ten-minute mile.

Doug breathed in a lungful of ash and doubled over in a coughing fit that racked his body with pain. He was alive, but this was it. He couldn't get up, couldn't walk, could barely breathe. This was where he'd stay.

"Oh, my God, is that you, Wilson?"

Gentle hands cradled his head and water dripped over cracked and dry lips. Doug swallowed it gingerly, his eyes opening. He hadn't been aware he'd closed them. The face hovering over him was soft and professorial, much older than it should have been on a platoon leader, almost thirty. Lt. Gordon Sutton was a schoolteacher and looked it, though if he lacked any sort of military demeanor or killer instinct, he made up for it by caring for his men as if they were his students.

"Where am I?" Doug wondered, the water bringing him closer to coherence.

"You're about a half mile from the trailhead, Wilson." Another face loomed over him, ugly and scarred from wounds taken in WW2. Master Sergeant Herbert, the company first sergeant. "Now what the hell happened out there?"

Doug twisted around, looking at the devastation behind him. Nothing was left. Not the aliens, not whatever spaceships had brought them both to Earth. Not the bodies of his squad. The only thing anyone would ever know about what happened was what he told them, and what he told them would determine the course of the rest of his life. He could still make something of himself, get into a good school and find himself in Africa, studying lions and elephants.

Or he could tell the truth and open the eyes of humanity to a new reality of existence, that they weren't alone, that there was a larger universe out there. And probably be locked away in a mental institution and pumped full of Thorazine.

"I don't know what happened," he told them, shaking his head. "I . . . got separated from the others during our patrol and then I heard this loud bang. I think maybe a plane crashed or something."

Or something.

Herbert frowned at him, skepticism in the tilt of his head.

"That don't look like no plane crash to me. Looks more like a damned nuclear explosion."

"Master Sergeant," Lt. Sutton interrupted, "we need the search and rescue out here. I'm going to go find the RTO and call them. Grab a medic and have Private Wilson seen to."

Sutton didn't wait for an answer, just took off back down the trail. Herbert watched him go before turning back to Doug, his glare filled with suspicion.

"Val is a friend of mine, Wilson," the old man growled. "If you know anything, you'd better tell me."

Herbert was a larger-than-life force of nature who'd always scared the crap out of Doug. Not today.

"Sgt. Val told me if I really wanted adventure," Doug said slowly, "I should have gone to Vietnam."

The master sergeant snorted, stalking away from him, throwing one last, bitter comment over his shoulder.

"Maybe you should have."

Doug laid back against the mud, staring unfocused into the gray haze blocking out the noonday sun.

Maybe they were right. Vietnam wouldn't have been so bad.

There were tigers there.

Bug Hunt

Melissa Olthoff & Nick Steverson

234 Velex-b
Sigma Outpost

"Welcome to your lovely tropical destination!" Gunnery Sergeant Sam Warrick bellowed, his baritone voice carrying across the hold. "Now get your asses off the shuttle!"

Lieutenant Zoe Callahan stood on the airfield and watched as her armed and armored Raider team hustled down the ramp. The ruddy light of an alien sun bathed her black battle armor, and her boots kicked up swirls of the blue-tinged dirt that had drifted over the cracked tarmac as she strode over to her gunnery sergeant.

"Was it necessary to rub it in, Gunny?"

"So to speak," Lieutenant Maryanne Bobbi Enoha, their assigned VTOL pilot, called out as she bounded down the ramp with a broad grin on her gorgeous face.

The older gunny flashed them a hard grin. "Builds character."

As Lance Corporal Vincent Moretti trotted past, he grumbled under his breath. "I don't know about you guys, but the Corps owes me a drink or three."

"Stow it, Moretti," Gunnery Sergeant Warrick barked.

"With little umbrellas, too," he continued as if he hadn't heard the reprimand. The fact that he raised his voice loud enough for them to hear as he moved farther away suggested otherwise. "On a beach fully equipped with top-heavy bimbos wearing less than bikinis."

"*Moretti!*"

"Shutting up, Gunny," he called back over his shoulder.

Callahan sighed. Moretti was a pain in the ass, but he was only saying what everyone else was thinking. High Command didn't care that their Raider company had just been in the thick of the latest Kyriel offensive, or that they had been on their way to some well-deserved downtime on one of the resort worlds. The only thing that mattered was they were the closest assets capable of investigating a backwater research station that had gone dark.

With a practiced flick of her eyes, she keyed up the command freq on her HUD. "Raider Actual, Charlie Six, on the ground."

"*Copy, Charlie Six,*" Major Dante Ramirez replied, his gruff voice calm but with an underlying current of urgency. "*Foxtrot Team will hold the perimeter. Get those supplies and our VTOL unloaded.*"

"Roger." Callahan jerked her chin at Gunnery Sergeant Warrick. "Let's get it done."

Callahan eyed Moretti as he trotted back up the ramp to unload supplies, muttering under his breath the whole way, and bit back a grin. On deployment, there were always constants—there was never enough ammo, the food always sucked, and Moretti bitched.

As Lieutenant Enoha guided the Bat, their VTOL craft, low over the deep blue-green jungle, Moretti caught the occasional flash of a diamond-bright river snaking through the thick foliage. His stomach lurched as the Bat rolled into a tight curve around a rocky outcropping, but he didn't mutter a word of complaint.

Sport bitching was for when they were safe, not when they were heading into a potential combat situation. The Kyriel had never penetrated this far into their territory, but he hadn't needed Gunny to point out the possibility.

Lieutenant Enoha's crisp voice came over the combat freq. "*Beginning approach.*"

The pilot pushed the VTOL into a gentle turn and circled Research Station Echo-3. Moretti's HUD *pinged* as she passed the whole team a live feed from the Bat's external cameras.

His jaw tightened at the level of devastation that had torn through the small research site. Blood streaked the walls of many of the single-occupant prefab habitats and a few bodies lay on the ground near the command post by the main gate. Blast holes in the prefab structures screamed of plasma weapons, and blackened craters were all that were left of the atmo and ground vehicles.

It was nothing they hadn't seen before. Regardless, he still hated the sight of it.

"*No heat signatures or signs of movement below,*" Lieutenant Enoha said, her tone hard.

"Take us down." Lieutenant Callahan swept her icy gaze over her team. "Gunny, Baker, Nguyen, you're with me. We'll start with the main building. Moretti, you take Hoosier, Hopkins, and Larson and clear the habs and the command post." Her cold blue eyes landed on his. "Search for survivors, but don't assume they're friendlies just because they're human."

Moretti held back a snort by a sheer effort of will. The LT might as well have told him water was wet. This wouldn't be the first time an outpost was hit by bandits who pretended to be the victims when the cavalry arrived.

Lieutenant Callahan's lips twitched in what looked like an aborted smile, so his face had probably been speaking for him again. At least Gunny hadn't seen it, too.

"Maintain IR contact." She frowned. "Something is interfering with our long-range comms. I had to tap into the Bat to reach Sigma. Stay close, stay sharp."

The door slid open with a faint *hiss* of hydraulics, and his LT leaped outside and hustled to the dubious cover of the research facility, Gunnery Sergeant Warrick at her six. Baker, their medic, and Nguyen, their comm specialist, ran after them. Moretti jumped out when they were clear and led his team in the opposite direction. Behind them, the whine of the Bat's impeller increased in pitch as the VTOL took off, heading back to pick up Foxtrot.

It didn't take them much time to clear the small compound. Whatever happened had happened days ago. Long enough for the blood splatter to dry. Long enough for the unarmored bodies near the main gate to swell and stink of rot. The command post at the main gate was empty, the security and monitoring equipment inside that could have told them what occurred destroyed, and the habs were empty but for one.

An old man had attempted to hide from the attackers under his bed. It hadn't saved him. Moretti grimaced at the bloated face and took a moment to be grateful to his armor's air filters before he used his HUD to scan the corpse.

"Damn it," he muttered when facial recognition found a match. "LT's gonna be pissed. That's one of our VIPs."

As they exited the hab, the faint whine of the returning Bat reached his ears. He sent a quick update to the LT and led his team along the perimeter fence. By the time they'd circled the compound and reported it clear, the VTOL had taken off again.

"Charlie Three, Foxtrot will assist with securing the perimeter," Lieutenant Callahan said. "Do another sweep and see if you can find anything. The research facility's a hot mess, but we haven't found nearly enough bodies."

Moretti grimaced. If the last two VIPs weren't among those casualties, the chances of them heading out into the brush on a wild-goose chase had just increased to a near certainty. "Charlie Three copies. We'll start with the command post."

A double click came over the comms, and he jerked his head at Hopkins, Hoosier, and Larson. They moved silently along the heavy-duty fence, bluish-gray dirt on one side, lush blue-green jungle on the other. Plenty of chirps, buzzes, and screeches drifted out of the dense foliage, but thick silence reigned over the compound, broken only by the quiet presence of the other Raiders.

"Fucking ghost town," Moretti grumbled as he slid along the back of the bunker-style command post. "If we find anyone alive, it ain't gonna be our missing scientists."

He edged a tiny camera around the corner and checked the feed on his HUD. "Clear."

He ghosted around the corner, rifle at the ready, his team hot on his heels. Each Raider swiveled in different directions, alert for threats.

"It's a research facility, not a town," PFC Danny Larson corrected.

Moretti didn't know him well yet, but despite looking all of sixteen, their new breecher carried an air of quiet competence. When he wasn't being a pedantic ass.

"It ain't no fucking beach either, Danny-boy," Moretti quipped, but he kept his eyes moving and his rifle up as he cautiously stalked around to the front of the command post, cleared it again, and moved on to the main gate.

"Are you going to bitch about that the *entire* time we're here?" Hoosier asked as he loomed over his shoulder. Moretti couldn't help but feel crowded—the heavy-weapons specialist was a large man by any standard. In his power armor, he was a damn tank. Even then, the big man still grunted as he adjusted the weight of his ZX75, a six-barreled kinetic rotary gun that fired .75 caliber rounds.

Moretti wouldn't want to carry that beast, but he was rather jealous of the M253 strapped to his back. The big bad brother of the old M153, that thing could bust a bunker or take out a tank, and he *wanted* one. Too bad the old sergeant who ran the armory hadn't agreed.

"I fucking might," he grumbled as he switched his HUD to thermal and scanned the jungle on the other side of the gate. Dozens of smaller animals up in the trees or hiding in the underbrush registered, but no threats. A glint of sunlight on metal where there should only be green caught his eye. "Shit."

"What is it?" Larson asked.

Moretti crouched down, reached into the tangle of flowering vines that had crept through the fence, and held up the bloodied, shattered remains of an infantryman's helmet. "Guess this means the guards didn't skip town. Unlucky bastards."

"God damn it," Hoosier hissed.

Semper Fi, brother. Hope you fucked 'em up good before you bought it.

"*Charlie Six, Charlie Three. Found a mostly intact helmet. We need Nguyen.*"

Callahan paused her fruitless search of the central lab of the research facility. Despite the limited damage to the exterior of the building, the interior was a mess, with cracked screens, destroyed consoles, and shattered glass littering the floor of every room. PFC Kim Nguyen was doing his best to resurrect the least damaged console, but judging by the wiry comm specialist's curses, it wasn't going well.

"Charlie Three, lock onto my location and bring it here." Callahan switched to the command freq. "Foxtrot Six, shifting perimeter primary security to you. Raider Actual, status?"

"*Charlie...ix...Raider Actual five m...out.*"

Callahan frowned at the static and glanced at Nguyen just as sparks erupted from the damaged console. She made a mental note to have him check the integrity of their comms when he wasn't putting out a small fire and replied, "Charlie Six acknowledged. Might have a lead. Standby details."

Static undercut the baritone rumble of Major Ramirez, but his response was clearer this time. "*Copy all.*"

Her frown deepened as she locked gazes with Gunnery Sergeant Warrick. "You get that static, too?"

He gave her a sharp nod, dark eyes steady. Before he could comment, glass crunched unpleasantly under armored boots as Moretti strode through the door, a battered infantry helmet carefully cradled in his arms.

Callahan's chest tightened painfully as she stared at the blood-streaked black composite and the shattered faceplate. For an instant, the sour tang of copper flooded her nose and the screams of the dying filled her ears. Tabahaa's helmet had looked like that when she'd stumbled over his body near the end of their last battle.

She shook off the memory. "Nguyen."

The wiry comm specialist jerked his head up from the smoking console. His eyes crinkled up in a wry grin when they landed on Moretti. "You bring me the best presents."

For once, Moretti didn't have a smart-ass remark ready, he just handed over the helmet with a solemn expression. Oblivious, Nguyen gently set it down on the central table and hooked it up to his combat slate. A holographic keyboard appeared and he bent over the screen with an intense look of concentration on his face, his fingers moving in a blur as he attempted to recover anything from the internal data storage.

The faint whine of the Bat's impeller intruded on the expectant silence. It increased in pitch before it spooled down into silence. "*Echo 21 on the ground.*"

As Callahan double clicked the comm in acknowledgment, Major Dante Ramirez marched inside. His cool green eyes met hers. "Report."

After she got her commander up to speed, she asked, "Did you catch static on the flight in, or was that just on our end?"

"The closer we got, the clearer your transmissions were. Sergeant Astin is looking into it." His gaze shifted to the comm specialist currently scowling at his screen. "Have you been able to recover anything, Private Nguyen?"

"Working on it," he mumbled, shoulders hunched as he typed furiously.

Gunny cleared his throat sharply, and the wiry comm specialist snapped straight as if goosed. Or in danger of being stuck on latrine detail for another month.

"Sir! I've isolated fragments of video. I'm stitching them together now."

"As you were," Major Ramirez said with a patient nod and what looked like faint amusement buried deep in his eyes. He keyed up the command freq. "Foxtrot Six, on me."

A few minutes later, Lieutenant Donnie Darken trotted in and came to a halt next to Callahan. Sweat ran down his face, but his breathing was steady and his eyes were sharp.

"Perimeter's secure sir," he reported briskly.

The major nodded once before he turned back to Nguyen. "Are we ready?"

He glanced up. "Almost, sir."

Callahan glanced sidelong at her fellow officer and whispered, "Hey, Double D."

Darken winked. "Having fun yet, Calla?"

"Be having more fun if we were on a beach," she muttered.

Standing off to the side, Moretti's whole face twitched as if biting back both a grin and a remark sure to get him in trouble with Gunny. Callahan kept her expression impassive, but Darken smirked.

Nguyen's fingers stilled as he let out a grunt of victory. "Done, sir. I recovered everything I could, but it's not much. Pushing it to you ... now."

A new message flashed on Callahan's HUD, and she accessed it with a practiced flick of her eyes. A fragment of a video played, jagged and over almost before it began. She frowned and looped it, studying the shaky footage recorded by the late owner of the helmet.

"What the hell is *that*?" she muttered. "It's not a Kyriel."

Darken frowned. "It doesn't look like any of their indentured races, either."

"It's not," Major Ramirez said firmly. "Whatever it is, I've never seen or heard of it before, but it's clearly sapient." His fingers tapped at his wrist slate as he manipulated the video on everyone's HUD. The footage paused and zoomed in on the lower left corner, where a second alien crouched on top of a trooper, firing some kind of plasma rifle directly into the man's face. "And definitely hostile."

With the ease of long practice, Callahan compartmentalized the horror of the trooper's destroyed face and studied the blurred image of his assailant. The alien bore more than a passing resemblance to an Earth beetle, with four angular limbs, a pair of upper arms, thick mandibles, muddled brown-and-green chitin, and a triple cluster of faceted eyes.

"They're wearing armor," Darken said thoughtfully.

Callahan tilted her head and caught the thicker line where the mandibles protruded past the chitin-like armor. She nodded. "And those rifles aren't other races' castoffs. Those were made for the ... whatever they are."

"Bugs," Moretti muttered under his breath, his eyes slightly glazed as he focused on his HUD. "Two-meter-tall *bugs*."

Major Ramirez eyed him briefly before he shrugged. "Good enough for government work. Bugs it is." He turned to both lieutenants. "How many bodies did you find?"

"Not enough," Darken said grimly.

"And only one who matched our VIPs." Callahan narrowed her eyes as she studied the bugs' physiology. "No obvious sign of how those bugs got in, but they might have just scaled the fence."

As Nguyen packed up his gear, his elbow knocked into the helmet. It crashed to the glass-strewn floor, bounced off a shattered monitor, and rolled to a stop in the far corner atop a pile of broken crates. Moretti jerked forward in reaction, but Callahan was closer, and she waved him off.

"I've got it," she said, already moving.

She knelt to pick up the battered helmet, and the boards creaked alarmingly beneath her armored weight. Her head snapped up, wide eyes locked onto Darken.

He lunged forward just as the floor gave way. "*Calla!*"

Too late.

Callahan fell, jaw clenched tight against the startled scream that wanted to burst free. She braced herself. Impact came a mere heartbeat later, and she rolled forward to disperse the force, coming back up to one knee. In the same motion, she pulled her rifle over her shoulder and snapped it up, searching for threats.

An empty tunnel stretching out into darkness met her sharp gaze. In the next instant, Darken leaped down next to her, with Gunny and Moretti right behind him. All three Raiders had their rifles up and ready.

"Negative contact," Callahan murmured over the comm for Major Ramirez's benefit when nothing emerged from the darkness to eat their faces. "I think we found where the bugs got in."

Her gaze landed on dark streaks smeared over the dirt. Cautiously, she reached down and brushed a finger through the substance. When she brought it up to the light, the black armor shone a dark red.

Darken grimaced. "And where they took the missing scientists."

"Callahan, take your team and scout it out," Major Ramirez ordered. "Darken, get the rest of the troops prepped to follow."

Before he climbed out of the tunnel, Darken's hard eyes met hers. "Be careful."

Callahan gave him a sharp grin as she rose to her feet. "Always am, brother."

"Damn." Moretti moved a short ways down the tunnel, peering through his scope. "They left a trail so obvious even an LT managed to find it."

Callahan resisted the urge to tell Moretti where he could shove his smart-ass comments. Instead, she arched a brow at Gunny, who promptly moved forward and slammed an armored hand onto Moretti's shoulder.

"Lance Corporal Moretti, thank you so much for volunteering to take point on our excursion into the bowels of this fine planet."

Moretti's shit-eating grin vanished as his shoulders slumped. "Happy to serve the Corps in any way needed, Gunny."

Nguyen dropped down into the pit to take up rear guard, and they ghosted down the tunnel on silent feet. Tension ratcheted up Callahan's spine as the tunnel stretched on and on, well past the point where ambient light filtered through the hole she'd punched through the entrance. There was a slight hitch in Moretti's stride, and then tiny lights embedded in his armor emitted a green glow just bright enough to enable the night vision on their HUDs.

"I feel like a fucking glow stick," he muttered as he stalked down the tunnel.

"Moretti."

"Shutting up, Gunny."

The blood trail proved sporadic. It gave Callahan hope they might find some of their people still alive, but when the tunnel angled up and spilled out deep within the jungle, there was no sign of them. The thick tangle of underbrush showed a clear trail leading farther from the research compound, bright splotches of blood decorating the deep blue-green foliage.

Moretti came to an abrupt halt at the tunnel exit and panned his rifle around the jungle. "Clear."

Callahan passed a progress report to Major Ramirez and waited for orders.

Once more, static undercut his transmission. "*Roger. Hold position. I'm sending the rest of Charlie and Foxtrot to you. Priority is to recover the VIPs, secondary is to get as much intel on this new race as you can. I'm setting up the command post at Sigma, there's too much interference here to reach orbital. Echo 21 will remain on standby at Sigma.*"

"Charlie Six, wilco."

Moretti glanced back at Callahan. "I'm still on point, aren't I, ma'am?"

She grinned. "What do *you* think?"

Moretti couldn't believe it. His mother had been right—his mouth really was going to get him killed. One little joke about lost lieutenants had landed him on point for a trek into the depths of an alien jungle chasing giant bugs who'd already slaughtered or kidnapped everyone in the facility.

As the other squad joined up on his, he glanced over his shoulder at the gunnery sergeant.

"Squad File, Gunny?"

Gunny nodded and slapped his shoulder again. "Squad File, Moretti. I'll pass it along."

As the gunny roared orders and the Raiders fell in behind him, Moretti resolved to keep better control of his smart-ass mouth.

"Bug Hunt Brigade on me!" he shouted over the IR. *Okay, one last quip.*

The thick canopy blotted out most of the ruddy sunlight, leaving the trail in deep shadow. Whatever was playing hell with their comms was also messing with his scans, so Moretti kept his eyes moving and his audio receptors maxed out. If something tried to sneak up on them, he wanted to at least hear it before it was too late.

Two klicks down the trail, Moretti held his fist in the air. Cautiously, he slipped forward on silent feet until he came to the object lying in the center of the path. He let out a sigh and scanned the area in all spectrums. Nothing.

"Clear. Regroup." As Callahan and Gunny approached, he held out a leather loafer. "I'm guessing this belongs to one of the VIPs."

"Confirms we're on the right track," Callahan said. "Let's keep moving."

"Structure one hundred meters out. Circular doors embedded in the mountainside," Moretti reported an hour later from the dubious concealment of a cluster of alien vegetation. The trail had ended in a small clearing under the shadow of a craggy mountain stabbing up from the jungle. "Think our VIPs are in there?"

"Safe assumption," Callahan said as she crept up on his left with Gunny at her side.

"I don't see any cameras." Moretti filtered through his HUD's different spectrums. "I can't get a proper read on the structure. Don't know if it's the interference or the composition of the structure."

Nguyen slithered forward to the edge of the clearing, his gaze focused farther up the craggy mountain. "There's some kind of array up on the bluff. Could be the source of the interference. If we blow it up, I'll know for sure."

Callahan sighed. "Let's not announce our presence just yet."

"Roger." Nguyen tapped the small screen built into his forearm and let out an irritated huff. "I'll see if I can find a work-around."

"Keep working on it," she said. "In the meantime, Gunny, I want that door open."

"Yes, ma'am. Moretti and Larson, you're on the door," Gunny Warrick ordered. "Hoosier, Hopkins, you cover the left. The rest of you fan out behind them in the tree line to our left."

"Manahue, Koit," Gunny Blathe said, "you two cover the right. The rest of Foxtrot will fan out to the right of our position."

"Nothing like a little cross fire." Gunny Warrick exchanged a serrated smile with Blathe before he turned to Moretti. "On your mark, Moretti."

Moretti nodded sharply and waited until Manahue and Koit had joined up with his fire team. He waved one hand forward, and they dashed across the exposed clearing in a coordinated rush. The two overwatch teams took up position as Moretti and Larson ducked under the stone overhang in front of the control panel.

"The fuck kind of language is this shit?" Moretti grumbled as he studied the panel. "These symbols aren't in the translation program."

"New race, new language," Callahan said calmly. "Can you get behind the panel and into the circuitry?"

"Wait one," Moretti said. He tried to wedge his armored fingers behind the steel plate, but there was no give. Upon further inspection, he realized there was no edge. "Negative."

"Copy. Larson, you're up."

Larson grinned and ran a hand over the seam running down the center of the circular door. "I'll try to pry it open. If that doesn't work, I've got a pretty aggressive universal key."

"I'd prefer stealth if it's all the same to you, Larson," Callahan replied dryly.

"Understood, ma'am. Just giving you the option if it comes to that."

"Try the quiet way first."

"Yes, ma'am."

Larson opened a compartment on his right thigh and withdrew two pieces of titanium. With a snap, the two parts became a single pry bar. He slipped the flat end into the seam and pulled. It didn't budge. He pulled again, harder this time, and the servos of his armor whined under the strain. After a brief moment, Moretti gripped the bar opposite Larson and added his own augmented strength. The door stubbornly remained sealed.

"LT, we might need to use Danny-boy's universal key. These doors ain't giving."

There was a moment of silence where he assumed she was going over their options with Darken and the gunnery sergeants. "Do it," she finally said. "But be ready for all hell to break loose."

"Oorah, ma'am." He raised his brows at Larson. "You heard the lady. Make with the explodey shit."

"I got just the thing." Larson produced a block of plastic explosives. He then pulled out another device with three tubes attached to it. One tube held a green liquid, one a blue liquid, and the center tube was empty. He pressed the device into the block.

"Uhhh, Danny-boy, what the hell is that?"

"This? Just something I came up with on my own."

The fact that Larson's voice was nearly an octave higher than usual did not fill Moretti with confidence. "Your own design, huh? I assume it's been approved by the Corps."

Larson darted a glance at him. "I mean, they haven't *not* approved it."

"Oh, yeah, that totally means it's not a complete violation of the regs."

"What they don't know—"

"Gets us blown up faster," Moretti finished, but gestured for Larson to do it anyway.

The breacher raised the questionable bomb up to place it as close to the center of the seam as he could. Before he could plant it, the doors opened vertically in opposite directions with a loud *hiss*. Larson froze.

Well, that's a stupid fucking door design, Moretti thought a split second before his brain caught up. On the other side of the doorway, a horde of bugs stared at them. The lead bug tilted its head and clicked its mandibles.

"Ah, fuck me." Moretti fired his plasma rifle three times into the confused bug's face. He didn't bother to watch the body hit the deck. Instead, he shouldered Larson out of the way and roared, "*HOOSIER!*"

With a deafening battle cry, Hoosier swung his bulk around the corner, leveled the ZX75, and unleashed hell, with Manahue only a beat behind from the opposite side. The machine guns screamed as .75 caliber rounds tore through the aliens. Within seconds, half a dozen were piled up at the entrance, blocking the other bugs from exiting.

"Raider Actual, Charlie Six, enemy contact." Callahan waited a beat and repeated her transmission. Unlike their trek through the jungle, where responses from Sigma Outpost had been full of static but otherwise unimpaired, nothing but silence answered her call. "Foxtrot Six, Charlie Six, can you get through to command?"

"*Standby, Charlie Six.*"

While she waited on Darken, she raised her plasma rifle to her shoulder and joined Gunny and the rest of her team in laying down covering fire. Moretti dragged Larson back from the door as their heavy-weapons specialists tore a swath through the bugs. After the initial shock, the massive beetlelike aliens had pushed through the blockage and poured out of their underground facility in a seemingly endless flood.

Over the command freq, Gunny Warrick muttered, "*It's like we just kicked over an anthill.*"

He wasn't wrong. Hoosier and Manahue retreated step by slow step, keeping up a steady rate of machine-gun fire, while Hopkins and Koit shadowed them with their plasma rifles. Callahan felt a flash of pride. Despite the overwhelming numbers of bugs, the two teams reacted with the training and discipline she expected from her Raiders.

"*Negative comms, Charlie Six,*" Darken reported.

Fucking hell. Callahan double-clicked to acknowledge and then pinged her comm specialist. "Nguyen, we need comms back ASAP. Get me a solution."

The wiry Marine shifted his rifle to one hand and bent his head over his built-in wrist slate. "On it, ma'am."

Without warning, Gunny slammed into her. They tumbled sideways in a tangle of limbs as a burst of plasma burned into the brush where she'd been lying prone. Moving quickly, they low-crawled to a fresh patch of cover.

"Thanks, Gunny," she said absently as she surveyed the evolving battlefield. The first wave of bugs had been unarmed, but this latest carried the plasma rifles she'd seen in the HUD video.

Gunny Warrick grunted an acknowledgment as he picked off a bug about to shoot Hoosier in the back. Callahan resumed firing as the familiar song of battle washed over her. The crackle of plasma weapons competed with the deafening rage of the ZX75s, all of it undercut with the curses and shouts of her Raiders.

And the screams.

A flash of yellow in her HUD warned her plasma rifle's power pack was nearly depleted. As she swapped it out for a fresh one with practiced efficiency, she studied the entrance to the underground facility. The flood of bugs pouring out of the facility had tapered off after the second wave, and no more had scuttled out in the last few minutes. It was an opportunity she couldn't ignore.

"Foxtrot Six, Charlie Six, you have command," she said.

"*Charlie Six, Foxtrot Six, wilco.*" Darken switched to a private comm line and added, "*What the hell are you doing, Calla?*"

"Accomplishing the mission objective."

Callahan couldn't see Darken through the thick brush, but the wry amusement in his voice came through loud and clear. "*Translation, you're doing something stupid.*"

A sharp grin creased her face. "Probably. Give 'em hell, Double D, but do me a favor and try to keep them from retreating underground."

A beat of silence, then a string of vicious swearing that would've burned her ears before she joined the Corps. "*Roger that. Don't die, you stupid bitch. You still owe me money from our last poker game.*"

"Only because you cheated."

"*Prove it.*"

Callahan rolled her eyes and switched back to the main freq. "Gunny, Nguyen, on me. Let's see if we can recover our VIPs while the bugs are occupied."

Next to her, Gunny Warrick calmly took out another bug before running a calculating gaze over the battlefield. A smile ticked up the corner of his mouth. "Charlie Three, Charlie Seven, need a distraction in left quadrant."

"Charlie Seven, Charlie Three, roger that." Down in the thick of the fight, Moretti pulled a pair of plasma grenades from his belt. "*FRAG OUT!*"

The lance corporal tossed them one after the other into the seething mass of bugs swarming the clearing. Chitin, armor, and black blood erupted from the impact sites, and the tide of battle flowed to the left—leaving them a mostly unobstructed path to the door on the right.

Callahan grinned in approval. "Nice work, Charlie Three."

"Happy to make myself bug bait to serve the needs of the mission! Eat shit, motherfucker! Uh, not you, LT."

Callahan exchanged an exasperated glance with Gunny.

"I'm on point." Gunny slithered out of the brush, and Callahan followed on his heels. "Nguyen, cover our six."

"Roger," the wiry comm specialist said as he fell in behind Callahan.

They skirted the far edge of the battlefield, staying low and sticking to the scant cover of the brush encroaching on the rocky mountain. They nearly made it to the entrance unchallenged. Callahan didn't know if it was the branch Nguyen stepped on, or just bad luck, but a bug at the back of the swarm spun around and charged right for her.

Rather than shoot it and call unwanted attention to their position,

Gunny Warrick hit it hard from the side, slinging himself over the mottled green-and-brown carapace and catching the bug's upper arms in a full nelson hold. Nguyen wrestled its plasma rifle away before it could fire, while Callahan yanked her Ka-Bar knife from its sheath, darted in, and slammed it into the bug's faceted eye to the hilt. When it didn't die, Nguyen burrowed his own Ka-Bar into a natural chink in its chitin, just below its twitching mandibles.

As the bug's legs folded beneath it in a slow collapse, Gunny rolled clear and shook his arms out.

"Strong fuckers," he said quietly as he took point again, his harsh breaths filtering over the comm.

They made it to the entrance without further issue. Gunny stepped over the bodies Hoosier and Manahue had shredded at the beginning of the fight, cleared the door, and led the way inside.

Over the command freq, Callahan murmured, "Foxtrot Six, Charlie Six, going in."

"*Charlie Six, acknowledged,*" Darken replied crisply.

The trio ghosted down the sloped tunnel in single file. Callahan noted the temperature readout steadily decreased the farther they descended, but the atmospheric composition remained constant. For the first hundred meters, it was nothing more than packed blue-tinged dirt, with a low ceiling and narrow walls that would've given Hoosier in his power armor trouble—exactly what Callahan would expect from an insectile race.

At one hundred fifty meters, they lost contact with the surface. Callahan jerked her head at Nguyen, who retreated up the tunnel until he could reestablish comms.

He trotted back after a brief pause. "We've got fifteen mikes and then Foxtrot Six wants a status update."

Callahan nodded, set a countdown timer, and they moved on.

At two hundred meters, the tunnel abruptly leveled out and widened, and something resembling duracrete replaced the packed dirt. A diffuse green light illuminated the underground complex, and their steps slowed as a number of branching cross-corridors came into view along with multiple doors along the main tunnel. There was no trail to follow, nothing to indicate where the VIPs may have been taken, and while their HUDs could keep track of their path, Callahan had no intention of getting cut off from the surface.

Her jaw clenched as she felt the pressure of time ticking past. *Fucking hell.*

"No help for it," she said after a moment's hesitation. "We'll clear each room as we go and hope we get lucky."

Gunny arched a brow. "Hope isn't a plan."

Callahan calmly gazed back. "Got any better ideas?"

"No, ma'am. Just pointing out the obvious," he said with a brief grin.

The older man positioned himself at the first door and made eye contact with Nguyen. The comm specialist nodded his readiness and flung the door open. Gunny swept right, Nguyen went left, and Callahan followed after Gunny.

She let out a slow, controlled breath when they were met with an empty room. Judging by the mostly empty racks in orderly rows, it was the bugs' armory. Gunny strode over to a rack in the far corner of the room that still held a handful of plasma rifles and mag-locked one to his back.

"Good thinking," Callahan murmured. Command would absolutely want to examine their weapons. "Let's keep moving."

The second and third rooms were empty of both bugs and any useful intel. There were only six minutes remaining on their countdown when they got lucky at the fourth room. Callahan grimaced at the ravaged bodies of the two men strapped down to identical tables in the center of the room. *Lucky being a relative term.*

Facial recognition confirmed the men were the last of the missing VIPs. Both bodies showed clear marks of aggressive interrogation. Gunny tilted his head toward the far corner of the room, where bloody clothes and shoes had been carelessly piled.

"I guess we know what happened to the rest of the research station personnel, too," he said.

A portion of the far wall slid up with a near-soundless *whoosh.* It was a door, so cleverly blended they hadn't even noticed it when they swept the room. A bug scuttled two paces into the room before it froze in evident alarm. Callahan had time to note it was unarmed and unarmored, and that it had a narrow metal band around its throat, before Nguyen opened fire.

The plasma bolt glanced off its carapace, leaving a blackened scorch mark against the mottled brown-and-green chitin. The bug screeched and moved with astonishing speed back out the door. Callahan snapped her rifle up and sidestepped until she had a good view of the new corridor. Unlike the main tunnel, this one was unlit, and the bug was quickly swallowed up by the darkness.

From the depths of the new corridor came a series of sharp clicks and a high-pitched buzzing that rose and fell in a rhythmic song. And then, in the midst of all that cacophony, an electronic voice called out, "*Leave.*"

Callahan's hands tightened on her rifle. She switched her HUD to IR, trying to spot the bug, but the corridor was empty as far as she could see. The clicks and buzzing grew louder, gained depth and variation. There was more than one bug down there. A lot more.

"*Leave. Leave now. LEAVE.*"

"Fuck this shit," Nguyen snarled. He switched his plasma rifle to full auto and lit up the darkness. "Die, you creepy motherfuckers!"

Barely ten seconds later, Nguyen's rifle fell silent, though his finger continued to hold down the trigger.

"Quit wasting plasma!" Gunny smacked him on the back of the helmet. "And swap out your power pack, you dumb fuck."

As Nguyen tucked his spent power pack away and slapped in a new one with shaking hands, the countdown timer on Callahan's HUD reached zero.

The noise coming from the corridor hadn't abated in the least. The mechanical voice kept saying "leave," over and over. Worse, more mechanical voices joined the chorus. A chill swept down Callahan's spine. The VIPs were confirmed dead. There was nothing left for them down here.

"Time to go, boys."

"Get some, you pussy-ass motherfuckers!" Moretti roared as another bug caught a plasma bolt to the face. A warning flashed on his HUD and he swapped his power cell with quick precision. He glanced to the side in time to see Larson drop another of the monstrous bugs. They hadn't made it back to the tree line yet as they couldn't abandon their heavy-weapon teammates. Besides, sticking next to the guy with the biggest gun was always a good idea. Looking away proved to be a *bad* idea.

A bug-shaped freight train barreled into him and slammed him into the dirt. Moretti rolled to his back only to meet the business end of his plasma rifle. He had dropped it in the collision. Behind it, the freight train leered down at him, pincers clicking. The foul creature leaned close and let out a high-pitched chitter that reminded him of the cicadas back home. A guttural growl replaced the chittering as it squeezed the trigger.

Click.

The bug's head swiveled down to the rifle, then back to Moretti. He could have sworn the thing grunted a confused "Huh?"

"Access denied, bitch!" Moretti gave a silent thanks for biometric safety features. His plasma rifle only fired when it recognized an authorized user either by their suit, or their DNA upon touch. Only a Raider could fire a Raider's weapon.

Faster than he'd ever moved in his life, Moretti buried his Ka-Bar deep into its armpit. While the bug howled in pain, he grabbed it by the back of its cranial armor and snatched it down toward him. His other fist came up hard and fast into the tri-cluster of eyes. The bug struggled to free itself but Moretti's grip was too strong and his blows too fast. Each time, his armored fist met chitin and eyeball with a sickening *thwack.*

The bug struggled less and less with each impact. Moretti didn't relent and slammed his fist harder and faster. There was a loud *crack* and then his arm sank elbow-deep into the alien's head. Thick, black fluid tinged with yellow and green oozed and drizzled down onto his armor.

"Fuck me, that's nasty," Moretti groused. "Goddamn, armor's never gonna come clean."

Without an intact brain to tell the alien's body to remain upright, it collapsed with all its considerable weight—right on top of Moretti. The impact caused more fluid to gush from the wound and completely coat his face shield.

"Oof!"

Even in his armor, the pressure was tremendous. Increasingly desperate, he tried to shove the dead alien off to no avail. His left arm was pinned to the ground, along with the rest of his body below the neck. With only his right arm free, he barely budged the beast.

"Really regretting my life choices right now," he wheezed to nobody. "Should've gotten the fucker off me, *then* killed it. Rookie Bug-Hunting 101. Don't die under the bug you just killed."

He felt the weight shift. Once. Twice. Then, suddenly, all the pressure blessedly disappeared as the bug was rolled off. He gratefully sucked in a deep breath and swiped a hand over his face shield to clear off the gunk. Gunny Warrick stood over him, the ruddy sunlight glinting off his armor like a scene from one of the old war vids.

"Gunny! You're my hero! Shining armor and everything!"

"Ain't got time for you to be takin' a nap, Moretti! Get your ass up and kill something!"

"Yes, Gunny!" Moretti answered as he rolled to his feet. "I was born to kill!"

Gunny bent over and ripped the rifle from the dead bug's limp and handed it to him. "Lose something, Lance Cor—"

A bug slammed into him from behind. The two rolled and the bug came out on top, a serrated blade held high.

"*Gunny!*"

Moretti took two bounding steps forward, lowered his shoulder, and rammed the alien with all the considerable augmented strength he could muster. There was a high-pitched squawk of surprise as the bug rolled, its legs flailing as it tried to find purchase on ground that was no longer there.

With a wild war cry, he leaped onto the bug's torso boots first and slammed the butt of his rifle down into the monster's face over and over. "COCK! SUCKING! BUGS! NOBODY! FUCKS! WITH! THE GUNNY!" The alien's limbs went limp, and Moretti turned to his NCO. "You good?"

"Didn't know you cared so much, Moretti." Gunny grunted as he tried to stand. "But don't think for a second that I'm gonna call you my fucking hero..."

The bug twitched again and Moretti's rage rekindled. With the object of all his problems at his mercy, he started beating the thing again. "I'M! SUPPOSED! TO BE! ON! A! BEACH! WITH! BEER! AND *TITTIES!*"

The stock of his rifle sank deep into the creature's face with the last word and the twitching ceased.

"You could have just shot him, you know," Gunny said as he finally made it to his feet, clearly in pain and favoring his right side.

Moving quickly, he recovered the gunny's rifle, shoved it into his hands, and helped steady him. "Yeah, but this was more therapeutic."

ZX75 fire, the screaming ordnance of M253s, flying plasma, and the war cries of Raiders and bugs alike combined as one in an ear-splitting symphony of destruction and chaos. Callahan appeared at their side, firing at yet another bug. Her commanding voice broke through the cacophony. "*Sitrep!*"

"Fucked, Lieutenant!" Moretti said as he and Gunny combined their fire with hers to down the bug.

"No shit, Captain Obvious!"

Moretti grinned. "Should I consider that a battlefield promotion?"

"Just fucking kill everything that isn't human, Moretti!" Gunny snarled.

Plasma fire whipped past their heads as a cluster of bugs charged their position.

"Screw this." Moretti yanked one of his last grenades from his belt. "Frag out!"

The lead bug whipped one arm out in a blur of speed and knocked the grenade high. It exploded a heartbeat later, and then the bugs were on them. Everything became a blur of plasma fire and stabbing blades.

"Everyone down!" Hoosier roared in warning.

Moretti's eyes widened as their heavy-weapons specialist brought his ZX75 to bear. Gunny, Callahan, and Nguyen dropped, but Larson was embroiled in a fistfight with a bug twice his size and either wouldn't or couldn't break free. Moretti tackled him from the side. A split second later, machine-gun fire cut a swath through the bugs, giving them some much-needed breathing room.

Larson didn't get back up right away.

Moretti extended a hand down to him. "Shit, Danny Boy, you okay?"

The baby-faced Raider glared up at him. "Fuckin' peachy."

Moretti winced. "Knees aren't supposed to bend in that direction, buddy." He spotted Larson's rifle and passed it to him. "Stay down."

"You think?" Larson propped his back against a dead bug, set his rifle to his shoulder, and shot the nearest bug in the face. "You owe me so many drinks when we get to that beach."

"We've got comms again!" Nygeun shouted. "Moretti, you lucky asshole! That grenade landed in the array and blew it apart!"

"Luck had nothing to do with it," Moretti said with a smug grin. "Totally meant to do that."

"You're so full of shit, Moretti."

"Sigma Outpost, Charlie Six," Callahan said. "I need immediate exfil, repeat, immediate exfil from signal location. Sending data burst now. Acknowledge receipt."

Enoha's crisp voice responded immediately. *"Echo 21 copies all. Launching."*

Thank fuck. A running retreat back through the jungle wasn't feasible. There were too many yellow indicators on her HUD signifying injured troops, along with three reds. Even as she glanced at the vital sign data, another icon turned red. *Nguyen.* She spun around in time to see the wiry comm specialist fall to his knees, the bloody tip of a serrated blade sticking out of his chest.

Callahan howled in fury and shot the bug who'd stabbed him in the back. Another immediately took its place. She shot that one, too. And the next. And the next.

"Charlie Six, Echo 21 airborne. ETE... twelve mikes."

Twelve minutes. They could survive twelve minutes. They had no other choice.

Callahan used her HUD to set a waypoint for everyone. "Retreat to rally point alpha. Baker, prioritize the wounded for evac. Twelve mikes."

She paired up with Gunny, retreating while he provided covering fire, then switching to laying down covering fire while he retreated past her current position. Her whole team slowly leapfrogged their way toward the tree line, away from the damn bug stronghold, except for Moretti, who dragged Larson by the carry strap built into the back of his armor. The young Marine's complexion was bone white, but he didn't stop firing.

Callahan fell into the disciplined rhythm drilled into them by countless hours of training and even more hours on the battlefield.

Shoot, retreat, repeat.

A plasma blast bit into the armor of her upper arm, scorching the skin and muscle beneath. She gritted her teeth, flexed the arm, and kept firing. Gunny was counting on her to cover him.

Shoot, retreat, repeat.

"ETE, seven minutes," Enoha said.

A flash of yellow in her HUD. Drop the spent power pack, swap it out for her last fresh one. Another flash of yellow. Hopkins stumbled, snarled, and kept firing.

Shoot, retreat, repeat.

"Charlie Six, Echo 21. ETE 5 min. Request LZ info when able."

Callahan shook off the haze of battle and double-clicked over the comm to acknowledge. Most of Foxtrot team had already reached the rally point and were doing a damn fine job of laying down covering fire. A glance at her HUD showed Darken's breacher among them.

"Foxtrot Six, Charlie Six. Need you to make a hole for the Bat."

"Charlie Six, Foxtrot Six, roger that," Darken replied with a slightly feral edge to his calm tone.

Several dead bugs later, a rolling roar of thunder punched through her chest. Out of the corner of her eye there was a flash of brilliant light and flames, and trees toppled on the slight ridge just beyond the tree line. Thick clouds of smoke billowed up into the air and there was plenty of debris on the ground, but Callahan had faith in her best friend's ability to handle the improvised LZ.

"Echo 21, LZ is a cleared field directly off your nose. Use caution."

The whine of the Bat's impeller was barely audible over the roar of battle as it skimmed the tops of the trees and dropped into the new clearing with its lights in the hot-load configuration. Before the wheels had fully settled, Baker hauled a badly wounded member of Foxtrot straight to the still-running VTOL. Seconds later, additional icons were marked for priority medevac. *Only room for three more? Shit...*

Callahan glanced at Moretti. "Get Larson loaded up."

"On it."

She glanced at Gunny, heavily favoring his right side as he fired at the swarm with disciplined, well-aimed shots. "You should be on that Bat."

"Noted, ma'am."

Callahan hadn't expected any other response. She flicked her eyes in a practiced movement and marked another Raider for medevac. Within seconds, the Bat was loaded up and climbing for the sky in a near-vertical takeoff. Before Enoha could get clear, a whole cluster of bugs raised their plasma rifles and opened fire.

The Bat lurched sideways. The breath froze in Callahan's lungs as it dipped dangerously close to the treetops, so close the wheels skimmed the blue-green leaves. In the next instant, it recovered, gaining altitude and airspeed as it tracked away from the battlefield.

"Echo 21, status?" Callahan barked.

"Alive with a limp." Enoha's voice was steady, but Callahan could hear the pain she tried to mask. *"Be back in approx twenty."*

"Fly safe."

Enoha didn't reply. Callahan grimaced and added her rifle to the cross fire. With four medevaced and three dead, they were down to only nine Raiders—and their power packs were rapidly depleting. She squeezed off a precise shot and put down a bug threatening Hopkins.

Twenty minutes. They could survive twenty minutes. They had no other choice. *Hurry, Eno.*

A bestial roar sliced through the air. The world seemed to shake as Moretti's suit struggled to compensate for the sheer volume. Avian life rose from the treetops and fled for their lives.

The battlefield became eerily quiet as the roar tapered off. As one, the bugs ceased their attacks and turned in the general direction of where the roar had come from.

"What the fuck was that?" Moretti asked. He licked his lips and tightened his grip on his rifle.

Clicks and chittering filled the silence as the bugs began communicating back and forth.

"Coming."

"Aliens less threat."

"Redirect fire."

"Prepare."

"The bugs have stopped," Callahan said. "Whatever it is has them spooked, too."

"Shouldn't we take that as a sign to haul ass, ma'am?" Moretti asked. He glanced up at the sky. *Lieutenant Enoha would be a sight for sore eyes right now.*

Another roar, this time from their rear shook the air again. A third to the right sounded a moment later.

Fuck, fuck, fuck, fuck, fuck. Moretti mentally chanted as he swiveled his weapon from one direction to the other. "There goes any chance of running away bravely. I can't tell which one's closer."

Jungle flora, chunks of splintered trees, dirt, and at least three bugs exploded into the air as an enormous rampaging nightmare burst from the tree line. Moretti had a blurred impression of a behemoth with curved horns stretching from its dragon-like skull down to its face as it bounded on all fours toward the mountain facility. The mass of jagged armor and tubular growths on its curved back strangely reminded him of a buffalo, though elephants also came to mind as the beast swung its head side to side.

Behemoth, elephant, buffalo . . . Bohemalo? Bug definitely won't work for that thing.

The demon halted its charge and roared again. Moretti winced as the deafening sound blasted through his helmet and straight into his eardrums. His jaw dropped as the Bohemalo rose up on its hind legs and towered over the battlefield. If it was five feet tall, it was fifteen. He caught a good look of what he'd taken for front paws and realized they were long, three-fingered hands. Each digit was tipped with curved black talons perfect for disemboweling Raiders.

In the distance, there was another roar, followed by gunfire and screaming. The beast pulled its upper lip back with a menacing growl just as Lieutenant Darken burst from the tree line.

"There's another one of these things on the way! It tore us apart! Smoke it!"

Shaking off his own paralysis, Hoosier raised his ZX75, the barrels already spinning, and opened fire in concert with the bugs. Hot lead and plasma bolts hit the Bohemalo. Whether it roared in pain or rage, Moretti didn't know, but it sent chills down his spine all the same.

Two more Raiders tumbled out of the jungle and caught it in a cross fire. The Bohemalo spun and swatted one with enough force to send them flying into a tree ten meters away. The snap of wood and bone alike was enough to snap him out of his shock. Moretti raised his rifle and fired as fast as he could. There was no way he'd leave his old battle buddy to stand alone. They'd kill this thing before the other one showed up.

The Bohemalo dropped to all fours again and rushed Hoosier. As big as it was, the monster closed the distance faster than Moretti thought possible. Its clawed hand flashed out and grabbed Hoosier's ZX75, stopping the spin of the barrels with a metallic groan.

"What the fuck?" Hoosier squawked as the machine gun was

ripped from his hands. In the next instant, he was swatted aside like the other Raider had been. Luckily, he didn't slam spine-first into a tree. Instead, he rolled like a discarded rag doll into the jungle brush.

A bug rushed up next to Moretti, its plasma rifle blazing away. The bug paused to swap out an empty magazine and, without thinking about it, Moretti provided cover fire.

"Looks like the bugs are friendly, or at least have a common threat, for the moment," Callahan shouted over the comm. *"Not sure how long it'll last, but let's not waste the support while we have it! Concentrate fire on the ... the ... whatever the fuck it is! Shoot the big monster thing!"*

"Kill the big monster. Got it, LT!"

His HUD sent a low-ammo warning. He slapped the bug on the shoulder and got an ugly set of pincers in the face for it. The bug's triple set of tri-cluster eyes seemed to narrow.

Moretti activated his external speakers. "Follow me! We gotta get out of the open!"

Without waiting to see if the bug understood, he bolted for a pile of fallen trees. At the last second, he dove over the pile, hit the ground rolling, then scrambled back up to the top. A heartbeat later, the bug lumbered over and joined him. Working in sync, they took turns firing over their cover. Twice, the bug tossed over what turned out to be grenades.

A thought occurred to him and he toggled his face shield setting to clear and looked the bug in the face. "While we have a moment—and we're on the same side—I'd like to take this opportunity to apologize for killing any of your friends or family out there. That wasn't like your brother-in-law or something I shot in the face, was it? If so, hopefully you didn't like him very much."

The bug's head tilted to the right, its eyes emotionless, and clicked its mandibles twice before skittering over the pile. The other bugs appeared to be out of ammunition and had resorted to swarming the beast.

"Was that 'Thank you,' or 'Fuck you'?" Moretti shrugged and kept shooting.

"Out of the way!" came the roar of a very pissed-off Hoosier. He had his ZX75 back in his hands and marched toward the bug-covered Bohemalo.

No sooner had the bugs skittered away than the Raider opened fire.

He stitched a line up the Bohemalo's back, forcing it to drop to all fours again. Even then its head stood ten feet off the ground. It turned and charged, bullets impacting all the while.

"Hoosier!" Moretti shouted. "Run!"

It was too late. The Bohemalo was on him. To Hoosier's credit, he held onto his beloved death machine a little longer this time before it was flung into the jungle. As before, Hoosier was backhanded by the beast. However, this time he managed to turn and deflect most of the blow, rolling only a few meters. Hoosier reached over his shoulder for his M253. Air was all he managed to grab. Moretti spotted it on the ground where Hoosier had been struck. The big man twisted and eyed the fallen weapon.

I know that look. Damnit, Hoosier.

"Run, you idiot!" Moretti bellowed as he leaped from cover and fired plasma shots at the Bohemalo's legs.

The bugs seemed to catch on and joined him. Hoosier let out a war cry and made a mad dash for the M253. The Bohemalo's gaze tracked his movement, and it dashed forward to intercept. As it charged Hoosier, one of their plasma shots hit a weak spot on the creature's thick, scaly hide and it stumbled as one of its back legs gave out.

It wasn't enough.

Hoosier's fingertips barely kissed the M253 before a massive hand wrapped around him. Razor claws punctured through his armor like it was made of tinfoil and the big man screamed. Blood poured over the Bohemalo's clawed fingers as it rose back to two feet, lifting Hoosier off the ground.

The mortally wounded Raider never gave up the fight.

Defiant to the last, Hoosier drew his oversized combat knife, flipped his blade edge up, and slammed it to the hilt in the Bohemalo's belly. Hoosier dragged the blade all the way up to the monster's sternum as he was lifted, cursing it all the while. Alien intestines spilled to the grass in a pool of black blood. The beast staggered but held Hoosier up to its face and roared. Hoosier roared back and jammed his blade into one eye socket. The Bohemalo loosed a final roar before clamping its massive jaws down on Hoosier's head. There was a *crunch* that would haunt Moretti for the rest of his life. The Bohemalo fell to the ground with a thunderous crash, Hoosier still in the grasp of both its jaws and claws.

Moretti's eyes burned as Hoosier's name turned red on his HUD. There were too many red names already. But this one...this one was going to hurt for a long time.

Goddamnit, Hoosier. You stupid, badass motherfucker. Semper Fi, brother.

His thoughts were cut short as another roar accompanied the arrival of a third Bohemalo. He turned to the other side of the clearing to see it snatch up Manahue like a club and use him to crush Koit like so much cannon fodder.

Hoosier's M253 gleamed in the ruddy sunlight like an answer from heaven. Moretti snatched it up, dropped to a knee, and set the sights on the charging alien. Just as he fired, something huge slammed into his side and sent him sprawling. There was a flash of smoke, legs, and fire as he rolled, but no scream of a dying Bohemalo. There was, however, another roaring war cry from the direction of whatever had crashed into him. He pushed himself up to see a dead Bug lying next to him. The rampaging Bohemalo had charged right past him and was tearing through the ranks of the Bugs. Another was embroiled in a fierce battle with a mix of Bugs and Raiders.

Moretti's gaze snagged on the Bohemelo lying dead on the ground, Hoosier still caught in its grasp. At a sudden silence to his left, he snapped his head around. The third Bohemelo was gone, a trail of dead bugs in its wake, but the thing had completely ghosted. No crunching leaves, twigs, swaying trees...nothing.

He had to clear his throat before he could speak. "LT, Gunny, be advised, one of those big fuckers is being a sneaky-ass in the bush. Repeat. There are currently two threats. Eyes on one, one dead, one unaccounted for."

"*Copy all,*" Callahan answered. "*We also have eyes on the second. No sign of the third.*"

Thundering footsteps caught Moretti's attention. He turned just in time to see the second Bohemalo shake two Bugs off its back and tear straight through several Raiders in a bid to escape. He was right in its path. He gritted his teeth and fired his plasma rifle only to get a warning after four rounds that his power pack was empty. He grabbed at his belt for a new one but found he was out.

Frantically, he searched the surrounding ground for something, *anything* he might be able to use against the monster bearing down on him. Then he saw it. A lump of plastic explosives with a device full of unknown liquids pressed into it. Larson must have dropped it when he'd shoved him out of the way of the initial Bug surge.

A fierce grin creased his face as he pulled the detonator off his belt. Before Larson had gotten on the Bat, he'd shoved the small device in his face—just in case. He fumbled for a split second and depressed the trigger.

Time seemed to slow to a crawl as the Bohemalo closed in. The fluids on the device merged in the center tube as the Bohemalo bounded over the bomb.

BOOM.

Moretti's HUD automatically dimmed down at the eye-searing flash, and he rocked back a step as the blast hit him like a physical punch to the chest. The Bohemalo was ripped apart in the middle, the back half raining down in small pieces all over the clearing, while the front half skidded to a halt a meter from his boots. The jaws snapped once, twice, then the vicious light in its eyes dimmed.

"Damn it, Danny-boy." Moretti brushed a stringy chunk off his shoulder. "That's twice I've been covered in alien guts today."

"Damn it, Moretti," Callahan grumbled as she wiped her faceplate clear of fluids she really didn't care to identify. "A little warning next..."

She trailed off as a ripple of blue lights played in the deep shadows of a thick grove of trees to her right. Something about the colors, or maybe the rhythmic pulse, pulled at her. She sidestepped, rifle up, until she had a clear visual.

It was the big fucker that had disappeared into the jungle.

The massive beast stood on its hind legs, arms spread wide, berserker eyes almost serene as a blue glow rippled over its crest, down its neck, and along its chest. Hopkins stood right in front of it, her rifle dangling from her fingertips, face slack, eyes blank.

Callahan took a step forward before she'd even made the conscious decision to move. Those dagger claws and razor-sharp teeth were no less terrifying, but that light... it was hard to look away. Her gaze was so focused on the dancing lights that she never even noticed the bug until it was too late.

It slammed into her side hard enough to make her stumble but not hard enough to hurt. It clacked its mandibles in her face and buzzed at her in a high-pitched cadence. Interspersed was that same electronic voice she'd heard in the underground facility.

"Light bad! No look at light!"

Callahan could see the light out of her peripheral vision. Blue rippled over the mottled browns and greens of the bug's face. She tried to look. The bug grabbed either side of her helmet and forcibly turned her face away.

There was no recognizable emotion in the triple cluster of eyes, but its agitation came through in the rapid click of its mandibles. *"No look."*

Callahan gave her head a violent shake, and her thoughts sharpened. There was a soft *thud* as Hopkins's rifle hit the dirt. A Raider *never* let their weapon fall, let alone in the face of an enemy. Something was very wrong.

"LT!"

Moretti slammed into the bug like a freight train and tackled it to the ground. Gunny was there in the next instant, standing at her shoulder, focused on the monster. Even as she watched, his expression slackened, and the tip of his rifle drooped. A glance to the side showed Moretti frozen, straddling the bug with one fist raised high but his gaze caught by the mesmerizing lights.

Moretti ran his mouth when he was scared. He didn't freeze. Ever.

The bug beneath him buzzed and clicked in a frantic cadence. The metal collar around its throat reflected blue. *"Light BAD!"*

Understanding shocked her into action. Her eyes flicked, accessing one of the submenus of her HUD. *Filters ... come on, come on. Where ... there!*

Her HUD adjusted in an instant, and her visual dimmed as it filtered out blue light. With another flick, she pushed out the change to everyone.

Moretti shook his head. "What the ... ?"

"Shit!" Gunny snapped his rifle up, but he didn't have a clear shot. "Hopkins, *move your ass!*"

Hopkins startled, her empty hands clenching and opening. Her gaze dipped, searching for her rifle. The light died. As the beast's jaw dropped in an overwhelming roar, Darken burst out of the brush. He didn't slow, he just grabbed Hopkins by the arm and pulled her along with him, yanking her clear.

Almost before they were out of the line of fire, the Bugs opened up on the enormous monstrosity. Her Raiders followed suit. It roared in pain and fury and dropped to all fours, shielding its more vulnerable belly. Still roaring, it snatched up one bug and bit its head off, then threw its body at Darken and Hopkins, knocking both to the ground. A trio of Bugs swarmed up its back, stabbing down at the thick hide with the same serrated blades that had killed Nguyen. The beast spun and stomped and slashed with flexible arms, catching all three with its long claws, carving through armor and chitin alike.

Gunny glanced over at Moretti. "Anytime you feel like joining the party..."

Moretti cursed, rolled off the bug he'd tackled, and stole its rifle. "Sorry, buddy. Should've added biometric locks if you didn't want somebody to steal it."

Gunny had also switched to the bug's plasma rifle that he'd tactically acquired from their armory. Callahan grimaced as her last power pack drained to nothing and fired one last shot. One by one, her Marines' weapons fell silent as their own power packs ran out. As the rate of fire dropped, the beast dashed forward with startling speed and caught up one of Darken's Raiders in one hand. The man didn't even have the chance to scream before he was torn in half. His icon turned red.

They were down to a handful of Raiders and maybe a dozen bugs. The countdown timer on Callahan's HUD for the Bat's return was still over five minutes. Callahan snarled as another icon turned red. By the time Eno made it back, there wasn't going to be anyone left for her to evac.

"*Down!*" Baker roared.

Their mild-mannered field medic lumbered up, one of the discarded ZX75s strapped to his chest, barrels already spinning up. Without looking, he tossed an M253 toward Callahan. She snatched it out of the air and braced it tight against her shoulder. It kicked like a motherfucker, but the round ripped a satisfying hole through the beast's shoulder. As machine-gun fire tore at its chest and legs, she adjusted her aim upward. Her next shot went through its lower jaw.

Its scream as its legs collapsed beneath it was a ragged, pitiful thing. Callahan didn't feel an ounce of mercy for the monster who'd killed so many. A high-pitched whimper escaped its shattered jaws. Coldly, calmly, she shifted the M253 and put a round through its eye.

It died without another sound.

Silence fell over the battlefield. Callahan snapped her head to the side as the bug who'd saved her from the light took a cautious step forward. Hands tightened on weapons as her Raiders shifted aim from the dead monster to the remaining Bugs. Tension wound through her, but she waited. They'd managed an unspoken truce up until now. If they could just hold it for a few more minutes, maybe she'd manage to keep some of them alive for Eno to save.

The bug clicked and buzzed, the mandibles on its face twitching with urgency. "Leave. Leave now. Big coming."

Callahan frowned. "Big?"

The bug's mandibles flexed, and it tapped at the metal band around its throat, frustration in its movements. Callahan glanced at the countdown timer. *Three minutes.*

A roar shattered the silence. It wasn't a sound. It was a force of nature, punching her in the heart and freezing the breath in her lungs in a primeval reaction.

The bug looked from the dead nightmare to her. "Big coming."

Moretti blanched. "Well . . . fuck."

Callahan tightened her grip on her rifle. "At least we found the VIPs before everything *really* went to shit."

Bug Out

Kacey Ezell

"Sigma Outpost, Charlie Six. I need immediate exfil, repeat, immediate exfil from signal location. Sending data burst now. Acknowledge receipt."

Lieutenant Marianne Bobbi Enoha shot to her feet and lunged for the radio receiver. That was her friend Zoe Callahan's crisp, no-nonsense voice on the line, and if Callahan sounded that calm, then shit was probably really hitting the rotary impeller.

Enoha punched the key to confirm receipt of the location databurst and send it to her Bat's onboard navigation system, then keyed up the mic. "Echo 21 copies all. Launching."

She didn't wait to hear any further transmissions, just slammed her hand down on the alert klaxon and took off running for the parking apron where her Bat VTOL sat waiting, composite skin gleaming darkly in the ruddy light from the alien sun.

Enoha pulled herself into her seat and donned her helmet in one smooth, practiced motion. She called out the steps of her checklist from memory as she toggled on the electrics and her display screens fired up. With quick fingers, she grabbed her kneeboard and strapped it to her leg, tapping the screen there to bring up the official copy of her checklist before she got too far into it. Straps came next, then the door, and then she did a quick visual check and hit the button to start the engine and get her impeller spinning.

The dirt on 234 Velex-b wasn't the same dull brown or gray common on Earth. Nor was it the red-tinged, iron-heavy dust of Mars. Here the dirt had a bluish cast, and somewhere in the back of her mind, Enoha's brain remembered that this rockball leaned heavily toward titanium and cobalt in its mineral composition.

"Focus, Eno," she told herself, and watched as her engine health readouts spooled up to normal operating levels. Temperatures and pressures all looked good, and the CF/FM navigational sonar was spooling up appropriately. Enoha flipped on her comm suite and keyed the mic as she smoothly pulled collective to lift her Bat into the air.

"Charlie Six, Echo 21 airborne. ETE"—Enoha darted her eyes to her navigation readout—"twelve mikes."

Callahan's short acknowledgment came through loud and clear, but once again her calm tone and brief reply pushed Enoha to nose down and pour on the speed. Something big was happening, and her friend was stuck in the middle of it. Situations like this were why the Raiders continued to pay and train pilots. No AI drone had the discretionary ability to respond in the rapidly changing environment of a hot extract.

No Raider worth their salt would trust a drone, anyway.

In seconds, the Bat passed beyond the fenceline of the outpost. Deep blue-green foliage swallowed up the terrain below, broken only here and there by narrow, twisty slashes of river.

"Not a bad-looking planet, overall," Enoha said out loud as she flew. She'd first earned her wings on the larger *Pelican*-class atmospheric craft, and had been used to working with a crew. Once she'd crossed over to Bats, she'd learned to handle everything herself, but she still disliked a silent cockpit. It usually meant things were about to go wrong.

"Navigation's on track," she said then, as she flowed into her cross-check. "Power margin's looking good. This atmosphere is rich with O_2. You like it here, don't you, sweetheart?" Enoha stroked the glareshield with her collective hand briefly before returning her fingertips to their resting place on the collective. She'd figured that the Bat's Aredyne 512 turboshaft engine would enjoy the atmospheric mix here. It was damn close to Earth's original ratios, which was part of the reason that Sigma Outpost had been established in the first place.

"And then something wiped out the scientists, and then they called in us Raiders, huh, baby?" Enoha rolled into a right bank and carved a turn around a large rock upthrust that broke through the surrounding canopy. She could have flown over it, but she preferred to keep her altitude low enough to avoid detection by most ground-based systems.

Something was out here. Something had wiped out the scientists... and something was engaging her best friend right now.

"ETE, seven minutes," Enoha said then, her eyes flicking to the navigation display before locking back outside, scanning for threats. Callahan hadn't sent any landing zone information other than the coordinates; she'd have to do a quick recon before she put the Bat down. If they were in a big enough open area, she might be able to check it out from the air and fly a straight-in approach ... but judging by the unrelieved canopy below her, that didn't seem likely.

She keyed the mic. "Charlie Six, Echo 21. ETE five min. Request LZ info when able."

Callahan didn't respond, other than a double click of the mic. It wasn't, strictly speaking, a standard response, but Enoha had told her how Bat pilots sometimes did that while flying in formation to signal acknowledgment while keeping comms clear, and Callahan had apparently remembered it—

Light bloomed out of the canopy in front of her as a column of flames shot skyward, followed by a thick, billowy ball of smoke that rose and dissipated in the light wind coming from behind the Bat's tail.

"Echo 21, LZ is a cleared field directly off your nose. Use caution."

Enoha snorted, and banked to the left to begin to circle around the field so she could land into the wind. "Cleared" was generous, for while Callahan's ordnance had brought down the canopy, plenty of debris lay over the floor of the so-called LZ.

Still, it was nothing she couldn't handle. Enoha fired off a call back to the base to let them know she was about to start her approach, and set herself up into the wind, on a descent angle that would have her skimming the tops of the trees surrounding the LZ.

As she drew closer, she could hear the discordant rhythm of concussive blasts, even over the Bat's impeller noise. She flipped her lights to the "hot onload" standard configuration to let Callahan's Raiders know that she wouldn't be shutting down the engine and toggled the cabin door controls to slide open just as she gently brought her wheels to touch down on the flattened jungle debris.

Baker, Callahan's medic, was first at the door. Enoha looked over her shoulder and jabbed a finger toward the bright orange comm panel hanging near the doorframe. Baker nodded, and Enoha heard the slight crackle as he came up on the Bat's intercom system.

"Priority wounded," he reported without preamble. "Forder took hits to helmet and center mass. I stabilized him for the time being, but he needs surgery ASAP. Uploading his suit data to your Bat now."

"He's the worst?"

"Yep. Not by much, though. How many can you take?"

Enoha looked at her fuel gauge and ran a quick weight calculation in her head. "Four," she said. "And those two crates in the back are ammo. Make sure you take 'em. They're not doing me any good and I need the weight. I'll be back with more."

"Might want to bring a crew and weapons next time, ma'am," the medic said. "The bugs are getting hot around here."

Enoha shook her head. "No time to reconfigure. I'll be back!" She waved Baker back as Moretti hauled the obviously wounded Danny Larson into place. She toggled the doors closed, ready to get out of there before the laser fire she saw crisscrossing the tree line turned toward her position.

She pulled collective, forced to do a near-vertical takeoff due to the proximity of the tree line to her position. It might have been her imagination, but Enoha almost *felt* the impeller strain under the increased weight of the now much heavier Bat. She kept one eye on her power readout and whispered sweet nothings under her breath as she approached her maximum power available.

"C'mon, baby. Just a bit more for Mama... almost there..."

A flash, and something hit her calf like a sledgehammer. Enoha jerked, and the Bat lurched to the right, dipping dangerously toward the tops of the trees currently just below belly-level.

"Fuck!" Enoha screamed, gritting her teeth against the pulsing pain that radiated up her leg as she centered the cyclic and pushed it forward to gain airspeed. The wheels definitely brushed the top of the jungle canopy, but more ground fire tracked toward their position, so a little leaf rub was the least of her worries.

"*Echo 21, status?*" Callahan's voice crackled through her helmet. She must have seen the Bat taking fire.

"Alive with a limp," Enoha answered, fighting to keep the pain out of her tone. "Be back in approx twenty."

"*Fly safe.*"

"Doing my best," Enoha muttered, but she didn't key the mic, so no one heard her.

Once she'd gained enough airspeed and distance to not get shot at again, she risked a look down at the agony that was her left leg. Her calf was a red-and-black ruin, edged with the crisped, frayed ends of her flightsuit. A small pool of blood lay beneath her boot, but there wasn't any flow . . . or worse, spurting.

"Energy bolt graze," she said out loud. "Painful as fuck, but not fatal. Damnit. This is going to make this next run trickier."

Without the tailwind helping her, the flight back to Sigma Outpost seemed to take forever, but eventually she shot an easy approach to the landing pad. She'd called ahead to let them know she was bringing wounded in, and so several corpsmen met her at the pad, ready to off-load her passengers while the maintenance bots handled the hot refuel.

"Need a quick burn-dressing kit!" she shouted at the lead corpsman, and pointed to her leg. Confusion pinched his face, and she waved him to walk around the nose of the aircraft and take a look. His eyes went wide when he saw the edge-melted hole in the plexiglass of her chin bubble, as well as the ugly burn on her leg.

"Ma'am, you need to shut down and come in!" he shouted over her impeller noise. She shook her head vehemently.

"We've got Raiders out there who need more ammo and they've got more wounded! Just slap a dressing on it and let me get back in the air!"

The corpsman shook his head, mouthing something about stupidity and brass ovaries, but Enoha didn't care. She was happy to let him think what he wanted as long as he did what she told him.

"You're good to go, ma'am," he shouted a moment later. "I did my best, but you really need to get that burn fully cleaned out so it doesn't get infected!"

"I'll do it as soon as I land," she promised. "Now get the hell back so I can take off!"

The corpsman stepped back, sketching a salute as she pulled collective. She answered with a nod, since her hands were full of the Bat's controls, and hurled herself back into the air.

The flight back wasn't any easier.

The ruddy sun beat down overhead, making sweat run down Enoha's face and into her eyes as she squinted at her nav readout. Agony wreathed her leg, pulling at her every time she moved her foot . . . which was often, since her pedals controlled her yaw and trim. Nausea rose up within her, but she swallowed it down.

"Focus," she snarled at herself. "Get this last lift, and then you can throw up and fall apart and cry. But just now, you gotta keep your shit together. Callahan and her Raiders need you."

Pain crowded in at the edge of her vision, and Enoha gritted her teeth as she set up for her second approach into the hot LZ. She didn't want to take the same ground track as last time, lest she be too predictable. This time, she came in lower, faster, intending to show up and be on the ground before the noise of her impeller really registered her position.

It wasn't an easy thing to do on a good day. With agony pulling at her attention, and her eyes scanning the tree line for more energy bolts . . . well. She might have hit a little hard. Not hard enough to put the wheel struts through the floor . . . but harder than she liked. The g-meter beeped its protest as she lowered the collective to flat pitch.

"Sorry, sweetheart," Enoha whispered to the Bat a heartbeat before she keyed the mic. "Charlie Six, Echo 21. Get your ass on this Bat before I pass the fuck out from blood loss."

"On it, Echo 21."

Forward and to her left, Enoha saw six figures rise up from the tree line at her two o'clock and come running flat out for the bird. Five of them looked familiar. One of them . . .

Enoha had her personal weapon out of its holster and pointed at the insectoid form before she really even registered what she was looking at.

"Don't shoot!" Callahan screamed. Enoha blinked. *Fuck, I'm losing time.* Apparently, Callahan had gotten to the Bat and come up on comms without Enoha noticing. Maybe she was hurt worse than she'd thought.

"Prisoner?" Enoha asked, returning her pistol to the holster mounted on her flight vest.

"Ally," Callahan said, turning to give Baker a hand as he helped a limping Gunny Warrick into the Bat. "It's a long story. I'll tell you in the air." She lifted her rifle and fired several shots back toward the tree line. The last Raider, Lieutenant Darken, the Foxtrot Team commander, popped up at the sound of Callahan's fire and ran flat out for the Bat. Behind him, the tree line shuddered.

The Bat's g-meter beeped again. Even though they were flat on the ground.

"Uh ... Callahan ..."

"DARKEN!" Callahan screamed as the tree line parted and something massive stepped out. The weird bug-ally-thing let out a keen that went almost ultrasonic and made Enoha's teeth ache in her skull. She squinted and did the only thing she could: pull in collective to get light on the wheels in preparation for takeoff.

"Callahan, we gotta go!" Enoha said. "I don't know what that behemoth is, but it looks pissed!"

Darken ran, stumbling the last few meters toward the Bat as the impeller's whine picked up volume with the increased pitch. The behemoth—whatever it was, Enoha could barely wrap her mind around what she was seeing—took another step out past the trees, letting out a roar that shook the Bat's entire frame.

"Let's go, let's go!" Enoha shouted, but Callahan couldn't have heard her over her own screams.

"DARKEN!" the lieutenant screamed again. "Come ON!"

But Darken didn't listen. Instead, he stopped, gaped. Enoha watched in time-dilating horror as he lifted his plasma rifle and began firing at the towering creature looming overhead.

It let out another bellow as Darken's fire seared a line up the side of one massive leg toward the torso.

"Flying machine. Fly. Fly now. Fly now!"

Enoha didn't recognize the electronic-sounding voice that came over her intercom, but she wasn't about to leave a fellow Raider behind. She raised her own near-useless pistol and pointed it at the monstrosity just as the thing swiped a five-taloned forelimb at Darken. One of the talons caught him just above his shoulder, and Darken's helmet flew off his body, trailing a red spray in a grotesque arc as it tumbled to the ground.

"DARKEN!" Callahan screamed one last time, and opened fire toward the massive creature. Baker grabbed hold of her arm and hauled her back and into the Bat, flinging them both to the floor. Enoha felt the *thump*, and spun back to her controls, holstering her weapon and pulling collective in one smooth motion as the lumbering creature turned its ... face? toward them.

"Going to max power," Enoha said through clenched teeth, hearing the impeller noise scream as she blew right through the maximum continuous power setting and settled at the very top end of the power band. She couldn't pull that much power for long before the Bat's engine would start throwing turbine blades, but she had a few seconds...hopefully enough to get them clear of the LZ and that... whatever it was.

The Bat climbed like it was on an elevator. The minute she could see over the top edge of the tree line, Enoha rotated forward, tucking her nose in order to pick up airspeed. She reduced the power back into the continuous range, which had them dipping back toward the tree line, but would be safer in the long run. The wide-leaved green branches began to rush by beneath them as the Bat accelerated—

Thunk.

Enoha slammed forward against her four-point harness, which fortunately locked its inertial reels and kept her torso from jamming the cyclic forward. The impeller and the engine screamed louder, higher, and a series of sharp *popopopop*s reverberated through the Bat's frame.

"What's happening?!" Callahan's voice cut through the impeller noise. Enoha's eyes flew over her gauges, but she didn't have time to register any information before the world tilted and spun.

"Autorotate!" Enoha screamed, slamming her collective to the floor. But the aircraft didn't descend, and the spinning stopped. Instead they...swung?

"Oh, bloody hells. It's grabbed us!"

Callahan's shout overlaid the sudden electronic screaming of the other creature in the cargo compartment: the one that should have been their enemy...maybe? Enoha's vision wavered, black crowding in at the edges as the Bat changed direction yet again, hurtling through the air and down toward the canopy below.

"Brace!" she yelled over the intercom, just as a particularly large tree loomed up ahead in her windscreen. It almost looked like it was reaching out for her, its branches spread in welcome—

Sound returned first. Besides the high, incessant tone that drove a spike through her skull, Enoha could hear the insistent beeping of her low impeller speed warning, and something that sounded like a ping of heated metal cooling. She heard a groan, too, and only a moment later realized that it came from her.

Enoha opened her eyes to complete blackness. Panic cut the edge of her throat. She flailed, clawing at her face as she fought to breathe and suddenly, a bar of light appeared below her.

Chill the fuck out! she ordered herself, splaying her hands and flattening them against her face—or what was against her face. *Your helmet spun around! Get a grip, Eno, and quit fucking panicking! That never helped anyone!*

With this pep talk ringing in her metaphorical ears, Enoha yanked on her helmet, managing to pull it off, despite the chinstrap that dragged up against her left ear. She immediately lost her grip on the unwieldy thing, and it flew up and out of her hands...

No. Not flew up. Fell down. She heard it thunk against several branches on the way down.

Enoha blinked, trying to make her eyes adjust to the weird mix of deep green shade and the spears of ruddy sunlight that penetrated the hole her poor Bat had made in the jungle canopy. She hung against her restraint straps, facing down into the shadows. She reached down into her leg pocket, wincing as her fingers found the graze against her calf.

Little deeper than a graze, she realized, gritting her teeth. *Okay, new plan. Get down. Bandage calf. Find team. Easy. No problems. Let's do this.*

With one more reach, she managed to get hold of the headlamp she kept in her pocket. Unfortunately, as she pulled it out, she realized that the energy bolt that got her had burned right through the headlamp's strap. The light still worked, though.

She clicked it on and shone the beam into the trees around her, twisting in her straps as best she could. From what she could figure, the Bat had snapped in half, separating her cockpit from the cargo compartment and the rest of the airframe. She hung in the trees, her seat and the remains of her cockpit wedged there about four meters or so above the jungle floor.

So where's the rest of my aircraft, and my team? She played her light down into the murkiness below, but she didn't see anything except the irregular ball of her helmet where it had fallen against the roots of the tree that currently held her up.

"Okay, Eno," she told herself. "Step one, get down." That was easy, at least. All she had to do was unlock her harness ... and then not fall four meters onto her face. That second part was harder, but ...

A plan slowly coalesced as she took a look at the interlocking web of branches between her and the ground. Slowly, very slowly, she reached her injured leg out, grimacing against the pain until the toes of her boot touched the next branch below her.

"Here goes," she said, and reached out with her left hand while twisting the harness lock mechanism with her right. Her straps released, and she fell. With a grunt, she slid her boot across the curving perimeter of the branch, letting it slam into her groin and belly as she collapsed onto it. White stars exploded in her vision, but she wrapped both arms around the branch and held on tight, panting through the pain.

Eventually her vision cleared, and she was free. Slowly, she lifted her head and looked down.

Okay, that got me maybe a meter closer. Progress. Next branch?

Tricky, but doable. At least with her arms and legs free, she could shimmy to the thick cylinder of the tree's trunk and use its rough bark to help her work her way down to the branch below.

Repeating the process one more time brought her to within a meter and a half of the ground, and with a sigh, she leapt down. The impact of her boots on the ground shot up through her injured leg and threatened to make her knees buckle. She bit back the curses that flooded her brain. The white stars flashed in her eyes again, but she shook her head and blinked them away.

Step one, complete. Step two ... find my team. Or, no, step two was bandage calf but ...

Enoha looked at her helmet, lying on the ground not far from where she'd landed. She hop-skipped over and picked it up. It was dented, and the smoke-colored visor was cracked, but it looked like it would still go over her head. Enoha took a deep breath and pulled it on, feeling the helmet's connecting pins make contact with their receptacles on the back of her armor's neck.

Her flight-crew armor wasn't as robust as Callahan's power armor, of course, but it still gave her some protection, and it still carried enough power to fire up her HUD and comms when she wasn't strapped into the aircraft. The HUD flickered annoyingly against the cracked visor, but it was usable. And more importantly, it showed that she had a clear channel on the command network.

"Charlie Six, Echo 21 ... you out there?"

A pause.

"Echo 21, authenticate with Moretti's favorite color."

Enoha's eyebrows went up inside her helmet. They knew she was out here, did Callahan think she was captured? Or that someone had lifted a voice print from the wreckage of the Bat? It was possible... probably... but would take a comms specialty team a hot minute to break the Bat's encryption and synthesize a message. How long had she been hanging in that tree?

"Charlie Six, Echo 21. Orange... or as he calls it 'ginger.'"

"Good to hear your voice, Echo 21. Can you burst location coordinates?"

"Yeah, stand by."

Enoha toggled the appropriate command, using the microswitches embedded in the fingertips of her flight gloves, and saw the tiny data icon in her HUD flash blue for a few seconds.

"Got it, Echo 21. Stay put. ETE five min. We're not far away at all."

Callahan hadn't lied. They were close. Moretti and Baker showed up about four and a half minutes later. Despite their size and armor, Enoha couldn't help but be impressed by the smooth, quiet way they moved through the undergrowth. Baker bandaged her calf and promised more thorough treatment back at their camp not far away. Enoha gritted her teeth and nodded, steeling herself for the hike.

It was slow going, but she made it to the little clearing they'd chosen. All in all, it was a good spot, next to a curve in a stream, with a break in the canopy and several large boulders dotting the terrain. They'd set up in the shadow of one of the boulders, and Enoha recognized the silhouette of Hopkins emplaced atop it. The red-tinged sun slanted through the tops of the trees behind him, and the growing shadows promised a dark night to come. Enoha was glad to see the glow of a tiny, sheltered fire reflecting off the bottom curve of the blue-gray boulder.

"Eno," Callahan said, coming forward to wrap her arms around her in a hug. "Damn, girl. The way the Bat split apart... I thought we'd lost you."

Enoha hugged her friend back hard, heedless of the strength of her armored arms. Callahan was wearing armor, too, and she could take it.

"I'm a tough bitch," Enoha said, swallowing hard against the emotions that threatened to rise up in her voice. "Can't get rid of me that easily. Got a little banged up, though." She dropped the hug and gestured down to her calf.

"I've got meds for you right over here, ma'am," Baker said, pointing to a spot next to the tiny fire where a large, open pack sat. "It should help a little, at least."

"Go get fixed up," Callahan said, slapping Enoha on her shoulder. "I've got to deal with our new *ally*. He's damn near hysterical, and I can't figure out why."

"Is it because we shot up a bunch of his fellows?" Enoha asked, dropping her voice. "Because we did, didn't we? I didn't imagine that?"

"No, you didn't, and yes, we did. But he doesn't seem to give a shit about that. It's almost like they have some kind of hive-mind thing, so the individuals don't matter as much . . . It's creepy as fuck, but I'm trying to understand. He's . . . well. You saw that thing."

"The monster that swatted my Bat out of midair?" Enoha forced her voice to stay dry and slightly sarcastic, lest it start to tremble with fear. "Yeah. I saw it."

"Yeah . . . this whole fucking thing is a mess, Eno. I just . . . Fuck." Callahan rolled her shoulders back and jutted her jaw forward in an expression Enoha recognized as her best friend's version of squaring up. "I'll handle it. You go get fixed up."

"I can talk it through with you later if you want," Enoha offered. "If you think another perspective would help."

"Yeah, it might." Callahan flashed her a grateful smile. "Thank you."

"Anytime, girl. Ride or die." Enoha stuck out one gloved hand.

"Ride or die." Callahan gripped her offered hand briefly, as if it were a lifeline. Enoha winked, letting her smile grow.

You can do this, Zoe girl, she thought. She knew Callahan wouldn't hear the words, but that her ultimate confidence in her best friend would shine through. Callahan's own lips curved in the smallest smile as she squeezed Enoha's hand once more before letting go and turning back to where the Bug crouched on the far side of the boulder.

"Moretti!" Enoha called as she started to limp her way toward Baker's station. "Unless you're doing something useful, come here. I have questions and you have a big mouth."

While Baker cleaned her calf, slathered it with numbing cream and anti-infection gunk, and wrapped it in a clean bandage, Moretti filled

Enoha in on what, exactly, had happened between her first and second lifts into that hot LZ.

"We saw how they concentrated their fire on your Bat the first time, ma'am," the cocky Raider said as he lounged beside her, idly chewing on a ration bar. "So when you called on final the second time, we were getting ready to lay down covering fire for you when that Bohemalo came—"

"Wait. Bohemalo?"

Moretti shrugged. "Yeah, it's like a cross between a behemoth, an elephant, and a buffalo. You probably didn't see it, but the way it swung its head as it passed through the trees was just like one of those old nature vids about African elephants before they went extinct in the wild. And it has this back hump like an American bison—I wonder if it tastes as good as bison does..."

"Your LT said that the Bug acts like it's sapient."

"So?"

Enoha snorted, and then shook her head. "Okay, Bohemalo. Fair enough. Go on."

"Well, it came barreling through the trees, and all of a sudden the Bugs turn like one creature and start firing at it. So we think...cool, right? But then it starts taking a swing at our guys, too. So fuck this thing, ya know? We lit his ass up."

"Okay, but how did we end up 'allies' with the Bugs?"

"Yeah, that was weird. Hopkins is still looking at it, but it looks like they have a translator-assist mechanism that learns our language as they hear it. So as our fight got closer and closer in quarters, they started shouting things in English."

"What were they shouting?"

"Mostly things like 'shoot it.'"

"'It' being the Bohemalo."

"That's what we figured." Moretti shrugged and took a swig from his suit's canteen hose. "Next thing I know, that one over there is climbing over its dead comrades and grabbing the LT. She was fucking hypnotized or some shit, I don't know. But the Bohemalo had these trippy light things, and the bug knew not to look at it. So we figure, fuck it, we'll take the bug back with us and come back with some real firepower if we need to. So you land, we load up. We take off and then..."

"It grabs us and flings us into the trees."

"Is that what happened? It was hard to see. Plus, I was too busy watching my life flash by to sightsee. It was mostly PT."

"Best I can tell, yes," Enoha said, rolling her eyes at the rest of Moretti's commentary. She shook her head again, trying to get her mind past the improbability of the sequence of events as they'd happened. But they *had* happened. "It grabbed us by the tail and flung us into the trees."

"There you go, ma'am," Baker said as he clipped the bandage closed. "You should be good to go. Just keep an eye on it if we have to do much more walking."

"Which we probably will," Moretti put in. "Since the Bohemafucker broke our Bat."

"Thanks, Lance Corporal Obvious," Enoha said. She rolled over from where she'd been lying on her belly and sat up. "That feels great, Baker, thank you," she added. A glance over at Callahan showed that her fellow lieutenant was still deep in discussions with the Bug. Enoha let out a sigh.

"Let's get some food going," she said, "while we wait for your commander to figure out what we're going to do next."

Enoha had just finished mixing her instant coffee ration in with her instant cocoa ration to make a surprisingly decent field mocha when Callahan stomped over and flopped down with an exhausted sigh next to her.

"Rough day?" Enoha asked, blowing the steam off her mocha before risking a mouth burn on the scalding beverage.

Callahan let out a dry laugh that held very little humor. "What is that?" she asked. "Smells good."

"Field mocha," Enoha said, handing the cup over. "Here. Be careful. It's hot."

"I don't want to take yours."

"I'll make another. Go on, you look like you need it more than I do." *Which is saying something, considering I had a . . . what did he call it? Bohemalo? Smack me out of the air today and break my Bat.*

"This guy is a grade-A, Galaxy-class pain in my ass," Callahan said as she lifted the mocha and sipped. Her eyes widened, and then rolled backward and she moaned in a way that had Enoha snickering.

"Careful," she said. "Your Raiders hear you making sounds like that, they're going to start thinking of you as more than the LT."

"Fuck, that's good," Callahan said. "How the fuck did you do this?"

"Seriously? Coffee ration, cocoa ration, water. You went to the same survival training I did, they didn't teach you this trick?"

"I must have blocked it out." Callahan lifted the mocha and drank again.

"So what bug is up our new ally's ass?" Enoha asked as she got started mixing up another mocha for herself. "See what I did there?"

"Yeah, you're a fucking comedienne. I don't honestly know. He's just ranting and raving how we have to hike back to the outpost right now. I finally told him that we've got wounded, and plenty of ammo to defend our position until it's light if necessary. Even against that..."

"Bohemalo," Enoha supplied.

"What?"

"Bohemalo. Like a cross between a behemoth, an elephant, and a buffalo. Don't look at me like that, Moretti named it."

"Of fucking course he did."

"Anyway, if the Bohemalo comes back?"

"If it comes back, we've still got Hoosier's rig. I don't care how big you are, a few of those '75s to the face is going to fucking hurt..." Callahan trailed off, her mocha mug hovering closer to her lips as her eyes stared sightlessly into the tree line.

"No argument there, but Calla... that thing *grabbed the Bat and pulled us down out of the air.* I don't—I'm not even sure how to think about that."

"I noticed that, too. Or at least, my gut did."

"So what the fuck does that mean? And what the fuck do we do about it?"

Callahan shrugged and drank the last of her field mocha. "I have no idea what it means. But we're going to camp here for the night, regardless of what our asshole ally says. Rest up, treat our wounded, figure out a route back to Sigma so we can let higher know about this Behema... Bohem..."

"Bohemalo."

Callahan sighed. "Fucking Moretti."

"What happened back there? Why did you turn and help us when the Bohemalo showed up?"

After getting fixed up, Enoha'd grabbed a spare weapon and limped over to the fire to get some chow, and saw Callahan there, talking with the Bug. Judging by the expression on Callahan's face, she wasn't pleased with the flow of the conversation, so Enoha had abandoned her ration and worked her way around the fire to come up alongside her friend. If Calla didn't want her there, she'd tell her to leave. If she didn't, it meant that she appreciated the support.

Callahan didn't say a word, just kept staring down at the Bug. Anger creased her face and turned her knuckles white as she crossed her arms over her chest.

"*Crackle pop* are bad. Criminals. Inmates. We good. Bugs good. Guards. Planet is prison for criminals." Enoha obviously couldn't read the Bug's body language, but it did seem to be shifting around a lot. The facets of its compound eyes glittered in the firelight as it scanned the tree line around them.

"Why did you attack us in the first place, then?"

"Did not attack. Retaliated. Aliens shot my people when doors open. We respond, think you enemy here to help *crackle pop*."

"That doesn't explain what you did to the research station and why you tortured the scientists."

"Much same. We go to facility to ask aliens to leave. Ships dangerous. *Crackle pop* can steal. Escape. Aliens refuse. *Crackle pop* attack next day. We go help, keep criminals on planet, aliens shoot us, too. We defend ourselves against both."

Callahan's eyes narrowed. "You tortured the scientists. I saw their bodies." Enoha swallowed against the rising nausea in her throat and kept herself, barely, from growling. Sigma Base hadn't been pretty when they arrived.

"Alien is mistaken. We study alien after it die. We try to save, but hurt too much. Die fast. We analyze species. Never seen before."

Enoha didn't buy it but held herself back from saying so. This was Callahan's show, her command, so she'd keep her mouth shut. Even when everything about the explanation screamed "bullshit" to her.

"So, what is our relationship now?" Callahan's voice remained empty and professional, giving no hint as to whether or not she believed a word the Bug said.

"Ally. Truce. Alien not hurt us, we not hurt alien. Wait for sunrise. Go to your command post, you leave. We stay, keep watch over *crackle pop."* Once again, the Bug shifted, looking past Enoha into the shadows beneath the tree line.

"What's to stop you from using us to get into our command post and killing everyone inside?"

"Will not. Allies. I leader. Send word to all: stand down, no kill, no harm. Protect. Keep safe. Truce, Alien."

"Lies..."

Before she could form a conscious thought, Enoha spun, bringing her plasma rifle up to her shoulder, aiming at the deep, almost subliminal sound that shivered out of the darkness at them. Behind her, the Bug began to shriek, but she didn't register words within its noise. She did hear Callahan shouting orders to the remaining Raiders as they, too, aimed their weapons into the murky gloom.

"What the fuck was that?" Gunny's voice, not far away.

"It lies..." The voice from the dark came once more, the sound making a weird reverb as it collided with the trees and boulders that formed the perimeter of their camp.

Enoha kept her muzzle on target, but glanced over at Callahan, who took a step forward.

"Who are you?" Callahan shouted, swatting away one of the Bug's limbs when it would have reached for her armored hand. "What are you talking about? What lies?"

"No!" the Bug shrieked. "No! Do not speak! Do not listen!"

"You are... deceived. The *crackle pop* are not criminals, we are prisoners of war. Taken illegally." The words took on more shape and form with every syllable. As if someone were training an assistive-translation device to speak in an unfamiliar language.

Callahan swatted the bug's grasping limbs away and turned with white fury on her face. "Who is that? What are they talking about?"

"No listen! I am your friend! I tell you truth! I only help!"

Come to think of it, that's how the Bug sounds, too. Enoha thought. *Only there's no way that tiny body is creating a sound like that. Too deep, and too... organic sounding to be something recorded or electrically amplified...*

"It lies," the voice said, and something small and brick-like arced toward them, catching the flickering firelight as it soared first up, and then down to thud into the dirt near Callahan's boots.

Nguyen's backup radio, still smeared with blood. Enoha watched Callahan pause, then slowly bend.

"No!" the Bug shrieked, reaching for her again with four of its six limbs.

Enoha swiveled, aimed, and stroked the trigger once to send a plasma bolt sizzling into the dirt between Callahan and the Bug.

"Ally or not," Enoha said, her voice icy as the Bug swiveled its compound eyes to focus on her, "you do not touch her."

"Call your comrades," the voice from the darkness said. "Learn the lies of the unclean."

For just a split second, Callahan met Enoha's eyes, and Enoha knew they shared the same sick feeling of dread slowly opening into a pit in each of their stomachs. Then Callahan blinked, picked up the radio, and keyed the mic in one smooth motion.

"Sigma Base, this is Charlie Six. Status?"

"*LT?* Thank God! Listen! Bugs . . . everywhere. Killing . . . everyone! Pretty sure . . . I'm all that's left . . ." Enoha felt the blood drain from her face as she met Callahan's widening eyes.

"Hold on, Danny-boy!" Moretti shouted. Enoha hadn't seen him approach, but he was suddenly there, leaning over Callahan's shoulder. "We're coming for ya!"

"That . . . Moretti? That's a . . . no-go, LT. There's bugs all over. I don't . . . have long. Bleeding out, and they're close. Gonna . . . find me. I'm hidden . . . one of the buildings. They found . . . everyone else." The radio crackled, and Enoha thought she heard a cough, or maybe a pain-soaked laugh. "You know what they didn't . . . find? My . . . ordnance."

"Larson?" Callahan's hand tightened around the bloody radio. "Larson!"

"Semper . . . Fi . . . motherfuckers!"

The sun burst over the horizon. Or at least, that's what it looked like as a distant explosion bloomed brightly enough to turn the night sky as bright as morning. Enoha just had time to gasp before the wall of roaring sound and the shock wave hit them hard enough to make her stumble.

"Semper Fi, Danny-boy," Moretti whispered as Callahan dropped the radio, her eyes like chips of ice. She turned, jaw tight, and in one smooth motion drew her sidearm and shot the still-shrieking Bug directly in one of its bulbous, compound eyes. It gasped, and then collapsed into a clicking, twitching pile of exoskeletal debris.

Callahan kept her weapon drawn and turned back to look into the darkness as the light from Danny's explosion faded from the sky.

"Show yourself," she ordered, her voice cracking like a whip striking flesh.

Slowly, a figure emerged from the closest trees. It moved with a fluid grace that belied its gargantuan size, and Enoha found herself struggling not to gape as the monstrous creature that smacked her Bat out of the air stepped into the flickering ring of firelight.

Fuck, it got close, Enoha realized, belatedly raising her pulse rifle back up to her shoulder. *Look at the size of that thing! How did none of us hear it?*

Callahan stared cooly at the Bohemalo. If she felt any of Enoha's awe, she didn't show it. Her jaw remained clenched with anger, her sidearm held low, but ready.

"You can understand me?" Callahan asked.

"Yes."

"Explain yourself. Why are you here?"

"War with Kyriel."

Enoha snorted softly. "Aren't we all?" she asked, speaking low. But the Bohemalo heard, because it swung its giant head to regard her with huge, intelligent—*but not friendly*—eyes.

"You war with them, too?"

Callahan's eyes narrowed. "Yes," she said. "For many years now. Why?"

The Bohemalo looked back at Callahan, then down at the fallen Bug. Its face changed, just slightly, as if the muscles beneath the tough-looking skin contracted to change what passed for a Bohemalo facial expresson. *Like a sneer*, Enoha realized.

"The Tanthupla are allied with Kyriel." The Bohemalo's words started out slowly, still in that low, rumbling tone. But with every word, the explanation picked up speed and intensity. As if the Bohemalo were becoming more and more passionate about the subject.

"Tanthupla experiment on *crackle pop* to make chemical weapons. Compliance chemical. Make slaves for war. Experiments make my... my male offspring... my sons mad, bloodthirsty. Cannot control urges. Irrational. Only feel bloodlust. They go to fight when they hear sounds of battle."

"So that's what they're called: Tanthupla," Callahan said. She didn't relax her posture in the slightest. "If they do experiments and make you irrational, why are you able to stand here and talk to me?"

"Affects female different. Brain structure not same."

"Right. You said sons. Only the males are susceptible?"

"Don't know. Maybe. Maybe Tanthupla just don't use compliance on me."

"Why not?" Callahan asked, suspicion thick in her tone.

The Bohemalo's expresson changed again, and Enoha could swear that it sounded almost wry. "Am mother. Too valuable to risk."

"So why talk now?" Enoha demanded, ignoring the look Callahan shot her way. "You knocked my fucking Bat out of the sky!"

"Was trying to kill Tanthupla commander. Your Bat was collateral damage. Came to kill all. Heard talk. Heard lies. Realized Tanthupla not truly your ally. Maybe we help each other."

"So now you're offering a truce, too?"

"Yes."

"And I'm supposed to take that seriously?" Callahan's hands tightened on her sidearm to the point where the metal grip groaned in protest. "You killed Darken as he was running for us! You took his head off!"

"Even the most rational in battle make poor decisions. Your Darken was trying to kill me in my pursuit of the commander. I retaliated. But I must do what is necessary to escape, especially now—"

"Why now?"

Silence for a long moment, broken only by the sound of leaves rustling in the night breeze.

"They took my children. For a very long time, they took them all. Every son. But now . . . now there is *she*."

"She? Another female? You have a daughter?"

"The Tanthupla will kill her or enslave her as they have done to me. I must protect her, as I have not been able to protect my sons. It is imperative. The loss of your warrior is regrettable."

"*Regrettable?* What the hell—"

Rustling all around. The Bohemalo's head snapped up, moving faster than Enoha would imagine possible for a being of that size.

"Tanthupla. Here! This is a trap. You must call your ship. We must escape. The Tanthupla come!"

Callahan looked around, listening to the rustling.

"Gunny! Get everyone emplaced for a fight. I want Moretti up on that boulder with the heavy. Eno, stay with me." Enoha nodded as Callahan locked eyes with her for a split second, and then returned her nod. "As for you," she said, turning back to the Bohemalo, "we'll discuss a truce and getting off this hellhole of a planet once we survive this. But you'll have to go through my superiors. I can't guarantee you shit."

"Understood." The Bohemalo ducked her head in what looked like an odd mimicry of their nods, and turned to face the tree line just as the first wave of Bugs boiled through.

A plasma bolt sizzled from the trees to their left.

"Moretti!" Callahan snapped on their local command net.

"On it." Moretti responded, and he swiveled the heavy machine gun in that direction, opening up with a spit of flame. A high-pitched screech came drifting out of the trees, and suddenly dozens of Bugs began to pour out of the jungle around them.

The Bohemalo let out a growl that the translator didn't catch, and she lunged forward, her long-taloned forelimbs extended. With sweeping slashes, she carved a bloody swath through the bugs ahead of them, even as Moretti mowed them down on her right.

"Tell your Raiders, cover my left," the Bohemalo said through the network. "Your Moretti has my right."

Enoha heard Callahan shouting orders to that effect and left her to figure it out. Soon enough, she could hear the distinctive sound of plasma bolts echoing out to the left as well, and someone threw a grenade in that direction.

"Frag out!"

"Hang on, concussion inbound!" Enoha warned the Bohemalo, though she wasn't quite sure why. The Bohemalo let out a sternum-vibrating hum and crouched as the grenade exploded, throwing wood shrapnel through the Bug bodies—alive and dead—that littered the forest floor.

"Go!" Enoha yelled then, as the Bugs reeled from the blast. The Bohemalo surged forward, stomping through the mass of Bugs, crushing them under her gargantuan weight as she surged toward the perimeter of their camp.

Or what had been the perimeter.

"Hopkins! Get over here and help me get this radio working! We gotta get word to the orbital!" Callahan yelled. "The rest of you, stay with the Bohemalo and help her keep those fuckers off of us!"

"Got it," Enoha responded to Callahan's barked orders. The Bohemalo hummed in response and crouched as she pulled back toward the center of the group. Off to her left, from his perch in a nest of boulders, Moretti opened fire, raining hate down on the swarm of Bugs that now surged toward them.

Enoha lifted her own rifle and joined in. She didn't have quite the volume of fire as Moretti's heavy rig, but her aim was good, and she had drilled enough to be a pretty decent shot for an aviator.

The world contracted down to the pinpoint focus of combat. Aim, fire, check charge, re-aim, fire . . . The thudding vibrations of Moretti's rig blurred into the background, as did the Bohemalo's hums and growls. Distantly, Enoha registered Callahan's voice shouting something, but none of it was directed at her, and the Bugs just kept coming. So she just kept shooting.

Aim. Fire. Check charge. Re-aim. Fire . . .

It wasn't enough. Her charge was running low. Moretti's rig barked out in short blasts, rather than an unending stream. *He must be low on ammo, too.* The Bohemalo drew closer, close enough that Enoha could see her skin rippling every time she moved.

"There's too many," Enoha said softly. "We aren't going to make it out of this."

"This is the problem with the honorless Tanthupla. There is always more. I am proud to die beside honorable warriors."

"Semper Fi," Moretti said as he opened up with the rig for one more long, burring blast before the rig fell entirely silent. The Bohemalo snarled and swiped out at the Bugs as they reeled back from the heavy machine-gun fire, but Enoha could see that her movements were slow, fatigued.

She lifted her rifle and fired another shot. Then another. Then she pulled the trigger and the plasma rifle let out the low tone that indicated it had reached the end of its charge. She was empty.

"Semper Fi," she said, letting the rifle drop on its sling and drawing the pistol she held in her vest. Below her, the Bohemalo let out an enraged roar as the Bugs began to swarm, crawling up her tree-trunk legs with their skittering, spindly limbs.

"Fuck no!" Enoha yelled, and began firing her pistol, trying to clear them off. Before too long, though, that weapon clicked empty, too. She didn't allow herself to think. She tossed the pistol away and drew her knife, then stabbed the first Bug she could reach. It fell, but another came scrambling up behind it. She could hear Moretti cursing as she stabbed that one, too, and lashed out with a booted kick to the one behind it. The Bohemalo bellowed again, trying to scrape the Bugs off with her huge taloned forelimbs. She decapitated several of them, and their bodies fell to the ground beside Enoha... but more kept coming.

Enoha wanted to say something to her, wanted to call out to Moretti, wanted to check on Callahan and ask what the fuck was taking so long, but she couldn't. All she could do was stab and kick and fight not to let the Bugs overwhelm her as they fought to down the Bohemalo beneath their swarming weight.

Her knife got stuck. She tried to pull it out. It wouldn't budge. Another Bug rushed up. Enoha kicked it, but it grabbed her boot, pulling her down. She hit hard on her shoulder and had to scramble to catch herself. The Bug wouldn't let go of her boot, and she felt her balance slipping—

Something grabbed her. The world tilted sideways. The sky lit up in blinding white an instant before something huge came down over her, sending her hurtling down a long tunnel into black oblivion.

"Ow. Fuck."

"Eno?"

Enoha blinked, wincing as pain rushed in from every cell in her body. Even her hair hurt. Wincing didn't help, either, and her head began to throb. She went to open her eyes, only to realize that they were already open, and she couldn't see a thing.

"Callahan?" she asked, her voice like sandpaper over a rusted-out fifty-five-gallon drum.

"Yeah, girl. It's me. How do you feel?"

"Like a three-day-old corpse. What the fuck happened? And...I can't see."

Callahan's humorless chuckle reached out to her, slightly muffled. "I don't think you're blind. It's dark as fuck under here."

"Under where?"

"Heh. She said 'underwear.'"

"Oh, cool, Moretti's here in the dark, too."

"Yeah, Gunny and Hopkins and Baker, too. She grabbed us all when the orbital strike came in." Callahan sounded exhausted, her tone soaked in pain.

"She ... the Bohemalo? She grabbed us?"

"Rolled us under her body as the munitions started to rain down, ma'am." That was Gunny's voice, off to her left. Enoha tried to turn her head to look that way, but realized that she actually couldn't. Something heavy held her in place, pressing her helmet toward her right shoulder. As soon as she thought it, pain flooded into her mind, along with throat-closing panic.

"We're trapped," Enoha whispered, hoping the others couldn't hear as she worked to push back against the fear. "She's too heav—"

Something shifted. The oppressive weight holding her in place eased. A thin line of light flooded in, and then illuminated another monstrous, huge, but oddly graceful figure.

The daughter.

"Crawl out. Pilot, get the LT," Gunny said. "I think her legs are hurt. Baker, you get Hopkins. C'mon, Moretti."

"I'm okay," Callahan said. She lay pressed in the dirt not far from Enoha. Enoha looked over at her friend's filthy, blood-and-dirt-covered face, and gave her a tiny smile.

"Yeah, you are," Enoha said, unable to contain the sudden effervescent joy and euphoria that surged through her. She knew it was just survival adrenaline, but damn, it was always a heady cocktail!

Though they moved as quickly as they could manage, the six of them were more than a little banged up, so it took a few moments to fully crawl out from beneath the Bohemalo's mangled corpse. Once they had, the corpse's daughter set her mother's body down with something that might have been reverence before turning to them.

Enoha felt her euphoria drain away, and she reached for her missing pistol only to remember that it was dead anyway. They were out of ammo, having expended it on hundreds of the Bugs that now lay piled in clumps all throughout the clearing. And that was *before* Callahan had called in the orbital strike.

The Bohemalo reached over and removed something from her mother's body, her graceful movements slow and heavy. *She's mourning*, Enoha abruptly realized. *That's her mother.*

"She is dead."

The voice was the same as the dead Bohemalo's . . . because the daughter now held the same translator in her forelimb. Enoha looked up, and then up some more, trying to meet this creature's eyes.

"Yes," she said, feeling her throat tighten. "She saved us."

"My mother would not have sacrificed herself without a reason."

Silence. Out of the corner of her eye, Enoha saw Moretti's hand reaching for one of the long knives he kept on his person.

"Are you allies of the Tanthulpa?"

A sharp, humorless bark of laughter cracked through the clearing, and Moretti surged forward, ripping his helmet off as he went. He swung both hands out to the side, turning in a full circle, one hand holding a knife, the other holding his helmet. "What do *you* think, bitch? Does this fucking *look* like we're allies?"

The Bohemalo turned its alien regard on Moretti, who stopped suddenly and stared back, apparently undaunted by her sheer size and destructive potential.

"What of the Kyriel? Do you serve them?"

"Fu—*mmph!*" Gunny's gloved hand wrapped hard around Moretti's unhelmeted face, dragging him backward until his legs buckled and he sat down hard in the churned-up mud. More muffled curses followed, but true to form, Gunny appeared unmoved and unrattled, merely looking over at Callahan.

"No," she said, stepping forward with a decided limp. "No, we're not. We've been at war with them for a very long time. So long, that some say we're probably going to lose. We might, but if we do, we're sure as fuck going to go down swinging."

The Bohemalo stared at Callahan for a long moment, and then took a single step forward before crouching so that her giant eyes were level with Callahan's face. Enoha stepped up beside her friend, though without a weapon, she wasn't sure what she could do. But fuck if she wasn't going to be there.

"If you fight the Kyriel," the Bohemalo said slowly, her deep voice vibrating through the ground under their boots, "we can help you win."

* * *

After-Action Report
234 Velex-b Sigma Outpost
Kilo Company, Dark Horse Raider Battalion

Outpost VIPs: Deceased
Outpost Personnel: Deceased
Kilo Company: 95% casualties, combat ineffective

Summary:
    Discovered two new sentient life-forms
    Insectoid species, code name Bugs. Responsible for Outpost casualties. Status: Hostile.
    Reptilioid species, code name Bohemalos. One individual recovered. Possesses intel on Kyriel. Status: High Value.

    Enroute to BN HQ on *TNS OKINAWA*. Request Intel/Xeno debriefing and further orders. Scientific outpost on 243 Velex-b destroyed by Bugs, likely by means of treachery, given the physical evidence left behind (no sign of outpost perimeter breach, etc.). Bugs appear to act in a manner consistent with allies/subordinates of the Kyriel, per intel provided by Bohemalo individual aboard. Request immediate debriefing with Dark Horse BN command, Intel, and Xeno to verify intel and determine path forward.

                    Lieutenant Callahan
                    Kilo Company

Concursante

Jason Cordova

The basis of the Explorer exam was simple: observe, record, and survive.

That last bit, though—surviving the seventy-two hours? Always the hardest part.

Even being permitted to take the exam was a sort of survival of the fittest. The adjudicators of the test accepted only ten percent of the applicants. And fewer than twenty percent of those lucky few who were selected survived the Dome. And among the survivors, barely half were given the opportunity to take the oath of the Explorers. In fact, it was becoming so difficult to pass the exams that many people simply gave up applying.

All these statistics meant little to me at the moment. I was in the midst of an artificially created biome, running for my life from some unseen creature that had ambushed us the moment we stepped out of the lift, and didn't have a lot of time to think about the odd vagaries of *why* I'd been selected in the first place.

I slid down an embankment and winced as my foot caught on an exposed root, twisting my ankle slightly. It didn't stop my progress, though it did slow me down a bit. Above and behind me I could hear panicked breathing and cursing as the surviving members of my exam group struggled to keep up. I was not about to wait around for them, especially after what had happened to Carino.

During the written exam four days before, I'd heard one of the unofficial rules of an Explorer muttered by an adjudicator: *You don't have to be faster than the predator, merely faster than the bait.*

I *really* didn't want to be bait.

Reaching the bottom of the ravine, I tried to move as quickly as I could away from the steep incline and into the thick underbrush of the jungle. The overhead canopy created shadows here, and it was slow going as I struggled to move through the underbrush without making too much noise. Somewhere in the distance I heard a startled cry, a scream, then . . . nothing.

Another one down, I thought. I had no idea how many others were still alive.

There was no way, with my ankle and level of exhaustion, I was going to be able to keep it up much longer. The pace I'd been setting was brutal, even by Explorer standards. I needed time to recoup, rest, and maybe figure out what to do next. Unfortunately, with some unknown alien creature hot on my trail, my options were limited. There was no way to outrun it. Others who hadn't been injured had tried, and I vaguely recalled their dying screams from somewhere out in the jungle.

There. In the middle of the ravine stood a massive kapok tree, one of those bizarre specimens that did very well on just about every human-settled world. At the base of it was a small alcove in the exposed roots, almost too small for a normal-sized human to fit into. However, thanks to growing up in the *bairro* and being somewhat poor, I was short and thin compared to the others taking the exam. I knew I could fit. Easily, too. Best of all, there were deep shadows there to hide me, all while giving me a decent view of the ridgeline I'd just fallen down. Whatever was tracking me, I would see it long before it saw me.

Crawling inside, I checked for any spiders or insects that could make my already threatened life even more miserable. I slid behind one of the larger roots of the tree and watched as another candidate went running past my hiding spot. He either didn't recognize the tiny alcove for what it was or, more likely, was simply too busy running for his life to care.

As quickly and suddenly as he'd appeared, he vanished out of view, his heavy footsteps fading as he sprinted south. I waited in silence before a terrifying scream erupted from the direction he'd gone. It cut off almost as abruptly as it had begun. The scream had sounded . . . *wet* at the end. There'd been no other sound after. None was needed. It was obvious what had happened.

Shivering, I pressed farther back into the shadows. As I sat there, it slowly dawned on me just how *tired* I was. Every single muscle in my body ached from the constant running. My stomach gurgled, reminding me I hadn't eaten since before the test began, and my hands were shaky. As slowly and quietly as I could, I reached into my pocket to find a hydrator bar. I had three, which would have been enough to keep me alive for the entire seventy-two hours of the test. A quick bite of the solidified nutrient bar and I felt much better almost immediately. I eagerly devoured the entire thing, not bothering to ration it. I'd been running on fear and adrenaline for so long now, I'd almost forgotten what food even tasted like—though I would never willingly call a hydrator bar *food*.

Sustenance might even be stretching it.

I pocketed the trash. Explorers tried not to disturb the natural fauna of a planet, and litter was frowned upon. Littering on a planet we were supposed to be evaluating was a PR nightmare. Plus, I didn't want to give whatever was hunting me an easy time of it. Of course, one could argue the tectonic probes launched into potential habitable worlds counted as litter, but those who made that argument weren't cut out to be Explorers, so their opinions were pretty much worthless.

As I pulled out a second bar and munched on that, I made a quick personal inspection. There were no visible wounds anywhere, though I had an aching pain in my ankle from twisting it when I'd fallen into the ravine. My left knee throbbed, but I couldn't remember hurting it. Probably when I ran from whatever had decapitated Carino over forty-eight hours ago. I had blood coating one of my green BDU—battle dress uniform—sleeves, but I was fairly certain it wasn't mine.

After a moment I remembered that the same thing that had removed Carino's head had also ripped the head off another man, whose name I didn't know. He stepped out the lift first. It had been such a hectic two minutes that I'd almost forgotten about the first man. The blood spray had splashed across the rest of us, a sort of gory starter pistol that had begun my wild escape into the dense jungle beyond.

It's strange how trauma affects the memory.

I'd lost my helmet and my rifle the day before, when I'd tumbled down a brush-strewn hill. If I survived, that might cause me to have some of my points deducted. There was no way of knowing where they'd ended up. My boots looked good, as did my pants. I had a tear in my shirt near the shoulder from snagging it on a branch, but it didn't appear to have broken the skin. Somehow, I was in one piece.

With nowhere left to run and my hunger and thirst temporarily sated, I settled into the small alcove at the base of the kapok tree and awaited my death with what little dignity I could muster.

My name is Edison Loret de Jacinto. My friends and family call me Edi.

Life on Nuevo Aires was tough for those of us who lived in the *bairro*, the workers' sections in the major cities on the planet. My father worked as a steelworker in a mill, and my mama was a substitute teacher. While I wouldn't say we were poor—we always had food, something not a lot of my friends could claim—we definitely weren't part of the *Nuevistas*, the ruling-class wealthy.

Well, they weren't really the ruling class, but it felt like it sometimes.

It was hard, but we were pretty happy. I had both my parents, which isn't something a lot of the other kids could claim. One of the other things that made life tough on Nuevo Aires was a lack of good jobs for those of us coming out of primary school. Sure, university was an option—if you were rich or had perfect grades, or played sports. Since I was none of those, my best hopes had been for getting a job with my father's company when I turned eighteen. Unfortunately, that'd been everyone else's hope as well, and there were no openings anywhere when I finished school.

So I did what every other kid in my district did...I waited for a job opening.

But one never came.

After five years of waiting, I finally had to make a choice. We had only so many years after finishing primary school to find work before we had to get on the dole. Doing this meant I would never have another shot at finding real work, having a shot at making something of myself. Going on the dole was pretty much a kiss of death. It was the last thing I wanted, but I was at a loss. All of my friends were going on it, but I didn't want to do that. I had hopes, dreams. But what could I do to give me a chance at a better future?

Two weeks before I had to register for the dole, my mother reminded me how much I'd wanted to be an Explorer as a child. It'd been all I spoke about as a little boy. Those childhood dreams had been tempered as I grew older, and more important things like girls and money took over my thoughts.

As far-fetched as my chances of making it as an Explorer were, it was better than the other option. Being an Explorer gave those of us without a guaranteed career the opportunity to do something with our lives. It was dangerous, sure. But so was staying in the *bairro* with no options to get out. With no other opportunities before me and time running out before I was required to go on the dole, I applied to take the exams.

One of my sisters asked me why we used Explorers to seek out new life and habitable worlds. She was worried for me. After all, successful applicants were few and far between. My death, it seemed, was a foregone conclusion.

When humanity first started exploring the systems to expand into, drones and automated sensors were used, and there was absolutely zero risk. The drones would come in, feed data to a relay satellite, and analysts would then dig into what was found to determine what the planet was best suited for—be it colonization, agriculture, mining, whatever. The system worked, too.

For about six years. Then... Plagamundo happened.

That's what it's called now. Back then, the planet was called Nuevo Muncie. The details of what precisely went down are still classified, even after all this time, but there is a pretty good theory of what happened. And nobody in the government ever actually denied said theory, so...

The drones missed *something* during their surveys. Only... nobody knew it at the time. Initial scans were promising, so it was deemed a good fit for habitation and colonization. One million colonists were shipped there as well as constructed prefabbed housing and buildings to start a new life. Everything was great for about six days, until the seventh day when every single one of the colonists fell sick and died within twenty-four hours. One million people, dead, in a single day. No clue. No cure. Nothing.

The planners didn't know what had happened. More drones were sent in, and nothing could determine what had actually taken place. They sent in another cluster of colonists—a much smaller one this time—with the same results. One thousand more, dead, without any outward trace on their bodies, exactly seven days after landing. A bio decontamination team followed and they performed a mass autopsy on every dead colonist. It was then they discovered that the drones missed something not in the air, but in the soil.

Drones could do a lot of things, but they could not test for some random toxic anomaly in the soil that only activated when it came into contact with certain mucous membranes in the lungs, which then sent a neurotoxin straight to the brain. The results? A viral hemorrhagic stroke that was one hundred percent fatal.

In order to avoid repeating Plagamundo, something had to be done. Humanity could not afford to stop seeding the stars, but new precautions were needed. After much hemming and hawing for almost a solid decade, a solution was born. A dangerous one, but safer. Thus, the Gasparan Explorers were commissioned into being.

One life versus a thousand? A million? The government jumped on board with this plan quickly. A single Explorer was more reliable on the ground than a drone. It wasn't safer, true, but it was more reliable. Drones couldn't detect what a failing body was able to find . . . even if it meant through illness, injury, or death. Explorers wore wrist comms that tracked their vitals, which was then relayed to geosynchronous satellites orbiting above. This way if something happened, someone would know *how* it happened and adapt accordingly.

But they learned very quickly that the testing process needed to be rigorous. The exams were created, then the Dome in Cidade Azula to host the testing process was built. The Dome allowed the adjudicators to design any sort of world environment they wanted within, and removed almost all the safeguards to make certain the proper candidates passed.

This winnowed down the numbers even further—which was for the best.

But . . . as always, the road to hell is paved with good intentions.

The exams became spectacles. Money was to be made, and adjudicators of the exam quickly realized there was a section of the populace who wanted to watch the danger and excitement of the *concursante* (the contestant) running in the Dome and trying to stay alive while taking the test. Ticket sales skyrocketed, and then it became the must-watch show on the vid network. Gambling focused on the exam, and schools started to open for those who wanted to try and become an Explorer.

It created a very dark underbelly, where kids either were accepted into the Explorers and then indebted to those who'd paid for their pre-exam schooling, or they died in the Dome. And even after some of them survived and made it to the selection process, they were washed out of the program. These poor unfortunates would end up as indentured servants to the schools for arguably the rest of their miserable lives. It made death within the Dome preferable.

I'd heard of a few even being turned into Thinkermen, which was enough to almost cause me to reconsider the exam completely.

I didn't go to any of the schools. None would accept me. I was small, after all. Skinny, short. The physical requirements of the exams, according to the school administrators, were too great for someone of my diminutive stature. Those they did accept were all bigger, stronger. So I had to find my own way to get accepted into the exam process.

Before I took my test, I read up on the few survivors who'd been washed out. Most people read about how the successes went on to make names for themselves as famous Explorers. I wanted to know why some of the survivors weren't approved. It was only after reading the story of a *concursante* named Miguel when I realized the survival part wasn't the challenge—it was doing the difficult job of being an Explorer *while* surviving. He had forgotten the mantra of the Explorers during his hectic seventy-two hours within the Dome.

Observe, report, and survive.

. . . for seventy-two hours.

I passed the initial exams easily enough and was chosen to proceed with the testing. For some reason, I thought I'd be different from the other *concursantes*, and I would simply rip through everything with ease until it came time for the Dome. I was smarter than the meatheads who'd taken the initial written exams with me. This fed the delusion I would do well, coast through, and succeed. Of course, this didn't turn out to be the case. Instead, it seemed my destiny was to die in the Dome, another failure in a long list of young punks who thought they would cruise through this when signing up.

No. I'm not dying here. And I'm not failing, either. I'm going to be an Explorer, and Explorers don't quit. Explorers observe, record, and survive.

The strength in my inner defiance while repeating the Explorer's mantra caught me off guard, it made me think. Just dying, going through the motions of life? Anybody could do that. Most people did.

But surviving? And not just surviving, but actually taking risks, accepting challenges, and rising above the station in life assigned to you? Facing a challenge head-on while finishing any given task? That was something not everyone did. Or even *could*, if given the opportunity.

Could I do this? Or did I just want to subsist on the government dole, a jobless voter, no hopes or future? Just another statistic in the *bairro*? Those were the questions. The answer was simple enough.

I had to finish the job if I wanted to be an Explorer, after all. And Explorers never quit.

Observe.

That part was actually pretty easy at the moment. Even deep inside my little hidey-hole at the base of the giant kapok tree I had a pretty good vantage point out into the clearing beyond, and the ridgeline past that. I could begin my tests here, then move out and explore. I checked my wrist comms—thankfully unbroken from my multiple falls. Testing the air, it was pretty obvious right out of the gate that the humidity in the Dome grew denser as the afternoon wore on. In my desperate scramble to stay alive for those first forty-eight hours, I hadn't taken note of the environment around me and had missed this. It was dense jungle foliage everywhere, with the smells and humidity designed to mimic random worlds an Explorer might come across.

The simulated planet was high in humidity. Oxygen was rich, which suggested dense foliage throughout the region, if not planet. It was very Earth-like, which meant it would be tagged for further exploration for potential colonization. Looking around, I couldn't see a nearby water source. There had to be one, though. Thick growth like this meant regular water, and unless there were torrential downpours on a regular basis and the soil was capable of storing it somehow, there would be water nearby.

Tapping in my notes, my eyes continued to flicker up and around, trying to see if any other life was out there. There were birds nearby, which sang and chirped noisily. There was no way to tell if they were predatory or not, so I marked it in my comms as "birds—unknown danger" and continued listening. There weren't any insects, which I found a bit odd. I'd expected mosquitoes in a place like this. With nothing but various bird species chirping and singing, I amended my note and decided to do a quick soil sample test.

I dug my scanner out of my hip pocket. Somehow it hadn't fallen out of my BDU during my mad scramble to evade whatever monster was hunting me. Silently thanking whichever saint my parents had lit a candle to before I set off for my test, I brushed it against the soil and took a quick sample. It took a moment before the readings appeared on my screen.

Favorable levels of nitrogen, phosphorous, and potassium. Good for growing crops. Moisture levels in the soil were adequate, too. Nothing out of the ordinary that the scanner could determine, minus a tiny bit of clay. I couldn't be certain if that was the soil of the simulated world, or remnants of Nuevo Aires. It didn't matter. I added it to my notes.

From out in the nearby jungle, a terrifying sound filled my ears. *Click. Click click. Clickclickclick.*

The noise was loud and instinctually *familiar*. I paused and held my breath, struggling to draw out some long-forgotten memory of vids I'd watched as a child in school. Seconds stretched into eternity as I racked my brain trying to figure out why the sound was so familiar before I remembered. Something out there was using echolocation, the same way dolphins did back on Earth. We didn't have dolphins on Nuevo Aires, but we'd seen enough vid replays of the aquatic mammalian from Earth back in primary school. Quite a few creatures in the universe hunted using it, but hardly any of them were dangerous to humans while on land. At least, from what we'd seen so far. Still, the test adjudicators had to capture something to use as "local fauna" while candidates attempted to do their jobs. Whatever they'd set loose in the terrarium was nearby, searching, and probably familiar with human behavior—which made it doubly dangerous.

Hunting me, and any other surviving candidates.

The adjudicators kept the testing groups small, and only ran the test every other year to discourage unqualified people from clogging up the testing pipeline. There were ten in my test group. Had been, rather. I hadn't seen any of them since I'd hidden inside the kapok tree.

During our mad scramble something *big* had ambushed the landing pad the moment we set foot inside the arena—undoubtedly to the enjoyment of the spectators seated in the arena stands just beyond the terrarium's forcefield bubble. None of us could hear them out there, but they could see and hear us just fine. They probably cheered when heads began to fly.

Me? I just remembered something big, and a *lot* of blood. And the confused look on Carino's face when his head was violently removed from his shoulders. Something *big* was out there, just out of visual range.

Hunting.

But if I wanted to be an Explorer, I needed to not only observe, but to *record*. Death could wait. Everything on a world an Explorer could potentially land on would try to kill us. From a gargantuan beast with fangs and claws, down to a tiny mosquito that could paralyze with a single bite, death was always at the ready. Expect death, hope for the best. That was the job. It's why the pay was so good, and why the test was so difficult.

But hope alone wasn't going to get me out of this mess.

The loud clicking noise faded into the distance somewhere off to my left. The creature was moving away. I kept my eyes tracking left and right, looking for any sign of the dangerous being in the testing area. Then, as suddenly as the original ambush had been, it stepped out into the clearing on an exposed ridge roughly one hundred meters away.

Immediately I began quietly tapping out more notes on the keypad as the monster continued moving, pausing only to sniff the air every few meters.

I already knew what it was. The universe was rife with them. The ultimate apex predator that humanity had stumbled upon on almost half of the colonized worlds, though nobody could quite figure out how they seemed to be on multiple planets throughout the explored universe. The scientific designation of the dangerous, highly intelligent creature was *Aich'Kandida*—but nobody ever called it that. Instead, people used the more popular term that arose soon after contact with the alien species—Star Demon.

Report.

Again, a difficult thing to accomplish given my circumstances, but not entirely impossible. Tapping my wrist comms, I tried to access the simulated satellites above planet. Theoretically, I'd deployed them before coming down from orbit to explore. Unfortunately, the canopy above was either too thick to transmit or, more than likely, the test adjudicators were making things difficult. I'd need to find an open clearing or climb a hill or a large tree in order to get clear of the interference.

The Star Demon was gone, moving away and over the edge of the ridgeline. There were no other observations I could make from the safety of the kapok roots. I needed to get out and explore the ten-square-kilometer dome—all while not dying. Which, admittedly, would take some doing. The Star Demon was out there, somewhere. Probably nearby. It had to know there were still survivors out here. Why else would it be lingering instead of going back to whatever the adjudicators were using as its makeshift den?

Aich'Kandida were smart, somewhere between 0.7 and 0.8 on the Hampson Sapience Scale. Almost as smart and aware as humans. Of course, I thought this was all scientific mumbo jumbo. If they were so smart, they'd have killed every Explorer who showed up on a world with them. A lot of vid reporters spouted off on the 'nets that the Star Demons were as smart as humans, maybe more, and were simply hiding just how intelligent they really were so they could infiltrate and kill us all.

Those darknet talk shows were too much for my non-tinfoil-hat-wearing brain.

There was no sign of this Star Demon, though, so I decided it was clear enough for me to do something other than hide. Moving quietly out from the cover of the kapok tree, I headed back toward the hill I'd stumbled down previously and started to climb back up. Once at the top, I paused and looked around. The birds in the trees atop the ravine continued to sing, either unconcerned about my passage or, more likely, not viewing me as the biggest threat in the jungle. Tapping my wrist comms, I continued to update my running log with notes about the local fauna and wildlife—notably, the birds.

They were loud but remained out of sight. Not that I could blame them. The Star Demon was a terrifying creature, and at a base level, every living being should be nervous whenever one was around.

Movement in the branches drew my gaze left. I spotted a *pollo verde*—more commonly known back on Earth as an iguana—moving slowly along a thick lower branch. They were everywhere on Nuevo Aires, brought in initially to serve as a food source for the early settlers. They were well-suited for the environment, long before real poultry was actually introduced. They'd taken to the jungles here and their population had exploded.

Plus, they were especially good barbecued and paired with a side of *ensaladilla rusa*.

However, seeing one in the Dome was a bit off-putting. They weren't native to any planet in the galaxy that we'd discovered thus far, indigenous only to Earth. This one had probably slipped in between builds for exams and had taken up residence inside the Dome. Still, I dutifully noted it and started to move on before I paused, uncertain. It took me a moment to realize the singing of the birds hadn't necessarily stopped, but had . . . changed somehow. There was a more rhythmic pattern to the chirping and singing now.

A tiny bird flew directly in front of my face and stopped, its miniscule wings beating furiously as it worked to hover mere inches from my nose. I stayed still. The petite thing wasn't a true bird, I realized as I carefully inspected it. Though superficially resembling a hummingbird, instead of a beak it had more of a mouth. Also, there were two eyes in front and one on each side of the head. No bird I'd ever seen before looked like that.

The *thing* chirped again, louder this time. Around me, more birds chirped in reply. The little bird analog sang again before pivoting in midair, its wings keeping it perfectly balanced as it continued to hover there. I slowly let out a breath as the bird appeared to look in the direction of the *pollo verde*.

The iguana continued to move along the branch, looking to climb higher into the tree. Or maybe it was searching for lunch. Either way, it didn't seem aware that it had drawn any attention. It stopped, tasted the air with its tongue, and continued to move along the branch. The iguana seemed to have found a beetle of some kind. It made a rapid diving movement and snatched up the beetle and began chewing, crushing the hard shell easily. I could hear the crunching sound over the shrill chirps of the surrounding birds.

The fast movement produced a rapid shift in behavior in the bird analog before me. The chirping of the winged animal changed to a shrill cry. Suddenly dozens of similar-looking bird analogs exploded out of the bushes and branches of nearby trees, none larger than my thumb, but all shimmering just as colorfully as the first. They began swarming in the air above, their shrill chirps growing louder with each passing second. Instinct told me to run, flee, but I stayed rooted where I was.

The iguana, though, must have recognized the danger and immediately began clambering up the large trunk of the tree. The movement drew the attention of the swarm. Dozens of them flitted past the iguana as it struggled to make an escape. It managed to get halfway up the trunk to the next branch before the swarm struck, each passing bird analog taking a bite out of the *pollo verde* as it flew past. The iguana struggled to defend itself but the winged creatures were too quick. Within a minute the stripped carcass of the iguana fell from the tree and landed on the ground, practically picked clean to the bone.

As quickly as they'd appeared, the swarm flew back into the thick branches of the trees around me. A few seconds later their songs began anew, hauntingly beautiful, a stark contrast to the violence I'd just observed.

Instead of panicking like I really wanted to, I began tapping more notes into my wrist comms. The bird analogs didn't *seem* like a threat to me but, if this was a potential colonization world, then they would be deadly to smaller, domesticated animals. I shivered at the idea of a swarm of those *things* getting hold of a baby pig.

Movement-based vision? I paused in my notes and thought about it some more. The first one *had* looked right at me. Either it hadn't viewed me as a threat or, more than likely, I was too big to be a meal. Considering they'd been no larger than my thumb, it made sense. However, they'd made short work of the iguana. Definitely something to make sure I noted.

Whatever this world is supposed to be simulating, make sure nobody brings a small dog during colonization.

I amended my previous note about the birds as well.

Definitely dangerous.

Clickclick click.

I froze. The Star Demon was nearby again. Time to vacate the area. But to where? Every person who'd run before had been easily chased down and brutally killed. Looking around, there wasn't any undergrowth where I could hide, nor a kapok tree to bury myself under. My eyes drifted over the carcass of the iguana, moved on, then came back to it. The birds were still singing in the trees, which meant the deadly little predators didn't view the Star Demon as much of a threat. Or, more than likely, didn't know any better.

But my eyes remained on the remnants of the iguana. Technically, it was an invasive species and probably not an official part of the test. It wasn't part of the simulated planet's evolutionary story, either here on Nuevo Aires, or whatever simulated world the Dome was supposed to be portraying. Most worlds did not offer a wide variety of divergent evolutionary traits. Was this one like all the others? Odds were good, but not great. Good enough would have to do.

The pseudo-birds—*bords?*—had only gone after the iguana when it had run. They hadn't even really noticed me when I froze. Were other creatures in the Dome similarly trained? Was there an evolutionary key I was missing here?

Clickclickclick.

It didn't matter. I was out of time.

No. It *did* matter.

Observe.

Explorers had an obligation, a duty. If I wanted to be one, then I had to do mine. Looking around, something interesting caught my eye. There was a small thornbush at the base of the tree where the *pollo verde* had met its gruesome death. Other than that, there weren't really any other places I could hide and still observe the Star Demon. The decision was easy and I hurried over to the thornbush. There was a tiny space between it and the tree. Once more my smaller frame served me well and I was able to squeeze in between without stabbing myself on one of the bright orange thorns.

With my sensor still in hand, I brushed the reader across one of the orange thorns. The readout was immediate. Toxic, in line with poison sumac, with tertiary contagion possibilities. Calamine lotion would help soothe some of the rash and itchiness, but only temporarily. No idea how long the symptoms would last. The sensor suggested I avoid contact with the plant until further studies could be made by remote scientists.

Good thing I didn't let one of those stab me, I thought and froze as the Star Demon slowly strode into the clearing, standing fully upright. It was the first time I'd truly gotten a good look at it. I really wished I hadn't.

The *Aich'Kandida* was over four meters in height, walking almost the same as a man. Claws as long as my arm gleamed wickedly in the patches of light that streamed through the thick canopy. The Star Demon was practically covered with corded muscle beneath its strange, reptilian blue skin. Its head almost didn't seem to fit its body, sitting atop a thick, slightly exaggerated neck. Long tendrils hung from the top of the head. Suspecting they might serve some sort of sensory purpose, I continued to take notes as slowly and quietly as possible.

Clickclickclick click.

The predatory muzzle of the Star Demon swung to the left, then right, searching. It knew something was close. After all, there'd been a lot of noise from this direction, courtesy of the pseudo-birds. It couldn't track the noise down, though. Snapping its fangs in frustration, it began slowly walking around the edge of the small clearing, clicking every few steps.

I stayed motionless behind the bush. The Star Demon *whuff*ed and swung its head low to the ground, dropping from its standing position to land solidly on the jungle floor. Its front claws dug into the soft ground with ease. It was the first time I'd seen it down on all fours. As far as I knew—or anyone else had recorded, for that matter—they were bipedal hunters, like humans. Were they more in line with the ursines back on Earth?

Observe.

Time was ticking. Not too much longer now until my seventy-two hours were up.

It quickly found the corpse of the iguana, and if the Star Demon had a facial expression, I would have classified it as *confused*. It sniffed it, then turned to look around. The clicking sound started anew. This close it was almost deafening. The face—for lack of a better term—of the Star Demon turned back toward me. For a moment I stared directly at where its eyes should have been.

It couldn't see me, I decided, confirmation of my earlier observations, making my heart beat rapidly in my chest. It had no eyes to see with, unlike the bird analogs that had devoured the iguana previously. It made me wonder if the exam was being based on what the adjudicators supposed the homeworld of the *Aich'Kandida* looked like. The Star Demon clearly used echolocation to help it hunt, and had been able to track the others when we'd fled into the jungle of the Dome. But up close, when I wasn't moving at all, with a partial obstruction in the way? The creature seemed to have trouble locking down my location. The Star Demon hadn't seen me when I'd been beneath the kapok tree, and couldn't track me down now. It *whuffed* again, swinging its head side to side as it scoured the ground near where I'd first fallen. Claws dug into the earth as the Star Demon continued to search in vain.

While the Star Demon was unable to find me, I couldn't stay in this position forever. Something was digging painfully into my rear, and those orange thorns of the thornbush were starting to press dangerously against my BDU. One wrong move and I could get stabbed, which could be bad. If I moved the branch away, though, the *Aich'Kandida* would hear me. My eyes slowly drifted back to its claws. They were long and sharp, designed to easily cut open their prey. I'd read about how on some worlds there'd been reports of said claws ripping through ballistic silks—which made sense, if anybody bothered to ask. Silks were designed to stop gunfire, not knives.

Or in this case, razor-sharp claws.

But could they hook, grasp prey? Were there opposable thumbs? That was an interesting question.

Risking a slight turn of my head, I tried to get a better view. Sure enough, they looked more for slashing than anything else, and were lacking any recognizable thumb, opposable or otherwise. Probably weren't good for gripping or hooking things, the way Earth-born ursines could. For the first time in my life I wished I could have afforded one of those fancy neural-uplink implants used to communicate with certain devices like my wrist comms. Transcribing planetary observations inaudibly would make things a lot easier.

As slowly as I could, I glanced to see if my wrist comms had connected with a satellite yet. Unsurprisingly, it hadn't. The canopy overhead was simply too thick. I'd need to get above it somehow. Perhaps climb a tree and hope for the best?

Inwardly rolling my eyes, I tried to think of a better way to solve my current problem than "hope for the best." Unfortunately, nothing else came to mind.

The Star Demon moved farther away, still searching. It was far enough away to tempt me into fleeing, but I remained still. The creature could easily chase me down from this distance. I needed to move, but I had to be patient. One false move, one premature step, and the chase would be on once more. And this time, I was fairly certain my luck would run out.

After a while I extracted myself from behind the thornbush. Every single movement was a trial of patience as I gingerly tried to avoid being stabbed or jostling a branch as I slid out from my hiding spot, every loose twig and dry leaf on the ground a potential land mine. Managing to make it out without so much as a scratch, I quickly scanned my surroundings. I could still hear the Star Demon to my left, out of sight behind a small cluster of what looked like more thornbushes. The coast seemed clear.

Another kapok tree was at the very edge of the clearing, on the opposing side and just beyond where the Star Demon had disappeared. Smaller than the one I'd hidden beneath earlier, it still towered over its neighbors. It was also noticeably thinner than its brethren, with branches low enough for me to reach. They looked sturdy enough to climb as well. I thought back to what I'd noticed about the Star Demon's claws.

They weren't designed for climbing. At least, they didn't look like it. There was no way for me to know for certain without testing my hypothesis. Being wrong could be painfully fatal. Nobody had ever recorded anything of the sort about them, either. What if I was wrong? Glancing back at the kapok tree, I frowned. I needed to get above the tree canopy to broadcast my report to the satellites in orbit. The tree appeared to be tall enough, and could protect me somewhat from the Star Demon. Provided, of course, I was right about the creature's claws.

Two birds, one stone.

The ground was soft here, which aided my attempt at stealth. I was still making more noise than I was comfortable with, though. The tree was less than five meters away. Looking at the bark on the tree, I could tell there'd be no way for me to climb it silently. My best bet was to get as far up into the tree as I could as fast as possible, and hope the Star Demon was slow to respond.

Hope is never a good strategy, but it's all I had at the moment.

Click clickCLICKclick.

The Star Demon was coming back. I needed to hurry.

Grasping the lowest branch I could reach, my shoulder made an audible crackling noise as something pulled inside. It took everything in my power to not cry out in pain and alert the Star Demon.

Apparently, I'd injured myself far worse than I'd thought during my previous mad dash. Gritting my teeth, I tried to use my other arm to pull instead. My left was weaker than the right, but combined I was able to swing my feet up and onto another branch nearby.

The edge of my boots' soles caught the tree bark. Pieces fell to the ground as my feet struggled to get on top of the branch. It made far more noise than I'd wanted. To my left there was a massive rustling in the undergrowth. The pseudo-birds went silent. The *Aich'Kandida* was back.

Moving as fast as I could, I kept climbing the tree. Every few branches I risked a glance downward as I continued my ascent. Sure enough, the muscular Star Demon was at the base of the tree, back to standing upright, the snout following my movement as the clicking noise intensified. It growled low, dangerously. The beast tried to climb onto the same branch I had scaled previously, but failed. It leapt up—a terrifying height—but the claws missed my legs by a few dozen centimeters.

I breathed a sigh of relief.

Report.

Below me, the Star Demon paced around the base of the tree. There was no way I could afford to slip and fall now, so instead of worrying about the beast below, I focused on climbing the tree to keep myself alive. Working my way up, I noticed the foliage of the pines and spruces surrounding the big kapok tree were rapidly thinning. Twenty, thirty, forty meters. It was higher than I'd ever climbed in my life. Even as a kid, what few trees we had in the *bairro* weren't for climbing, but to give the oxygen-starved inner city a needed boost. In the various dwellings where I grew up, we always had been on the lower floors, and were never allowed to go up above the third level. Looking down, I was suddenly and acutely aware of a newfound fear—heights.

Fear wasn't a stranger in my life, though. This was simply a newer, spicier version of it.

Swallowing to relieve the constriction in my throat, I grasped the sturdiest branch I could find to balance myself. I stretched out my wrist comms and waited. The indicator still showed red. Growling in frustration, I shimmied a little to reach out a bit farther. My reward was more red. I wanted to kick the kapok tree in frustration but managed to restrain myself. After all, there was a huge likelihood I'd fall to my death if I did anything that stupid.

Tick-tock. Time, as they say, is fleeting. My seventy-two hours were almost up.

There was another branch above me, not too far, which looked like it could hold some weight. Another one—this one no thicker than a twig, and more like a vine—extended out above it. If the bigger of the two could hold my weight, maybe I could hang onto the vine for balance to get me out past the last bit of canopy blocking my comms signal. Then, *maybe*, I could relay my report. It was worth a shot. Exhaling slightly, I continued my climb.

Reaching my destination, I looked back down. This would be classified as a *mistake*. Swallowing the sudden urge to vomit from fear, I pressed hard against the trunk of the kapok tree. It took me a few deep, calming breaths to quell the terror in my guts. Risking a quick peek at my wrist comms, it still showed red. It looked like the adjudicators were not showing me any mercy.

So be it.

Reaching up, I grasped the vine for support before I slid a foot out onto the branch. Closer to the trunk it felt sturdy, but farther out? How far would I have to go to get a signal?

One foot in front of the other, the vine slid through my hand as I squeezed, then let go as I moved on. My eyes flicked constantly between my wrist comms, the branch beneath my feet, and the swaying of the spruce tree next to me. Red indicator light, vine in my hand, branch beneath my feet, another step.

The indicator light flickered. Red, yellow. Back to red.

Then green. The satellites above had received my report. I almost whooped with glee. I'd done it. The report had been delivered.

It was at that moment the branch beneath my feet snapped and gave way. The vine in my hand decided to break as well. Screaming, I tumbled out of the kapok tree and fell toward the ground.

I crashed into the thicker branch I'd stood on previously, a sharp pain in my ribs flaring upon impact. The wind was completely knocked out of me as my diaphragm struggled to keep me breathing. My feet were suddenly pointed toward the sky, then at the spruce tree, back up at the sky, before my head crashed into a somewhat soft branch. A small part of my brain analyzed the impact and decided I'd hit it on the spruce tree.

I landed on my side, my right shoulder taking most of the impact.

The spruce tree broke my fall. Instead of landing fatally on the soft dirt of the jungle floor, I was deposited gently there by the loving whorled branches of a giant Colorado blue spruce. It still hurt—everything did at this point—but I was still breathing. Well, struggling to breathe. My diaphragm was refusing to work properly. I gasped and gaped like a fish out of water, willing my lungs to suck in some air, to breathe, anything.

Clickclickclick clickclick.

Oh. Right. The Star Demon.

Great.

I looked straight ahead as the giant face of the Star Demon came within centimeters of mine. It sniffed once, twice, and clicked again. Too tired and in pain to do anything else, I simply lay there, wheezing, trying to breathe. It nudged me with its jaw, and I swear upon *mi familia* and my honor that it . . .

. . . *smiled?*

The pain was causing me to be delusional. That was it. Nothing else could explain the absurdity of an *Aich'Kandida* freaking *smiling* at anything other than its lunch. My head must have hit that spruce tree harder than I thought. Closing my eyes, I waited for my death.

It didn't come. Still, I waited.

Nothing.

After what felt like an eternity, I grew impatient and cracked open my eyes to look around. The Star Demon was gone. I'd never heard it leave. Indeed, I was alone.

But *why* was I alone, and still alive? It boggled the mind. Had the Star Demon gone to another part of the jungle, looking for . . . what? Less beat-up prey? Maybe food that wasn't concussed?

I chuckled at my own cleverness, then groaned softly as a new wave of pain ratcheted up my back. The landing had really done a number on me. Or maybe it had been the dozen or so branches of the neighboring spruce tree that had helped break my fall—and from the pain, half of my body with it. Either way, for some reason, I was still alive.

Bruised, bloodied, battered, and a general disheveled mess, I rolled on my back and looked up at the sky—or where it would have been, if not blocked by the thick jungle canopy. More pain. It was welcome. This probably meant I was still alive. Wincing, I tried to do a mental checklist to see what hurt the worst. After a few moments I decided that it was my left ankle. And I was in shock.

A slight rustle of leaves nearby caused me to open my eyes. The Star Demon . . . was it back? Too sore and tired to get up and flee, instead I turned my head just as my wrist comms beeped three times.

Odd.

To my surprise, I saw the exam adjudicator stride out from behind the very kapok tree I'd climbed—and fallen from. I had no idea where he'd come from. As far as I knew, the boundaries of the Dome were still a kilometer or so away. How long had I been lying there, anyway?

He wore a huge smile on his face and it no longer mattered where he'd come from. None of the pain mattered anymore. It was gone the moment I saw that grin. The cost to my body had been worth it. The bruises would fade, the cuts would heal. I'd succeeded.

Observe, report, and survive.

The mantra of the Explorer.

My mantra, now. There was no way they would fail me. I'd accomplished all of the mission parameters, including the most important one—*report*.

Sudden energy and excitement flooded through me. Sitting up, I could hear the raucous cheering of the people in the stands surrounding the Dome at last. I couldn't blame them. They'd been given a fantastic show, mayhem and carnage, survival against all odds. It was the type of show that they'd talk about for years to come. In their minds, the story would definitely be worth the pint of watered-down beer at the government-sanctioned bar, spending their monthly dole while living vicariously through others, month after month, year after year. Unending, unceasing, and without dreams.

I pitied them.

Let them keep living their lives on the dole, secure in their provided comforts, being told when to do what and how to do it by a faceless bureaucracy that cared only how our votes are counted. That kind of life wasn't for me. It never was, and even my parents knew it—though they were loath to admit it out loud. They knew it from the time I was a child. What I'd just accomplished merely drove home their belief in me. Most people from my *bairro* were more than happy to be nothing more than drones, going through the motions of life without ever living, doing thankless jobs as nothing more than cogs in a giant machine. Not me. I was given the burning desire to explore, to search, to strive and be *more*.

Wiping the blood from my face, I grinned as the adjudicator helped me to my feet. As soon as I was upright and steady, I saluted sharply.

Pain be damned. I wanted my first time to be *perfect*. It was returned just as crisply. He then offered his hand, and we shook. The adjudicator was clearly pleased with my actions. "Congratulations, *Explorer*."

My heart swelled with pride. I was no longer a *concursante*, a mere contestant. I'd made it, achieved a childhood dream . . . something I wouldn't have thought possible six months before. Sweeter words my ears had never heard. Dipping my head, I spoke the words that had been smoldering in my soul since I was a child, only for the flames to be rekindled when desperation had truly taken hold.

"Explorer Edi Loret ready to deploy, sir."

The Butcher
A WarGate Story

Jason Anspach & Nick Cole

"You're dangerous ... because you're honest, Butcher."

The words hammered in like driven nails on some lonely job site where the work would never end. The structure never finished. As though the project was just make-work, and never really intended to be finished at all.

Like that guy who'd push a stone up a hill he could never get to the top of. Forever.

Hopelessness written into the blueprints somewhere by other unseen *someones* who were cold, calculating, and viewed everyone else as just a piece to be moved on the board in a game no one but them really knew the rules to at all.

They were the only sound in the dark heat of the Central American night, in a stinking military junta jail cell, hot air so thick you could drink it, not that you'd want to. The air was so fetid and warm with diseases, to stay here long was to court long-term illness.

A Green Beret light colonel spoke those words, while nearby a three-man Ranger team pulled security and watched the walls out there where the guards were slowly turning into ... monsters. "Simple as that, Butch," said the Green Beret officer as one of the two searchlights that scanned the main prison building passed over the bars and cells, making strange shadows shift and lean in the passing. "And even so ... we need you now again. One more time. Last time,

227

soldier. They're calling the bullpen for the Butcher to come and do what he does. You down, John? This one's for all the marbles."

The message was an offer of salvation delivered to a former Ranger scout known as Master Sergeant John Butcher, Ranger Regimental Scout Team leader. Delivered all the way from on high and deep down in unseen doomsday bunkers where the shadows were darker, but the air was cool and climate-controlled as all the pieces got moved and the schemes of power and design were adjusted by the seconds left in the game. They came from there, brought by an old friend and teammate, all the way to here. And where's here? The hot, sweaty grounds of the rendition prison that didn't formally exist, and neither did Master Sergeant John Butcher anymore for that matter. A quick desperate message and an offer that, really... couldn't be refused as the world came apart at the seams all around and everywhere across a war-torn little globe with bigger problems than old enemies and new ones too.

The world that would soon be the world that was... it was on fire with a fever that would see the end of it.

Literally.

Soon.

The colonel spoke these words, his jump boots grinding into the rotten cement of the dank and dark cells now that the searchlight had passed and everything was shadow and blue.

Again, Colonel Crowe was wearing bloused jump boots with his dress greens. Another detail as to how long the man had been inactive. They must've called him up, thought Butcher, just to come make the offer.

This was serious.

The object of their transmission sat on a steel, mattress-less bunk, hulking and triangular, hands held down and head bowed as though in deep thought.

The man other Rangers called the Butcher had wondered why they'd brought him out from the deep, dark hole to receive the message from an old... *friend.*

He'd been sure that today, tonight at the end of another hot, stinking, long day in a jungle prison cell, was that last day he'd been expecting for more years than anyone could count. That it was finally here. When he was finally going to get backed up against an old crumbling bullet-riddled wall and done.

Cleaned up as it all came apart.

Business finished before everything was wrapped up, and the world that was ... faded over the hill, and into history.

He'd made those kinds of enemies. But that was another story, not this one.

The world that would soon be ... was coming apart. You could tell. Even down here in the forgotten deeps of the Latin American jungle, buried alive as it were inside a place that didn't exist and wasn't acknowledged.

By anyone. Ever.

That's the kind of enemies the Butcher had made.

He'd accepted the terms of the deal. And when they'd locked him up and thrown away the key he'd muttered uncharacteristically, because he was a man of few words ... "Worth it."

He had a gravelly voice, deep as a grave. And quiet as one too.

Bureaucracies and civilizations were like that. Cleaning things, and problems, up. Especially the bad ones when they knew they were on the way out. Into the dustbin of history if there was even gonna be one. They'd see to the last details, even though those problems didn't matter much anymore. Somewhere, someone—and Butcher had a few ideas who wanted it done—didn't want his loose thread jamming their chi.

He had enemies. Real ones.

So he'd assumed, when he got pulled out of the hole in the sweaty twilight by the guards who were beginning to grunt more and more like animals, not like pigs, but maybe apes, that he was getting cleaned up finally.

But then his old team commander showed up in the meeting cell from SMU. Special Missions Unit. Older now. Still in uniform. Class A's. Greens, in fact. Boots bloused. A Green Beret exactly as one should be, which was the final formal thing that could be acknowledged about his presence here.

Though in truth nothing could be *acknowledged*. Nothing was official.

Even as the whole mess came apart at the seams.

It was a Green Beret light colonel he'd once known and worked with in places no one remembered anymore.

The rest was shadow and redaction.

Even here in the Devil's armpit of some Latin American hellhole that didn't technically exist, either. But the CIA knew it did. Knew where it was. And where the Butcher was stashed until a doomsday arrived that needed his skill set—and that's why he was here.

The light colonel.

I'm on ice, the Butcher had had to tell himself some days. Or...

Waiting for that explosive and unexpected *bang* to the back of the skull. Or...

To be needed just one last time.

And other days it was just waiting for the last day to be maybe this one.

"Ain't that how it always is, Colonel," John Butcher muttered low under his breath. "For all the marbles."

The man who'd once been a Ranger scout team leader said this *patrol low*. Like a hiss. So low the little brown guards beginning to grunt like apes and grow sharp fangs, surrounding the colonel and the Ranger extraction team in the cell, out there in the shadowy stinking halls, didn't even hear. And maybe neither did the younger Rangers with the comm gear, ear pro, the trio watching the walls and the shadows, the avenues of approach too, noting targets and sitrepping one among the other the increasingly bad situation they were finding themselves in as it devolved by the second. Getting worse as the night came just as it had for two weeks now.

But the colonel heard the Butcher and said nothing.

Most of the prisoners who'd been here with the Butcher were gone now. And over the course of those two weeks as the world that would soon be caught its fever...the Butcher had smelled human flesh.

Roasting.

Out there in the jungle.

Even the birds had gotten quiet, and that was saying something for this kind of triple-canopy jungle.

The Butcher figured the situation, still as a stone statue, and waited for the offer he'd begun to doubt some days would ever come.

He knew out there in the jungle, somewhere nearby, was a designated LZ as black as night. A Special Operations Black Hawk, 160th most likely, would put down on it once the trio of Rangers had called for an exfil and departed the facility.

You couldn't get a helo in here. This place was so tight and lost in the jungle. The Butcher's Pathfinder training had made that clear.

But right now, in the deepening dark hell as night came on and the little brown guards grunted like hungry mad apes and there was no scent of roasting human flesh in the hot still air ... the Black Hawk was life.

Even the trio of Rangers, stone-cold killers all of them even though two were young and probably on their first enlistment, even they wanted on that bird when it was time to go because you could feel the madness brewing out there in the jungle dark.

They wanted on the bird if only just to get back to their Ranger brothers who were probably knee-deep in it somewhere around the world. Not on some babysitting detail on the wrong side of the action with an over-the-hill Green Beanie officer no less.

Go to a prison with some spooky Green Beanie and extract an HVI. High-Value Individual. Then get back in the action. That's what these three wanted.

You're gonna get action here, Rangers, the Butcher almost muttered, listening to them ID targets and develop the situation as it got progressively worse by the second.

The ape-men who'd once been human guards were starting to bark and howl.

Just like hungry baboons in the night.

There was a Ranger staff sergeant leading the three-man extraction team. Normally there'd be four, calc'd Butcher. The team leader was Mississippi-mud brown. Lean and rangy like a Ranger should be. Jocked up and ready for battle against overwhelming odds because that's every pump-day for a Ranger *and sometimes twice on Tuesday* as a Ranger NCO the Butcher once knew used to tell his section.

All insignia and unit, even the nametapes were pulled. Just rank in the new way the kids started wearing it during the GWOT.

Global War on Terror.

An SSG. A specialist on the SAW—Squad Automatic Weapon. Cold and already *been there, done that* with a calloused sneer about it all. That's the gunner, thought the Butcher. And a very young PFC runnin' hard with an M4.

Tough as nails because he's been through RIP ...

They call it RASP or something now, the Butcher reminded himself. He knew that.

Whatever, he grunted internally. Tough because the kid's been through RIP, or RASP, or whatever the name-changers have come up with this week. Maybe tabbed already. He's nineteen running on pure testosterone and hate. He's trained, can run like a gazelle, and he'll fight anything anytime just 'cuz.

He's as close to pure predator as it gets, and he doesn't know it, and that somehow makes him more dangerous than most because he's looking to find out just how deadly he is in the hierarchy of killers that is the military.

John Butcher didn't say much. But like every scout he was a thinker. He studied everyone. Relentlessly.

That was his job.

And ... it was life and death in what he'd done and how he'd lived.

Fourth man was missing, assessed the Butcher. And to an old scout that spoke volumes.

They'd been in it already on his op.

Their mission had most likely been to get the light bird in his dress greens, no time to drop into fatigues from wherever he'd been found, summoned, and then sent to where he needed to deliver the offer. To get the old soldier—old to them, to the Butcher too—to deliver the message. The offer.

And then get an answer.

They'd sent someone John Butcher had been ... *in it* ... with. Once and a long time ago. So the offer was legit. And it was serious.

No expense was spared.

What was said was "patrol low" between the two old pros. The colonel, and the Butcher, had patrolled much, once and long ago way downrange and far beyond the wire of polite civilization in very dark and unfriendly places they ... were never supposed to be in at all.

In the silence of the quiet and mostly unspoken negotiation, the *been there, done that* gunner spoke through the dip in his cheek.

"Orcs at the front gate are startin' up, Sar'nt. Now they gesturin' our way. Get-it-on-thirty approacheth."

Orcs, thought the Butcher. What's an orc?

New slang for the kids, he guessed.

A long time ago it was *Ivans*. Then *hajis*. Now ... *orcs*.

Whatever, thought the veteran Ranger who'd been locked away since ... well, a long time ago.

Butcher didn't need tabs or scrolls to know they were Rangers too.

They had the gear and the carriage. And he was one of them. But from a long time ago. He could practically smell them. Knew the *hard* in their terse communication and the way they hugged wall and embraced the shadows, focused like hunting cats on their targets, their sectors, and what they were here to kill.

They were killers.

That is ... what Rangers do.

Even the PFC.

"Copy, Specialist," said the extraction team leader in a drawl that matched his Mississippi-mud-brown skin. "Hear me now, Ranj-uh ... they move up on us aggressively, we go to guns and make sure there's a hole outta dis hellhole. Feel me?"

One Ranger at the window to the cell. One in the hall beyond the bars. The extraction team leader at the door to the cell.

Two old soldiers, one a Green Beret, the other the Butcher sitting on opposite ends of the prison bunk in the dirty, stinking cell lost in the jungle.

In the half-light of the watchtower moon-bright searchlight scan that filtered into the cell, the gunner smiled grimly at the targets he'd chosen and adjusted his stabilization on the SAW that commanded the field of fire in his sector.

"Solid copy, Sàr'nt."

That's Rangers, thought the Butcher. The order to murder in bulk was issued and received with zero emotion, and yes ... a quiet kind of enthusiasm to get it on one more time and see who was meaner than it.

A different life and he would have been their sergeant major.

Now he was just a nameless prisoner in a third-world hellhole, awaiting quick death in the heat of the sweltering day and the insect-ridden night.

It was early night now. Deep blue, and the jungle an unkempt silhouette of tall canopy out there, and perhaps the stars above if they could be found at all.

There had been gunfire at times out there in the jungle. Over the weeks of increasing madness as the world out there lost its mind from a fever, and the fever was so bad it had made its way to all the forgotten places just like this rendition prison. More and more so as the days passed. But it wasn't the sounds of battle. The Butcher knew those well.

Had known them before Panama '89. But these had been sporadic, loud pray-and-sprays. Full-mag dumps against something that didn't seem to obey kinetics and physics, or the insistence of high-dosage gunfire applied in adult-sized party packs. Shooting at . . . *something* . . . that didn't need to respond in kind.

Something that roared like a lost titan of an elder age never known by the men of now . . .

And then there'd been deep unsettling silences in the aftermath as though it was clear the gunfire of the becoming-ape-guards speaking local Spanish had not prevailed.

"That's the offer, Butch," said the colonel in his clear officer's official voice. "Best I can do."

The prisoner in the shadows of the cell watched the gunner standing near the lone barred window and listening to the night, smelling it, watching what he could see out there in the darkness where the hot bright moonlight did not penetrate, didn't move.

He knew exactly what was running through the kid's mind. *Kill. Survive. Do it again.*

"No one . . ." began the colonel and seemed to halt for half a second as he sighed. Butcher could tell the clock was ticking.

For the colonel.

And for them.

"No one disputes why you did *what you did.* Smoking a CIA officer running an op with . . . with that sorta damn heart o' darkness going on and that filthy Deep State lizard telling everyone to just look the other way . . . *this is how the steaks are cut* . . . no one disputes the smoking as righteous, John. Guy had it coming, and you were the only honest guy on the X. It wasn't always that way. Things have gotten worse. More . . . more out of hand than I ever thought things would become. It used to be *right* and *wrong* and the battle between good and evil, John. Now . . . it's just power and who can sink the lowest to get it done and grab what they can on the way to the bank. No one in the community disagrees with what you did. And that's what makes you more dangerous than other men. To them, John. To them."

Silence.

"But you did it, John. And they had to make an example out of you, which is why you've been left to cool your heels down in this cursed hellhole. They don't want the rest of us getting ideas about things like *right* and *wrong*. Good and evil. We do the dirty work and that's all they want out of us. John Wayne days are over. Even for Special Operations, John. But now you got a shot to get out of this and that's why I asked to be the one to come all the way down here and make the offer. All the bad they get up to, it's still going to go on. I can't lie to you about that. You made your point now. You wasted one of them. A real up-and-comer too. They were sore about that. Now they need you so bad they're willing to let it go and set you free for what remains of the world. That's a pretty solid deal, Johnny. I'd take it. As your former commanding officer . . . I can't order you to take it, but hell, John, I'd take it. So take it, man! Get out of here and just live. Or go do it again. There's enough of them to still get your kill on. Okay? Let's walk. Right now. I'll go all the way with you and if you get done what they want done bad, and on the other side of it you still want that revenge . . ."

The colonel paused.

Another shadow in the dark.

He was standing now. His speech had taken him to his boots. His body bent in its classic dress greens, and yeah that's how long he'd been out. Colonel Crowe hadn't been active since they'd updated the uniform. And there were all the ribbons he'd earned doing all the dirty work for the powers that be, seeming somehow a bright spot in the shadows of the present.

There were a lot of them. The ribbons. Awarded in files attached to reports that were blacked out. Redacted, they called it.

And yeah . . . each one was earned.

The Butcher had been there for some of them. So, he knew.

Now the shadow colonel stood.

Serious.

"Then I'll pick up an AK just like Tehran, John. I'll be on your six and we'll get out of there even if they've declared us KIA and saturated the whole site. We'll go for it even if it's no fail. Again. John. You have my word."

And to the Butcher, few men had words worth meaning anything. He'd seen too much of the world to believe anything different.

But the colonel was not one of those men.

He owed his life to this man. A few times over.

"What about her, Colonel?"

Master Sergeant John Butcher spoke, and his voice was gravel and hard-bitten road. It was cold winter stalks and burning desert hells where nothing moved and even the lizards couldn't stand the heat. Long patrols and hand signals for days without seeming end. Few words used and exchanged that spoke volumes about targets, intents, capabilities, and next moves.

Actions on the objective.

How far you were willing to get it done to make it happen.

The Butcher, as Lieutenant Colonel Crowe knew, was the best scout he'd ever worked with in his long career on the dark side of Special Operations Command.

But the Butcher was more. Much, much, much more. And the powers that be had decided to trade him his freedom, for one last run.

One last op.

But the Green Beret colonel, receiving his mission from on high from the real dark powers that ruled the collapsed nation once called America, knew freedom wasn't enough for the Butcher.

"Hell," Crowe had told them when they told him to go deliver the message and the offer. The colonel's voice a hard, barking trumpet in the vast stillness of the SCIF. "He's only sitting in that cell because he knows what you can do to the last person he cares about. Give him thirty minutes and he could clear those walls and be gone like a ghost in the dark and you'd never see him again unless he decided to come looking for you. Hunt him, and he'll kill everyone you send after him plain and simple, gentlemen. But wait, there's more, kids..."

The colonel was feeling his own as he began to roll, and he hated everyone in the room too. So there was that. Especially the suits with the "problem" glasses and bespoke three-piece suits that were all the rage among the political class here at the end of things. But the SOCOM colonel had been knee-deep in expended brass in enough third-world hellholes to get away with his speech because they needed him to convince the one man who could get what they needed done, whom they'd iced for a special very bad occasion just like the one they found themselves in right now, to be a team player and work for them one last time.

"Once he figures out, gentlemen, who's calling the shots, then he'll come for you. Even if you are way down in this deep-down, under-all-the-rocks pneumatic bank vault door the size of a house, surrounded by the best of the best of operators... John will come for you. And there won't be a damn thing you can do about it. You can't buy your way out of this one, he can't be reasoned with, and he definitely can't be stopped until he's dead. And if that's what you're thinking, then get in line because there's a long list going way back to the Cold War who failed to kill him. Hardship, on levels you have no conception of, is every day for him. Hell is where he's happiest, if . . . if he even knows what happiness is. Incoming doesn't bother him even when it's so thick you can look up and see the bullets cutting jungle like fast-moving hornets. Believe me, I've been there with him. He thrives in bad odds and especially mean little brawls gone real, real bad, gentlemen, because you people have messed things up once again for the umpteenth time. He's a ghost, a killer, a shadow you can't shake and a knife in the dark. He's unstoppable with what you've got on hand here in this bunker that makes the president's security force look like bad mall cops. If you were smart, and this one's for free, gentlemen . . . you'd run a Spectre gunship down there and light the whole prison up with everything you had and make sure the bird was on station for a good thirty minutes until all the thermals cooled. You are . . . playing with fire in even mentioning his heavily redacted records jacket. You may be irritated by what I've just told you, even offended. I don't care. This is the truth and that's what you hired me for."

Then the colonel stared at them all and waited for them to order the ex-SEALs they had all around them acting like some kind of praetorian guard for Global Domination scumbags to just waste him on the spot.

But no one in the cool dark shadows and heavy plush furniture of the secure room said anything. Then, one of the faceless and expensive suits cleared his throat, like they do, and asked a question.

"Then what buys us his services, Colonel?"

The Green Beret light bird looked around and then straightened his dress greens with a roll of his shoulders.

"World's going to hell!" he practically snapped at them, willing himself to calm. "This virus is out of control, and I know about Operation *Special Delivery*. I get you've selected your teams and detachments to go forward in time and secure your place after the effects of the plague wear off. I get that an old soldier like me doesn't have a slot on that particular ride. I get that."

The colonel leaned forward and put both of his hands on their dark polished obsidian briefing table, West Point ring flashing in the overhead subdued lighting.

"The one he cares about. Her. She gets a slot on the ride out. I'll go down and get him out for you. Make the offer. He'll do your devil's deal to get her a ride out. Like I said, that's why he's doing you a favor and just riding pine in the hellhole you put him in. Because of her and her alone. Otherwise you'd all be dead."

He'd told them that.

He'd bargained for the one thing the Butcher would come out of retirement for.

The most dangerous man the colonel ever knew. If only because he was so damn honest in a world of shadows and lies.

Now, in that hellhole jail cell in the hot dark of the sweaty Latin American night, watching the moonlight, the searchlight dance, and the shifting shadows, as the barks of the ape-men began to grow, the Butcher spoke.

"I go with you, and she gets a ride out of the end of the world, Colonel?"

"Yeah, John. She does. You have my word."

The Butcher turned toward his old team leader.

"Who do I gotta kill, Colonel?"

"It's a what, John. Not a who. I'll explain on the ride out of here. But if you're down to depart, these Rangers are gonna get us out of here and to the exfil bird two klicks down that road. Once we get to the airbase we'll brief you on the target."

From the SAW gunner near the shattered and barred window that watched the front gate came a quick sitrep, small and terse as Rangers do.

"We got movement, Sar'nt. Those boys at the front gate got ideas and I don't think we're gonna like 'em too much."

The Ranger team leader stepped to the window, staying in the shadows, and eyed what his specialist was seeing.

"Light 'em up loud. We goin' hot now. Colonel... don't mean no disrespect... but is his decision for Christ made? 'Cause them guards are going feral now and we gotta cut bait and fish."

The colonel turned back to the Butcher.

The Ranger team was removing their suppressors. They wanted maximum noise and violence to scare off the feral guards that were turning into something not quite human anymore.

Since the GWOT, unless it was a straight-up Fallujah II-style slugfest, all the Special Ops units ran suppressed right from the start as a default setting.

The Butcher noted the change in SOP and tucked that info away for whatever game he was being offered a chance to play in.

"I promise, John. She gets a tomorrow. The rest of us, you, me, we're going down. We don't. Is that enough?"

The Butcher nodded. His angular lean face, hard and unshaven, like some desperate wolf's in the night.

✳ 2 ✳

The Green Beret, checking his watch, turned to the Ranger team leader.

"Cut us a way out of here, Sergeant, and tell the pilot we're on the move to the LZ."

The Mississippi-mud Ranger NCO stepped away from the fractured window. The specialist with the squad automatic weapon was already smashing glass from and landing the barrel of the gun against the crumbling windowsill of. Stabilizing the gun and readying to engage targets out there in the hot night.

"Cowboy, this is Python Two..." The NCO was handing ear pro to the colonel and the Butcher. Nodding at them to get them on. "Gonna be loud."

The SAW gunner engaged with a short burst, finding his range as he landed rounds among the clustering bandy-legged guards, misshapen and demonic in the dark.

Brass clattered on the floor of the cell as the thunder of the gun echoed off through the rotten halls of the ancient building that served as a prison. "Cowboy, we on the move but we're gonna have company fo' sho'. LZ in fifteen if we make it. Python out."

The gunner opened up in full and carefully murdered the first cluster of "orcs" who'd gotten it into their deranged and changing feral minds to go in and take what they could from the team that had come for their most highly guarded and valuable-above-all-others prisoner.

And the main thing they wanted, snapping their drooling and

hungry fangs, was flesh, for they had grown quite fond of it in the changing of the last two weeks as the plague did its work.

"Movement down the hall, Sar'nt," said the PFC with the M4 who'd been on rear security. "More comin' in now."

"Do 'em, PFC. We goin' that way PDQ," ordered the rangy dark NCO.

All the Rangers were in full battle rattle. FAST helmets. Plate carriers with mags and gear attached. Comm and rucks most likely stuffed full of extra ammo and high-ex. Each had a large IFAK strapped to his body armor and a sidearm on his battle belt, and because they were Rangers, more than an above-average number of knives.

Down the hall, barking feral cries rang out, echoing madly off the depths of the dank, dark, jungle-shrouded walls. The cries were more animal than Guatemalan peasantry turned tyrannical guards of the Deep State's secret rendition prison.

The Ranger NCO turned toward the Butcher as the team readied itself to move.

"Heard you was scouts back in the day, boss?"

Butcher said nothing, only nodding.

"Wasn't authorized to arm you till we make the bird, but way I see it now, we gonna be in it jes' to get outta here and make the LZ, boss."

The E-6 reached over his shoulder to his swollen assault pack and shucked the breaching shotgun he had there.

"Read in your file that you ran the SPAS like back in the old days. This ain't one o' those, but it's a good combat shotgun. We use it for breachin'. Loaded with slug right now, but there's shot and dragon all up along the sling. Red for dragon. Green for shot. You good, boss?"

The Ranger extraction team leader thrust a tight Italian shotgun he identified as the Beretta 1301 at the prisoner in the shadows.

The colonel watched the Butcher take the weapon and study it for half a second. They had been through much together in past lives not this one anymore. Redacted lives that never happened as the world slept and never knew how close it'd come to nuclear annihilation back in those long-gone days. On the way down, Colonel Crowe had wondered what he'd find left of the man he'd once known. But in that moment, as John Butcher handled and checked the weapon, he was reminded of who the Butcher was, and of one thing he'd heard, online, some meme or something, that epitomized his . . . friend.

Beware an old man in a profession where men usually die young.

"We go all the way, John. That's how this one goes. All the way."

But the Butcher was already in "cleanup" mode, assessing the situation and positioning himself to meet the enemy head-on from where they least expected him.

The PFC with the dialed-up M4 began to engage someone, or some*thing*, coming down the dark, dank corridors of the fetid prison on this level. More gunfire from the SAW, destroying whoever had tried to cross the overgrown courtyard that still smelled of the smoke of the previous nights' barbecuing.

"Group in the yard's clear, but we got bad guys all over this place, Sar'nt," muttered the SAW gunner. "We gonna have to blast our way outta here."

The Rangers were flipping down their night-vision optics.

"Jes' Tuesday for us, young Ranger," rumbled the NCO.

The Butcher was already moving to the hall, shotgun forward and following the front sight, shifting expertly in sidestep to the shadows along the wall where he would be unseen.

The NCO gave his orders for movement as Butcher and the PFC covered the exit. "We move out here, Hopkins, you on anchor. I'll take point. Rogers, you got rear security once I get past you. Colonel... fall in if you please, on my right. Boss... you got my left. We stay in wedge and make for the chow hall out back o' the prison. Priority is to get this man on the bird. Rest of us die doin' it, then command says tha's the way it gotta be. Way Catfish see it... we all gonna make it on that bird. Screw da end o' the world. My NCOER up and I need a good one if'n I even gonna make sergeant first class and get my twenty done as a eight."

Butcher smiled as he heard this. The E-6 running the extraction team probably wasn't even born when Butcher was a lowly two-oh-three gunner just out of RIP with Second Batt back in the day.

Time passes and soldiers wonder why they're still alive.

Hopkins was the gunner.

Rogers was the PFC with the M4.

A thin trickle of sweat ran down the Ranger team leader's muddy face in the pale moonlight. It was sweltering. It would be a long hot night in the jungle even if they only had fifteen minutes to reach the bird.

But then again, wasn't every night in the regiment?

And that fifteen minutes was gonna be long.

The place must have once been some old coffee plantation main house turned into a prison long ago by whichever junta had gotten around to it.

They threaded the dead they found down there. Five in all. The Ranger PFC had fired down the hall before they'd begun to move, engaging bandy-legged, snarling, smaller men who now had misshapen heads and fangs. His NODs, his targeting laser, the powerful illuminator, and the good marksmanship that had been drilled into him through Basic, Infantry School, RASP, and range time in the batt had put accurate fire on the five ... ghouls ... that's what Butcher thought as they threaded past the drooling corpses in the moonlight.

Not "orcs," whatever that was, but *ghouls*.

They were still wearing shreds of the former guards' uniforms. Some of them still had weapons but they looked badly used as though they'd been turned to clubs instead of firing. But their skin was now dark like charcoal. And of course the bright and shining fangs. Their eyes were narrow lifeless slits that seemed more animal than the human they'd once been.

They weren't men any longer.

That was reality now, thought the Butcher. He had no idea what was going on, what had happened to the world. But if this was reality, and it was, then he'd deal with it on his terms. He covered the dead with the shotgun because he'd seen "the dead" pull the trigger on a live man before. But they were still, if one allowed one's mind to think of it that way, they were still *like* men. Guatemalan soldiers, wearing the Halloween costume masks of children playing at being ghouls, or goblins in the dark, or some such make-'em-up make-believe.

It didn't make sense.

Their squat brown faces, brutalized by years of sun, sweat, scars, and the acne of bad diets and American soda, were made even more horror-show now by the fangs they were growing. Their noses widening like a gorilla's. Brows overdeveloping almost like ... cavemen.

By the pale moonlight bathed in the stinking heat, the ever-present flies already seeking the bodies, darting and dancing from drooling wounds of ragged gunfire leaking blood, to the quick congealing dark pools of the stuff forming like black in the shadow ponds in the gray dark, even by that pale-gone-white moonlight, their brown-hard Guatemalan skin was turning charcoal on some, and on others it almost seemed dark green like the Hulk in the comic books of long ago.

And in these ruined frames, there were two such among the green dead the Ranger PFC had gunned down as they came down the hall, dragging their AKs and barking, with their jungle butcher's knives and machetes all the jungle-fighter Lanceros liked to carry strapped upside down on their chest rigs . . . the muscles of these two were unnaturally bulging, making their hulking torsos swole above the rest.

As though they were pack leaders.

Animals.

Their eyes, even in death, even as the blood drained and made their green-colored skin pale lime and ashy, their eyes were still distant and focused on some hatred. Some demonic malice they'd been dreaming of.

"World's changing, John," said the colonel as he came alongside. "I'll explain it all on the bird out. Now, we just gotta make it there."

The Ranger NCO was ahead and almost at the shadowy stairs where the firefight would come at them.

But in that brief moment, free finally after years he'd lost count of, John Butcher did something he rarely did . . .

He spoke.

And in his usual terse way, it was just a question. A question for a human killing machine that needed to know what it needed to know so it could go on doing . . . *what it did.*

Killing.

The Butcher.

"What are they, Colonel?"

The veteran Green Beret officer, whose time went as far back as the old Cold War and operations when the players were different but the game was still the same somehow, studied the Butcher as images from those past pumps crossed his mind like slide-projected images from some long-lost age of technologies. Missions and ops that still, to this day, remained classified and unacknowledged though most if not all involved, except the last two remaining here in this stinking jungle prison, were dead now.

"Long story short, John," whispered the colonel, two killers watching the Mississippi-mud-dark Ranger thread the dead bodies and approach the landing at the top of the stairs littered with ruined inhuman corpses.

"Good shootin', Rogers," mumbled the NCO.

The shadows of bars and the bone moonlight made the tall and lanky Ranger like a specter. And it was clear he was in it to win it, determined that his team and those who were his responsibility were going to survive this hump through a hell straight out of Dante's *Inferno.*

If only to take on the next nightmare. And the next, and the next one after that. That was how Rangers are, thought Butcher as he watched the man.

And he was cool with that.

This is how it would be now, and that was clear, as though the ghost of the dead Bard whispered his ancient lines about all our tomorrows coming in day in and day out. Same as it ever was. Same as it ever would be.

"Remember the doomsday project called Jump Start, John?" hissed the colonel in the dark as he stepped around and through the dead. "One of the monsters...the smart kids...let's call her 'Spider Queen.' That's her code name. One of the monsters they bred to be a scientist in the doomsday tomorrow they were planning for, well, this one tested off the scale. Like a savant, but orders of magnitude beyond measurement. Once they figured her out, they segregated her away from the tacticians and the warriors in the project. Then, apparently, they supercharged her, just to see if they could. In ways they probably shouldn't have, Johnny. Turned her into a vegetable, like a zombie really, extreme autism...but she could still do things. Amazing things beyond current levels and even human comprehension. Code was her specialty. Coding.

"She escaped. Turns out she wasn't as dead inside as everyone thought she was. Felt the US government was owed some grudge about being pulled away from the Day After test site and inserted in a deeper, more hidden program with more diabolical intents and purposes. All those other kids who had no clue their perfect life was one giant lab experiment to save civilization from the end of the world. She wanted payback, John. On the run, she got loose in the Deep System and ran amok on some nano-weapons that never should have been made in the first place. Then she released a plague on the whole world. What you're seeing in those dead Guatemalan 'orcs,' as the Ranger kid called them, Johnny ... it's spreading. It's contagious. It's turning the whole world into her own personal payback. A nightmare."

Butcher nodded. He understood.

He'd had the same thoughts someone in ... the Spider Queen's position, would've had.

Payback.

Letting the world burn.

But he'd had a doomsday he couldn't afford. And so he'd let them live.

As long as she was safe. They could live.

"So ... this girl ... she's destroying the world now?"

The colonel shook his head in the hot sweaty darkness as they neared the stairwell leading down into the depths of the forgotten prison, through the levels of hell that was the rank jungle fortress where men were sent to be forgotten and die.

"Negative, John. She's *remaking* it. Turning it all into a roadside circus attraction of horror-show freaks and monsters straight out of some science fiction novel. Or rather ... a fantasy. Like *Lord of the Rings*. But it gets worse ..."

The Ranger NCO raised one assault-gloved hand, held it out, and made a slow and purposeful move to one of the grenades on his rig. Letting his rifle dangle.

His movements were slow at first, then all at once they accelerated into a practiced swiftness as the Ranger NCO plucked the grenade free of his harness, popped the spoon, and deftly dropped it over the rail at the top of the stairs.

Butcher's keen eyes, even in the barred shadows and bone-white-moonlight-bright dark caught the Ranger mouthing *Have a nice day* silently as he danced away from the ledge, covering his ears even though he had ear pro on.

The explosion, though just from a small fragmentary device, thundered through the old, moldy, jungle-rotten concrete of the fetid rendition prison. The sound of its blast echoing and rebounding throughout the structure and wandering off through the other levels of empty cells.

Those places were now emptier and more forgotten than they

already had been. The guards, for the two weeks since things began to get weird in the prison, had been taking the political prisoners, thieves, and pimps who filled the secret jail off into the jungle where they never returned after the smell of roasting flesh and the smoke that lingered and never quite seemed to go away.

Butcher had been on enough battlefields with burning tanks and cooking off ammunition, both main gun and personal defense from the coaxial machine gun, to know the scent of burning human flesh all too real.

Tankers got trapped when the A-10s and the Apaches made a Highway Hell.

The Butcher had been forward with his team. Lasing the targets and making sure the destruction was more than complete.

But in the prison over the last two weeks even down in the dark hole, he'd gathered enough evidence to know things were getting... *strange*. The Butcher was getting ready to either make his move... or it was clear he'd end up like the others taken off into the jungle to roast and smoke.

He stayed, even though he could have got free, because she was the threat they used to keep him in place.

Her life.

For his.

Even in a forgotten prison it was easy to see that the world was breaking down in some catastrophic way it never had before.

But now the game had changed, and the Butcher was on the move, armed, and ready to give her one more chance at life.

Like he always had done.

✻ 3 ✻

Contact came in the form of a brutal gunfight. A pure no-holds-barred slaughter took place in the ruined central hall after the team made it down the central stairwell. This was an area of the prison John Butcher had rarely ever been taken to. Mostly he was kept in extreme isolation due to the nature of his high-priority incarceration.

The guards in their now feral form were barking and rushing in, smelling blood and wanting flesh. AKs rattled off but that seemed more for noise and show than accurate rounds on target. This seemed to make sense in their new "orcish" minds.

The team replied with applied gunfire in high doses and began to stack almost from the get-go. But it was clear the numbers were against them.

The Rangers were actually getting pushed by the dozens of once-humans the gunner and the PFC were calling "orcs" even as they blasted away at them. Their NCO ran the fight, called the sectors, and managed his charges, keeping them back and out of the action even though all eyes were on a swivel as bad guys were coming from every direction, and even at times through the walls and down off the rents and cracks in the ceiling above where once the guards had walked the walls and rusty iron catwalks as the searchlights crawled and reminded all there was no escape from this hot, stinking, jungle hellhole.

"Orcs on the right, lift and shift, PFC Rogers!" barked the NCO, losing his muddy drawl.

When the Butcher gave the colonel a look asking what this meant, the colonel held up a hand and indicated he would explain later.

"One very pissed-off woman with an axe to grind against almost everyone, and it doesn't help matters her intelligence is untestable and off the charts in every measurable form. Bitterness is a hell of a thing, Johnny. But of course, you'd know all about that more than anyone, wouldn't you?"

The Butcher said nothing and moved off under a sudden fusillade of some orcs' badly aimed fire to get closer to the team leader, Staff Sergeant Hunter. Nearby, the hard-eyed gunner burnt a pouch, ruining orcs on the far side of what had once been the prison's main chow hall for general population.

This area was nothing more than wooden tables now, smashed chairs, shadows, and lonely darkness. It was lined with bent bars and ruined cages the inhuman guards were trying to push through any way they could find.

The orcs, impossibly, were bending those ancient rusting bars and climbing through to get at the Rangers, who were trying to make a hole out of the prison through the front door and get their HVI out as per the order.

High-Value Individual.

Orc gunfire resounded off the distant halls and interrogation rooms, reaching as far as the commandant's "palatial" quarters along the top floor, where whores would often be driven in from the villages for his pleasure on the weekends, but which were nothing but brutality and heat for the rest.

"They're pushing on the right!" shouted the PFC and almost at the same time, "Mag change, cover my sector!" He burned a mag keeping them back, the suppressed fire hissing and spitting off into the darkness like it was full of all the focused hate and energy the kid could put out.

But the tension was clearly getting to the PFC, and the "tough Ranger" exterior he was learning was getting replaced by the very real fear that all of them were starting to get trapped in here, more and more so by the second, and . . . might never exfil.

Rangers are used to this moment, thought the Butcher in some distant part of his mind as he worked the angles and tried to figure out how to get them all out of here alive. But that takes time and experience, and the kid was getting that live fire right now.

If he survives, he'll learn. If he doesn't . . . then it don't matter.

"Un-alive-ing yer sector, Rogers! Head down, kid—'bout to lay some Big Box hate forward your position!" the gunner shouted raggedly and heaved his SAW up, its suppressed barrel smoking. He worked it by its sling and dumped the rest of his next pouch on the misshapen shadows of the small hulking simian orcs as they pushed through the bars, smashed the tables, and raced for the kid reloading and doing a stand-up job of keeping-it-Ranger despite the developing bleakness.

Hot five-five-six ripped those orc bodies to shreds . . . and they still kept coming, barking like the animals they'd become. They waved fractured machetes, bent pipes, and even the weapons they'd once used to maintain control of the prison population as they died.

As clubs and no longer firearms.

Occasionally a round would explode from a chamber, or someone's misshapen black booger-hook would squeeze too tight and dump what was left in the muddy magazines.

But the black and green barking orcs took rounds and pushed forward even as the gunner ruined them and went dry all of a sudden.

Staff Sergeant Hunter was putting accurate fire on a group of shadowing hulks guarding the "galleria" that was the prison's sole entrance and exit. The Rangers had intended to use this exit to extract their VIPs now. When they'd first entered the prison, after being inserted by the Black Hawk now on station above and orbiting out over the jungle, most of the guards had been absent. The few who remained weren't as changed, but they definitely seemed odd and uncomfortable, allowing cash to be thrown at them in order for the team to gain entry to the prison, then disappearing off into the complex where insane laughter and ominous hooting seemed to erupt.

The plan had been to simply leave the same way. The clock was ticking. The asset of time wasn't in great supply.

But it was clear the way in was now no longer an option as the way out.

The exit from the prison beyond the bars and cages on this floor, holding cells for the other deeper, danker horrors within, was now swollen and choked with more and more "orcs" coming out of the jungle night. The loping creatures were threading the downed wire and pushing through the main gate, crossing the tall unkept yellowing grass in the moonlight, and waving strange axes and machetes like some Bronze Age horde of savages come for civilization itself.

The Black Hawk that was their ride out of this bad business passed suddenly overhead, its heavy engine thundering as the blades beat air and thumped jungle.

"Pythons, you got bad guys all over the way out . . . suggest you fade for the rear of the prison, come around the hill, and get down to the LZ ASAP. Jungle's alive tonight and it don't look like something we wanna play with too long."

That was the Black Hawk's pilot over the radios the Ranger team had strapped to their plate carriers.

"Copy that, Cowboy. Can you dust the party that's occupyin' the tee? See what that might do on our behalf?"

A second later: *"Roger, Python team leader . . . Hold position and stand by for fire support."*

The noise and engine of the Special Operations Black Hawk warped and shifted across the soundscape of gunfire, jungle, and the barking within the shadowy prison . . .

They were coming around for a pass with the gunners.

Outside, the searchlights on the prison walls rotated madly now as though operated by sugar-filled children with severe attention-span problems.

Then one of the Black Hawk's gunners dosed the whole prison courtyard beyond the rotting walls of the main building with minigun fire for eight long seconds of continuous *BRAAAAAAAAAAAA AAAAAAAP*.

The Ranger gunner shouted something enthusiastically, but it was lost in all the Black Hawk's outgoing on the Ranger extraction team's behalf.

That sound of minigun fire replaced everything else, and it was clear a force of tangos was being ruined beyond the walls of the central prison.

Heavily, and savagely.

Then the pilot was back on the radio.

"Cut some of the local pop down, Python Leader . . . but ain't enough to get you outta there. More pushing on your loc now. Suggest you fade before you're stuck."

"Copy, Cowboy . . . workin' it," muttered Sergeant Hunter. Then he covered the mic with one assault glove and turned toward Butcher and the colonel. "Exfil says we all covered up and gotta find a new way out. You been here the longest, old man—what's da best way off dis *X*?"

Butcher thumbed shot rounds into the 1301 off the sling, his face a stern mask of problem and solution.

Then . . .

"There's a yard out back, a prisoner cemetery really, three levels down, on a terrace in the hill this facility is built on. To get there we gotta go through an area of cells called 'The Slums' by the locals. The guards just threw prisoners down in there and forgot all about them. Other side of the Slums we can blast through the exterior wall to exit into the cemetery, if you got the high-ex to do the job."

The Butcher didn't tell them of the long years he'd spent collecting odd bits of info regarding the layout of the prison, planning the escape he might one day need to make. There were places he'd been inside, and places he'd never been. But he'd played a game of knowing everything by hook, crook, observation, and even deeds done, to find out what he could about where he was kept.

And how one day . . . he would leave.

SSG Hunter nodded to himself as he digested all this.

"Oh, fo' sho' we got the high-ex to do that bastard and mo'."

"I figured you did. Gimme your chemlights, Sergeant. I'll head down through the cells that way and mark a path."

"You a Ranger, boss. You know that and I know you had the skills once to find us a way out. So we'll go with that plan. We'll anchor and draw here, you mark a trail out through down there, and we'll follow and bleed 'em. How many minutes you need to get us to that exterior wall, boss?"

"Seven," stated Butcher. "Four and you start moving and following the chemlights. Get your explosives ready, as these guys don't look like they're gonna let you break contact easy."

SSG Hunter turned and surveyed the fight. A round smacked into the wall right near his head. He didn't flinch as he turned back to the Butcher. Apparently some of the orcs could still fire their weapons, if badly. But they could and that made things even more dangerous.

"No worries, boss. We roll a gunfight better than most. We gonna learn 'em along the way. They gon' learn not to follow Rangers when it's time to go!"

Then the Ranger extraction team leader shoved a handful of red chemlights into the Butcher's scarred and weathered hands and the meeting was over.

"On your six, John," said the colonel a second later. "Just like the old days."

The colonel was holding a silver-plated .45 he must've hung on to from the old days. He'd already smoked a few orcs that had gotten a little too close to the team. "Three mags left, didn't think I was gonna need 'em, but... hell, never know, Johnny, when the day's gonna brighten up and you get to shoot some dumb bastard that thought you were just old and retired. We'll pick up a pickup somewhere in there, I suspect."

The Butcher nodded, and then they were off into the shadows, following the blunt end of the combat shotgun the Butcher was holding, into the darkness.

✳**4**✳

The Slums.

It was a nondescript door to the jungle hellhole prison's *oubliette*...a forgotten place...and it was already banged open and ruined like it had been bent open from within when the two men made it down the hall to that section of the prison.

In the distance the Rangers worked suppressed, laying down gunfire as the insane barking of the surging orcs grew and grew like madness itself.

Inside the Slums there were monsters, and almost immediately the Butcher opened fire with the 1301 at near point-blank range, shredding and tearing at the plague-made monsters that had once been human wrecks cast into this dank and deep place within the jungle prison.

It was dark down there. An utter darkness, and the colonel had taken the first chemlight, snapped it to red-lit life, and held it above and up for illumination. The two men had no comm gear or night-vision devices like the extraction team had been carrying. They would need this thin wavering light to find a way through, and out. Or they'd all end up part of the scenery if the insanity and gunfire behind them was any clue.

But they had no idea *why* what they'd face down here had become what it had become in the lonely dark of this abandoned place within the prison.

The Slums.

They knew nothing, not even the colonel did, really, of what the intelligence agencies had tagged *The Spider Queen*. A girl with an axe to grind who'd coded a devastating nano-plague that turned people, and animals, into real live monsters. Her motives—and motives they seemed to have been—for the most part held no detectable rhyme or reason for what she'd coded.

But they were there. And so were the monsters her plague had made.

Back in the world, in what some had once called *civilization*, these real live monsters were taking over the cities. Gang members and prisoners and even certain religions were rapidly shedding their humanity and becoming... orcs, gnolls, ogres, hobgoblins. And worse than that. Strange, mythic creatures from the times of legend and fable.

Some were beginning to become elfin.

Others taking the forms of monsters of fey and imagination not known to but a few who'd read strange works of fiction and fantasy, or played games set in fantastic realms, rolling funny-shaped dice or using keyboard and mouse to thread some beautiful and unreal digital video-game world of traps and magic.

Lawyers became vampires.

Corporate overlords, werewolves.

And beyond this...

Others acquired magical, almost superhuman powers. And still others became minotaurs or fiends that defied easy definition. Lions at the zoo were growing bat wings and becoming manticores. And still many, many more strange creatures were... *becoming*... running amok as civilization simply broke down and became little more than chaos and disorder. Rape. Murder. Rampant looting. The military and the government were collapsing.

Strange cults arising.

Technology breaking down.

And as the scientists and the government struggled to find an answer, some answer, any answer, or just understand why the plague the Spider Queen had coded was doing what it was doing...

The world was falling into ruin. Becoming this orc-overrun jungle prison of madness and danger.

And there was no answer. No answer as to why what was done... was done. For the Spider Queen was gone now. And in her absence, all that was left was... survival.

The Slums.

The criminals who'd been thrown into the darkness of the Slums, they too had evolved, just like many across the darkening globe once they'd been infected by the near-invisible nanos of the plague.

This jungle rendition prison wasn't actually part of the local government of Guatemala. It was a secret off-books CIA prison. The prisoners, for the most part, were political enemies of the powers that be. And they'd been disappeared here to be well-forgotten as all tyrants do when they don't like the words being used against them.

But the Slums of the jungle prison were different from the rest of the rotting, stinking complex they'd thrown the Butcher into and tossed away the key until the day, the doomsday, they'd needed him.

The Slums were a different, *local* arrangement. Equally off-books.

The governor of the prison, a lover of kidnapped whores in the jungle night and heat, a callous man and indifferent-to-the-sufferings-of-others villain, had started a little side business on his own, housing the local criminals, local problems from the surrounding villages, in his "Slums."

The forgotten place where those who were to be forgotten . . . were thrown into.

He was paid by the various mayors to house these minor problems—robbers, pimps, killers and debt collectors, parasites of society even if society was a third-world country in the hell of a jungle . . .

Here they were forgotten.

Down in the dark. Of the Slums.

Unfortunately, the governor was paid neither to feed them nor care for them. They were on their own once they were tossed in and the door was closed.

Desperation and survival in the dark at the pro level was what happened next. Sociologists in big-brain universities would have been surprised at what really happens in such situations. But then again, most people would be too.

So as *the world that was* was beginning to collapse, to be replaced by the world that would be, as the guards turned to simian-like orcs feeding on the rest of the prison population, those down here in the dark . . . just died.

And then . . .

. . . they became *ghouls*. Literally so.

Ghoul. An evil spirit or demon in folklore believed to plunder graves and feed on corpses.

A grave robber.

One who delights in the revolting, morbid, or loathsome.

There was a dark science at work. Whatever that vengeful wronged little girl the national intelligence agencies called the Spider Queen, whatever she'd coded into life and reality itself to exact her dark revenge on the world . . . it was at work down here too, in the dark of the Slums with the forgotten. Nano-plague and mRNA and other technology combined with the vast data-beast information behemoth she'd hacked into, it tore things and people apart, and remade them as she intended.

And in the months and years to come . . .

Things would become strange and fantastic indeed.

She'd coded for effect, then she'd released her doomsday weapon on all the world, letting the algorithms and nanites sort as they would.

Within the Slums, even as the world changed, scarred pimps,

remorseless serial killers, cunning robbers, and the rest of the worst of the worst of the local jungle villages slew each other, robbed the mass graves in the yard out back of the prison, and all the while made their nightly forays off into the jungles and the villages and the rotting cemeteries, yes even those in the jungle, and delighted in the revolting, the morbid, and the loathsome.

There'd always been a way out of the prison for some, through the broken pipes and the waste pools at the very bottom and against the back wall, if you had the smokes or hidden cash to pay the guards for a moment of deliberate "inattention." But that had been a price few had been able to pay. Now that they were become monsters, guard and prisoner alike, things were different. The prison had become a lair. A hiding place. A feeding place to bring their victims back to, and a place to cache their stolen hoard.

A home.

They were ghouls now. Come out of the dark to haunt the jungle and the nights.

The first of these to come at the Butcher and colonel, appearing out of the dark, was a pimp named Reyes Alamogordo. Back on the streets of Punta Real he had been known as "the Carver." Each girl in his stable of girls had his symbol carved into her once-pretty face, just below her left made-up whore's eye.

To mark her and show her, and everyone, she was his indeed.

The world's an awful place like that.

And since the plague and his personal infection had begun, Reyes had been making nightly jaunts out into the villages he'd once run his trade in, first to take the whores that were his, and marked as such, back for a feasting among his ghoulish kind deep down there in the Slums... and then out to the graves on the edges of the villages to dig up the whores he'd once murdered long ago in another life, not this ghoulish one.

He'd carried their rotting corpses, and sometimes just their body parts, back to his dark lair down there in the Slums, muttering the dark rites and phrases that had begun to occur in his fevered dead mind of late. Words from other worlds... other realities... *other-words* he was thinking as they ran across the chalkboard of his screeching ghoul-mind.

His flesh was rotting.

His fingers were turning to long claws.

In direct sunlight, which he'd once loved and now hated, his skin was becoming pale and corpse-like. In the dark that he now loved, and felt as though he bathed in cold waters within, his skin was green down there in the Slums the colonel and the Butcher now made their way into.

Holding out a snapped red chemlight to see by.

Reyes the ghoul's teeth were jagged and broken from the rotting bones, fresh and old, he'd been gnawing at, and the dead and living flesh he'd been tearing at.

Down there in the dark, his eyes were alight with a new malevolence and strange mischief much more than they'd been in life.

He was no longer tall.

He hunched, slavering and mumbling. His belly was growing into a pot-shape, instead of the once-lean taut pimp's abs he'd draped in red silk gaudy shirts that contrasted against his olive-tan skin, black hair, and almost aquiline Spanish fine features much different from the squat, stocky frames of most of this region's native inhabitants.

He'd always—and truth be told others had too—fancied himself a Romeo. Of sorts. But with a switchblade and fast backhand.

That's how he'd gotten into pimping.

Now, down there in the dark of the Slums, Reyes and the other ghouls, twelve in all who'd fallen under his sway, even though in reality he'd quietly fallen under the sway of something darker down below in the basement, they'd all listened, hunched and trembling, claws opening and closing, to the sounds of the battle between Ranger and orc up there in the prison above. And somehow, the dark whisperings within their ghouls' feverish minds, as though there were some minor deeper-down-below demon lord of the ancient jungle all about, was telling them who they were becoming in the revealing that was overtaking them day by day, and night by night, whispering that the battle above would soon come to them.

And... that there was no escape for their prey up there in the shadowy searchlight-washed halls, and that the prey would soon seek their ghouls' dungeon out as a way of escape from the fray.

From the battle up there...

The murder of ghouls gibbered like hideous baboons and cackled insanely in sharp burping hiccups, readying their prison shivs and shanks and all the other varieties of weapons they'd made down there during all those years of forgotten survival in the Slums, readying them to take the night's feast that was even now coming their way.

Reyes spread his fellow ghouls out to take the extraction team in a trap. But he had it in mind to feed first, and so he placed himself where he thought best, mumbling those mad words he was hearing in his fevered mind of late.

But . . .

It was too bad, for Reyes the ghoul-pimp, too bad the Butcher had come down for them this night. Any other man and maybe the murder of ghouls would've had a chance at the meal they'd been lusting for as the battle raged in the rotting prison above the Slums.

But a Ranger, and a scout at that, is a survival machine in situations most would never dare. And this one, this one had once been a legend at such dire endeavors. The dark and the dangerous was his home and natural to him even if it was filled with grinding, gibbering death.

Shivs out and waiting in the dark of a long-forgotten place that smelled of wretchedness and death.

In the long years in the prison, the Butcher had always smelled the death that came from these lower quarters. The Slums. He'd known something wasn't right down there and had expected nothing but a fight to escape if it was through that dark maze he chose to go.

Even though throughout those long years he'd had no intention of leaving the prison because of the deal he'd been forced to strike with those that imprisoned him here . . . he'd made his plans for escape nonetheless.

Because that was all he knew.

Those plans had involved the Slums and the external wall he'd need to get through to reach the cemetery terrace cut into the hill on the far side of the jungle-prison where the guards dug shallow graves and covered up their crimes with loose and loamy black dirt and rotting vegetation.

So, he'd had a plan to go through here anyway.

It was Reyes the ghoul who appeared first down there in the dark, thinking easy prey had come his way and that all his fellow ghouls would help once he'd had his first take.

But, down there in the dark, the Butcher pulled the trigger first on the combat shotgun and blew off most of Reyes's hunched shoulder and rotting arm in one fierce blast as all the ghouls surged like a nightmare shadow, hiss-howling madness all at once.

The fiends were on the move in an instant, howling from dark passages and unseen shadowy alcoves.

Reyes screamed and threw the other arm wide, the one holding the deadly sharpened lawn-mower blade he'd traded the guards a pound of smuggled cocaine for to make a shank out of for his protection down there in the Slums. And as the battle broke out there in the short set of steps that led down to that floor of the place, at the back of the prison, the deadly wrap-handled lawn-mower blade swung in, a slicing arc coming at the old Ranger scout.

Unlike the M97 he'd once worked, the Beretta 1301 was an automatic combat shotgun. No need to rack another round.

Butcher centered the barrel and pulled again on Reyes center-mass. He blew the ghoul-pimp end over end, destroying most of his rotting chest and neck in an instant of explosive fury.

But more ghouls were coming in at the two men seeking to map a way out. By the red light of a broken chem-stick, the pimp's odd-angled head hung weirdly. The neck was mostly shredded, but still attached. The spine was blown apart. But Reyes's eyes were yet alive with malevolent intent. Raging and angry.

Still, the body... was ruined. The sanity, if there'd ever been any... was gone now. And despite Reyes's still-living undeath... despite his murder-rage eyes... he would never move again down there in the dark.

In the hours that followed, the ghouls that survived deeper down, running off and hiding from the Butcher's fury, deep down in the catacombs of this jungle dungeon, they would return to feed on the pimp, even as his eyes watched them do so, his ruined body unable to deny them.

They would feed on him.

As ghouls do.

But now the battle there in the first steps of the Slums was underway and other ghouls were now setting upon the two men who'd come there. The colonel blazed away with the roaring 1911, striking the ghouls that seemed to barely react other than jerking their bodies at the sudden fast-moving impacts of the heavy-hitter .45 rounds blazing forth from the barrel.

Four died in the gated hallway that led into the cells between the Butcher and Colonel Crowe.

John Butcher worked the combat shotgun, kicked those he could, and butt-stroked one, breaking its fanged jaw to ruin and clear it off. As fast as the sudden brawl had begun, ghouls were howling, gibbering like the deranged, and running off into the shadowy darknesses beyond the red wash of the broken chemlight down there in the dark.

When it was over, Butcher grunted, thumbing more rounds into the Beretta from off the sling.

"Mark it," hissed the Butcher at Lieutenant Colonel Crowe. They were less than fifteen feet into the prison dungeons called the Slums.

Now they had to find the way to the outer wall.

Working quickly, they made their way through twists and turns, popping chemlights as they moved toward the back of the jungle fortress, probing into the darknesses down there.

They found other ghouls.

Enclaves of them, hissing and leering in the dark like craven things as they were suddenly bathed in the hellish glow of the broken chemlight the SF colonel held aloft with one hand, .45 in the other.

The Butcher didn't leave them alive to be a nuisance once they'd passed. He blasted them with the smoking barrel of the 1301, shredding them with shot rounds and leaving no enemy along their back trail that might be a problem for them later, or for the Rangers coming along behind them shortly even as the battle raged in the main prison above. The sounds of cacophonic gunfire made it clear the Rangers were on the move now, fading and making the orcs pay for any pursuit through the cells and halls.

There was the sudden thunder and rumble of an explosive being used in the levels above, and the dust and concrete of the main floor rained down on the Butcher and the colonel as they delved deeper and farther into the Slums, looking for the back wall to the prison.

The last obstacle they needed to clear lay inconveniently along the very wall they sought.

This area was little more than an underground, fetid, swampy miasma that was the most forlorn reach of the forgotten realms the jungle guards had dubbed the Slums beneath the old prison.

Los Barrios Marginales.

There was nothing marginal about this area as the Butcher worked the corners and scanned the shadows, waiting for more of the ghoulish once-humans to come slavering out of the dark. Coming again as they'd just done a few turns back as the dungeon got lower and they followed sloping passages and crumbling stairs that must have been part of the original architecture of the old Spanish territorial prison the place had been built on the foundations of long ago.

They'd gone down a blind passage that looked promising when the Butcher caught the scent of some bit of "fresh" air smelling of the jungle and the night, and not so much decay and death.

But it was a dead end and in an instant more ghouls sprang their final trap coming from half-buried recesses in the walls.

"They're all around us!" shouted the colonel and stuck the .45 right into the top of the forehead of the first one that came straight for him, the danger and trap was that close... and pulled the trigger on the .45, volcanoing the rotting brains of the feral ghoul straight out the back of its green and lumpy, almost hairless, scalp.

Its eyes rolled white as it simply fell over backward and into the dark beyond the red chemlight's circle of illumination.

Two more of the fiends were already on the Butcher and it was the biggest, and last, mistake they'd ever make of their lives.

The Butcher couldn't get the shotgun around on either because the passage was too tight and he was oriented forward and scanning the darkness right up until the last second when they'd come face-to-face with the dead end down there in the dark.

The trap of ghouls had eased in behind them, creeping through the shadows and surrounding them in the warren of old crumbling passageways.

Butcher butt-stroked one savagely with the composite stock of the combat shotgun and broke its misshapen nose with a suddenly loud and fierce *snap*, driving the gun for all he was worth right between the thing's hideous eyes like it was a steel spike.

There was a savage crunch as though some too-dry deadfall had suddenly broken on a lonely winter's walk in some distant wood.

Then both ghouls were rasping and hissing, reaching out dirty claws that had once been fingers to tear his face off and rip the Butcher's throat out even though he'd just messed one up badly.

The first "ghoul," some human wretch that had run afoul, or been a problem for, the local potentates, got rocked by the butt-stroke to the broken jaw and that gave the Butcher room to push himself into the stinking thing, jerk the shotgun backward, and pull it hard into his own stomach to give him some room to get it to bear as he let the other hideous thing have it point-blank right in the guts with a blast.

That one howled and fell backward and away from the fight, flailing into its ragged stone cubby, yowling inhumanly like some feral cat mortally wounded forever.

By the red light of the chem-stick, the Butcher could see that one had built some voodoo-like shrine within its recess, a collection of trophies from its prowling out through the hole in the prison and into the local surrounding villages.

Photographs.

Perfume jars.

A rotting woman's slender hand missing a finger or two.

Rings.

Teeth strung in a rude necklace.

Now Butcher was free to deal with the one whose gruesome nose he'd shattered. He pushed the shotgun into the thing's throat like a bar, choking out the undead life within, crushing its neck and trachea as brittle bones broke and the thing gagged and rasped horribly. The malevolent light within its dark eyes faded, and it simply flopped over ... dead. Again.

Other ghouls died too and as the thunder of the .45 faded into the deeps of the Slums, the colonel shot two more quickly that had tried to come in behind them.

Breathing heavily, the two men continued forward for there was no time to lose, and they found another grim shrine in the dark once they'd made their way out of that area and found another passage they thought would take them to the outer wall of the prison down here.

That other shrine was lit with small greasy candles, and under it sat a ghoul in a kind of dreaming lotus position. As though it were in a trance. Bloody cinnamon-stained scratch marks like words were written in Spanish along the ancient rotting concrete of the walls.

They were clearly warnings of danger. Of some kind.

Danger of what? Butcher wondered and continued on, shooting the dreaming ghoul, for he would leave nothing alive in their wake.

Just as they'd done in other wars, and other forgotten places.

For the colonel, and the Butcher, it was as though no time has passed. As though they were made for such situations, even if it was the end of the world.

Or so it was seeming.

In the passages beyond the last shrine, they found the last obstacle they'd been warned of by the undeciphered bloodstained cinnamon-crimson scratch words along the walls of the small shrine.

The Mind Whisperer...

The tentacled feeder in the darkest, deepest part of the Slums. Where the swampy water table began in the base of the prison and the old stones there were black and moldy...and even the ghouls had been devoured by the thing that games of funny dice and paper once called...a neo-otyugh.

A feeder in the darkness.

✳ 5 ✳

Jorge Escudo was the local banker of a small town near the river. Rio Maria. And to have once called him "a banker" was to have used a loose grip on terms and words and their exact meanings.

He was more of a loan shark. A lender at exorbitant interest rates with a slew of leg-breakers at his disposal who didn't mind disappearing the family members of his clients off into the jungles to feed the local alligator population so that debts, or really the crushing interest on them, were and was serviced on time.

He was an excellent businessman for a monster.

He was corpulent, sweaty, stinking to the point of foul because of his diet of sweets and grease, and despite all this, still considered himself a ladies' man.

All four hundred and fifty-eight pounds of him. He smelled bad, and his office, a repossessed hacienda of a once-prosperous family whose remains could be found at the bottom of a deep and lonely lagoon twenty miles distant from the village, was a hoarder's paradise.

Or goal to be aspired to.

Often, he took whatever in exchange for whatever interest on the debt had accumulated—family treasures, tools, collectibles, and other weird items to delay the leg-breakers paying a visit. The interest didn't stop, though. So the villa had ended up stuffed with a collection of curious knickknacks, gaudy heirlooms, and dusty gewgaws.

Eventually, Jorge had been betrayed by one of the leg-breakers who henched for him and had learned the business just enough to take over badly and make do without Jorge's disgusting habits like devouring at least three chickens, bones and all, a day, not to mention a never-ending supply of pastries delivered courtesy of the local baker who'd tried to poison Jorge Escudo a number of times, and failed.

The baker's daughters had been disappeared into the nearest big-city brothels, sold to pay on the interest of a loan.

Jorge shrugged off the final attempted poisoning with an epic case of dysentery and flatulence tasted and felt by all houses on the block where the villa lay. And he survived.

His constitution was considered iron and he thrived, florid-faced, despite his health, weight, and appetites.

Then the chief leg-breaker tired of the game at his rate and took the whole thing for himself, selling Jorge out.

After being turned over to the Federales, Jorge Escudo was then handed over to the prison commandant because the Feds didn't want to deal with the problems Jorge came with, and so was the fat man thus disappeared into the lowest levels of the Slums to be lost, and hopefully forgotten, forever.

Beaten and abused much, at first, Jorge retreated deeper and deeper into the Slums, diving down past the "graveyard" the prisoners maintained and finally reaching the offal pile that was the make-do plumbing system for the Slums given the official installed system had given up its efforts years ago.

From here, he maintained his existence for six months and details are best left out, but in that time, the Ruin . . . that is what the fantastic world that would follow the collapse of the present one would call itself—*the Ruin* . . . the Ruin began to do its revealing, and who knows the *how*s and *why*s of the Spider Queen's nano-plague and why it made some this, and others that. But Jorge began to change along with the rest of the world.

Lawyers becoming vampires.

Hedge-fund bros turning into bloodthirsty werewolves.

Government workers parasitical life-forms, and even around some of the major capitals, vast hordes of zombies feasting on the flesh of the living and the politicians who'd once wielded them against the populace.

Fantastical beasts of some, and orcs of others.

Wights, chimeras, sphinxes, minotaurs, giants, and many, many others. Maybe even a giant floating eyeball monster.

Who knows why...

But in the case of Jorge Escudo, he became what the programming and coding of a manufactured nano-plague demanded. What the Spider Queen had coded for with her vast databases of DNA, information, records, spites, grievances, prejudices, and final judgments of.

Jorge Escudo became a neo-otyugh.

A neo-otyugh is a repulsive monstrosity of many legs and slithering tentacles. It is a beast of chaos and therefore highly weird. Example: the body parts don't always add up. There ain't always two legs or two arms or equal parts. A strange thing indeed, as weird in fantasy as Jorge Escudo was in life. So it was an odd misshapen beast, vexing to the rational mind to behold, that the "banker" became, and if that wasn't enough, if that wasn't bad enough, opening wide from its main pestilent pus-filled reeking body was a hideous fanged "mouth."

A giant maw of a thing that drew the eye in all its mind-numbing horror of disbelief that such a thing could exist.

Jorge was now truly the monster he'd always been. Fully revealed.

They say, in the years to come within the Ruin... *The Ruin Reveals.*

A neo-otyugh loves the filthy foul-smelling places, and where Jorge had retreated into, deep down in the depths of the Slums, was such a place. Since the revealing work of the plague had done its work on Jorge Escudo, the awful neo-otyugh had begun to ambush and lure victims among the prison population that was dwindling by the day, the ghouls gathering and growing by the night, and occasionally the stray "orc" guards who were foolish enough to descend to the deeper levels of the rotting Slums where Jorge ruled the waste-filled pools and forgotten ruins.

And just as in life, he'd begun to gather his little treasures that he could find among their torn-apart bodies, and his own waste where sometimes he'd chewed and swallowed too fast and missed an important treasure. A shank. Cached prison currency. Gold and sometimes even jewelry taken from the dead that had been robbed either in the night, or from the grave.

Here at the bottom of the Slums, Jorge buried himself deep as he changed, and grew even larger, becoming that hideous bull-sized thing he soon would be. Becoming a fantastic monstrosity of lore and fantasy once found in some forgotten game of what would all too soon be long ago.

Jorge had always been naturally smart, a learner of systems, a schemer of ways, and a reader of the hearts and wants and, yes, even dark desires of men's minds and the desperations that would send them seeking the services of the malignant moneylender at truly exorbitant rates to feed these appetites.

So, Jorge Escudo was an especially crafty monster, Ruin-revealed, and just as he'd preyed well on the living as a loan shark, now he went to work on the local population as things began to quietly, and then not so quietly in recent weeks, change.

His mind could listen, and sometimes talk to his soon-to-be victims, and Jorge thought this was delicious and he slavered with delight as he thought how best to apply this new skill to feed his wants and desires.

Along with the other effects of the plague, he'd come to have . . . *powers* now. Later, some would call those powers . . . *spells*. Though in Jorge's case it was more of a mental power, like psionics.

These—the spells, the psionics, and other abilities far stranger still—were powers the secret labs of the military called DARPA had once explored and developed. And the Spider Queen had access to those files and labs too.

Her hacking skills were, not an understatement here . . . without peer.

So Jorge had *powers* now as he sat there, slavering in the dark, undulating his snakelike tentacles and great bulk as he bathed his feverish mind and throbbing muscles in the warmth of a feces-filled cesspool, undulating his odd-numbered tentacles to caress his collected treasures and the rotting carcasses of his most recent victims along its edge and cached down here in the stinking dark at the back and bottom of the Slums.

A couple of ghouls he'd lured here, infiltrating their minds and commanding them to come to him in a dreamlike state via his powers, were ready to be finished off as soon as he made room for their consumption by expelling a massive fart that had been tormenting him for some time. Also on the menu of impending consumption was an orc-ling, one of the thieves the guards had once used as intelligence gatherers within the rendition prison, who'd come delving down into these low depths for scraps of food and information. Jorge had Held him too with the sheer force of his mind.

The power to *Hold*. This also was one of Jorge's powers. He could read minds, listen to them really, and then, sometimes, dominate them and make them do small tasks he wanted done. Commanding them. Come to Jorge so he could devour them down there in his stinking pool. Ripping their flesh with his tentacles, gobbling with his fangs, his grotesque bulk trembling with delight as he did so.

Swallowing his meals too fast, then digging through what came out of him for the "interest" they owed him, his mad mind chanted over and over as things got sicker and weirder by the day.

"Hold!" he'd thought at the orc who'd once been a pickpocket in the village of Sinta, over and across the jungle-covered mountains to the north. And the orc had held, frozen in place, unwilling and unable to move.

Then Jorge's tentacles, now ropy and powerful and thick, strangled the man who'd become, revealed as it were, an "orc" now. Jorge fed on him—some; that giant fart was already killing him by then—then stashed what was unfinished in the offal pile that was the prison's waste collection area, saving some for "*a snack for later*," even as his other tentacles searched the cooling half-ravaged corpse for what baubles and treasures might be added now that things had gone . . . well, the way they'd gone.

Yeah, that's dark.

Right about now, one might ask how all this had come to be the way it had. You, like the Butcher, will find out more than you'd like to know. In time. But right now, let's just say that the Spider Queen . . . once, many years ago . . . the Spider Queen, not yet a Spider Queen, played a game one summer in her youth between being a girl and becoming a woman. A game of dice and monsters, paper and fantasy. Dungeons . . . and dragons. Of course.

And heroes.

Just some twelve-year-old girl with severely Asperger-like tendencies and an incredible off-the-charts IQ even before the powers that be jacked her up for a government experiment to unlock the potential of the human brain.

She and everyone around her in that planned community were part of a vast experiment to survive some promised Nuclear Doomsday the Cold War had assured everyone was coming with drills of *stop, drop, and roll* and movies and books of a postapocalyptic tomorrow that would be more horrible than anyone ever knew.

It was a giant experiment to find and develop warriors to fight for the rise of a new civilization, and tacticians to lead them, and yes scientists to give these warriors and tacticians greater weapons than ever imagined to perhaps someday end their civilization's global enemies, or destroy the world all over again.

Same as it ever was. Civilizations end all the time.

But in that group, that summer, in what was supposed to seem a "game store," she found a boy, a hero, a someday warrior when the bombs would surely fall, and as girls do . . .

She fell in love.

First love.

They kissed. Once.

But alas, when the summer was done, she was taken away for further testing, deeper down into the unseen bunkers beneath the community, the perfect planned neighborhoods, and of course to that powering up that would make her lose her mind . . . and become the Spider Queen, in time.

For one second, one moment, she'd had love. And the potential to become something other than what she would become . . . was possible. In a kiss.

Just a boy and a girl.

Old as time.

But she was taken away. The powers that be ordained it be so.

And so it was.

That's how it is.

And for a lost kiss . . . she burned the world. The whole thing.

She bore them a grudge now, and this plague was her payback. In full. And that game she'd once played with a handsome boy . . . it was a future that would never be, and a future she felt we all deserved now, making monsters, and magic. And yes, perhaps even . . . perchance if we can be poetic . . . heroes, even.

Perhaps even love?

As though she was daring the universe to prove there was such a thing as heroes, and true love, and fragile princesses who were taken down into a doomsday bunker and made into a doomsday machine to win some game for the end of the world, someday.

All that is another story for another time, and you just need this bit to explain here how Jorge Escudo the ruthless loan shark and generally terrible human being became a monster in the dark. We'll get to the rest . . .

And how magic became real.

And monsters.

And how heroes were needed, desperately perhaps, even now in the dark of humanity's last hours.

Elves and orcs and monsters were becoming all too real as the world that was became the Ruin that would be. A Forgotten Ruin.

So as Butcher and the SF colonel approached the neo-otyugh that was once Jorge Escudo down there in the basement . . . Jorge the horrible thing was already digging into the two men's minds. Listening to their thoughts as he sought some way to manipulate them now before the inevitable happened and they came into his stinking foul lair with guns to ruin him.

Jorge was a survival machine too.

It was clear their intentions were to escape the prison. It was also clear they were dangerous and violent, armed with weapons.

And Jorge was hungry for warm flesh and not just the cold rotting remains he kept near the waste-pool that was his throne of horrors.

For a moment, the neo-otyugh considered crawling deeper into the recesses of the foul-smelling stench that was the cesspool where most of the Slums' "plumbing" had run down into it finally. It could crawl back in there, pull the reek and filth of human and now-inhuman waste over itself, and just hide and let these two escape. Pass on. Pass by. Live.

And then Jorge could rule and feast on those who could not leave.

The ghouls that had fallen under its powerful psychic sway were now all dead. He could no longer hear their thoughts in his insane mind. *Best to hide*, some small part whispered inside his brain.

But Jorge was hungry.

He was always hungry now, hungrier than he'd ever been, and even more so now that he'd become what he'd . . . become.

The Feeder in the Dark.

The Ruin reveals, as they say.

So perhaps then . . . he would hide here in the shadows of the basement, burrow into their minds when they passed by, and perhaps grab them with his magnificent, and putrescent, sucker-laden tentacles. Then pull them to his hungry mouth.

Yes . . .

Jorge gave a terrific and triumphant victory fart that resonated off the lonely basement walls underneath the collapsing and fetid prison in the jungle, feeling relieved and confirming that his trap was good.

He would do it.

He would take them.

He would . . . *consume them* . . . over many days.

That would be . . . good, thought the hideous neo-otyugh. Its former humanity almost shed now completely. It would love nothing more than to just rip their flesh open and gorge itself on the tasty organs, slavering and cracking their bones and sucking at the marrow as it pitched chunks of flesh and other broken limbs into its mouth with other revolting tentacles.

Here we go . . .

The Butcher heard the thing in his head. Digging around. Listening. Trying little spidery whispers . . .

Except the Ranger scout didn't recognize that what he was experiencing was a thing with a mind. In the dark, as he and his former team leader waded through the half-sunken chambers of the lowest level of the old prison, approaching the outer wall . . .

. . . sporadic gunfire off in the distance as the Ranger extraction team followed the trail of snapped chemlights and made orcish guards pay a heavy price for the chase . . .

. . . John Butcher felt an animal in the darkness of the jungle.

Another predator, just like him. Out on the stalk and hunting. Recon men were no stranger to coming across other predators late in the night, beyond the wire and downrange.

He'd been doing recon all his life, or so it seemed. In the darkest night, in jungle and enemy nations sworn to hunt and kill intruders, for a scout, the ability to feel danger in the night, even where there seemed to be none, wasn't just critical...it was a way of life. And continued existence.

"Something's down here with us," muttered the lieutenant colonel, feeling it too because he was also a recon man, despite the silver oak leaf clusters and the green beret, but nothing like the Butcher who was considered by even the best...as *gifted* at the art of reconnaissance. The colonel ejected the weathered old mag on his retirement 1911 and confirmed the number of rounds he had left to get it done by.

"I got five left, Johnny."

Butcher had one slug and four shot shells in the 1301. More rounds on the sling and ready when needed. Dragon's Breath too.

There were two chemlights left, and Butcher had been counting off steps to calculate in his head how close to the outer wall they were now. They'd entered some vast awful-smelling basement where there was nothing but darkness, and the Butcher had never been to this part of the prison. But he had a pretty good mental map developed over the long years of forced incarceration at the hands of leaders who'd once considered him a valuable asset, and then a dangerous liability they were willing to live with until they might need him again someday.

And now was that rainy day they'd feared ever needing him again.

The colonel was holding up the last chemlight, giving them some illumination.

The surrounding swamp and the water table surrounding the old prison was causing the cursed old rotting place to sink into the swampy grounds. But the smell was worse than just those elements. There was something else here that was...unclean. Horrific with corruption. It was...as bad as burn pits and somehow...even worse in a way that couldn't be sensed and was more felt.

There wasn't just human waste down here...there was something...like *death*.

"Smell that?" hissed the colonel.

The Butcher grunted.

For a moment the Ranger scout thought the hair on his skin had just stood up, or like someone had just caressed the back of his neck causing an electrical response, a thrill almost...but instead of being a delight it was mentally slick and viscous and...*deeply foul*.

He worked the barrel on the shadows and corners, pointing it where he thought an attack would come and willing to destroy whatever it was as fast as he could work the trigger and keep the barrel pointed in the right direction.

He'd ride the thunder and kill it fast.

But somehow, he had the feeling he'd need more than just the shells in the deadly combat shotgun, and not for the first time in a long time he wished he had his old scout knife on his rig.

But he didn't.

Hadn't seen that in years.

The sensation of the unclean caress along the back of his neck was so real, Butcher removed one hand from the foregrip of the 1301 and ran it back there to see if some deadly local horror-show spider or some poisonous snake had dropped down from the roof and into his clothing.

They did that. This was the jungle, after all. That's why scouts wore boonie hats on the stalk.

But there was nothing there.

The neo-otyugh whispered in his mind...

"Over there..."

As though someone had called to him from one of the deepest darkest corners of the deep dark hole he and the colonel found themselves in now.

Butcher turned his head slowly, feeling like he was being pushed to perform this very action and knowing it was... somehow wrong.

Didn't feel right.

Then the first tentacle came whipping out of the dark beyond the red wash of the chem and slapped him like a suddenly sprung deadfall trap, powerfully, knocking him off his feet and at least ten feet to the side of their course.

He went down in foul dark waters.

A second tentacle surfaced out of those same waters, curled around the colonel's legs, and dragged the SF officer to the sunken floor of the basement.

At the same instant, a quivering mound of total and utter revulsion surfaced within the now turbulent dark waters along the floor where most of the pool of nightmares had collected through abject ruin and long years of waste collection.

This was like something out of a horror movie or a Cthulhu novel. The hideous mass was a quivering green mound adorned with dripping filth and foul-smelling water, and really it was nothing more than the giant fanged-mouth gash of razor-sharp terrors that opened and gnashed hungrily in the obscene pool's direct center.

And there were also two... human... eyes just above this.

Feverish. Burning with desire. Darting this way and that as though in both delight, and fear.

The transformation of Jorge Escudo had been painful indeed. But to the few tormented shreds of the man's mind that still remained, loosely gripping to sanity and rational thought like some high-wire trapeze artist, this was the moment to act. Hunger and the will for total domination, even in this basement turned public sewer, drove Jorge, and divested him of all care for the surrounding dead ghouls and the stray orc-lings that'd wandered down this far. He was no longer in some deep of the most forgotten place on Earth, in a prison so distant from the minds of men that it wasn't even listed on any maps and was in fact blotted by algorithms when satellites crossed high overhead.

This was the feasting table of Jorge Escudo's Throne of Corruption. The banquet where the lonely fat man is already considering his next meal even as he consumes the one he's at, because that's all there is to him, and in time... in time he would devour the whole wide world.

And perhaps even that... *would not be enough.*

Those satellites... they were starting to fail.

The ruin was starting to become the Ruin.

Technology was... breaking down all around them. The world was going Bronze Age fantasy, and monsters and magic were becoming all too real.

The Butcher kept his scarred finger off the trigger of the combat shotgun as he rolled from the impact, saw the hideous quivering thing that was impossibly Jorge, and came up on one knee. No need to comprehend the impossible monstrosity he was witnessing, he was a killer. He was the Butcher. And he'd been killing monsters long before they became what they truly were inside.

He fired the first slug and missed. The heavy round thundered and struck some unseen wall, exploding rotten stone and grit where prisoners had once been beaten, interrogated, beaten some more, then shot.

But the Beretta 1301 combat shotgun the Ranger NCO had handed the Butcher didn't come with just one shell. There were four more ready to go, and it didn't need to be racked like the old M97 the Butcher had once preferred for certain scouting and infiltration missions in the event things went pear-shaped, or the green light was given to go into the dark and unknown and terminate the target.

This shotgun fired as fast as the trigger could be pulled.

Successive blasts of sudden thunder erupted from the barrel as the Butcher focused all his rage and anger on the two feverish eyes dead center of the quivering mass that was the neo-otyugh that could barely be seen in the dim submerged wan red light of the sunken-beneath-the-foul-waters chem-stick the colonel had dropped when dragged off his feet by the hideous tentacles of Jorge the Neo-otyugh.

Jorge the Victorious.

Jorge the Triumphant.

Jorge the *Very . . . Hungry!*

The thundering blasts seemed to have no effect on the horrible mind-numbing thing.

At first, as the Butcher got to his feet, dripping corruption and filth from the ancient cesspool, he'd thought there were more assailants already on him. Some pulpy body had come in contact with his as he'd struggled out of the waters, but it was only a half-eaten ghoul that Jorge had been unable to resist when hungry a few days back.

John Butcher grunted at the utter horror of this and began pulling the trigger as fast as he could on the abominable thing attacking them.

The tentacle holding the colonel was now dragging him toward his razor-fang-laden mouth, which was already working its hideous jaws open and closed like it was some comedy-funhouse-of-mirrors trapdoor that must be part of this carny-ride of roadside terrors. It was clear to the Butcher that in just seconds the fanged gash would crunch down and bite his former commanding officer right in half.

Then that unclean voice whispered within Butcher's mind . . . but now it was not a whisper when it landed right in the center of his brain, going off like an artillery strike close at hand.

"Detener!" shouted Jorge the Horror-Thing.

The neo-otyugh.

This was a new ability in the becoming of Jorge that the neo-otyugh had learned. It could, once it had a firm foot, or mental tentacle as it were, inside a potential victim's mind . . . it could freeze them in place. *Hold* them. Not as though paralyzed, but unwilling to move unless it was told to do so by Jorge. The neo-otyugh.

That command to *Hold*, to *Stop*, was so utterly powerful, dominating even, that any lesser man not used to the hardships, adversity, and levels of sheer suck beyond imagination that had been the Butcher's career as a scout for the Rangers, SOCOM, and other darker government powers, would have frozen, or hesitated for a fatal second of inaction.

But the Butcher was not other men.

When the others froze, he was on the move.

When one-chance opportunities opened within impenetrable defenses, he slid like a shadow into the cracks and was gone like a ghost.

When the chance to fire a shot at extreme distances, surrounded and in high winds was needed . . . he took the shot.

And then . . . gone like a ghost in the night.

This, and other well-supported reasons, were why he was known in the community that was SOCOM as . . . the Butcher.

He was quick, precise, and deadly.

And these were exactly the reasons why he'd ended up here, in a rendition prison that didn't exist on any of the maps of men, in the first place. Perpetually waiting to be executed so that *she* . . . could live.

That was the unspoken deal that had been made.

All bets were off now. He liked freedom, hadn't tasted it in a long while, and now . . . awakened to it in just the few minutes since he'd been offered the deal in his cell . . . he was intent on going all the way with it this time.

Farther than they knew. Or even expected.

He'd do this deal, find her, and keep her safe. The world was ending. The deals were off and new ones were possible.

He closed the distance in the dank basement with footsteps that might as well have been artillery walking the earth as he started pulling the trigger fast and dead center on Jorge the Neo-otyugh's impossible still-human eyes above that gaping gash of horror that was its hideous mouth.

Jorge, or whatever he'd become now, his power to *Hold* . . . failed and now he was being shredded to pieces by the individual and rapid blasts of the fast-working very deadly combat shotgun in the hands of the man called the Butcher by the few who knew he even still existed.

And that the Butcher was death itself, or so some said.

The first blast to hit, thundered and burst Jorge's eyes. Pulping them instantly. The hideous horror heaved, expanding its horrid hide and forcing its vital organs closer to the skin. Subsequent blasts tore deeper into the monster's carcass and shattered its massive heart, tore apart its foul bulging organs, and slashed open the profane contents of its four stomachs, spilling out more half-eaten ghoul.

A blasted tentacle flung itself wildly and writhed in pain as the one around the colonel tightened and tried to strangle him through sheer raw feral strength.

The Butcher slung the now-empty still-smoking shotgun and grasped the tentacle as it slithered around the colonel's chest. Seizing it with both of his scarred hands, John roared and pulled in both directions, ripping the grotesque and unholy thing apart, causing the rest of its length to recoil in searing pain as the last death throes of Jorge Escudo began down there in the forgotten basement beneath the prison that didn't exist.

Jorge's wails of pain and torment became gurgles of the last of himself as he sank into the putrescent pool and down beneath its black foulness.

Moments later, the three Rangers of the extraction team entered the basement, staring in stunned awe and amazement at what was revealed in the gray-green of night vision and thermal.

Neither Colonel Crowe nor the Butcher had night vision to see the place fully. But the Rangers did.

There were half-eaten inhuman bodies everywhere, floating among the flotsam and debris of the ancient sunken room. And then the remnants of the giant obscene thing that was the neo-otyugh, blasted hither and thither by the Butcher.

Even just what was left of it ... defied explanation and understanding of any rational kind.

Colonel Crowe was getting to his boots as the HVI helped him out of the coils of what looked like oily and bloody shredded fleshy ropes. With small suckers that still gasped and closed as though seeking life to feed on even in death.

These things were clearly not common things at all to even the

Ranger who'd seen many strange things of late in these uncertain and dark days as the world didn't end . . . but became something else.

Something ruined.

"Looks like we missed the party," said the Ranger team leader. "This da outer wall?"

Butcher nodded and began to thumb Dragon's Breath rounds into the 1301.

It was all he had left now for the final push to the exfil site.

He studied the wall for a long minute, comparing it against his suspicions and the mental map he'd made over the long years of his imprisonment.

Years of horror.

Years of brutality.

Years of . . . hope.

It was time to leave.

"That's it. Breach it and we'll be in the yard as best I can tell, Sergeant."

There was the other exit if things went south. The one through the waste pools that the prisoners used. Those with coin or trade, and later, the monsters. But John Butcher was no longer a prisoner, and if he was a monster, it was of a different kind. A much more dangerous kind. He'd swim through waste if that's what it took, and had, but better to keep the weapons dry.

On the other side of this wall, they'd be needed.

Staff Sergeant Hunter was down on one knee and into his ruck, getting the necessary demo out despite the filth and ravaged bloating bodies of the ghouls. And even the obscene thing floating among the dead, drooling darker blood into the dark waters on thermal vision within the night optical device he wore.

"Ain't da end of our problems by half now, boss, but we almost there. Jungle's alive with dem things and the bird's already on the LZ and getting pushed. Gotta hustle now, Rangers. Stand by to breach."

✳7✳

"Execute, execute, execute!" shouted PFC Rogers as the old outer wall of the rendition prison blew suddenly outward, pushing rotten debris and time-ravaged concrete dynamically forward in a wide spray across the old sunken cemetery. An "informal" burial place that had once been a manicured garden long ago in a more genteel lost colonial plantation age, but after that ... a disposal yard for dirty secrets in a less polite time.

Shattered, featureless tombstones, already leaning through rot and carelessness, tilted yet farther away as though recoiling from the offense caused by the Ranger extraction team's high-ex as they detted the outer wall in order to make their escape and reach the LZ before it got overrun by the changeling denizens of the hot jungle night currently surrounding them and blocking their escape.

Sergeant Hunter had walked the PFC through the emplacement and employment of the explosives, to train the kid, and keep his hands on carbine in case more ghouls, or orcs, came out of the dark at them.

Rangers are always learning, and learning on the job is just as much a part of the process as class time.

"No better time than now to indoctrinate ya into the Cult of High Explosives, PFC. This here is how we gon' do it . . ."

Then it got done, the wall got blown open, and a hole was made.

The graveyard beyond the smoke and debris in the jungle night was filled with leering ghouls, aghast that they were disturbed in their work, and wretched zombies, the ghouls' work, being dragged from the deep graves by the ghouls in some dark effort to create an ad hoc army to block the escape of their next meal, the extraction team and their HVI. The Butcher.

The blast thundered, ripping through rotting and upright walking corpses with fast-moving high-ex-driven debris, shredding some, ravaging others, barely touching the rest for reasons physics didn't feel it needed to explain.

The Rangers came out shooting into the yard behind the old plantation turned prison. Ghouls and their zombie foot soldiers got dusted with precise gunfire delivered with maximum speed and violence, quickly.

The Butcher, in his own stoically grim way, was glad to see the inheritors of the scroll he'd once paid the rent on a long time ago, still embraced the concept of Violence of Action. Headshots to rotting skulls were handed out as the three Rangers cleaned the yard and kept moving for the exfil.

The Butcher picked up a fast-moving ghoul trying to flank the wedge and shotgunned the thing with a blast from the Beretta 1301.

The rotting, hoary old thing flat-out came apart in several pieces, disintegrating even as the thunder of the gun faded off into the jungle.

The Butcher and colonel picked up the rear as the killing wedge moved through the plague army force of ghouls and zombie foot soldiers, leaving a wake of dead-again corpses as they made for the jungle clutch and the edge of the hill that would take them down toward the LZ, and extraction out of this nightmare. The wedge of two riflemen, Sergeant Hunter and PFC Rogers, and Hopkins the SAW gunner moved forward like a relentless force that could not be stopped by undead or nightmare-creatures today, or any other day. These were Rangers on the move, shooting, communicating, and picking up targets as they eliminated all who dared oppose their exit off the X. Roman legionnaires would have applauded the efficient killing and learned a thing or two along the way, as the normally easygoing Sergeant Hunter ran his team like a quarterback calling plays in clipped, definite, military commands.

Nothing was left to chance.

Nothing survived.

Spent brass dribbled into the wet grass and open graves, and more gunfire wiped out the rest of the tangos here.

This was not the extraction team's first rodeo with zombies and ghouls, but that was another story, not this one.

The yard cleared through lethal force via kinetic violence, the extraction team and their HVI were on the move as they hit the jungle at the edge of the prison, threading a long-downed wire fence. Now, above the simian barking and snapping of gnashing fangs of the orcs within the prison, and all across the dark in the night all around them, the team could hear the beat of the Special Operations Black Hawk's powerful blades beating jungle along the wide river below the hill where the plantation once lay, surveying its domain, and in time … becoming a prison for the forgotten, allowing the triple canopy and dense press of the flora and fauna all around to hide it, to contain the dark purposes within of the Deep State and those who would rule the world from the shadows.

Down there along the river, the sound of the mounted miniguns the door gunner and crew chief were working, was constant.

"They gettin' pushed real hard," said Staff Sergeant Hunter. "Let's get on the hump fast now. They gonna need to give them bad guys a break to allow us onta the LZ."

They were on the move, and any orcs they encountered in the night, pushing toward the bird, got the same treatment the ghouls and zombies back in the yard had received.

Tangos died, stumbling and tumbling, shrieking in horror at the wounds that had suddenly been made in them by the stalking wedge of the Ranger fire team.

But ahead it was clear there was a major force surrounding the Black Hawk.

"We in it now," whispered Sergeant Hunter. "Ain't no way out but through all dat."

But...

...there was one last predator out in the night that night. A hulking giant of a thing. Twisted and cruel, it was inky, and oily, and its tough, almost leather hide seemed to be made of hideous ropy vines of the jungle, but that was not the case.

The creature, large, had followed the team as they left the prison and disappeared downslope. It stayed back, trailing along the ground and using the huge jungle trees to hide as it watched.

Those ropy features along its dark, oily, almost leathery hide, were the ugly creature's lean, twisted muscles, entwining about its massive frame.

It was easily twelve feet tall.

It listened to the orcs gnashing their teeth, barking wildly down there in the jungle and along the river, occasionally aimlessly firing now-meaningless automatic weapons, rifles, and pistols they still possessed. Still more streamed down the hill, away from the prison now, heading toward the developing battle at the LZ where the transport helo waited.

The thing in the forest watched and waited for its moment, just as it had before it had become what it had become, plotting its next move.

This was... a *troll*.

The troll had lingered, hanging back in the hot sweaty night... just as it had done in its human life, waiting for just the right moment to cause its special and particular brand of mayhem. And to take what it wanted for a nice and tasty meal.

Sweat dripped down its ugly skin as it breathed heavily and chanced getting closer to the Rangers and their HVI as they made their way to the LZ.

Decision time was imminent...

"Now or never," it rattled gutturally and considered what it might attack them with. A tree. A boulder. Perhaps...

It selected a good-sized stone, quietly and quickly pulling it up from the moss it lay entrenched within along the jungle floor. A dozen deadly pulpy shining black spiders scurried away from the stone, terrified of what they were beholding in the terrible troll.

The troll cast one of its glaring and malevolent yellow cat's eyes at the fleeing men, weighing the stone and considering what it might do with just this. It laughed, and its laugh was hitched and clunky and sounded like a dog coughing.

It was not a good thing to hear in the jungle quiet.

It was a laugh that had never known real humor or joy. It was the sound of something that delighted in the suffering and misfortune of others.

Now it was getting abundantly clear to the stupid yet crafty thing that was the troll that its opportunity to consume living, real, and still-human flesh...was slipping away quickly now.

It was tired of orc.

At first, once it had reached its full height, and power, it had been taking orcs, picking them off down by the river and on the way out to the nearest town that was rapidly disintegrating into violence and mayhem as strange creatures began to appear there. Using its great stealth, its ability to be almost unseen in dense jungle night, and using sometimes even the river and the bridge it had begun to live under after being forced from the small city the troll had once lived in before the Ruin began to do its revealing work... using these talents, the troll had been able to throw its voice, or even small stones, causing the changeling guards, and local villagers, to fight with one another. Hostilities erupted, and in the end, someone was always left alone.

Out in the jungle or some other lonely place.

Then she came for them. Dragging them under, off into the brush with her troll's claws, to have her way with her unfortunate victim. And her way...was feasting. Cracking the bones, sucking the marrow, drinking the blood, then licking it off her claws. Saving the best, the brain, *oh the tasty sweetness of the brain* ... for last. In this she burped loudly, picked up the ragdoll lifeless corpse of her most recent victim, then just simply bashed the skull against a nearby rock, and ... slurped up the brain as though it were one of the cookies she used to have when doing her work as a simple telephone operator, for a party line that served a few local down-and-out villages.

Before the Ruin began to be revealed. Before the world that was, became the Ruin it would be ...

Back then she used to love to sit and just listen to all their secrets, and dramas, who was cheating on whom, who was pregnant by whom, who'd murdered someone, or who had stolen from someone else, all those people on her lines. All the while eating her sweet, lemony-frosted cookies, licking off the icing and making hot cloying tea she listened, keeping notes on a small prized battered laptop she'd bought secondhand ...

And then would come the blackmailing she began to get up to once she had all their secrets marked down.

At first this had just been a hobby. Before the blackmail. Listening in. Then the listening led to sowing discord, just for fun. She was quite amused to watch, from a distance, as affairs were discovered and lives ruined. That was fun, and she laughed her choking laugh in the silence of her crummy hovel, thinking how superior she was to the ones whose lives she'd ruined. Then one dark and stormy night in the jungle, late by the clock, as she sat and waited for someone, anyone, to talk and no one was talking that night because of the storm, she figured just how she could turn all this wonderful gossip into ... profit. Money she so desperately craved to prove to them just how much better she was than they were.

And have fun doing it. So that was a bonus.

She was a troll, of sorts, even though she didn't live under a bridge like she soon would when she was revealed to be what she would become, later, because it was dark there and she could listen to the roadway above and that was just like listening to the telephone system that had begun to fail as the Ruin began to turn her ...

It was horrible. The revealing.

And though she didn't snatch children and murder them, like she did as a troll now ... hadn't she been doing that all along, murdering with her silent whispers and lies, stealing away lives with her well-laced divisions, and more gossip spread just right?

She was a troll even before all that would happen ... happened.

But what really made her a troll, long before she became one, was "the Facebook" as she called it in her third-world patois. "The Facebook" was where she had the most fun because even though it was the jungle in Latin America, believe it or not, people had "the Facebook" pages, and so did small communities she ran the telephone lines through and along.

Using the comments section, and her vast knowledge of all their dirty laundry, she spent hours tracking everyone down, day and night, identifying their Facebook pages by what she knew of them from the calls she'd eavesdropped into ...

And in using the comments section ...

... well, that was when she truly became a troll.

Example.

Someone might post they had a tractor for sale. *Used of course, but working hard for the community.*

And the Esmeralda Reale who would soon become a real-life troll would simply comment, *Much like your whore wife and the many of your neighbors she's with when you're not around, including even your closest friend, Tomas.*

She had a fake-name account. They could never find her, who she really was in the comments sections, and in time many followed her to see just what tasty tidbits she would drop that day, or night, and hopefully nothing about *them* as only the lives of others were ruined, outed, held up for public inspection, true or not.

The best trolling was when she began to just make stuff up and was taken at face value due to her credible "reporting" in the past.

A mayor was shot in the face and killed on the lie that he was stealing from the public trust and spending it on a whore in Calle Via.

He had five children. He'd never been to a whore in Calle Via.

But who cared. The lie was delicious and the man who shot the mayor believed the money had been stolen.

Then the nano-plague began to spread ...

And things began to change.

Esmeralda Reale began to change. The fever that began the changing was incredible. Her bones ached like nothing she'd ever experienced. As though they were being stretched on a torture rack. At one point she was in a delirious coma for more than a week, and when she awoke her skin was oily and dark, leathery patches spreading like a rash, her features misshapen. Her brow heavy like an ape's. Her eyes wide and glittering, malevolent in her shadowy room.

She could now see clearly in the dark. And by then, she was two feet taller.

For the next few weeks she grew, first eating everything she could get her hands on, then sleeping for long periods of time as her chest heaved with heavy, rapid breathing.

She would wake up drenched in sweat and thinking only of eating food.

She took to robbing her neighbors' chicken coops in the night. Eating a whole cow, bloody and raw, in the next. And finally, catching a late-night drunkard coming home from the cantina . . . *well, why not*, thought Esmeralda Reale and attacked the man along the misty jungle road, knocking him to the ground and throwing herself on his flesh, so very hungry.

She ate him right there in the road. Sucking the marrow of the bones she broke open as though what was within was calling to her.

And when she finally discovered the treat . . . of the brain . . .

It reminded her of those lemony-frosted tea cookies she'd once nibbled on, and sometimes gobbled by the tinful, listening to all the dirt on the lines she was tasked to watch over.

She was a troll now.

She didn't know that. Didn't know what a troll was. She wasn't educated. And not well-read at all.

She didn't care.

What she'd become had given her so much more raw power than she'd ever possessed as a frail, almost middle-aged woman listening to the lines and connecting calls local and international.

Now she could throttle a man, in the night, and eat him.

She grew and grew the more stray drunkards she attacked, but by that time the world was breaking down and descending into chaos as the Ruin became what it was.

"Orcs" were appearing.

She ate those too.

The villages grew silent. Strange and dark things were going on there.

There were other strange creatures out in the night now.

The orcs tried to kill her. She killed many of them in a pitched battle along the quiet road two weeks before the battle at the rendition prison. Then she followed them back to their lair and lately, after a few nights of hunting them, they'd begun to give her sacrifices.

Hoping to appease the terror of the troll.

Esmeralda Reale liked that very much.

"In time," she rumbled, for her voice was now a deep hollow rumble under the quiet of the bridge she'd made her lair. Her home. "They'll worship me."

The troll liked that a lot.

But now, as she'd stalked the outskirts of the battle, watching the Rangers and the colonel and John Butcher escape through the back of the prison, the hunger of weeks ago had awakened in her once again.

She was tired of stringy stinking orc.

Why not... some good old-fashioned human? While it lasted. Who knew how many were left?

The Ruin was doing a lot of revealing these days...

As though it were meat on sale just like in the *carniceria* she'd once gone to for her hamburger. Before they'd driven her out of the city, in those first days when she looked like some Black Plague victim. She'd yet to grow tall, or have claws or fangs...

They thought she was sick, and the potential for infection was high. The government was falling apart. So they drove her out.

After all she'd done to them. The nerve.

I should go back there, she thought as she watched the soldiers, John Butcher bringing up the rear, moving closer now for she had crept ahead of their position, padding quietly alongside, for despite her bulk she was as stealthy as she had ever been with her fake-name account, unable to be tracked down and appearing only when and how she chose.

The soldiers swiveled their heads and scanned the night as though they sensed her out there, somehow, that she was watching them.

"Taste their brains," she gutter-muttered, then she hefted that good-sized rock and just whizzed it angrily, thinking of her former neighbors who'd chased her from her home. The projectile rocketed downslope from the jungle hill she watched them approach beneath her from. It whipped through the canopy and struck the gunner right in the chest.

Specialist Hopkins. Though she didn't know that. She saw only meat on the menu. She watched one of the shadowy figures fall. Her prey.

Perhaps, she thought, remaining still and not knowing they were Rangers, *they'll fight now, and I can pick one of them off for a nice snack. Oh, those brains . . .*

She drooled a thick, viscous rope of saliva from between her huge fangs.

✳ 8 ✳

The rock came out of the dark and slammed right into the gunner's plate carrier. Dead center.

There was an audible *crunch*.

The kid swore, was on his knees instantly, and it was clear from the get-go he was already having trouble breathing.

Staff Sergeant Hunter was on his troop like white on rice. The veteran Ranger NCO ran his hands around the kid's torso and fatigues and rig, checking for blood.

Nothing.

The PFC was scanning the jungle with his night optics. Rifle ready to come up and engage anything as lethally and as quickly as possible. "I got no one, Sergeant," reported Rogers as the NCO continued to try and figure out why Hopkins was struggling to breathe while still on his knees.

It was clear something was wrong more than just having the wind knocked out of him.

"Can you make it, Hopkins?" asked Hunter, quickly and almost making it sound like a challenge.

The SAW gunner nodded his head that he could, furiously, and tried to get to his feet still holding the gun that was slung about his shoulders.

But he couldn't.

He was back on his knees, gasping about not being able to breathe.

"Aw hell..." grunted the Ranger extraction team leader. "Ain't got time to treat a tension pneumothorax. But that looks like what it is. We gotta hustle and we can get to it on the bird. Rogers...gimme a hand with him."

"Here," said the colonel, deftly inserting himself into the chaos as he moved to unsling the SAW over the gunner's head.

"Negative, sir. We got quick disconnects now. Here, like this. After your time, sir."

The SF colonel said nothing and took the SAW.

"Y'know how ta use that thing? Sir," asked Sergeant Hunter.

The colonel glared at the team leader in the dark and muttered, "Go to hell, Sergeant. I'll take point. Tell the pilot to cool the guns... we're coming in. Johnny..." the SF officer said, turning to the Butcher. "Hell of a rescue...you're on cleanup. I got a feeling something's back there and it's coming for us."

"Ain't seein' nothing on any light spectrum, sir," volunteered the PFC.

"Yeah, maybe, kid. But I been in enough bad situations to know we ain't out yet and we got something followin' us. Live long enough and you can maybe be as paranoid as I am, kid."

PFC Rogers fell silent as the colonel hoisted the gun and straightened the linked ammo.

"C'mon, quit yo' jawin'. Sir...you on point. Get us in there. PFC Rogers, let's get our man to the bird."

Then the team leader was on the radio telling the pilot they were coming in now and the compass heading they'd be approaching from.

They took ten steps toward the bird, which was just down the road, down a steep embankment through triple canopy and then farther below at the LZ in a shallow river with enough clearance for the blades.

The gun on the Black Hawk closest to them fell silent and they could hear the orcs roaring and barking out there, heaving whistling spears, their former firearms, rocks, and whatever they could get their hands on at the crew of the extraction bird.

The team took ten steps before Esmeralda made her move, realizing they weren't going to fight each other, or blame each other, for her hurled rock, and then separate so she could pick them off one by one.

"They're leaving. Together," she gargled in her gutter-growl, indignant. Hissing as she dripped spit from her massive jaws.

She'd crack their bones and suck...

The troll charged furiously like a mad thing down the slope above like some unseen bull elephant raging and emerging from the brush, coming for them like a freight train that couldn't be stopped.

She was huge.

The colonel swore when he saw her. Turning, he immediately opened fire with the SAW, sending a staccato burst of accurate fire into the troll as it came for them even though his eyes desperately didn't want to believe what his mind was telling him.

The world was getting stranger... and stranger.

This was clearly one of the monsters the briefings had been warning them all about. But in real life... it was worse than could be conveyed. It was huge, tall, and moving fast. It didn't have to beat them to death... it was simply going to run them down and mow them over.

Butcher turned and fired a Dragon's Breath round into the troll as it closed on him, then dove to the side just to get out of its way as it thundered down upon them all. That was all the time he had to do anything as the massive oily black thing thundered past him in the night, reeking of the fouler parts of the jungle, and the bodies she'd devoured, making for their dead center where Colonel Crowe was firing up and at this hideous behemoth.

He heard the wet slap of fast-moving five-five-six slapping her hide, but... it didn't slow her down in the least or do anything much at all.

But it was dark, and the action was chaos and blur in that sudden instant of ambush.

The troll was bull-mad now, and that was all that was clear.

"Move, Rangers!" shouted the team leader as the colonel continued to fire the SAW center-mass on the huge wild-haired troll with massively thick muscles, despite the ineffectiveness of his fire so far.

Colonel Crowe did the math instantly. He'd seen enough contact and combat in his life to know what was gonna happen like it was second nature.

He'd stand his ground and dust her with all he had. Give the Rangers time to get to the bird. Maybe.

The Rangers hustled down the road, helping the wounded gunner between them, and were at the edge of the embankment leading down to the burbling stream where the orcs were still throwing themselves against the idling Black Hawk when the SAW went dry and the troll simply snatched up the colonel from the ground, reared high and terrible like the monstrosity of nightmares it was, and heaved Crowe off into the jungle, the SAW cartwheeling off in another direction into the bush.

Esmeralda's thought had been to stash this one by hurling him aside with all her might, probably badly injuring her next meal and caching him for later when she could get around to him after she'd dealt with the rest and taken what she could of them.

But the throw was bad and ended up being a little more than a toss.

Where the Butcher's first blast of Dragon's Breath had caught her on the ropy, black, foul-smelling, oily armor that was her outer skin, flames had ignited and sprung up, burning her nerves and causing her to squeal pathetically as the fire grew, illuminating her massive size by its red light in the night beneath the towering canopy.

Smoke and burnt flesh were everywhere all at once.

The colonel smashed through branches and slammed into a tree trunk, fracturing a rib, smashing his head, and going unconscious for about thirty seconds.

The Butcher saw all this. Where outgoing five-five-six had done little to the massive beast that was the jungle troll, the hot breath of incendiary shotgun rounds had ravaged the thing's leathery hide.

He didn't have many Dragon's Breath rounds left.

He thumbed the top-offs in and got to his feet as he watched his old commander go spinning off into the night-lathered jungle. Shadowy orcs raced past him, either fleeing the LZ or following the fight to the troll. He butt-stroked one, knocked it to the ground, then slammed his boot against its neck, breaking its windpipe suddenly. He needed the incendiary rounds for the troll. The Butcher knew the imminent threat to their survival was this massive thing . . . whatever the hell it was.

He didn't need to slam-fire like he'd worked the old M97 as he got ready to attack the dark, oily giant in their midst, looking wildly about for something or someone to attack next. Again, the Beretta 1301 was a mere trigger pull, and a solid delivery of what looked like sparks, flame, and smoke peppered a cone of fiery destruction over the massive twelve-foot hoary and hideous leathery-skinned thing.

The Butcher recovered his stance, landed the combat shotgun on the hulking thing, its massive dark chest heaving, its huge, narrowed eyes like yellow beacons of malevolence in the night, and started firing fast, closing the distance quickly.

He'd ruin the thing, the Butcher told himself, making a plan. Then he'd recover the colonel and make for the LZ.

Maybe they'd make it.

Three shells of Dragon's Breath, and Esmeralda was on fire across most of her chest and arms, a dozen small flares breaking out across her massive frame. With the fourth shell she simply turned and ran, her huge and powerful legs turning into giant pistons, taking herself off into the jungle like the freight train of pain and nightmare she was.

In an unbelievably sudden instant, she was gone.

At the edge of the embankment leading down through more jungle to the LZ on the river, the Ranger team leader turned back, still humping the wounded gunner between him and the PFC...

The man's mouth opened as though to ask what they should do now. Though he clearly knew what to do. *Get to the chopper.*

But the colonel was off in the bush. Somewhere.

And there wasn't much that could be done about that due to one of the wounded Rangers, his soldier, having a collapsed lung that was starting to push on the heart. The trachea had shifted, and Hopkins was starting to hack and cough. Death would come quickly without immediate treatment in the next few.

And this wasn't the place.

In minutes, without help, and a really big fat needle, Hopkins was gonna be dead.

"Move!" thundered the Butcher at the team leader. "We'll meet you on the LZ!"

Then the Butcher was gone off into the jungle in the direction the colonel had been flung.

It took a hot minute to find his downed former commander, and John Butcher moved through the jungle dark, eyes roving and searching the trail and the ground.

Another orc ran past him, breathing heavily, so heavily it sounded like a steam piston. The thing spotted him, turned savagely, inhaled, and made ready to scream as it bared its simian fangs.

Butcher shot it in the chest.

The 1301 exploded in sudden rage, covering the orc in flame and blast-fire. Thirty seconds later, he spotted the colonel's legs and found Colonel Crowe near the tree he'd gone into.

The wood was soft.

If it had been some jungle hardwood the man's brains would be drooling out the side of a fractured skull.

The colonel came to life as Butcher hauled him to his boots.

"Wind…" the man gasped and hacked, coughing. "Outta me."

"You mobile?" asked the Butcher, scouting the darkness all around them. Along the jungle trails more orcs were now streaming away from the LZ they'd tried to overrun.

They were giving up. The battle was too much for them. There were too many enemies out tonight.

The M134 Miniguns had been too much for their force.

The colonel nodded.

"In it…" he gasped again, "to… win it… Johnny. Let's…"

And then he nodded toward the LZ. "Let's… go."

They hustled through the rotor-blade-driven jungle as though struggling against some sudden typhoon that had come up.

Ahead they saw the hulking Black Hawk ready to lift off.

In sight of the stream and the bird, seeing the subdued marking lights and the glow of the instruments, the greenish light coming from behind the gunner's NODs, the Butcher more heard than saw the massive tree Esmeralda suddenly hurled at them from the jungle behind, where she'd been hiding.

In an instant Butcher dove on the colonel, crushing him beneath his own body as the tree sailed over them, barely missing.

The tree was huge, and it seemed impossible that even such a giant creature could have uprooted it and hurled it at them.

"Keep goin'!" Butcher shouted as he dragged the colonel to his feet, then pushed the man toward the waiting Black Hawk.

The crew chief was pumping his fist.

Esmeralda came for her last charge, and the Butcher faded back to the LZ working the combat shotgun and putting rounds into her, causing more flames and fire to cover most of her hideous form.

He had one round left.

She was aflame, on fire like some massive burning effigy that the rational mind kept screaming was impossible that it should move and attack, and live, like it was doing. And yet she thundered across from the jungle clearing, splashing into the river water to reach the Black Hawk like some savage giant that would ruin them all.

"I've had nightmares that weren't this bad," said Sergeant Hunter as he turned and got to work on Hopkins, who was starting to convulse.

"Go, go, go!" shouted the crew chief, and the pilot didn't need to be told twice to do so. The Black Hawk heaved itself heavily up from the river as the gunner went hot again and dosed the rampaging closing troll with as much as the minigun could do in a hot second of target engagement.

Esmeralda reached them just as the Black Hawk began to clear canopy, her head just below the deck, her hand literally reaching up to grab the bird as it made for the night sky.

The crew chief swore and grabbed on to the airframe.

The Ranger PFC shouted, "We're not gonna make it!"

Staff Sergeant Hunter, regardless of the chaos, already had Hopkins on the deck, clipped into the airframe, and with his body bracing the convulsing gunner, was peeling gear and trying to get a needle ready to do a decompression with the other hand.

Esmeralda roared savagely, titanically, like some lost beast from an elder age, raging above the Black Hawk's turbines. The pilot begged for lift, found some, and tried to escape.

But it wouldn't be enough.

Her giant claw was about to smash into them.

The Butcher grunted, "Ain't over yet!" while still holding the emergency handle he'd hauled himself onto the deck of the Black Hawk with, raised the combat shotgun with the other hand as he held on, pointed it at Esmeralda's hairy black troll's claw... and blew it clean off with a single blast from the shotgun.

Then the helicopter was over the jungle and climbing for the starry night, turning and heading back to base.

The crew chief whooped as Sergeant Hunter got ready to save Hopkins's life.

They were clear, and the Black Hawk thundered off into the Latin American night.

An hour into the flight, Hopkins was stabilized and the colonel was holding his head with one hand. The SF officer looked at the Butcher, who sat stoically next to him, still cradling the empty shotgun and staring into the nothingness ahead.

Ready for whatever came next.

Which was his way, thought the colonel as he observed his soldier for a long moment.

They were both jacked into the bird's comm system now.

"Wasn't much of an extraction, Johnny."

John Butcher turned and gave that grim half smile, not really a smile at all, he'd once been known for. He was a man of few words. The men he'd once shared them with were mostly gone now.

But...

"The world's gone strange... sir."

For a long moment Colonel Crowe looked at the man he'd always thought of as... a son.

He'd never told him so. Maybe now was the time...

He'd felt that way about all the men, or most of them, on his teams. Teams that were now long gone.

The world was changing. Growing stranger. But hadn't it always felt that way to old men?

The colonel nodded and massaged the growing bruise on his scalp. He winced. It was tender.

The crew chief had given him a cold pack to put on it.

"Yeah, John. It has."

The night was dark beyond the doors of the thundering Black Hawk. The Rangers had done their job. Somewhere out there was someone the Butcher cared for. The world had gone strange. And she was getting a ride out of the madness because of the skills the Butcher possessed. If he could provide a service for the dark powers that be... she would live.

And that's all that mattered to him.

He was willing to take that shot. For her.

He'd always been.

The man called the Butcher nodded once but not in response to what the colonel was saying to him about time remaining, schedules, the next landing field, rearming, and getting ready for the mission they had for him. And of how much precious little time remained before the world went completely sideways...

The Butcher was settling his mind on a point.

He'd go all the way for her. This time. And maybe... just maybe, however impossible it was, maybe he'd get to see her someday. He'd always wanted that.

He highly doubted it would happen.

He was the ultimate realist in ways few were.

"All that," said the colonel, jerking his thumb toward the rear of the beating, rumbling Black Hawk, indicating the strange nightmare creatures they'd left behind in the jungle and on the LZ. "Yeah, Johnny... *strange* doesn't describe it by half."

He paused.

Then...

"I won't lie to you, John. What you're headed into this time... makes all that look like a company soccer picnic. There's every chance you won't make it this time."

The Butcher laughed. It was that same grim and halfhearted smile.

One of the not-dead from the teams, one of the few that was still around, a guy named Sloan, Delta operator, he'd said the Butcher was the only man who smiled and made you feel like you were in the presence of death itself.

"How many times did they tell us that, sir?" asked John Butcher. Making up his mind he'd go all the way for them. For her. Just this time.

The colonel didn't laugh. He just stared back at the man whom the files and those who knew called... *the Butcher*.

Heavily. Redacted. Files.

"I'm serious, Johnny. What's ahead is stranger than anything we can ever imagine. I've seen things... things even I still can't believe. This is for all the marbles this time."

The Butcher turned and looked at his old commander, seeing, for the first time, the old man Crowe had become in all those years of incarceration.

In John Butcher's mind he'd only ever seen Colonel Crowe as a man who seemed older when they were younger, but they were both much older now than the officer had once been back then in those long-ago times lost to now.

"She gets a ride out." It was a statement. Not a question.

The colonel nodded.

"Deal's a deal, Johnny. You make it happen for them and she gets a ticket out. And there aren't that many left. Best I can do."

The Butcher leaned back against the firewall and closed his eyes.

He needed sleep now.

There wouldn't be much ahead if the schedule and timetables he was being told of were any indication of what he was getting himself into in all that *strange* ahead.

He'd always been able to sleep anywhere. Instantly. Soldiers are like that. Even the ones that seem like death itself.

"Then that's all that matters," grunted the Butcher, eyes closed, slipping into dreams of another place, another time, not this one anymore.

Her.

He would go all the way. And in time, he would realize he'd had no idea what that meant. How far he would go. And what that would cost.

Her.

He was a dangerous man.

And not just because he was honest.

About the Editor

Jason Cordova was born in California way back in 1978. He has had his novels published in multiple languages around the world and is both a John W. Campbell Award and Dragon Award finalist (though not in the same year). Jason is the author of *Mountain of Fire*, coauthor of *Monster Hunter Memoirs: Fever* with Larry Correia, and the editor of *Chicks in Tank Tops* (all from Baen Books).

Along the way he has also been published in over forty anthologies and penned over twenty novels across many genres, including YA, horror, science fiction, and urban fantasy. A huge history nerd, Navy veteran, former teacher, and retired esports pro (don't ask, long story), he currently resides in North Carolina with his muse and a plethora of animals.

About the Authors

Shane Gries is a retired soldier, former diplomat, student of history, and Dragon Award finalist. He spent over eighteen years serving overseas in Europe, Asia, and Oceania, and can order beer in several languages.

Shane started his military career as a young enlisted man and was later commissioned as an infantry officer. He's a graduate of Airborne School and Ranger School, earned the Expert Infantryman Badge, and did some time in combat.

He's even got a family hanging around someplace that continues to put up with his nonsense.

David Weber is an American science fiction and fantasy author born in Cleveland, Ohio, in 1952. His most popular and enduring character is Honor Harrington, whose story, together with the "Honorverse" she inhabits, has been developed through twenty-three novels, seven shared-universe anthologies, a five-book young adult series, and "Honorverse historical" Manticore Ascendant series, written with Timothy Zahn and Tom Pope. To date, David currently has over seventy book titles and twenty-one separate series that he has written or cowritten.

David currently lives in Greenville, South Carolina, with his wife Sharon, three dogs, and four cats. You can keep up with David's busy schedule by following his Facebook page, visiting www.davidweber.net, and on X/Twitter @davidweberbooks.

Marisa Wolf writes SFF that ends with hope, no matter how hard the circumstances. She has a number of coauthored novels in shared universes, solo novels in her own worlds, and a plethora of short stories. All contain various levels of snark.

After several years living on the road in an RV, Marisa, her husband, and their high-maintenance rescue dog are currently based in the woods of New England—but it's anyone's guess where in the country she is at any given moment. More at www.marisawolf.net.

Blaine L. Pardoe is a *New York Times* best-selling author. For over three decades he was a writer of BattleTech. Now he is the primary writer for the Land&Sea and Blue Dawn series, and has a new series, Tenure, which he's writing with Mike Baron of Punisher fame.

Joelle Presby is a former US Navy nuclear engineer and a recovering corporate consultant who grew up in West Africa. Her first-reader husband works for NASA, but he has yet to build her a space elevator.

She began her writing career publishing in David Weber's Honorverse and joined him as a cowriter for the Multiverse novels. After over a dozen short fiction pieces in other people's story universes, she has started a series of her very own, Sadou's Rings, with the novel *The Dabare Snake Launcher*.

She lives in Ohio with her husband and two children.

Jacob Holo has been a recreational geek since childhood, when he discovered Star Wars and Star Trek, and a professional geek since college, when he graduated from Youngstown State University with a degree in Electrical and Controls Engineering. He started writing when his parents bought that "new" IBM 286 desktop, and over the years, those powers combined to push him to the next level of nerddom: a sci-fi author who designs intricate worlds and tech systems...and promptly blows them up in a string of nonstop action.

He is the author of over fifteen books, including the best-selling Gordian Division series (with David Weber), *Time Reavers* (a *Kirkus Reviews* Best Indie Book), *The Wizard's Way* (with H.P. Holo), and *Monster Punk Horizon: Excess* (with H.P. Holo).

Edie Skye wrote *Titan Mage* as a joke and, in doing so, discovered that while she likes writing smart stuff, she also likes writing smut. Pretty spicy smut, too, 'cause if you're gonna do it, you might as well do it *hard*.

Specifically, she enjoys spinning fun (and funny) adventure fantasies about badass women with giant robots and giant...plots, and the equally badass dudes who want to do them. Vigorously. There's action, airships, monster fighting, and mech-upgrading galore, with a substantial side of harem and fun-for-all-involved graphic spice. (Which is to say, it's super NSFW. Unless your workplace is, like, cool with that.)

Sign up for her newsletter and learn more about her work at https://edieskye.com.

Rick Partlow is a native Floridian. He attended Florida Southern College and graduated with a degree in History and a commission in the US Army as an Infantry officer.

His lifelong love of science fiction began with the Heinlein juveniles and traveled through Simak, Asimov, Clarke, and on to Gibson, Walter Jon Williams, and Peter F. Hamilton.

He has written over seventy books in a dozen different series.

He lives in northern Wyoming with his wife and a goofy blackmouth cur. Besides writing and reading science fiction and fantasy, he enjoys outdoor photography, hiking, and camping.

Melissa Olthoff is a science fiction and fantasy author, a military veteran, and a self-proclaimed mocha addict. In 2023, she took second place in the Baen Fantasy Adventure Award and won the Imadjinn Best Short Story Award. She is published by Baen Books and Chris Kennedy Publishing and is best known for sneaking romance into everything she writes. Her first Baen novel, *Rise from Ruin*, was published in 2025.

Nick Steverson: A blue-collar truck driver from the Panhandle of Florida, Nick Steverson is the winner of the 2023 Imadjinn Award for Best Science Fiction Novel. He has nine novels in the soon-to-be-cinematic Salvage Title Universe as well as multiple short stories. More of his work can be found in the Four Horsemen Universe, This Fallen World, Starflight, Ashes of Entecea Universe, and Last Brigade Universe, and he also coedited the *Thirteen Stories of Horror* anthology.

* * *

Kacey Ezell is a retired USAF helicopter pilot who writes emotionally charged adventure fantasy and science fiction. She is a two-time Dragon Award Finalist for Best Alternate History and has written multiple best-selling novels published with CKP, Baen Books, and Blackstone Publishing. Find out more and join her community at https://kaceyezell.net/the-dragons-horde.

Nick Cole is a former soldier and working actor living in Southern California. When he is not auditioning for commercials, going out for sitcoms, or being shot, kicked, stabbed, or beaten by the students of various film schools for their projects, he can be found writing books.

Nick's book *The Old Man and the Wasteland* was an Amazon Bestseller and #1 in Science Fiction. He is a two-time Dragon Award-winning author (*CTRL ALT Revolt!*, and *Savage Wars* with Jason Anspach).

The Galaxy's Edge series and the Forgotten Ruin books have sold millions of copies.

Jason Anspach is the award-winning, *Associated Press* best-selling author of *Galaxy's Edge*, *Wayward Galaxy*, and *Forgotten Ruin*. He is an American author raised in a military family (Go Army!) known for pulse-pounding military science fiction and adventurous space operas that deftly blend action, suspense, and comedy.

Together with his wife, their seven (not a typo) children, and a border collie named Charlotte, Jason resides in Puyallup, Washington. He remains undefeated at arm wrestling against his entire family.